Erica James is the number one international bestselling author of twenty-two novels, including the *Sunday Times* top ten bestsellers *Summer at the Lake*, *The Dandelion Years* and *Song of the Skylark*. She has sold over five million books worldwide and her work has been translated into thirteen languages. Erica won the Romantic Novel of the Year Award for her novel *Gardens of Delight*, set in beautiful Lake Como, Italy, which has become a second home to her. Her authentic characters are thanks to her fondness for striking up conversation with complete strangers.

Chat to Erica online:

www.ericajames.co.uk
@TheEricaJames
@EricaJamesAuthor
@the_ericajames

Letters From the Past

ERICA JAMES

ORION

First published in Great Britain in 2020 by Orion Books,
an imprint of The Orion Publishing Group Ltd
Carmelite House, 50 Victoria Embankment
London EC4Y 0DZ

An Hachette UK Company

1 3 5 7 9 10 8 6 4 2

A CIP catalogue record for this book is
available from the British Library.

ISBN (Hardback) 978 1 4091 7385 4
ISBN (Export Trade Paperback) 978 1 4091 7386 1
ISBN (eBook) 978 1 4091 7388 5

Typeset by Input Data Services Ltd, Somerset

Printed in Great Britain by Clays Ltd, Elcograf S.p.A.

www.orionbooks.co.uk

*For Edward and Samuel, and Ally,
Mr T and the newest recruit to the family,
my granddaugther.*

Chapter One

Out in the garden Evelyn Devereux could hear ringing from inside the house. With an energetic step, she dashed up the lawn, assuming it was one of the children calling to say which train they would be on. But by the time she lunged for the telephone on the hall table, she was too late.

Oh well, if it was Pip or Em, they would probably try again. Meanwhile, she would make a drink for everybody; they had certainly earned it. Noticing there had been a second delivery of post, she picked up the letter from the doormat and went through to the kitchen.

She filled the kettle and put it on the gas stove. From the kitchen window she watched her husband, Kit, carrying some chairs across the lawn towards the marquee which was still in the process of being erected. Alongside him was her brother, Edmund; he too was carrying chairs. They were both laughing about something and clearly enjoying themselves. Particularly Kit. And nobody deserved to be happy more than he did. Not after everything he had suffered.

Back in 1939 and desperate to do his bit for King and country, and with the RAF unable to train pilots fast enough at the start of the war, Kit had taken matters into his own hands by going to Canada to learn to fly. Evelyn knew that his desire to go had been fuelled partly by his need to impress her. Oh, how she wished he hadn't been so impetuous!

Returning home the following year, he'd been on board the *Arcadia* and while crossing the Atlantic the ship had been torpedoed by a German U-boat. When news of the sinking had reached them in the village, they had all believed Kit was dead. They had even held a memorial service for him. But miraculously he'd survived. Appallingly burned from when the *Arcadia* had been hit, he'd been in the most awful pain when he'd finally made it home to Melstead St Mary, mental as well as physical pain. To this day he couldn't fully remember what had happened to him, only what he'd been told, that a passing American merchant ship had rescued him. He was transported to a hospital where he was treated not just for his injuries, but for amnesia. It was weeks before his memory returned, and partially at that.

It had taken him a long time to recover and he'd bravely endured countless excruciating operations to repair his scarred flesh, vowing after each visit to the hospital that he'd never go through it again. But somehow he'd found the strength to do so, and gradually he'd regained some of his old self which had been buried beneath the layers of pain and horror of what he'd gone through.

Evelyn liked to think she'd played her part in his recovery, but really it was his stepmother, Romily, who helped the most by encouraging Kit to join her in the Air Transport Auxiliary. He refused on the grounds that he wasn't fit enough, but Romily wouldn't accept no for an answer and kept on at him. 'Good God, Kit,' she exclaimed, 'we have pilots with missing limbs and Lord knows what else, poor devils! Of course you're fit enough!'

In the end, as he still liked to joke, he waved a white flag of surrender and agreed to give it a try. Never did Evelyn consider that it had been easy for Kit to fly again, but being useful gave a much-needed boost to his self-esteem.

There had been an assumption, once Kit was safely home in Suffolk, that he and Evelyn would marry, but they didn't. Instead, Evelyn went to do her bit for the war effort, which meant she was no longer living in the village. But the real reason Kit wouldn't propose to her was because he flatly refused to believe that anybody, least of all Evelyn, would want to marry a gruesome wreck like him. He just couldn't believe that any woman could love him when he was so badly disfigured.

But in October 1942 they married and the following June Evelyn gave birth to twins, Philip and Emily. It didn't seem possible that those babies were now nineteen and enjoying (maybe a little too much!) student life at Cambridge University. What a joy they had been for both her and Kit. He adored them, there wasn't anything he wouldn't do for his Pip and Em. He was so very proud of them. And of Evelyn, he never tired of telling her. Which was why he had insisted on throwing a lavish party to celebrate their twentieth wedding anniversary.

Watching her brother emerge from the marquee along with Kit, the pair of them still laughing over something, Evelyn thought what a shame it was that Edmund and his wife, Hope, hadn't had a child of their own. Of course, he was utterly devoted to Annelise, their adopted daughter, but he had once confided in Evelyn that he would have loved a house teeming with boisterous children. 'That's so typical of a man,' she had gently chided him, 'not thinking of the actual work involved in caring for a brood of children. Not to say the pain of giving birth to them!'

One or two very quiet well-behaved children might have suited Hope, but a rowdy houseful would have been torture for her. Evelyn had long since come to the conclusion that while Hope, a prolific children's author, wrote so imaginatively for her audience, almost as though she were a child herself and inhabited the world she created for them on the page, she didn't enjoy their company very much. She found them exhausting to be around, always preferring to escape to her study where she could pour her energy into her work.

Evelyn meant no criticism of her sister-in-law in believing this, it was merely an observation. Hope was also Kit's sister and they had been friends since they were children themselves, so there wasn't much they didn't know about each other. Their being married to each other's siblings had a satisfying sense of symmetry to it, and perhaps a sense of rightness, of how it was always meant to be.

She went over to the fridge for a bottle of milk and after filling a jug, her eye caught on that day's copy of *The Times* on the kitchen table. Neatly folded, it was where she had left it at breakfast that morning, the cryptic crossword only half completed. Time was she would have done it in the blink of an eye. It was her ability to do this, coupled with her love of mathematics, which was what she had studied at Oxford, that led her to do the work she had during the war.

Nobody in the family, or her current circle of friends, had ever known exactly what she did, and because she had signed the Official Secrets Act, it had to stay that way. She told people then, and even now, that it was clerical work for the Ministry of Defence she had been assigned to do, that it was all a bit hush-hush. 'I was nothing but a glorified paper-pusher,' she would explain to anyone who asked what she did. 'Utterly boring, but it was essential to keep the wheels running for the war effort.'

Like many of those she worked with at Bletchley Park, her recruitment had come by way of an old college tutor. Out of the blue she had received an invitation from Dr Goulding to meet up for a drink and a chat. Several days after seeing him in Oxford, she received a letter requesting her to attend an interview in

London. She was happy enough teaching at the village school, but sensing an opportunity to be free of the drudgery of looking after her ungrateful and ill-tempered mother, and to give Kit time to adjust to the direction in which his own life had gone, she leapt at the chance to escape. Within the week, and leaving her furious mother in the capable hands of a nurse, she arrived at Bletchley Park and started work as a decoder in Hut 5. It was the most satisfying work she had ever done, the most exhausting as well.

She had a feeling that Romily had guessed that she was doing a lot more than mere clerical work, because she once asked if Evelyn had ever come across an old chum of hers called Max Blythe-Jones. In fact, Evelyn knew Max well, but all she said to Romily was that the name rang a bell. As for everyone else, they took her at her word, that it was tedious filing she mostly did.

She still missed those days at Bletchley. She missed the camaraderie and the knowledge that she was doing something vital. Marriage and motherhood, and a return to teaching, had been life-changing and rewarding, but it wasn't the same as being part of a close-knit team put together to decode ciphers and save lives. Nothing else she had done before or since could compare.

Had she not married Kit, she would have continued working at Bletchley Park. Her old tutor had even contacted her again in 1949, hoping she might like to join in with what he referred to as 'the fight against the USSR'. Despite the temptation to be a part of something important and potentially exhilarating, she had to decline: she was a wife and mother by then. The Cold War would have to be fought without her assistance.

The whistling of the kettle on the gas ring roused her from her reverie. She made the tea in the largest pot they had, and mentally counted how many mugs she needed for the workforce in the garden. She then added the biscuit tin from the pantry, recalling all those years of rationing when the humble biscuit had been such a treat.

She was about to take the tray outside when she remembered the post. It probably wasn't anything important, but she might as well open the letter before Pip and Em arrived and it was lost in the melee of party preparations.

Taking a knife, she slit the envelope open and took out the piece of paper. She frowned at the sight of the glued-on letters cut from a newspaper. Was it a prank of some kind?

But when she read the words she knew it wasn't a joke. It was deadly serious.

YOU'RE A HARLOT! WHAT WOULD YOUR HUSBAND SAY IF HE KNEW HE WASN'T THE FATHER OF YOUR CHILDREN?

Chapter Two

Island House, Melstead St Mary
October 1962
Hope

Hope had lost track of the time. Something her husband, Edmund, frequently complained that she did. It infuriated him, especially if she forgot they were going somewhere, or had guests coming for dinner.

She never used to be like this, but her busy work schedule meant that every minute of her day was devoted to the children for whom she wrote. If she wasn't writing her books for them, she was replying to the hundreds of letters she received from all around the world.

Her various publishers and agent applauded her for her prodigious output, but it was the children's applause that mattered most to her. When she received a letter from a young child thousands of miles away in Nairobi, she knew then that she had done her job.

She hadn't always been a children's author. In what felt like another life, she had been an illustrator after going to art school. Her early work had included illustrating wildlife books for children. It was during the war that she had changed direction and commenced writing the series of books which was to make her name. Based on Stanley, their young evacuee billeted at Island House, and his devoted dog, Bobby, she had created Freddie and his faithful mutt, Ragsy.

Of course, in the end Freddie had to grow up and she had to find new characters with which to amuse her readers. Her agent urged her to be more like Enid Blyton and feature a group of friends who together solve mysteries. She went along with the suggestion, but on the understanding that she would include two girls within the storyline who would show just as much pluck and intelligence as the boys, if not more. After all, hadn't women shown their mettle during the war just as much as their male counterparts, women such as Hope's sister-in-law, Evelyn, and her stepmother, Romily? While they had been away doing their bit, Hope had had the job of maintaining order at Island House and writing her books. For some of her storylines she rifled her own childhood for inspiration – ghastly Nanny Finch; the mother Hope had never really known; the distant father who was always away and the siblings who found it so difficult to get on. Although thankfully she and Kit had never fallen out with each other.

As well as this hugely successful series of books, Hope also wrote for much younger children, featuring imaginary woodland folk who inhabited Sweet Meadow Wood. These shorter and much simpler stories were influenced by the imaginary world into which she had escaped as a child, and they soon became as popular as her other books. Next she devised a range of board games and jigsaws based on Sweet Meadow Wood, and in recent years she had created a new series of *Tales from Pepper Brook Farm*.

Everything she had written had been an attempt to entertain and brighten the lives of the children for whom she wrote. It had been to lighten the darkness they had endured during the war, and long after it was over. The relief that the fighting had stopped had soon given way to another battle, that of the country rebuilding itself while still making do with rations. The thorough drabness of it all had worn people down. Maybe not so much for the Romilys and Evelyns of this world who always seemed to bounce along with whatever was thrown at them. But for someone like Hope, who didn't have the same resilience, it was a bleak and depressing time.

She could remember in the harsh winter of 1947 sitting at her desk, and wrapped in so many layers she resembled a barrage balloon, feeling unutterably miserable. Through the window, and listening to their happy laughter, she had watched Edmund playing in the snow with Annelise and envied his ability to enjoy life in a way she found so difficult. Sometimes she wondered if she'd been cursed by being given the name Hope, she seemed to have so little of it.

Removing the completed page from her faithful old Corona typewriter, she placed it in the box file along with the rest of the chapters she had already written. If the coming days weren't going to be so busy, she would be able to complete this latest Pepper Brook Farm book and send it off to her agent, but it would have to wait for now.

Reluctantly she stood up and looked out of the window at the garden and the large pond and recently rebuilt boathouse. She was a middle-aged woman in her late forties, but when she looked at the garden of her childhood home, and despite the changes Romily had made to it during her ownership, Hope was a girl again remembering how she and Kit used to hide in the bushes from their older brother, Arthur. How he used to love to torment them. What sport he made of exploiting their weaknesses for his own sick pleasure. She had never forgotten what he'd done to her pet canary. He never admitted it, but she knew that he had crushed the little bird and left it for her to find.

Undoubtedly his wanton cruelty played its part in shaping Hope as she grew up, but essentially, she had already been marked out as being destined always to think and fear the worst. Losing her mother at a very young age could have been the start of her problems, and certainly her widowed father had been ill-equipped to cope with three small children, but then why did her younger brother, Kit, not suffer in the way that she did? Yes, he lacked confidence at times, but invariably he was the most positive and cheerful person she knew.

Maybe she had merely been born unlucky. That's how it had felt when, back in 1938, and after only two and a half years of marriage, her first husband, Dieter, tragically died from TB. A German living in London, he'd left his country of birth because he was afraid of what Hitler was doing there. He had been the kindest and gentlest of men. Hope had met him during a lunch-time concert at the Albert Hall. When the recital had finished, and with a shyness that had touched her, he had struck up conversation and asked if he could accompany her to another concert one day. Charmed by his accent and impeccable manners, she had readily agreed. Before long they were inseparable. But then the genuine happiness she had experienced for the first time in her life was snatched away from her when he fell ill and died.

Everyone told her that in time the pain would lessen and despite not believing a word of what they said, they were eventually proved right when Edmund, her childhood friend, achieved the impossible and brought a lightness back into her life. They married when the war was over, and he had been her constant and loving companion ever since. But never far from her thoughts was the fear that she might lose him, just as she had Dieter. Or maybe he would simply tire of her.

She and Edmund had been staying at Island House for over a month now while work was finished on their new home. They had sold their old house surprisingly quickly and had to move out before Fairview was ready. Romily had come to their rescue by offering Island House as a temporary home. 'I shall be away in America, so why not make use of it yourselves?' she'd said with her customary logic, not to say generosity.

Technically Romily was Hope's stepmother, having married her father, Jack Devereux, but being only a few years older than Hope, they had been more like friends, or even sisters. Romily had inherited Island House – so named because of the stream that fed the large pond and which skirted around the house down into the next valley – when Jack had died shortly before war broke out, but the family had always been made to feel welcome. Well, everyone except for Arthur.

Despite their initial reserve at having a stepmother not much older than themselves, Romily soon came to be a breath of fresh air in their lives. She was, even in her grief at being widowed, a tour de force and a great example to Hope, who was still mourning Dieter. But somehow Romily, with her can-do approach to life, had nurtured and encouraged Hope. It was thanks to Romily, too, already an established and successful novelist herself, that Hope had become a children's author. She doubted she could have done it without her stepmother's help and support. Kit often joked that the Devereux family could never do anything by halves. 'Why have one bestselling author in the family when you can have two?' he'd say.

It had been Hope who had wanted to sell their old house on the edge of Clover Woods. Edmund had been happy to stay, but she hated the way it was no longer so private. The woods she had played in as a child had been partly cleared to make way for the building of a new development of houses. It was just one of the many changes going on in the village. It was called progress and she didn't like it. She blamed it on the war; it had altered things, not just here in Melstead St Mary, but everywhere. People's expectations had changed; they were dissatisfied with the old, they wanted newer, bigger and better.

The main street in the village had seen a turnaround in shops. There was still Minton's bakery and the butcher's shop, but where there used to a hardware store, there was now a supermarket where customers wandered the aisles with a wire basket, filling it themselves. The choice of food available was greater, but the service was less personal.

The one addition that Hope actually approved of was the small library which she and Romily had helped to get off the ground.

Knowing how resistant to change she was, Edmund had been surprised when Hope announced that they should move. He had been even more surprised when she had suggested they build a new house to live in. He had gone along with her wishes, but hadn't shown the same level of enthusiasm in the design process as she did. Her main priority was to find somewhere that was in no danger of being overlooked, and she had made doubly sure of that by buying the surrounding land from the farmer who owned it. Initially he had refused to sell, but when she offered an amount well over the odds, the farmer agreed. She kept that from Edmund because she suspected he didn't always like the fact that her writing earned her the kind of money it did.

Throughout the war Edmund had worked as a hospital doctor in London. He had wanted to enrol as an army doctor, but with so many already gone, his skill was needed to treat all those injured servicemen who were sent home to be patched up. They married in 1945, three months after the end of the war, and he immediately left his post in London and took over the practice here in the village when Dr Garland moved to Norfolk.

Edmund had been keen to have a child of their own, but

it was not to be. Tests proved that Hope was the one at fault, though no doctor used that word. She was secretly relieved. The thought of being weighed down by the needs of another child had frightened her. She had done her best with their adopted daughter, Annelise, but she knew deep in her heart, she was not the maternal kind.

In August 1939, just days before Hitler invaded Poland, and a year after Dieter died, Hope had travelled to Germany to visit his family. It was in Cologne when she went to see Dieter's sister, Sabine, and her Jewish husband Otto Lowenstein, that they begged her to save their only child by taking her to England. Hope tried desperately to convince them to come with her, to escape the fear of living in Nazi Germany, but they wouldn't leave Otto's parents. With a heavy heart, and fearful of the enormous responsibility laid upon her, Hope returned to England by train and boat, pretending the ten-month-old baby was her own. It was the longest journey of her life. Sabine and Otto's fear at what Hitler might do was justified; they both perished in the Holocaust. But thanks to her, Edmund would remind Hope whenever she felt she had failed Annelise, their precious child had survived.

Edmund had proved himself to be a wonderful father to Annelise and Hope would always be grateful for that. He was also an excellent uncle to their niece and nephew, Em and Pip.

Downstairs, she spotted that afternoon's post on the hall table. She flicked through it, putting aside most of the letters that were for Romily, then found one that was for her. It was handwritten and with a local postmark. Absently, she tore it open as she began moving towards the drawing room. She had taken no more than a few steps when she stopped dead in her tracks.

Stunned, she realised she was looking at a poison pen letter.

The words – in a jumble of cut out newspaper print – leapt off the page at her.

YOU NEED TO BE A BETTER WIFE
AND PAY MORE ATTENTION TO
YOUR ADULTEROUS HUSBAND.

Chapter Three

Quince Cottage, Melstead St Mary
October 1962
Florence

Normally Florence Minton told her husband everything. Well, almost everything. Some things were best left unsaid. Was the letter something she should keep quiet about?

EVER WONDERED WHY YOUR HUSBAND
IS SO POPULAR WITH THE WOMEN
IN THE VILLAGE?

Whoever had sent it had to be sick in the head. Billy was no philanderer. He would no more betray Florence than she would him. She trusted Billy completely. With her life. With their children's lives come to that!

The letter had arrived in the post that morning long after Billy had begun kneading the first batch of bread dough in the bakery, and just as Florence was about to set off for work at Island House. She had worked there for Romily since before the war and her job had changed many times over the years, from general housemaid duties, to nanny and now overall housekeeper and personal assistant. 'You're indispensable to me,' Romily often said, 'my secret weapon in keeping my life on track.' Florence had always felt honoured that Romily regarded her the way she did, and that she insisted Florence

15

use her Christian name. There had never been any standing on ceremony between them. Now, with Romily currently away in America, Florence was tasked with looking after Island House while Hope and Edmund Flowerday lived there temporarily.

When she had opened the envelope, she had initially stared in confusion at the cut-out letters of newspaper print which had been glued onto the paper. Then slowly, as if word by word, it had dawned on her what she had in her hands – a poison pen letter. She had shaken her head in disbelief.

'Rubbish!' she'd declared aloud. 'Disgusting filth!' She'd then lifted the lid on the range and tossed the letter in. 'That's where rubbish belongs,' she'd muttered, ever the pragmatist. For good measure she had added the envelope, but not before examining the handwriting to see if she recognised it. She didn't.

If she had believed burning the letter would put a stop to her thinking about it, she was wrong. All morning at Island House while she went about her duties, she couldn't stop wondering who could have sent it.

There was only one person who she could believe might want to cause her trouble, and that was Billy's mother.

Ruby Minton had never thought Florence was good enough for her precious Billy. Maybe the nasty woman was right, but they had been happily married for two decades and had given Ruby two wonderful grandchildren, George and Rosie. Even so, Ruby could still find fault with anything she did or said.

In the early days of their marriage, Florence had hoped the antagonism her mother-in-law displayed towards her would lessen as the years went by, but it didn't. Since Billy's dad had passed away, Ruby's behaviour had escalated, and she brimmed over with venomous resentment for Florence. But would she stoop to this? Did she really hate Florence that much? And if Ruby wasn't the culprit, who did hate Florence to the extent they wanted to cause trouble between her and Billy? Was it some jealous woman who had designs on Billy for herself?

Oh, if only Romily was back at Island House and not still in America! She was the one person in the world in whom Florence felt she could confide about this. She would know what Florence should do. That was the thing about Romily, she was always so clear-headed and always knew just how to deal with a crisis.

Chapter Four

Casa Santa Rosa, Palm Springs,
October 1962
Romily

Lost in thought, Romily Devereux-Temple stood in her night-clothes on the terrace of the guest house at Casa Santa Rosa. After a restless night, she was pondering the wisdom of her being here. She couldn't help but think it had been a mistake to extend her time in America by accepting the invitation to spend a week in Palm Springs. But everybody had been so persuasive.

Or was it her flattered ego that had been so persuasive and overruled her common sense?

That was the thing about Hollywood, people there could twist your arm to make you do things you wouldn't ordinarily do; they could sweet-talk you into believing anything was possible. It was the place where dreams were made, and shattered.

Following a lengthy tour of speaking engagements, Gabe and Melvyn Correll, the brothers who ran Starbright Picture Studios, had approached her to discuss their idea about filming the first in her series of Sister Grace books. Since her debut novel was published almost thirty years ago, and to great acclaim, she had written twenty-five detective novels, all of them widely sold around the world. She had only tried her hand at writing because she had hoped it would help fund her then two big passions in life – motor racing and flying. That was when she'd been in her twenties, and what an age ago that felt!

Sister Grace was a fairly recent addition to her canon of sleuthing detectives and after half a dozen novels the rebellious nun with a twinkle in her eye had become a firm favourite with her readers. Romily was rather fond of her too, which was why, when the idea of a Sister Grace film had first been mentioned, she had dismissed the suggestion out of hand. Apart from her being an author and not a scriptwriter, therefore not suited to the job of adapting the novel for the screen, she had felt protective of her protagonist and hated the thought of her creation being spoiled. But then the persuasion, encouraged by her agent back in London who loved the idea and claimed it was high time one of her books was made into a film, had begun. And before she knew it, following a few too many Manhattan cocktails, she had agreed to delay her flight home to England in order to consider the idea in more depth. Gabe and Melvyn had said they had just the man to help her turn her novel into a film script. 'His name's Red St Clair and he's a terrific scriptwriter,' Gabe said, 'a genius for getting to the heart of a thing. The pair of you will get on like a house on fire.'

So here she was, a guest in Gabe and Melvyn's sprawling Palm Springs home waiting to meet said 'genius'. Much as it galled her, she had to admit that she was now experiencing a flutter of excitement at the prospect of seeing her novel *Sister Grace Falls from Grace* turned into a film. Which just went to show, even a grounded fifty-five-year-old woman like her could be seduced by the bright lights of Hollywood.

With a wry smile, she leaned against the stone balustrade of the terrace. In front of her, and fringed with tall palm trees, was a sweep of lush green lawn and a turquoise swimming pool with sunbeds placed invitingly around it. Vibrant flowers of scarlet and fuchsia pink tumbled from stone urns and classical statues stood guard at strategically placed points.

None of which, to Romily's mind, could compete with the

natural beauty of the mountainous backdrop. In the early morning light of dawn, Mount San Jacinto glowed in the roseate blush of the rising sun. High above it was an unbroken sky washed with pale lavender. It was an astonishingly beautiful sight. The arid air was already warm and fragrant with orange blossom. The guest house in which she was accommodated was entirely separate but lacked nothing in the way of comfort or luxury. A maid – a middle-aged Mexican woman called Clara – had shown her from the main house to where she was to sleep and had impressed upon her that if there was anything she wanted, any time of the day or night, she had only to pick up the telephone and ring through her request.

For all its impressive extravagance, Casa Santa Rosa didn't feel real; it resembled a film set. Any moment she expected to see actors take up their positions and cameras start to roll.

She stepped back inside the guest house and telephoned her request through for her breakfast. Minutes later she reappeared on the terrace in her swimsuit, a towelling robe slung over her shoulder. An early morning swim seemed entirely appropriate. Especially as it would be something she wouldn't be able to do once she was back in Melstead St Mary.

She swam with a determined front crawl stroke, length after length, her arms slicing through the water, her legs kicking hard. She was perfectly used to spending long periods of time away from home, whether it was doing book research, or carrying out speaking engagements while promoting her latest publication, but for some reason she felt she had been away too long this time.

Island House had been her beloved home for more than two decades; it was the longest she had lived anywhere. Prior to that she had lived a nomadic life. The place held so many memories for her, some heartbreaking memories, but many happy ones too. It had been an oasis of respite during the war, not just for

Romily, but for all those she had taken under her wing – those who worked for her, like Florence, Lottie and dear old Mrs Partridge; her stepchildren Hope and Kit, and their extended family, including Annelise and Isabella, and not forgetting Stanley, the evacuee. He had come to Melstead as a nine-year-old boy, stick-thin and homesick for London, thoroughly convinced he would never get used to living in the country. Now he was a grown man of thirty-two who said he could never live anywhere but Melstead St Mary. Island House had been the making of him, he often said. It had been the making of them all, Romily believed.

Bored with front crawl, she flipped over and proceeded to swim on her back, her gaze fixed on the cloudless blue sky above her. Stretching her arms over her head, her thoughts reverted to the reason she was here.

According to Gabe and Melvyn, Red St Clair had written for three of the major studios, Paramount, MGM and Columbia. 'Of course, he's never really needed to work,' Melvyn had said, 'not after inheriting a fortune from a printing company founded by his grandpappy.'

'And don't believe all the stories in the gossip columns about him never being seen unless it's on the arm of some glamorous socialite,' Gabe had added. 'He's really not that superficial.'

He sounded like trouble to Romily. Big trouble.

When finally she'd tired of swimming, she swam to the shallow end of the pool and stood in the sun squeezing the water from her hair. Going over to where she'd left her towelling robe, she wrapped it around her body. For a woman of her age she liked to think she was in reasonable shape. Her legs (one of which bore a pale six-inch-long scar) and arms were still toned, and her stomach was pleasingly flat. She was lucky that she had one of those metabolisms that magically kept any excess pounds at bay.

She was just thinking she should telephone home to see how everybody was, when Clara, the maid from last night, appeared with her breakfast. Placing the tray on the table in the dappled shade of the orange tree, the woman passed Romily an envelope. 'This just arrived for you madam. It was hand delivered.'

Alone, Romily opened the envelope.

Dear Romily,

Unavoidably delayed! Will have to delay our meeting this morning until one o'clock. I'll book us a table at La Bella Vista. You can't miss it, it's next door to the El Mirador on North Indian Avenue.

See you there!

Red St Clair.

Unimpressed by the appalling handwriting, and by the rude and presumptuous content of the brief message, Romily's hackles rose skywards. This, she thought grimly, did not bode well. Mr St Clair was clearly far from reliable. And far from being a man of good manners. *See you there,* indeed!

Once more she doubted the wisdom of being here. She should have stuck to her original plan and flown straight home to Island House.

Chapter Five

Melstead St Mary
October 1962
Annelise

The train journey home from Oxford was always long and tortuous and when Annelise stepped onto the platform at Melstead St Mary and saw Stanley with his dog waiting for her, her spirits lifted in an instant. She didn't have that many friends, not what she would call close, but she counted Stanley as her oldest and dearest friend. She hadn't been home since Easter, so she was particularly pleased to see him again.

Putting down her suitcase, and after making a fuss of Tucker, she hugged Stanley warmly. 'You look well,' she said, taking in his collar-length hair, open-necked shirt and sandy-coloured corduroy jacket.

'And you look tired,' he said, holding her at arm's distance and studying her face with a frown. 'You've been overworking, haven't you, burning that candle at both ends?'

'You're a fine one to talk when it comes to working long hours.'

'I guess we're just two of a kind,' he said with a grin. It was a grin she knew of old. As children, she had always looked up to Stanley, eight years her senior, like she would an older brother. She must have made such a nuisance of herself, always trailing after him, wanting him to play with her. All these years on she could remember so vividly him pulling her along on a sledge in the snow of the garden at Island House. Or teaching her how to climb a tree or ride a bicycle. Not once could she remember him ever telling her to leave him alone, not even when he became a teenager and the age gap showed obvious signs of widening. Then, as if out of the blue, he was suddenly a man, whereas Annelise was still a child. She smiled to herself, thinking how eager she had been to catch him up, to be an adult too.

Carrying her case for her, his arm linked through hers as Tucker scampered on ahead, they walked out of the station.

'New car?' she asked, when Stanley unlocked the boot of a pale blue Triumph Herald and stowed her luggage inside.

'It's not actually brand new,' he said, opening the passenger door for her, 'I bought it second hand from Wally Stimpson's garage.'

'That old rogue? Are you sure it's safe?'

Stanley laughed and after Tucker had squeezed in between them, he slipped into the driver's seat. 'Safe as houses. And it handles like a dream.'

'Does that mean you're about to drive us to Island House with ambitions of being the next Stirling Moss?'

'Don't worry, I have no intention of crashing the car like he did his Lotus at Goodwood.'

As good as his word, they set off at a sedate speed, following behind the local bus while Stanley told her all he knew about the arrangements going on at Meadow Lodge for Kit and Evelyn's party. Which was the reason Annelise was home. She was disappointed to hear that Romily wouldn't be back to attend the party along with the rest of the family.

'How's it going with Mums and the new house?' she asked.

Now a fully trained architect, Stanley had designed Hope's dream house. It was Edmund's house as well, of course, but he had sensibly left most of the decisions to Hope. He was all for an easy life.

'Haven't they told you?' said Stanley.

'Oh, I get the usual thing from Mums, that it's all going much too slowly.'

He glanced sideways at her. 'She's not unhappy, is she?'

'Come on, Stanley, you know as well as I do, Mums is not the greatest of advertisements for the state of happiness. She just can't allow herself to be truly happy. And don't look like that.'

'Like what?' he said.

'As though I'm a fine one to talk.'

He smiled. 'If the cap fits.'

He was right, of course, the cap most certainly did fit. She might not be biologically related to the woman who had brought her up, but she did suffer from the same inability to enjoy life to the full. Always there was the feeling that she didn't deserve to be happy. How could she when almost every member of her family in Germany had perished at the hands of the Nazis during the war?

Annelise had no memory of her mother and father. Everything she knew of Otto and Sabine Lowenstein was what she had read in official reports during trips to Germany to uncover the truth about her family. Hope had also helped to fill in the blanks.

Hope's first husband, Dieter, had been Sabine's brother and while their parents – supporters of Hitler and the Third Reich – had disapproved of Dieter's choice of bride, an English girl, they had been horrified that their daughter wanted to marry Otto Lowenstein, a Jewish doctor. When war became increasingly more likely, and with Jews being regularly rounded up and sent to labour camps where they were never heard of again, Sabine and Otto had pleaded with Hope, not long widowed, to take Annelise to safety.

On her tenth birthday and with Hope now married to Edmund and knowing that Sabine and Otto had not survived the war, they legally adopted Annelise. They also changed her name from Lowenstein to Flowerday. In the preceding years, before knowing the fate of Annelise's parents, Hope had wanted to believe that they might have survived the death camps and would one day claim their daughter.

It pained Annelise to wonder how she might have reacted if that had happened, when she had known no other life than the one in Melstead St Mary. How would she have coped with being uprooted to live with strangers, to leave behind all that she knew and loved? To be parted from those who had enriched her life beyond measure?

One of whom was Romily. Without doubt Romily had been an enormous influence in her life. The extraordinary woman had been friend, aunt and mentor all rolled into one. There had been times as a young child when, in need of help or advice, Annelise had turned to Romily instead of Hope or Edmund. More often than not, Hope was unapproachable, the door to her studio firmly shut, blocking out all distractions.

Annelise knew that she had a similar tendency to distance herself from others. It took a lot for her to open up to people. Recently she had begun to do just that, and with one person in particular. His name was Harry, and such was the strength of her emotions for him, he would dominate her thoughts far too much if she allowed them to.

She was twenty-four and some would say laughably inexperienced when it came to matters of the heart. Until now romance had not been a priority for her. She was a scholar first and foremost and loved her work as a junior research fellow in German History at St Gertrude's College in Oxford. Which was where she had studied, just like her aunt Evelyn.

She was proud of what she had achieved, but viewed it very much as the start of greater things. She wanted to make Hope and Edmund proud of her. Romily too.

Nothing annoyed her more than not being taken seriously. It

happened a lot, primarily because of the way she looked. She was blonde with a petite build that made her appear younger than she was.

'So, tell me, how *is* the new house coming along?' she asked, feeling Tucker nudging her elbow with his nose, as though letting her know that she had let her thoughts wander.

'It should be finished within a month,' replied Stanley.

'I can't wait to see it.'

He briefly turned his head. 'We could take a detour and go and see it now, if you'd like? I don't have a key on me, but I could show you the exterior.'

'Why not?'

For answer, he checked the way ahead was clear and put his foot down to overtake the bus. She had joked earlier about him turning into Stirling Moss behind the wheel of his new car, but he was actually one of the safest drivers she knew. She trusted him implicitly, and in all things. She always had. If she was brave enough, she might even tell Stanley about Harry, having told no one else about him.

Chapter Six

Fairview, Melstead St Mary
October 1962
Stanley

The house was approached via a long straight driveway flanked by lawns and newly planted beech trees. Hope and Edmund had bought the three acres of land because of its convenient proximity to Melstead St Mary and unrivalled views of the softly undulating landscape. Hope had insisted that the house be positioned squarely in the middle of the plot, as though deliberately isolating it from everything around it. With its partially white stucco walls resplendent in the autumnal sunshine, it stood majestically before Stanley and Annelise.

'It's very impressive,' Annelise said after a lengthy pause. 'And bigger than I thought it was going to be.'

'It was always going to be this big,' Stanley said, watching Annelise carefully to see what she really thought. Her opinion always mattered to him. As did the need to please her and gain her approval. If he could only convince himself that he had her total respect and admiration, he might believe he stood a chance of being her equal. Which in his heart of hearts he knew could never be. Just as he knew it was futile to hope that one day they would be more than just good friends. To Annelise, and many others, he was destined always to be Stanley Nettles, the grubby illiterate evacuee from the East End of London who'd made good.

The plain truth was, despite the education he'd been given and then the long hard years studying to be an architect – all thanks to Romily's generosity and encouragement – a girl like Annelise would always be out of his league. They moved in very different circles. While she mixed with academics in the rarefied atmosphere of Oxford, a world which, if he were honest thoroughly intimidated him, he preferred his life here in Melstead St Mary with his old village friends.

London had been fine when he'd been studying, and for a brief period after he was qualified and working for an architectural firm, but it hadn't felt like it would ever be his true home. He was happiest here in the Suffolk countryside, where he'd lived since being put on a train as a nine-year-old boy and subsequently deposited at Island House. He'd hated it initially; he'd been terrified of the big empty sky, the wide-open spaces and the unnerving silence. He hadn't missed his cruel and sadistic mother, though, and when he realised he wasn't going to be beaten or locked up by anyone at Island House, he grew to love the place.

Now, and working on his own as an architect, he made a decent living here in the village, sufficient for his needs at any rate. The commission from Hope and Edmund to build them a spacious six-bedroom house with echoes of the Arts and Crafts movement was by far the biggest commission he had been given to date.

He took Annelise down some steps in the garden so that she could have the best view of what he'd designed. Once again, he examined her face for her reaction.

'It's beautiful,' she said at length. 'And quite unique. I love how the ground floor seems to be made almost entirely of glass, and curves in that sinuous way, and the way the two wings reach out like a welcoming pair of arms.'

He hardly dared ask the question, but he had to. 'You approve of it, then?'

She turned to look at him, her blue eyes wide and clear in the afternoon sun. 'What a strange question, of course I do. I love it! I can understand now why Mums is in such a hurry to move in.'

Filled with relief, and pride, he said, 'Talking of your mother, I'd better get you to Island House before she starts to wonder what's happened to you.'

'I wouldn't worry about that,' Annelise said, still staring up at the house. 'She's probably working and lost track of the time.'

'What time is Isabella arriving?'

Annelise smiled. 'I've no idea. But you know Isabella, there's no pinning her down.'

No, thought Stanley, but then the same was true of Annelise.

Chapter Seven

London to Suffolk
October 1962
Isabella

As an actress, Isabella Hartley was more than used to being stared at, but the man sitting opposite her in the first-class train carriage was making her feel distinctly uncomfortable. Ever since he'd removed his raincoat and dumped it on the seat next to the one he was occupying, he hadn't stopped staring at her while pretending to read his crumpled copy of the *Daily Mirror*. He might just as well have had flashbulbs going off in his eyes for all his subtlety. Some men really had no self-respect.

Mind you, when she thought about some of the things she'd had to do to get where she was, she wondered about her own self-respect. All those slobbering men she'd had to charm and flutter her eyelashes at. But if that was what it took to get to the top, then she'd grit her teeth and do it. Though she had her limits. Her compliancy only went so far.

Acting wasn't for the weak; she'd learned that when she was at RADA. It was a world in which only the fittest survived, and she had no intention of not surviving. She wanted to be the best. She wanted the kind of stardom she had always dreamt of since being a child, and nothing was going to stop her.

The man opposite her was still making a lousy job of pretending to read his newspaper. There was a strong smell of alcohol coming off him and a dusting of dandruff on his shoulders. He had moved his legs so that they were stretched towards hers. She pulled her fur coat around her as though it would shield her from his gaze, and pointedly jerked her head to stare out of the window at the passing countryside.

This was a rare few days off for her; it was ages since she had last been home to Melstead St Mary and she was looking forward to seeing everybody. People often didn't believe her when she said her work schedule was so demanding. But it was. At the theatre six days a week, she seldom made it back to her flat before one in the morning. Her habit was to sleep in until nearly midday, unless it was a day when she had a matinee performance to do as well as the evening one. It was an antisocial way of life.

But for all the hard work and frustration, she had to confess that she loved what she did. Particularly seeing herself on screen. She knew just how to make the most of her looks. Her striking face with its wide cheekbones, full lips and sultry eyes, together with her long dark wavy hair and curvy body, were her greatest assets. She had been dubbed the British Sophia Loren, a moniker she was more than happy to play up to.

She was now beginning to be recognised when she went out. She loved it when she was asked for her autograph and always made a point of smiling and exchanging a few words with the person who'd asked for it. It was possible that the man looking so lasciviously at her knew who she was.

Lulled by the rhythmic clackety-clack of the train, she wanted very much to close her eyes and sleep for the rest of the journey, but there was something about the man in the compartment with her that made her reluctant to do that. She decided to go in search of another compartment, hopefully one that was empty. She was just reaching for her suitcase in the overhead rack when the man sprang to his feet. 'Allow me,' he said, his hand on the handle of her case.

'I can manage,' she said.

'I'm sure a beautiful woman like you could do just about anything she wanted,' he said. 'Especially with the right encouragement.'

There was a sheen of sweat above his top lip and she could smell the sourness of his beer-soaked breath. Revolted by him, and what he was implying, she snatched her suitcase from his grasp, slid open the compartment door and hurried away down the narrow corridor of the train.

Changing her mind about wanting to find an empty carriage where the man might follow her, she headed to where the second-class seats were located.

'Isabella? Is that you?'

She glanced at the young man who had just called her name.

'It's me, George,' he said.

She stared at him blankly as the other passengers looked up interestedly. Then she smiled. 'George Minton,' she said, 'fancy seeing you here.'

'Are you going home for the party?'

'Yes,' she replied. 'You too?'

He nodded. When he indicated the empty seat next to him, she declined. 'Come with me,' she said, leading him to the empty first-class carriage she had spotted before.

'But I don't have the right ticket,' he said.

'Don't worry about that, I'll buy you one if the ticket collector comes round again.'

When they were settled, and grateful for his company after her encounter with that repulsive man, Isabella tried to remember when she'd last seen George. 'Was it Christmas when we last saw each other?' she asked.

'It probably was,' he said.

'And how are your parents?' She felt badly that she didn't make more of an effort to stay in touch with Florence.

Some of her earliest memories were of sitting on Florence's lap and being cuddled. That was during the war when she lived at Island House with Florence, Annelise and Hope, along with Stanley and dear old Mrs Partridge, their cook. Florence had run the household while Romily was away flying with the ATA. There had also been an Austrian refugee who had helped with the chores, leaving Florence to look after the children. Later memories included Isabella playing with George, and then his younger sister, Rosie, when she was old enough to join in with their games. Her cousin, Annelise played with her too, as did Stanley. Isabella and Annelise referred to each other as cousins, but strictly speaking they weren't related.

Isabella's connection to the Devereux family was complicated, and had, if she were being objective, all the makings of a great film. Her mother, Allegra Salvato had been the illegitimate daughter of Harry Devereux, Jack Devereux's ne'er-do-well brother. When Jack had learned that his brother was dead, and of the existence of a young child living in an orphanage in Italy, he had felt duty-bound to give Allegra a home at Island House alongside his own children, Arthur, Kit and Hope. But just as soon as she was old enough, Allegra went back to Italy to embark on what she had hoped would be a successful singing career. When Jack was dying, and now married to Romily, Allegra, down on her luck and pregnant, returned to Island House and married her childhood sweetheart, Elijah Hartley. It was not to be a happy ending for them, though. While Elijah was away fighting in the war, poor Allegra died giving birth to Isabella. In his absence, Romily was made Isabella's official guardian.

Elijah had been a wonderful man. A soldier with the Suffolk Regiment, she had scarcely seen him for the first five years of her life, then when the war was over, and he came home for good, she moved out of Island House and into Winter Cottage

34

with him. It had been a strange and bewildering time for her
– he was her father, so she had been told from the earliest age,
but she didn't actually know him. As for her biological father,
she never knew who he was and had no inclination to track
him down.

In those initial weeks of living with Elijah she had often cried
in her bed at night wanting to be back at Island House with
Florence and Annelise and Stanley. Poor Elijah, he didn't know
what to do, other than let her spend time back at Island House.
After a while she made the adjustment, as did he. It couldn't
have been easy trying to be her father. But she never doubted
that he loved her, and she grew to adore him. He had made
such a sacrifice taking her on, not that he ever said as much.
He always said he had loved her mother and was determined
to marry her despite knowing she was carrying another man's
child. How many men would do that? He had been exceptional in all ways. Isabella doubted she would ever find a man to
marry who would be as good as he was.

His death when she was seventeen had left her bereft and
unable to talk about him. She locked away her love and grief
for him deep in her heart, where it could never be lost. It was
that which she tapped into if an acting role she was playing
called for her to cry. All she had to do was force herself to think
of her grief for Elijah and the tears would flow. Somebody once
said of her that she actually turned deathly pale when she cried
on stage.

'My parents are very well,' George said, breaking into her
thoughts, 'and both as busy as ever – Mum at Island House and
Dad at the bakery.'

'And how's university going for you?' Isabella asked. She
knew how proud his parents were that he was the first of their
family to go to college. 'Remind me what you're studying?'

'It's going well, and I'm reading Chemistry.'

She smiled. 'Quite the boffin.'

He laughed. 'Not at all. By the way, I loved your last film. You were marvellous in it.'

'Thank you.'

They talked some more and then George took out what looked like a Chemistry textbook with incomprehensible symbols littering the pages. 'You don't mind if I read, do you?' he asked.

'Be my guest. It gives me the chance to snatch a quick forty winks.'

Her eyes closed, she thought of the weekend ahead and of her disappointment that she wouldn't be seeing Romily. It was very unlike Romily to miss a family get-together. All Isabella knew, based on the telegram she had received, was that 'something unexpected had cropped up' and Romily would be home a week later than planned.

Well, that was Romily all over, the unexpected was her speciality. She coped with it better than anyone Isabella knew.

Chapter Eight

Palm Springs
October 1962
Romily

Romily had asked Clara the maid where she should go to have her hair done and having taken her advice, she was now back from the salon. The hairdresser, who had wielded the tools of his trade as though conducting an orchestra, had made an excellent job of trimming and setting her hair into a stylish wave that was swept back from her forehead. She felt better for going.

However, the slapdash nature of Red St Clair's note earlier that morning still rankled. She wished she could summon up more enthusiasm for meeting him, but she couldn't. Even so, she was determined to look her best, and most businesslike. This was a business lunch after all. She put on her favourite cream Chanel suit and silk blouse, and a pearl necklace. She applied her make-up with care, slipped on her butterfly-wing sunglasses, and then scooped up her handbag to go across to the main house.

But the moment she stepped outside she realised the dry arid heat of the day had increased and she was going to be far too hot. Back inside the guest house, she threw off her suit and put on the red and white candy-stripe boat-neck dress she had earlier dismissed as being too informal. She then hunted for the handbag that matched the dress and her red peep-toe sandals, then reapplied her lipstick. This time a deep red.

'All set,' she declared, reaching for her sunglasses once more and appraising her reflection in the mirror. 'Showtime for Mr St Clair.'

She apologised to the taxi driver who had patiently waited for her, and following a short drive to La Bella Vista, she was told by the maître d' – a suave Italian with an impressive moustache – that her dining companion had called to say he was sorry, but he was running late. Resisting the urge to turn on her heel, Romily politely allowed the man to show her to the table that had been reserved for them. It was outside in the garden in the shade of a vine-covered pergola.

'Would the *Signora* like an *aperitivo* while she waits?' he enquired.

'Yes, the *Signora* would indeed like an aperitif while she waits. She would like a vodka martini with a twist of lemon. Shaken not stirred.'

He smiled. '*Subito, Signora. Subito.*' He hurried off, clicking his fingers ostentatiously to attract the attention of a waiter.

While waiting for her drink, Romily turned her attention to the other diners. They were mostly couples enjoying what appeared to be a romantic lunch. Seated at the table nearest to her was a young woman about Isabella's age staring adoringly into the eyes of her dining companion, a man old enough to be her grandfather. She was talking about them playing tennis later that afternoon and him taking her dancing that night at somewhere called the Thunderbird Country Club. The man looked the sort to want a nap after lunch, never mind exerting himself on a tennis court, or dance floor.

It was a sight Romily had often witnessed in Hollywood, young girls throwing themselves at older men who they believed would further their careers. Or those who hoped for marriage and a life of wealth and luxury. But there were, of course, plenty of rich and powerful men who took advantage of these wide-eyed ingenues for their own ends.

Romily recalled her own relationship with a much older man all those years ago and thought of the many people who had believed that she married Jack for his money. She smiled to herself thinking of the old biddies in Melstead St Mary, long since dead, who had considered her a scarlet woman. They had most assuredly assumed the worst of her. But they couldn't have been more wrong.

God how she had loved Jack! And what a passionate romance they had shared together. There had been no one like him since. Yes, she had been involved with a number of men in the intervening years, but no man had possessed her heart, body and soul the way Jack had. Now, at the age of fifty-five, she was content to live as a single and carefree woman. She had her work and her friends and a family whom she loved; what more did she need?

As though in answer to that question, the young waiter who had been assigned the task of bringing her vodka martini took that moment to materialise. '*Signora*,' he said deferentially, setting down the tray containing her drink, along with a dish of plump olives and salted almonds.

'*Grazie*,' she responded, although she could see with his pale freckled complexion he was about as Italian as she was.

Her drink had been perfectly mixed with just the right amount of vodka and she relished the sublime dryness of it while reading the menu.

Her glass was almost empty, and she was contemplating ordering a second drink, when she was aware that she was no longer alone.

'I bet you've been sitting there wondering what kind of a worthless fellow has the audacity to keep you waiting so long.'

From behind her sunglasses, she raised her gaze to the man

before her. He was so tall and broad in the chest and shoulders he eclipsed everything around him. 'And you would be who exactly?' she asked.

'If you don't mind me saying, that is somewhat ingenuous of you, but just so as you know, I'd get down on my knees and beg your forgiveness if I could.' He held out an oversized hand. 'Red St Clair at your service. Can you forgive an ignorant Yank such appalling behaviour?'

She shook hands, her own disappearing into his. 'If you really are such an ignorant Yank,' she said, 'I doubt we have any business to conduct.'

He smiled and pulled out the chair to the right of hers. His enormous body instantly dominated the space, making her back away from him.

'Have you decided what to eat?' he asked, indicating the menu in front of her. 'I can recommend the sardines followed by the *linguine al frutta di mare*. They're both favourites of mine.'

'I thought I'd have the *ravioli e limone* followed by the veal escalope,' she said, perversely changing her mind from her first choice of sardines and linguine.

'An excellent choice too.' He raised a large hand into the air, instantly attracting the attention of the waiter who'd brought Romily's drink to her.

'Hi Danny,' Red said to him, 'how're you doing?'

'I'm very well, sir.' The young waiter beamed, his pen and pad poised to take their order.

Red glanced at Romily and indicated her glass with his finger. 'Another of the same?' Before she had a chance to reply, he turned back to the waiter. 'Make that two, I have some catching up to do.'

'Certainly, sir. Have you chosen what to eat?'

Red rattled off their order, along with the request for a bottle of Barolo Marchesi.

If there was one thing Romily could not abide, it was a brash, self-important man treating her as though she wasn't capable of ordering her own meal, or deciding which wine to drink with it. If this was how it was going to be, working alongside Mr Red St Clair, Gabe and Melvyn Correll would have to think again! What was more, she was going to have to make things very clear to the man himself. She drank what remained of her martini and very slowly counted to five. Then: 'Mr St Clair,' she began, 'I think we need to—'

'Hey, please, call me Red.' He shifted his chair so that he was sitting at a ninety-degree angle to the table, an elbow resting on it, his legs stretched out languidly in front of him; they seemed to go on for ever, like a pair of Red Wood trees. 'Go on,' he said, leaning back in his seat, causing her to wonder if it could bear his weight. He wasn't fat, simply a colossus of a man. 'What do we need to do?' he asked. 'Other than write a cracking script. Have you ever co-written anything before?'

'No, and I'm really not convinced that—'

'That it's a good idea?' He laughed. 'You may well be right.'

'Then why are we—'

'Sitting here at all?'

She stared at him hard. 'Are you going to interrupt me all the time by finishing what I'm about to say?'

Drawing his thick brows together, he frowned, as though having to tease out the meaning of her question. 'Maybe that's a good sign,' he said, at length. 'It means we're tuned in to each other, that we're on the same wavelength.'

She pursed her lips. 'I think that highly unlikely.'

Their young waiter appeared with their martinis and after he'd placed them on the table and they were alone again, Red drummed his fingers on the table. 'Tell me if I've got this wrong, but I suspect we've gotten off on the wrong foot, haven't we?'

She gave him a pitying look. 'Goodness, do you really think

so? You delay our meeting by several hours and then can't even be bothered to turn up for lunch on time. What kept you, a round of golf, or a game of tennis at the Racquet Club?'

'I said I'm sorry, didn't I?'

'So you did. But it didn't have the slightest ring of sincerity to it. And if that's how it would be for our working relationship, then I'm afraid there's little point in us continuing with this conversation.' She stood up abruptly. 'Good day to you, Mr St Clair. I believe we've said all we need to say to each other.'

'Wait,' he called after her.

But she didn't. She kept on walking, right out of the restaurant until she realised she was on the street and with not a taxi in sight. Damn and blast, she would have to go back inside and ask for somebody to order her a car.

She pushed open the door and found Mr St Clair blocking her way. 'Please,' he said, 'would you give me the chance to explain why I was late?'

'It won't make any difference,' she said, 'I can't imagine for one moment that we could work together.'

'That might be true, but I'd like the opportunity to apologise properly to you.'

Reluctantly she followed him back through the restaurant and outside to the garden area. Other diners were looking at them curiously. Over on the far side of the pergola, tucked away in a discreet corner, she spotted Lucille Ball and her husband, comedian Gary Morton staring directly at her. And was that Dinah Shore on the table next to them? She suddenly felt mortified at the spectacle she had made of herself, and with such an illustrious audience. Dear God, what had got into her?

It was only when they neared their table that she noticed Red was limping. Yes, she thought cynically, he'd probably strained a muscle in bed with some young socialite.

He held her chair out for her, in spite of it already being some distance from the table. Obviously he was trying to prove he was a gentleman.

Once he was also seated, in the same way he was before, at ninety degrees to the table, he nudged her drink towards her. 'Cool your pistons with a sip or two, and then let me apologise for making such a poor impression on you.'

Cool her pistons? Oh really, these Americans had such an absurd way of speaking! She took a sip of her martini, and then another. She unexpectedly had to force herself to suppress a smile, but failed. The truth was, she did need to cool her pistons.

'There you go,' he said, noticing her lips twitching, 'I've always been of the belief that there's nothing a good martini can't cure. Now then, as to the reason I so rudely delayed our meeting, which I am genuinely sorry about, I'm afraid it was beyond my control. The thing was, I had an early call from the doc at the hospital that he couldn't see me tomorrow as planned, only this morning.'

'Are you ill?' she asked doubtfully. He didn't look like he had anything wrong with him. Far from it. She put him in his early fifties, and everything about him spoke of him taking good care of his appearance. In a cream pair of trousers and a short-sleeved Fred Perry T-shirt, as though he'd just come off the tennis court, he appeared the absolute picture of health – tanned, fit, strong and virile, bursting with energy. There was no doubt in her mind that he would be considered an extremely good-looking man, with the type of effortless sexual allure that would attract attention wherever he went. Without meaning to, but out of habit, her eyes drifted towards his left hand. There was no wedding ring.

To her annoyance she saw that he'd noticed her glance. 'No, I'm not ill,' he said, a smile playing at the corners of his full lips. 'And I'm not married either.' He tapped his leg that was

43

nearest to her, and which was stretched out in front of him. 'But I had to have a new prosthetic leg fitted this morning.' He shrugged. 'It's not the way I'd ideally like to spend a morning.' He smiled. 'Not when I'm supposed to be spending it with a beautiful English woman. But it was the only time this week the doc could see me. He was then delayed by an hour, so I just had to wait my turn. Am I forgiven?'

The humiliation Romily had experienced a few minutes ago was nothing to what she was now feeling. Never had she felt such excruciating shame. She was furious with herself.

'Hey,' he said, holding out a fork for her to take when she didn't say anything, 'just in case you think this is some kind of elaborate ruse on my part, try pushing that into my shin to prove to yourself that I'm speaking the truth. Just be sure to stab the correct leg!'

'There's no need to be quite so—'

'Melodramatic?' he finished for her.

'And there you go again,' she said, 'interrupting me.'

He grinned and raised his martini glass to her. 'How about we drink to many more occasions when I can finish off your sentences?'

'Let's just see how lunch goes, shall we, Mr St Clair?'

'I told you, call me Red. And talking of lunch, here's our *antipasti*. I don't know about you, but I'm famished.'

Once they were alone again, Red said, 'You haven't asked how I lost my leg, and from what I know of you Brits, I know that's a British thing, a display of good manners by avoiding the blindingly obvious.'

'What precisely do you know about us Brits, then?' she asked.

'I spent time there during the war flying with Bomber Command. Unfortunately I let everyone down by getting blown out of the sky and ending up in northern France with a shattered leg.'

44

'Well, that puts me resoundingly in my place.'

'Hey, don't sweat it. It's my special skill to rub people up the wrong way. You're not the first to have their hackles ambushed, and you certainly won't be the last, you can bet on it. How's the ravioli?'

'It's delicious. Do you always flit from one subject to another?'

'Only when I'm nervous. And right now, I'm as nervous as two world leaders playing a deadly game of nuclear poker.'

His throwaway remark was a chilling reminder that the world was currently balanced on a knife edge. Which was hard to believe sitting here in such beautiful surroundings. For days now the news the world over had been consumed with what was being called the Cuban missile crisis. Last week President Kennedy had made a lengthy television broadcast informing America that Soviet ships were carrying weapons to Cuba and that the US would do all it could to prevent that happening. US warships were now in position. Who would blink first was the question on everybody's lips, Kennedy or Khrushchev?

'I suspect you don't know the meaning of being nervous,' she said. 'You strike me as having an excess of confidence and chutzpah.'

'Appearances can be deceiving, you know. How about you tell me three things I should know about you? Other than you can't abide lateness in a person, rudeness, or a brash Yank.'

'How very perceptive of you.'

'That's me. Perceptive as hell beneath the dumb exterior.'

'Seeing as you have me thoroughly sized up, why don't you tell me three things I should know about you?'

'Fair enough. Firstly, and to quote your Oscar Wilde, I can resist anything except temptation. Secondly, I always tell it how it is; I never beat about the bush. Thirdly, my golden rule in life is, if in doubt, do it. Which is why I think we should—'

'Work together,' she finished for him.

45

'Got it in one kiddo.'

'Don't ever call me kiddo,' she said sternly.

'Yes ma'am,' he replied, giving her a salute. 'I mean, no ma'am. So are we on? Are we going to do this thing?'

Chapter Nine

Melstead Hall, Melstead St Mary
October 1962
Julia

DO YOU THINK YOUR HUSBAND
COULD REALLY LOVE A PATHETIC
NOBODY LIKE YOU?

The words of the anonymous letter had taunted Julia Devereux ever since that morning when she had opened it after breakfast, and thankfully when her husband wasn't around. All day she had wondered whether she should tell Arthur about it, but in the end had decided not to. Not when it might send him into a furious rage.

She hated it when he was angry. And besides, it wasn't good for his blood pressure. Better to keep quiet about the letter, to throw it on the fire and pretend it had never existed. More than likely it was the work of that careless girl who Arthur insisted Julia sack after she'd burned the cuff of one of his shirts.

As was often the way of their evenings, when he was home, Arthur was downstairs in his library and Julia was in her upstairs parlour. It was her favourite room in the entire house. During the day it gave her a beautiful view of the rolling parkland that surrounded Melstead Hall, all one hundred acres of it.

She had been married to Arthur for eight years, yet she still had to pinch herself that her life had been so transformed. One minute she had been a lowly nurse living in a two-bedroom semi in Bayswater, and the next she was the wife of Arthur Devereux.

Her father had always said that marriage wasn't for her, that no man would treat her as well as he did. Her duty, he would repeatedly say, was to be a dutiful daughter and remain at home to look after him. He had encouraged her to become a nurse so that when the time came she would be better equipped to take care of him when he was old. He had been dead a year when she met Arthur and oh, how she wished he could see her now, mistress of Melstead Hall no less!

Listening to the carriage clock on the mantelpiece chiming the hour, she hoped that when Ralph, Arthur's son from his first marriage, arrived later that evening for the weekend, he wouldn't antagonise his father. He had a habit of provoking Arthur and creating an unpleasant atmosphere.

She put away her sewing kit and once more examined her stitchwork closely. Arthur liked his clothes to be just so. 'I might well be rich enough to wear a new shirt every day of the week, but I'm not a spendthrift,' he would tell Julia. 'People who are careless with money don't deserve to have it.'

Satisfied that the button she had sewn on was perfectly straight and secure, and that it would meet with Arthur's approval, Julia put it ready for her to iron in the morning. After being forced to sack the servant who normally did the washing and ironing, it was now down to Julia to take care of the laundry, and any sewing that needed doing.

'You're the only one I can trust to care for my clothes properly,' Arthur had explained to her. 'I know I'm fastidious, but I can't help the way I am. You understand that, don't you?' She had told him she understood perfectly.

There were many other tasks he didn't trust the household

48

staff to do and Julia willingly did them, wanting so much to please her husband.

A strict disciplinarian, her father had brought her up believing that nothing mattered more than obedience and duty. 'No matter how insignificant the task is, or how difficult, it should be done to the best of your ability,' he would say. For as long as she could remember, this was what Julia had tried to do.

So when Arthur insisted that she make a weekly inventory of the contents of the pantry and his extensive wine cellar, she did it with painstaking attention to detail. 'This way,' he claimed when he was checking the ledger books into which she recorded the inventories, 'the household staff can't pilfer from me and think they can get away with it. It's important for me to have somebody running the house in my absence whom I can trust.'

That Arthur trusted her to carry out these jobs and not Miss Casey their housekeeper, filled Julia with pride and the determination to do everything just as Arthur wanted.

She wouldn't dream of telling anyone this, for fear of appearing paranoid, but Julia could never shake off the suspicion that Miss Casey watched over her. She was convinced the woman looked down on her, and that the other members of staff talked about her behind her back. She often heard them whispering amongst themselves, but they fell instantly silent when she walked into the room. She never mentioned this to Arthur for fear that he might sack every member of staff, leaving her with all the work to do. She wasn't scared of hard work. Not at all. It was just there were only so many hours in the day and this house was so very big to run. It was a maze of rooms and shadowy corridors that were difficult to heat. In winter, and when Arthur was away in London, he instructed that the heating was turned down. Ice would form on the inside of the windows and winds, straight from the North Sea, whistled through the gaping cracks.

'A hale and hearty girl like you can withstand a little cold, can't you, Julia?' he would say. 'I wish I had your constitution,' he would add, 'but as you know all too well from when you nursed me, I'm not blessed with good health like you.' That was how they met, when she had nursed him through a severe bout of pneumonia.

She once remarked that their son Charles would fare better with a little more heat, but Arthur chided her for spoiling the boy.

This was Charles's first term away at boarding school and Julia missed him terribly. He was such a sweet gentle boy.

'The worst thing you can do to that boy is mollycoddle him,' Arthur had claimed when she had suggested there was no hurry to send Charles away to school.

Julia would have liked a daughter. She felt sure Arthur wouldn't talk of toughening up a daughter by sending her away to school. Every month that went by, Julia hoped that she was pregnant, but it hadn't happened. Now that she was thirty-seven, time was running out for her. Perhaps it had already. For Arthur too, given that he was now fifty and his health was not as it should be. He really ought not to eat so much, but the slightest hint from her on the subject and he would fly into a rage.

When Arthur had bought the Hall from Sir Archibald and Lady Fogg and driven Julia here for the first time to see it, he had been jubilant in his ownership of the house. Taking her upstairs, he had insisted they make love straightaway in what would be their bedroom. 'Start as we mean to go on,' he'd declared as he instructed her to remove her clothes and lie down on the dusty floorboards. Their noisy coupling had embarrassed her acutely as the thump-thump-thump echoed around the empty house. She had been grateful nobody else had been there to hear.

His appetite for sex matched that of his love of food and she worried sometimes that she wouldn't be able to satisfy him. But as always, and remembering her father's stern edicts, she performed her duty to the best of her ability and with exacting diligence. She never complained about the bruises to her body with which she often woke in the morning, or the pain that accompanied them. Complaining was not something she did.

And why should she complain when Arthur had given her so much?

Chapter Ten

London and Suffolk
October 1962
Ralph

Ralph Devereux would have set off earlier for Suffolk, but he'd had some unfinished business to attend to. That of ending things on the telephone with a girlfriend who'd started to imagine the ringing of wedding bells. The thought of marriage appalled him. He was twenty-two, had only come down from Cambridge this summer, and had no intention of settling down for a very long time yet.

His smart leather valise now packed, he locked the door of his Chelsea mews and hopped into his awaiting MG Roadster. With its 1600 engine, it packed a satisfying punch, and hopefully, given it was eight o'clock in the evening, the roads would be clear enough to give him the opportunity to get his foot down hard. He turned the key in the ignition and roared away down the cobbled street, taking a sharp right, and then an equally sharp left, the tyres squealing in protest.

Once he was out of London and had the open road ahead of him, the real fun started as he revved up the engine. Funny to think of Romily having been a racing driver when she was young. He had to admire her for that. Not that he'd ever say anything in her favour in front of his father. Arthur Devereux hated Romily, really hated her. He resented her for so much, but mostly for marrying his father, Jack Devereux, and, as he saw it, for stealing Island House away from its rightful heirs. This, Ralph was convinced, was the reason Arthur had bought Melstead Hall. It was his way of putting Romily in her place.

Situated a short distance from Island House, and easily the largest and most imposing property in Melstead St Mary, Dad revelled in the status the house gave him. He enjoyed lording it over the rest of the village, especially the rest of the family.

Ralph hated it when anyone in the family so much as hinted that he was a chip off his father's block. He may have inherited the old man's cunning for manipulating people to do what he wanted, but physically he was nothing like Arthur Devereux. He was taller and a lot slimmer, and a hundred times fitter. His dad was hugely overweight. He smoked too much and he drank too much. He had a vicious temper that frequently gave way to explosive outbursts, which doubtless sent his already high blood pressure soaring. In short, he was a heart attack waiting to happen.

The person who bore the brunt of his temper was Julia, his third wife. Much younger than Arthur, she had always struck Ralph as a very improbable choice of wife. She was, it had to be said, a rather pathetic creature who was firmly under her husband's thumb.

When Dad had announced he was marrying for the third time, and to the nondescript nurse who had cared for him when he'd been ill with pneumonia, nobody was more surprised than Ralph. Quiet and timid, she was the last woman anyone would have expected Arthur Devereux to install as his wife at Melstead Hall. She lacked class or wealth, both things the previous wives had possessed.

Within a year of marrying, Julia dutifully produced a new son for Arthur. Charles was now seven years old and experiencing his first term away at boarding school. Ralph had been the same age when he'd been sent away.

During the few occasions Ralph went home, he saw how his father treated Julia more like a servant than mistress of Melstead Hall. For instance, he insisted that she lay out his clothes every morning for him. They had any number of servants to do such a menial task, including Miss Casey the housekeeper, but for some reason Arthur made it clear that Julia had to do it.

Ralph could not imagine his previous stepmother ever agreeing to do that. Arthur had married Caroline when Ralph was six, just a year after he divorced Irene, Ralph's mother. Irene's name was never to be uttered again in Arthur's presence, and apart from a few letters, Ralph had no contact with her from the day she left their house in London and went to live in Paris with the man with whom she had been having a long-term affair.

For some time it was just Ralph and his father, along with the household staff, a nanny, and a stream of women who came and went. But then along had come Caroline Thurlesford, the sole heir to Thurlesford Brewery in the Midlands. She was a vain, vacuous woman who had no interest in Ralph. Ralph had always been of the opinion that his father married Caroline because she was so wealthy and would, one day, be wealthier still when her father died.

That day came sooner than anyone anticipated, but with a twist – both Caroline and her father died in an avalanche while skiing in Chamonix. As a result, Arthur inherited a considerable fortune and immediately gave up his cushy job with the Civil Service. The last thing he wanted to do was take on the running of the brewery, so he sold it to a competitor for an obscene amount of money.

If Ralph played his cards right and stayed in his father's good books, he would one day receive a decent share of the Thurlesford inheritance. God knows he could do with it.

With only ten miles left before he would arrive at Melstead Hall, he thought about the weekend ahead. Before or after the party at Meadow Lodge he hoped to persuade his old man to increase his allowance. It was ridiculous that he should be so penny-pinching when he was loaded to the extent he was. He'd grumbled endlessly when Ralph had come down from Cambridge and asked if he could have his own place in London. From the way Dad reacted anyone would think Ralph had asked if he would buy the Taj Mahal for him. The wrangling had gone on for weeks until finally the old man had extracted a promise from Ralph; that he would put his expensive education to good use and find himself a job.

The promise made, Ralph moved into 4A Caiston Mews. Furnishing it had cost him an arm and a leg, and the house-warming parties he'd put on for his friends had made a huge dent in his dwindling finances. He had yet to land himself a job; not that his hunt for one had been that exhaustively thorough, and he had reached the unavoidable conclusion that he had to ask for an increase in his allowance. It would be a temporary arrangement, he planned to say this weekend, just to get him on his feet. It wouldn't be easy and all he could do was hope to catch his father in a rare good mood.

Putting aside the slim chance of that actually happening, he contemplated his Plan B, that of approaching Julia. She must surely be given an allowance for the running of the household, as well as her own personal use, so it was just a matter of him applying his legendry charm and persuading her to lend him some money. It was a long shot, but worth a try. It would have to be an arrangement which they kept very much between themselves.

Chapter Eleven

Casa Santa Rosa, Palm Springs
October 1962
Romily

Darkness came early in Palm Springs and with surprising swiftness. The sunset, as glorious as it had been, had been fleeting and now the opaque velvety sky was studded with diamond-bright stars. With the air still scented with orange blossom, it should have been the perfect setting for a relaxing evening. But Romily was thrumming with restless energy.

Lunch with Red had gone on for some hours, during which he'd made it clear that he would enjoy the challenge of working with her.

'What have you got to lose by giving it a go?' he'd asked when she repeated her desire to think about their writing together. Which was her polite way of stalling, before finally ruling out the project.

'My sanity,' she'd told him, 'that's what I'd lose. Working with you would drive me mad.'

He'd laughed. 'I've gotta give it to you, you tell it straight. I like that in a person. And I suspect you do too. Which is why I'm gonna urge you to loosen up and have a shot at relaxing. When was the last time you had any fun in your life? And I mean real fun?'

His question had outraged her. How dare he presume her life lacked fun! He'd been in her company for no time at all and had the temerity to think he knew anything about her. In short measure she had informed him that she was perfectly happy with the quantity of fun in her life.

'I'm delighted to hear that,' he'd said. 'Care to share with me the last thing that made you laugh out loud?'

To her great discomfort she had not been able to answer him. Not honestly.

It was that realisation that was causing her to pace like a caged panther on the terrace of the guest cottage at Casa Santa Rosa. When had she last laughed to the point her sides ached? Was that what age did? Stripped a person of the ability to laugh?

No! Age had nothing to do with it. Besides, fifty-five was not old. Jack had been older than she was now when they'd met and their brief time together had been full of laughter.

'When I look into the mirror I see an ageing man with his best years long since past, but I look into your eyes and see myself still in my prime, young and invincible!'

Jack had said this on the eve of their wedding day, and just a few weeks before he'd died from a stroke. The age difference between them had never bothered Romily; all that mattered was that they loved each other and were happy together. And made each other laugh.

The ringing of a telephone from inside her guest accommodation interrupted her thoughts. She went to answer it.

'Hey, Romily, is that you, honey?'

'It is,' she said cautiously, unsure who it was.

'It's me, Gabe. How'd it go today with Red? Did you get on like a house on fire, just as we said you would?'

'I'm afraid not.'

'Oh?'

'I might just as well be perfectly honest with you, Gabe, our writing together won't work. We're just not . . . we're not *simpatico*.'

'Simpatty what?'

'Not compatible. We're two very different people and I'm absolutely of the opinion we wouldn't get the best out of each other.'

'Now Romily, honey, are you sure you gave Red a chance to prove himself?'

'I don't think for one second Mr St Clair needs any encouragement to prove himself.'

Gabe guffawed. 'Are you saying he tried it on with you, Romily?'

'Certainly not! And had he done so I would most assuredly have put him in his place.'

Gabe let rip with another guffaw. 'I don't doubt that you would have! You're one scary dame when you want to be.'

'What on earth do you mean?'

'Ah, c'mon, you know jolly well what I'm saying. Now look, get down from your uppity high-horse and give the guy a break; he's a war hero, you know. He's not some nobody with straw behind his ears. Sit down together and—'

'We've already tried that over lunch today.'

'So what the hell went wrong? Did he use the wrong cutlery or something?'

'Gabe, are you trying to imply that I'm a shallow snob?'

'Well, you Brits get pretty hung up on all that etiquette stuff, don't you?'

'I'd like to think I'm above such things.'

'I'm glad to hear it. Now do me a favour and meet with Red tomorrow. Loosen your stays and go have some fun together. And bear in mind the old cliché, Romily.'

Every ounce of her body fizzing with indignation, she said, 'Which would be what exactly?'

'Honey, even you, with your will of iron, must accept the

most obvious goddamn cliché in the book, that opposites attract. *Ciao* for now!'

Very carefully Romily put down the receiver, resisting the urge to hurl the wretched device across the room.

Within seconds the telephone rang again. 'Yes,' she snapped, 'was there something else with which you wanted to harangue me?'

'Not as far as I'm aware.'

'Who is this?' she asked, thrown off guard.

'It's me, Red. Have I caught you at a bad time? Or is it always a bad time for you?'

Romily inwardly groaned. 'I'm sorry,' she said, 'I thought you were somebody else.'

'Whoever it was, I wish him luck when he does call you. Do you give all the men in your life a hard time?'

'Why do you think I was expecting a man to be at the other end of the line?'

'Just a wild guess on my part. So, do you?'

'Do I what precisely?'

'Give the men in your life a hard time?'

'Only the ones who go the extra mile to annoy me.'

'In that case, how am I doing?'

Recalling Gabe's request for her to be nice, she said, 'Barely registering.'

'Gee, I'm hurt.'

'Did you ring for something specific, or was this just a social call?'

'I was wondering if you'd reached a decision about our working together.'

'I'd like to sleep on it,' she said. Another prevaricating lie. Why didn't she just get it over with and flatly refuse to consider the project any further?

'Look, I know I'm as pushy as hell and as subtle as a typhoon, but I have to tell you, I have a good feeling about a collaboration between us.'

She suddenly thought of his words at lunchtime – *If in doubt, do it.* It was exactly the kind of thing she would normally say. And hadn't she always enjoyed the challenge of deliberately flouting convention and doing something for the sheer hell of it?

Just as she couldn't recall the last occasion when she'd truly laughed and had disgraceful fun, she tried to remember when she had done anything for the sheer devil-may-care hell of it. Drawing a blank, she recoiled at the awful conclusion that somewhere along the line she had become an anathema to herself – boringly conventional. Where had her spirit of adventure gone?

'Red,' she said on impulse, 'do you have plans for the rest of the evening?'

'A whole ton of nothing. Why?'

'I'd like to experience the desert at night while I'm here.'

'With me?'

'Yes. If it wouldn't be too much trouble.'

'No trouble at all. I can't think of anything I'd like better: you, me and the desert stars.'

Chapter Twelve

Palm Springs
October 1962
Red

It was a hell of thing. This being with a woman who intrigued him the way she did.

To his bemusement Red hadn't felt like this in a heck of a time. He could not have felt himself more precariously placed had he been carrying a large tray of glasses while walking a tightrope in a gusting wind. He suspected a lot of men had experienced the same reaction on meeting Romily Devereux-Temple for the first time.

Usually he didn't give a damn what people thought of him, and nor did he usually have any trouble in persuading them to do what he wanted. But Romily was a whole different ball game. Which meant he had thrown his reliable rule-book out of the window for the simple reason he gave a *huge* damn about what she thought of him.

And that was based on three things.

Firstly, she was damned easy on the eye, a classy regal beauty who held herself tall and proud.

Secondly, when she'd removed her sunglasses during lunch today – the better to scrutinise him, he'd imagined – he'd been struck by the extraordinary violet hue of her irises.

And thirdly, what really piqued his interest was her blatant disdain for him. This was a new phenomenon for him, and he'd be damned if he didn't rise to the challenge to win her round, to make her think well of him.

He had picked her up at Casa Santa Rosa half an hour after calling her, and had been gratified by her reaction to his Alfa Romeo. 'A Giulietta Sprint convertible,' she'd remarked, when he'd held the door open for her to get in. 'I fancied one of these myself. Does she handle as well as I've heard?'

'Like a dream. The clutch is as light and fluid as it comes and she holds the road like a barnacle clinging to the hull of a boat. You're welcome to drive if you'd like?'

'No, no, I'm happy to be a passenger.'

He'd sensed her politely doing her best not to watch as he'd eased himself stiffly into the driver's seat. Her only comment was to observe how accommodating the car was for a man of his height. 'It's a damned miracle, given the build of your average Italian,' he'd quipped, turning the key in the ignition and firing up the engine with a satisfying throaty roar.

He'd driven her along empty roads that were as familiar to him as any he knew, and out to his favourite spot in the desert. It was where few other people ventured. Most visitors to Palm Springs, particularly the ritzy crowd, didn't go more than a few hundred yards from where they were staying, going only as far as the golf course and tennis courts, and the shops on the main strip, and the currently fashionable hotel bars, restaurants and nightspots. The artificial Palm Springs as he called it. They didn't come to see the real desert by taking time to explore one of the many trails, either on foot or horseback, where they could enjoy a picnic beside a creek and breathe in the scent of wild tarragon. The thought of having a close encounter with a rattlesnake or scorpion put a stop to them experiencing the true majestic beauty of the mountains, where even in June there could be snow at the summit of Mount San Jacinto.

'Do you trust me?' he asked Romily when he brought the car

to a halt on the side of a narrow dirt track, and switched the engine off, plunging them into sudden blackness.

'It would appear I have no choice,' she said, peering into the dark.

'I promise no harm will come to you. If it does, Gabe and Melvyn will come for my scalp, and toss my carcass to the coyotes.'

'Then we'd better do all we can to avoid that happening,' she responded with a wry tone to her voice.

Out of the car, he popped open the trunk and retrieved a duffle bag and a folded travel rug. He then proceeded to light a kerosene lantern. 'Are you bothered by snakes?' he asked.

'Not particularly.'

'Good,' he said with a laugh. 'You can protect me from them.'

'How about I carry something?' she asked as he began slinging the duffle bag over his shoulder.

'No need, I can manage.'

'But it might be easier if I take something.'

He relinquished the rug to her and carrying the lantern, he led the way up a gentle, but rocky incline. 'Watch out for the barrel cactus,' he warned her, 'their needles are lethal.' As they climbed higher, he willed his leg with its new prosthetic to comply. Goddammit, he'd sooner gnaw off his good leg than admit he was in pain. A man has his pride, after all. And he was determined, at whatever cost, to make a good impression tonight.

He found his preferred spot in a semicircle of towering rocks that provided both shelter and warmth. With the sun beating down on the rocks all day, they acted as a great heat source at night.

He began assembling a campfire on the ashes of the last one he'd lit a few nights ago. Behind him, and in silence, Romily laid out the rug. When the first flames of the fire took hold, he joined her on the rug and waited for her to speak. It wasn't in his nature to hold his tongue, but he was giving it his best shot in this instance. But then the desert had that effect on him, it slowed him down, gave him space to think.

The silence deepened between them. Staring towards the mountain, its shadowy broad outline just discernible against the dark sky, Red heard a rustling sound in the scrubby undergrowth. A lizard perhaps. Or maybe a scorpion.

'I feel as though I can see every star in the galaxy,' Romily murmured finally, her head tilted back as she took in the infinite sky above them.

'Did you know the Milky Way contains about a hundred billion stars, give or take?'

'No I didn't.'

'Now isn't the best time to see it, spring is better. You should come again then.'

She said nothing.

'I love being up here,' he continued, his voice low. 'I usually come alone. It's where I come to get a fresh perspective. Especially if I've just spent any time in Hollywood. What's your opinion of Tinsel Town?'

She sat up straighter, drew her knees in the cotton slacks she was wearing towards her chest. 'It is what it is,' she said, staring at him, her hands clasped around her knees. 'It doesn't pretend to be anything other than a brash carousel that never stops revolving.'

'You like that in life, do you? Transparency?'

'Yes. I can't abide affectation, people pretending to be something they're not.'

'But isn't the movie industry based on that? Nothing but lies and illusion?'

'My ward Isabella is a young actress, and she tells me that to be a great actor, to get the most out of the part you're playing, you have to be yourself and forget about acting.'

'She's a smart girl. It's the same with writing. You and I both know that it's got to be authentic, and from the heart, otherwise it's a load of horse—' he hastily checked himself, 'a load of baloney.'

'Horse shit will do just fine,' she said, 'no need to stand on ceremony with me.'

'Strangely that's exactly what I thought I had to do.'

She looked at him more intently in the flickering firelight, her eyes shining, her pale skin radiant with a roseate tint, a few strands of grey in her dark hair resembling threads of silver. 'Is your leg troubling you?' she asked.

Too late he realised that unconsciously he had been rubbing at the painful area where his stump and new artificial limb met. 'It's taking some getting used to,' he said with a shrug. 'It generally does.'

'I'm sorry. I shouldn't have imposed on you tonight.'

'I could have said no.'

The corners of her mouth lifted. 'I would hazard a guess that's something you rarely do.'

He smiled. 'Like I said at lunch, if in doubt, do it.' He rummaged in the duffle bag next to him. 'I brought you a sweater in case you got cold.' He held it out for her and she took it.

'Thank you,' she said, draping it around her shoulders, 'that was kind of you.'

He rummaged some more in the bag and pulled out a plastic tub and a bunch of wooden skewers. 'Now here's the most important question of the night – how do you like toasted marshmallows?'

She smiled. 'I like them a lot.'

He went to move nearer the fire, but she held out a hand. 'Why don't you let me do it?'

He was smart enough to know that allowing Romily to be

more than a bystander would go a long way to improving relations between them.

'Tell me about yourself, Red,' she said, when she had the marshmallows placed on the end of the sharp pointed wooden sticks and held them a short distance from the glowing embers of the fire.

'What do you want to know?'

'When did you develop an affinity with the desert here?'

He retrieved a bottle of bourbon from the duffle bag, along with two billy-cans.

'During the war. The El Mirador Hotel was turned into a hospital – the Torrey Army Hospital – and that was where I was sent to recuperate after I'd had my leg amputated. Drink?'

She nodded. 'That must have been a difficult time for you.'

He shook his head. 'There were men worse off than me. I was one of the lucky ones, I was soon able to hobble around on crutches and used to get one of the orderlies to take me out in his time off. He was a local guy, a Native American who knew everything there was to know about the wildlife and local traditions that were so important to his people. He'd drive me here, and I'd go as far as I could on my crutches. Each day I came he'd teach me something new and I'd push myself that little bit further.'

'You're a determined fellow, then?' She took one of the mugs from him and in exchange passed him one of the marshmallow sticks.

'I'm as stubborn as hell,' he said, 'and some. As you've already found.'

'You should know that I'm also as stubborn as hell.'

'I already figured that.'

In the quiet that followed, and worried that the cooling air temperature might not agree with Romily, he added some tinder-dry twigs on the fire, together with some larger pieces of tree branches that he'd gathered and hoarded during previous visits.

'I'm just a caveman at heart,' he said when she commented how organised he was. 'Or maybe I'm instinctively preparing for my own funeral pyre.'

'What a strange thing to say.'

'We're all nothing but a heartbeat away from death. I have no problem accepting my life is finite. Who knows, it might be tomorrow for us all if Kennedy can't stop the Soviets from plunging the world into a nuclear war.'

'Some deaths you just never see coming,' she said thoughtfully.

'Yeah,' he agreed. 'Like Marilyn Monroe's. When she died back in August, you'd have thought the world would stop turning such was the shock.'

'Did you ever meet her?'

'Sure, a few times.'

'Was she as beautiful in real life as she was on the screen?'

He shrugged. 'I guess.'

Romily raised an eyebrow. 'You must be one of the few men in the world not to rave about her exceptional beauty.'

'I am that rare man who prizes brains above beauty,' he said with a smile. 'Not that she was stupid. She wasn't.'

'The gossip columns would have us believe otherwise, that you prize beauty above all else.'

He laughed. 'Have you been doing your homework on me?'

'I found a pile of old magazines in the guest cottage in a cupboard. You're quite the ladies' man, aren't you?'

'You should know better than to believe a word of that trash. But enough about me, I'm much more interested in hearing something of your wartime escapades flying with the ATA.'

'How do you know about that?'

He tapped his nose. 'I've been doing *my* homework.'

'In that case you know all you need to know.'

'Hardly.'

'Why would you want to know any more?'

'Because I'm genuinely interested. Because we're two friends sitting in the desert getting to know each other over a mug of bourbon.'

And because I could sit here all night chatting with you, he thought. Or did he mean sparring?

Chapter Thirteen

Hamble, Hampshire
April 1944
Romily

The day had started off just as any normal day did; that is to say, I had no idea what to expect. Ever since I'd joined the Air Transport Auxiliary, no two days were ever the same; we took whatever was thrown at us.

It had been a busy period for me. According to my logbook, in the last six weeks I'd delivered a total of sixty-one military aircraft from British factories and maintenance units to RAF airfields. I'd flown Mustangs, Mosquitos, Spitfires, Hurricanes, a couple of Grumman Avengers and a Corsair, and my most hated of machines, the Walrus. I had also notched up ten taxi-days, ferrying pilots about the country.

Much to my amusement, there were still some RAF aircrew who resented a woman in the cockpit, believing we should be at home darning socks and making jam. But as with all my female colleagues, I took the sneers and put-downs in my stride. We had more important things to worry about.

For some weeks now, large-scale military exercises had been taking place on the south coast in readiness for the much-talked about Allied invasion of Europe. The trains were full of troops moving about the country and roads too were congested with military vehicles. I knew from Florence's husband Billy, and Isabella's father, Elijah, that they had both been deployed there,

69

though naturally their exact whereabouts was secret.

I was not normally a pessimist, but I worried about the chances of a successful outcome to this planned invasion. I worried about Billy and Elijah in particular. I kept my concerns to myself and put on an upbeat appearance at all times. I suspected that most people were doing the same. We were all so tired of rationing, of listening to the news and clinging to the hope that the war would soon be over. How absurd it now seemed that in the first few months after Neville Chamberlain addressed the nation to announce that we were at war with Germany, people had said it would be over by Christmas. That was four and a half years ago.

Funnily enough, I wasn't the least bit pessimistic when I was airborne. It didn't matter what plane I was flying – other than the dreaded Walrus – once I was up in the air, I felt elated. Even when it was freezing cold, or conditions made flying extremely risky, such as flying through dense clouds and relying solely on the instruments, I never lost that sensation of feeling utterly free. At the controls in the cockpit I felt all-powerful. Which I knew was dangerous; it could lead to a careless mistake that could cost me my life.

Which very nearly happened that morning.

Having cycled the four miles to work in the rain, I received my instructions from our commanding officer, Margot Gore. Margot was one of the most organised people I knew and was hugely respected by us all at No. 15 Ferry Pool, Hamble-on-Solent. Nothing passed her notice and she saw at once the expression on my face when I read the chit she handed me – I was to deliver a Walrus to RAF West Raynham. 'Everybody has to draw a short straw now and again,' she said pleasantly.

The reason most of us dreaded flying this single-engined amphibian plane used by the Air-Sea Rescue, was because take-off was akin to riding a bull at full gallop, and once in the air it rolled like a galleon on the high seas, rendering me as sick as a dog. No other aircraft had this effect on me. And no other plane forced me to crawl on my hands and knees through the hull to reach the cockpit. This involved pushing my way through a plethora of anchors and cables and anything else that was cluttering up the space, as though the aircraft was used like an old barn in which to store things. The alternative was to climb inelegantly up the outside of the hulking great beast.

By the time I was ready for take-off, the fine drizzling rain of earlier had ceased, but the wind had risen. I always imagined the Walrus as a cussed brute that sulked its way reluctantly off the ground and up into the air, but not before the control column had repeatedly bashed against my chest as the wheels went over the bumps of the runway.

All had been going well, when, and approximately ten minutes from my destination, I suddenly felt, and heard, an almighty clunk beneath me. The instrument panel gave no indication as to what had happened, but something was obviously amiss. When the engine began to cut out, I knew I had to land as quickly as possible. Checking my position, I calmly accepted that I wouldn't make it to the airfield.

The essential thing was to find somewhere clear of any buildings. I'd previously carried out a number of emergency landings, it wasn't new to me, but I'd never done one in a Walrus before. And a Walrus with a failing engine. Keeping the brute steady, I looked out for a handy field that was obstacle-free. I spotted a field fringed with trees and a large hay barn to one side, just as the engine made yet more ominous sounds of conking out and a plume of smoke appeared. Beggars can't be choosers, I thought, the field would have to do. I pumped away to lower the wheels and prepared to land.

I was about six feet from the ground when a cross-wind buffeted the Walrus. With its double wing structure, this was the last thing I needed and sure enough, the aircraft damn near performed a pirouette before heading straight towards the barn.

Chapter Fourteen

Palm Springs
October 1962
Romily

'What happened next?' asked Red.

'As you can see, I survived,' Romily said matter of factly.

'It must have been a hell of a hair-raising experience.'

'Yes. But it was one of many close calls. We were all like cats ticking off our nine lives.'

'So why tell me that particular incident?'

His question poked at an achingly tender spot. 'It's . . . it's the most memorable,' she answered.

'Why's that?'

She hesitated with her reply and tore her gaze away from the campfire. All the while she had been talking she had been unaware of where she was; she had been lost in the past, transported back to a time when she had never felt more alive. Flying with the ATA had been as exhilarating as it had been exhausting. Yet it had never entirely assuaged the pain of losing her beloved Jack, as she'd hoped it would.

Jack's oldest friend, Roddy, sadly no longer alive, had once made Romily promise him that she would let go of Jack and live life to the fullest.

Would he think she had?

Compared to most people she had lived an extraordinarily full life, but what did that really mean?

With the soft cashmere of Red's sweater resting against her neck, the sleeves tied beneath her chin, she could smell the heady scent of his cologne, a citrusy fragrance combined with bergamot and sandalwood. It made her look at the man sitting a few feet from her. In the peaceful silence of the desert, the dancing shadows of the dwindling firelight gave Red's face the look of being carved. He had a strong and determined profile, a pronounced square jaw and lines deeply etched around his eyes and mouth. His hair was thick and bordering on unruly, much like him, she found herself thinking.

He was a man who doubtless did things his way. A man who was spontaneous and resisted conformity. Why else was he sitting here in the middle of nowhere with her?

'Because of what happened next,' she said finally in answer to his question. Then taking hold of a stick, she poked at the glowing embers of the fire. 'We should go,' she said. 'It's late.'

'What?' he exclaimed. 'You're going to leave me hanging just like that?'

'That's the job of a storyteller,' she said, 'to leave the reader wanting more.'

He smiled. 'Well, take it from me, this guy definitely wants to know more.'

Chapter Fifteen

Island House, Melstead St Mary
October 1962
Isabella

'Mmm ... something smells good,' remarked Isabella as she, together with Stanley and Annelise, entered the gates of hell – otherwise known as the kitchen at Island House, and where Mrs Collings ruled supreme and with a fist of iron.

The formidable woman swung round from the stove, a wooden spoon clenched in her hand. 'What's this then?' she demanded. 'A deputation in my kitchen?'

Stanley laughed. 'Only you could hold a wooden spoon and make yourself look dangerously armed.'

'Is it any wonder I arm myself when you pop up looking more and more like one of those dreadful *nitbeaks*. Just look at the state of your hair! Any longer and people will think you're a woman!'

'I think you mean *beatnik*, which I'll take as a compliment. So what culinary delights have you in store for us for lunch?'

'Cheeky beggar,' said Mrs Collings. 'You have chicken and mushroom pie with mashed potatoes and green beans and carrots.'

'And for dessert?'

'Apricot tart. Now out of my way so I can get this meal served.'

'That's why we're here,' said Isabella, stepping forward, 'we're here to help.'

'And who says I need any help?'

'Hope thought you might like it, seeing as Florence is over at Meadow Lodge getting things ready for the party,' said Annelise.

'And taken Beatty the new maid with her,' said Mrs Collings, disapprovingly.

'But here we are,' said Stanley 'all three of us present and correct, just waiting to do your bidding.'

'In that case, if you can be trusted not to drop anything, you can make a start by taking these plates through to the dining room. Annelise, you can fill the water jug, it's over there on the draining board and then put it on the table.'

'What about me, Mrs Collings?'

She gave Isabella a look as if to say, *And what about you?* Isabella could become the most famous actress of the day, but this harridan of a woman would still treat her as the naughty teenager who had once secretly stirred salt into the custard Mrs Collings had just made. 'You can fetch the butter from the pantry,' she instructed, 'and add a knob of it to the carrots and beans when I've drained them. If you're sure you won't make a mess of it.'

'I'll do my best,' Isabella said, tempted to tug on her forelock and throw in a curtsey for good measure.

They had the last of the dishes on the table with Mrs Collings fussing over where they should be placed when Edmund arrived back from doing his morning rounds. 'Any chance of some mustard to go with your delicious pie, Mrs Collings?' he asked.

She scowled. 'I'll see what I can do,' she said.

'If it's not too much trouble,' Edmund said, with the kind of smile Isabella knew could warm the coldest of hearts. Not for nothing was he known in the village for having the best bedside manner this side of Dr Kildare.

'Honestly, I swear that woman gets worse,' muttered Hope, when Mrs Collings had gone. 'I don't know why Romily keeps her. She's not a patch on Mrs Partridge.'

'You know Romily has a weakness for lame ducks,' said Edmund.

'There's nothing lame about Mrs Collings,' asserted Hope.

'It must be difficult for her, knowing she has such a hard act to follow,' said Annelise.

'Yes,' agreed Stanley. 'Mrs Partridge was like a grandmother to us all.'

As they all did, Isabella had many affectionate memories of the big-hearted woman who had presided over the kitchen here at Island House for as long as she could remember. Sadly, she had died peacefully in her sleep two years ago.

'Mrs Collings is all right,' said Edmund, indicating everyone should sit down, 'her curmudgeonly manner is merely an act. She's a pussycat really. You just have to know how to handle her.'

Hope rolled her eyes. 'And you would know all about handling women, wouldn't you? You have every woman in the village of a certain age at your beck and call.'

'Not quite *every* woman,' replied Edmund lightly. As light as his voice was, Isabella caught the frown on his face. They were quite used to Hope's occasional bouts of crabbiness, but her remark, along with a couple made last night during dinner, seemed unusually sharp. Perhaps she was working too hard. That was the excuse they all used for Hope when she became tetchy.

Isabella clearly wasn't alone in thinking Hope had been unnecessarily unkind to Edmund, because the room had gone deathly quiet. It was as if nobody knew what to say. In the awkward silence, Mrs Collings bustled back in with the requested pot of mustard. Edmund thanked her and she huffed her way out again as though she had just been forced to tramp across the Himalayas.

Hope issued another tut, but before she could say anything, Edmund said, 'It's lovely to have you girls home for the weekend. We don't see enough of you these days. Not nearly enough.'

'Oh, please don't make me feel any worse than I already feel,' said Annelise. 'This term's just been so busy. I would have come home if I'd been able to.'

'For heaven's sake, Edmund, don't nag the poor girl; you said much the same thing last night. She has her own life to lead in Oxford.'

'I'm not nagging anyone. I wouldn't dream of it.'

Once more Isabella saw the frown crease Edmund's brow. Something was going on. Had Hope and Edmund had a row?

Ignoring her husband, and while they all began helping themselves from the dishes, Hope turned to Stanley. In a classic example of there being no such thing as a free lunch, Hope had invited him to join them so that she could go over some detail or other about the new house.

Observing Stanley across the table, Isabella acknowledged that longer hair suited him, as did the black polo-neck sweater he was wearing. There was a markedly more urbane air about him these days. She wondered if Annelise had noticed it. Possibly not. It was obvious to Isabella that Stanley worshipped the ground Annelise walked on, but Annelise being Annelise, she was completely blind to it.

The conversation around the table had now moved on to America and the Soviets battling it out over Cuba. Isabella took the view that if the world was about to end, she would make damned sure she enjoyed her last days on earth. Trying to lighten the mood again, and interrupting Hope, she asked Stanley if he was taking anyone to the party at Meadow Lodge that evening.

He looked uncomfortable at her question. 'No,' he replied, his eyes downcast, lost behind his fringe.

'Well, you are now, you can escort Annelise and me.'

'Isabella!' remonstrated Annelise. 'You can't railroad him like that. Now he'll feel obliged. And anyway, I'm quite capable of attending a party unaccompanied.'

'Oh, for heaven's sake, I haven't railroaded anyone. Do you feel obliged, Stanley?'

He looked uneasy. 'If Annelise would rather I didn't take her,' he said, 'I'd quite understand.'

'Why did you have to make me look so ungracious?' Annelise demanded when lunch was over and she followed Isabella upstairs to what had been her old bedroom before she went to live with Elijah. Downstairs Hope was still bending Stanley's ear, and Edmund had returned to his surgery.

'I think you'll find you did that all by yourself,' said Isabella. 'Honestly, why did you have to be so churlish? I was just trying to make lunch a bit jollier. What's going on between Hope and Edmund?'

'What do you mean?'

'Goodness, Annelise, for such an intelligent girl you can be remarkably obtuse. Hope keeps sniping at Edmund. She did it last night too.'

'You know what Mums is like when she's under pressure; she gets all cranky. As soon as she's finished this latest book she'll calm down. She's a perfectionist, that's the trouble.'

'No,' said Isabella, joining Annelise at the window where she was looking down at the garden, 'the real trouble is, she doesn't know how to relax. When was the last time she cleared her diary long enough to go on holiday with Edmund? Or even go to the theatre for that matter? She does nothing but work. It's like a drug for her. An obsession.'

'It's her passion. It always has been. I would have thought you of all people would understand that.'

'Of course I'm passionate about what I do, but I still want to have fun in my life. Otherwise what's the point? And you know what, Romily used to have fun too, but I've noticed lately that work dominates everything she does. Look how she was meant to be home this weekend for the party, but she's allowed work to keep her there in America.'

'We don't know that it's work.'

'What else could it be?'

'Even if it is, you and I would have done the same. It's called seizing an opportunity. As women we have to work that much harder in our chosen professions to get where we want to be.'

Isabella hated it when Annelise was right, but unable to let her have the last word, she said, 'And where do you want to be, Annelise, in, let's say, five years' time?'

'With Castro urging the Soviets to attack America with a nuclear missile, I don't think there's much point looking too far into the future, do you?'

Isabella tutted. 'In the hope that doesn't happen, where do you see yourself in five years?'

'I don't know. But one day, when I'm a lot older, I'd like nothing more than to be the Dean of St Gertrude's. What about you?'

'Does marriage not figure in your ambition?' Isabella replied without answering the question.

For a split second, Annelise's expression faltered. 'I don't think I'm the marrying sort,' she said, running a finger along the windowsill.

Storing away that hesitant response from Annelise, Isabella smiled. 'Well, I plan to marry at least three times. The first time to further my career. The second for money. And the third for love.'

Annelise's face was a picture of scandalised shock. 'That's dreadful, even by your standards.'

Isabella laughed. 'I'm joking! You really need to lighten up; you're much too serious these days. Which brings me back to Hope. She needs to watch out, because if she's not careful, she'll push Edmund too far. I've seen it happen with my own eyes, or more precisely, I've been on the receiving end of a neglected husband's need to feel wanted. It never fails to amaze me how fragile the male ego is.'

Annelise looked aghast. 'You can't possibly think Edmund would stray. He's not like those unprincipled actors you mix with. He's a decent and honourable man, the epitome of a loyal and utterly trustworthy husband. What's more he loves Mums.'

'All of which may well be true. But a man can only be pushed so far before his principles fly out of the window.'

'I can't believe you're talking this way. You've become so cynical.'

Accepting there was no point in going any further with the conversation, Isabella decided to change the subject.

'What are you wearing for the party tonight?' she asked. 'Can I see? After all, we don't want to clash, do we?'

Chapter Sixteen

Island House, Melstead St Mary
October 1962
Annelise

Alone in her bedroom, Annelise stood in front of her writing desk with its view of the garden. The leaves on the trees had turned, and in the afternoon sun, rich autumnal hues of rust, copper and gold were perfectly reflected in the still surface of the pond. She loved autumn.

She was about to turn away from the window when she saw Isabella in the garden below. Annelise watched her walk across the lawn, then disappear through the archway in the hedge. She knew exactly where Isabella was going; she was following the path that led to the churchyard where Elijah and her mother were buried. She went there every time she came home. It was a pilgrimage for her.

Isabella may not have known the woman who had given birth to her, and given her own life in the process, but she had a tangible connection, a gravestone she could touch, a place where she could lay flowers. Annelise envied her that. She had nowhere close at hand where she could go to mourn the passing of her parents.

Thanks to the meticulous records kept by the Nazis, Annelise knew that her mother had been sent to Ravensbruck, where eight months later she had died of typhus. Her father had been sent to Buchenwald to work in the infirmary of the camp, but died two years later of hypothermia. He had been forced to stand naked in the snow for disobeying an order.

In Oxford Annelise had been encouraged by Rebecca Hoffman, a friend and colleague at St Gertrude's, to observe the Sabbath, the Jewish holy day. Rebecca had invited her to join a group to celebrate Shabbat. She had accepted the invitation in the hope that she would feel some kind of connection to the people and the ritual, but mostly she had wanted to feel connected to her parents. But she had felt nothing, other than that she was an outsider, as though she were a spectator watching a performance that had no relevance to her life. Rebecca had sympathised, saying it was the lack of familiarity that had made Annelise feel the way she had, that regular attendance would change how she felt.

It was thanks to Rebecca that everything did indeed change for Annelise, just not in the way she could have foreseen.

Forever saying that Annelise didn't go out enough, Rebecca one day insisted that she accompany her to Blackwell's for the launch of a new book – *The History of Jews in Italy* – written by Professor Harry Knoller, a Fellow in Politics at Merton College. Reluctantly Annelise had agreed to go.

Her friend had been adamant that they arrive early for the event and had grabbed two seats on the front row. From the moment the author of the book had started speaking, Annelise could see that he was an immensely charismatic man who enjoyed the sound of his own voice. He spoke eloquently and with searing conviction, and it was obvious that he wanted his audience to be in no doubt that he possessed a ferocious intellect.

From her front row seat, and being in such close proximity to the speaker, it was impossible to avoid his gaze as it swept around his audience. More often than she was comfortable with, Annelise found his powerfully searching gaze settling on her. It made her wish she were seated at the back, safe from his scrutiny.

In his mid to late thirties, he had a full head of wavy dark brown hair, a narrow face and blue-grey eyes behind tortoiseshell-framed spectacles. He wore an open-necked shirt and a tweed jacket, which she noticed had a button missing. He looked every inch the college professor, but there was something overplayed about him. His performance, and that's exactly what it was, reminded Annelise of a play she had seen Isabella in. The leading actor had been hamming it up something awful, to the point that his character was wholly unconvincing.

As thought-provoking as she'd found the talk, Annelise had no wish to join the long queue to buy Professor Knoller's book, but Rebecca wasn't leaving empty-handed. They joined the queue until finally, in a gush of breathy admiration, Rebecca had her chance to request the great man's signature.

'What about you?' he said, pointing his fountain pen at Annelise, 'don't you want a book like your friend?'

'No thank you,' she said. 'I have enough to read at the moment.'

He considered her answer for a few seconds. And then: 'What did you think of my talk?'

'It was interesting.'

'*Interesting,*' he repeated. 'Is that all?'

'What's the answer you would rather I gave you?'

'The same as any academic would want. I want you to tell me that I'm sensationally brilliant, that my thought process is unique, and it had you on the edge of your seat, hanging on my every word.'

'If you need somebody to worship at the altar of your cleverness, I suggest you look elsewhere. After all, brilliance is not in short supply here in Oxford. And sadly, nor is sycophancy.' In any other situation she would have been appalled to hear herself being so extraordinarily rude, but she couldn't stop the condemnation pouring out of her.

But he just laughed. 'A straight-talking undergraduate, that makes a refreshing change.'

'A straight-talking *Junior Fellow*,' she corrected him. 'And really, we mustn't monopolise you anymore, you have many more people queuing to buy your book.'

'Won't you tell me your name?' he said.

'No need. Our paths won't cross again.'

She had been wrong. Three days later he appeared at the main entrance to St Gertrude's while she was checking her pigeonhole for mail.

'At last,' he said, leaning against the stonework, 'I've tracked you down.'

As startled as she was, she kept her expression indifferent. 'Which raises the question, how *did* you track me down?' she enquired.

'I remembered your friend's name from signing my book for her and asked around. May I take you for lunch?'

'I was planning to eat in hall.'

'Is that an unbreakable plan?'

Before she could reply, he said, 'Please say yes, I'd like the opportunity to prove that I'm not always an arrogant buffoon.'

'Whatever my opinion of you is, I wouldn't have thought it would matter to you very much. If at all.'

'Come on, you know what it's like for us narcissistic academics, we need everybody to love us.'

She couldn't help but smile. And with that, she allowed him to take her for lunch. And for dinner the day after, and to bed the following week. Only then did he tell her that he was married. By then it was too late.

So when Isabella had spoken about an unhappy and neglected

husband straying in search of emotional comfort, Annelise knew all about that.

But Edmund? Surely he wouldn't do that to Mums? No, Isabella was wrong about him. They must just be having a private disagreement over something. Perhaps Edmund had been trying to get Hope to ease back with her workload, worried that she was overdoing it and would make herself ill again?

From downstairs Annelise could hear the telephone ringing. It rang and rang, and when she realised nobody was going to answer it, she went to do it herself. She reached the hall just as the telephone stopped ringing.

She was about to go back upstairs to her room and do some work on the paper she was writing, when the telephone rang again. She picked up the receiver. 'Island House,' she said.

Seconds passed. Then came a voice, a man's voice: 'Is that who I think it is?'

Her heart leapt.

'Harry? Is that you?'

'The one and only. Are you missing me?'

'Not at all.'

'Liar.'

She smiled to herself and pressed the receiver against her ear, as if that would bring him closer to her. 'Are *you* missing me?'

'Of course I am. I want you here with me. How could you think otherwise when you know I'm crazy about you?'

Her body absorbed his words like a sponge soaking up water. But she made light of it. 'I'm glad to hear that,' she said.

'See, that's what I love about you,' he said with a chuckle, 'you're always so cool and distant with me. And always ready to put me in my place.'

'Somebody has to,' she teased.

There was a rustling sound in her ear, followed by a silence, and then Harry was cursing under his breath.

'What is it?' she asked.

'It's Miriam,' he said in a low rasp, 'home earlier than she said she would be. I'm sorry, I have to go. I'll see you when you're back. I'll book us a room, usual time and place. Be good without me and don't let some ardent young tyke steal you away from me!'

As he hastily rang off, she whispered into the receiver in her hand. 'I love you, Harry. I love you more than you'll ever know.'

Just a few moments ago she had been elated at the sound of his voice, that he had somehow found the telephone number for Island House, but now, as she climbed the stairs up to her bedroom, her heart felt as though a heavy weight was pressed against it.

She was tired of being his mistress, of making do with snatched moments behind his wife's back. On the one hand she lived for those moments – to hear his voice and to see him – but on the other, it simply wasn't enough. Isabella had said work was like a drug for Hope, an obsession; well, that's what Harry was for Annelise.

For six months she had waited for him to keep his promise that he would leave his wife. Every conversation they ever had, she waited for him to say the magic words, that he had asked Miriam for a divorce. She knew better than to push him, to force him to make a choice. Do that and she would lose him.

She had told Isabella earlier that she wasn't the marrying kind, but it was a lie. She wanted to marry Harry, to be his wife. And for that to happen she had to be patient. And careful.

Chapter Seventeen

Island House, Melstead St Mary
October 1962
Hope

Stanley had left a short while ago and Hope was now upstairs trying to work in what had been, a very long time ago, her childhood bedroom. She and Edmund slept in the main guest suite further along the landing. This room was her private space, her sanctuary. But try as she might to work, she just couldn't concentrate. Twenty-four hours ago this book had seemed to be writing itself. As most of her books did.

Her writing day usually started after an early breakfast when she would sit at her desk, her fingers poised over the typewriter. All she had to do was close her eyes and magically the words and ideas would flow. On her desk, next to the typewriter, would be a thermos flask of coffee, which she drank from until it ran out and she stopped for a short break to eat lunch. Afterwards, and switching to a thermos of hot tea, she would return to her desk until six o'clock. She hated for her routine to be disrupted and people knew better than to interrupt her with anything trivial.

But since reading that anonymous letter yesterday afternoon, she had written no more than a couple of pages. She simply couldn't think straight. Inside her head there was a clamour of voices vying to be heard. All telling her that of course Edmund was running around with every woman in the village, that it was glaringly obvious that the women would be falling at his feet in their droves. He was an attractive man. Intelligent. Thoughtful. Charming. And very caring. She was a fool to believe that he would have remained interested in her after all these years. Of course he would have strayed! And straight into the arms of someone so much more interesting and beautiful than she was. Didn't this confirm what she'd always feared, that she would lose Edmund? She was cursed! Always to be denied happiness, never to have peace of mind.

She sighed and clasped her elbows as she sat back in the chair. She had always been plain. Even as a child. A dull withdrawn child who had lost herself in roaming the lanes and meadows in search of wildlife to draw. Sometimes she would drag her younger brother, Kit, along with her.

She thought of Kit now. Could she confide in him about that anonymous letter? She shook her head. She couldn't bear for him, or anyone for that matter, to feel sorry for her. *Poor old Hope*, they'd think. Poor old pathetic Hope, so wrapped up in her work she had been blind to what had been going on right under her nose.

And yes, she knew she was guilty of putting all her energy into her work. But it gave her so much pleasure. And let's face it, she earned far more money than Edmund ever would as a GP in a small village. Would that be his excuse? That she had diminished him?

Unclasping her hands from her elbows, she stood up and opened a window. She then pulled out one of the desk drawers, and from the back of it took a packet of cigarettes, a lighter and a small enamelled ashtray, the sort that had a lid and could be carried around in a pocket or handbag. When she had the cigarette lit, she inhaled deeply on it, filling her lungs and letting the nicotine flood through her before exhaling and watching the smoke escape out of the window in one long stream. She had taken to smoking to calm her nerves – *to prevent another downward slide* – pretending to Edmund that it was no more than the occasional cigarette. The truth was, it was a lot more than that, but she kept that from him, knowing he would be cross with her.

But what right did he have to be cross if he was cheating on her? And on their own doorstep? Didn't he stop to think of what Annelise's reaction would be? The poor girl would be devastated. She had always been so fond of Edmund.

Hope shuddered with horrified disgust. Oh, it was all so sordid! How could he have cheapened himself, and their standing in the village? Scandal about a husband and a wife, it was the stuff of every gossiping tongue. Were they all talking about them in the village, and worse, laughing at Hope behind her back?

How could she face everybody this evening at the party? She felt sick at the prospect. Perhaps she could cry off, claim she had a bad headache. God knew she suffered enough of them. But why should she miss celebrating Evelyn and Kit's twentieth wedding anniversary? She had done nothing wrong. It was Edmund who should be hiding. And hanging his head in shame!

For the briefest of moments she contemplated confiding in Evelyn. They had known each other since childhood, and Evelyn was one of the most down-to-earth people Hope knew. But she was Edmund's sister, so how on earth could Hope tell her an anonymous letter was calling her beloved brother an adulterer?

Or did Evelyn already know what Edmund was getting up to?

Chapter Eighteen

Meadow Lodge, Melstead St Mary
October 1962
Evelyn

There seemed no escape from the bedlam going on around her; every which way Evelyn turned, somebody was pestering for her advice or opinion.

Right now one of the caterers was complaining that the oven didn't work. She was a young blonde woman with a waxy complexion and the affected manner of somebody who was used to working in far better surroundings. Well, that wouldn't be difficult, the kitchen at Meadow Lodge was practically a relic from the last century. Not like those swish kitchens she'd heard about on the new estate in the village. Breakfast bars were all the rage there, along with Formica counter tops and stainless steel sinks. It was a far cry from the antiquated appliances she made do with here – a refrigerator that conducted its own orchestra of hums, rattles and buzzes, a washing machine that leaked, and a moody oven that played up at will.

Pip and Em were constantly on at her to modernise Meadow Lodge, claiming that they might not keep losing the girls who came to clean for them if she did. Gone were the days of obliging and reliable housemaids; now Evelyn had to make do with a turnaround of young married girls from the estate who liked to earn a bit of pin money.

She and Kit could well afford to splash out on new appliances, but the trouble was Evelyn had little time, or inclination, for anything of a domestic nature. She was the sort of person who once she was used to something was resistant to change it. Although she wasn't bad at fixing things if the situation was dire enough. As it was now.

'I'm afraid it's a temperamental beast from the days when Noah was kitting out his ark,' she explained while on her knees and thrusting a lighted match into the back of the cavernous oven. 'One of these days I shall get around to replacing it. I think the problem is something to do with the pilot light. There, that's got it.'

She shut the door carefully. 'It helps not to slam it,' she said to the waxy blonde, 'despite how tempted one might be. And keep an eye on the temperature. The longer it's switched on, the hotter it gets.'

The woman regarded Evelyn and the oven with a sceptical eye. 'In that case, I can't be held responsible if the canapés don't come out as they should,' she said primly.

'I'm sure everything will be absolutely delicious,' Evelyn replied, seizing her chance to escape so she could go and change.

Parties used to be so much easier to arrange in the old days, and by 'old days' she meant during the war. Back then everything was in such short supply people were grateful for whatever they were given. Some of the best parties she had ever attended had been at Bletchley Park. They had been spontaneous get-togethers with just a few bottles of sherry and whisky to share, along with a plate of hastily made sandwiches, provided they could get hold of any bread or fillings. Nowadays expectations were so much higher.

Why, oh why had she agreed to let Kit organise this party? And why was she letting a condescending caterer intimidate her?

It was because she was not herself. Since yesterday afternoon and reading that anonymous letter she had been in shock. Who on earth could have sent it? The handwriting on the envelope was unknown to her, and the only clue she had was that the postmark was Bury St Edmunds. It wasn't much of a clue though.

She had barely slept the previous night, unable to stop thinking that somebody was out to cause trouble for her. But who? And why? Did the sender of the letter plan to blackmail her? Was that it? Would there be more vile letters?

The worst of it was she didn't dare share the letter with Kit. If the seed were sown in his mind that Pip and Em weren't his children, he would never be free of the doubt. He would forever be left to wonder. What man wouldn't? And Kit was such a worrier.

Their roles had been very clearly defined before they were ever married. Her job had always been to reassure and encourage Kit. Growing up without a mother – and a father who was distant while coping with his grief – had left Kit with a lack of self-belief and the need to prove himself.

Before he'd gone away to Canada and returned a broken man, she had begun to imagine a future with him, perhaps because she could see how much Kit needed somebody strong like her by his side. Somebody who could guide him towards achieving goals he'd never thought possible. Some might say that had been arrogant of her, but she saw it as her role in life, to inspire others to achieve their dreams. It was why she had become a teacher in the first place.

In his desperately dark periods after returning home to Island House, Kit had pushed Evelyn away, saying he couldn't bear for her to sacrifice her life for his sake. 'You could marry any man you wanted,' he would say to her, 'why settle for a pathetic crock like me?'

'Because I love you,' she'd said.

93

Whether or not she really had at that time, she couldn't say with a hundred per cent certainty. Perhaps she had loved him, but had not been *in* love with him. But what she hadn't doubted was that her feelings for him would strengthen in the years to come, that they would become something truly meaningful and lasting. Moreover, he had needed to know that he was still capable of being loved, and she was the one to prove that to him.

It was during one of Kit's dark periods that she had been approached to work at Bletchley Park. Feeling it might be good for them to have some time apart, if only so that Kit could come to terms with his situation on his own, she had accepted the post.

Her recruitment had happened so quickly she had scarcely any time to speculate what she was letting herself in for. But from the moment she arrived at Bletchley Park, she realised nothing could have prepared her for what lay ahead.

Chapter Nineteen

Bletchley Park
August 1941
Evelyn

In common with most arrivals at Bletchley Park my first thought was what a hideous house it was. A hotch-potch of architectural styles, it was, I came to know in the coming days and weeks, a reflection of the varied mix of people who worked there. It wasn't at all unusual to be chatting with a lady someone-or-other in the queue for lunch one day, and a GPO engineer the next. From all walks of life, we had been selected to do one job, to defeat Germany, and in total secrecy. Everyone had to sign the Official Secrets Act on arrival and we all took that oath seriously. Even to this day I have never once spoken of my time at Station X, as Bletchley was known back then.

I was billeted for my first night in a crowded boarding house in the centre of the town. I shared a small room with a girl who snored like a rumbling volcano threatening to erupt and who kept me awake until I shoved my head under the pillow. Although I was tempted to use my pillow to smother her!

The next morning my snoring companion offered to give me a lift on the back of her bicycle to the Park, and so off we went with her pedalling hard while effectively sitting on my lap. Somehow, I managed to keep hold of my small suitcase and handbag, which constituted my worldly possessions.

Strangely I never saw The Snorer again during my time at

Bletchley, which went to show just how many people worked there. It was also true that people often disappeared, never to be seen or heard of again. Given the intensity of the workload, burnout was a common problem and judging it to be bad for morale, those who couldn't take the pace were quickly despatched back to their civilian lives. Of course, on that particular August morning as I was directed to Hut 6 to begin my duties, I had no idea how hard I was destined to work.

Instructed first to go to Registration Room 1, I found I was one of many new recruits, the majority being graduates from Oxbridge, as well as a few other universities. I was older by about five years, and was reminded of being back at Oxford, surrounded by linguists, classicists, and mathematicians like myself. I concentrated on what was being explained to me, which was an overview of what went on in Hut 6 in relation to the whole of Bletchley Park. Cogs and wheels came to mind, and on a vast scale. I learned that all over England and Scotland there were wireless stations intercepting enemy messages. These were then couriered by motorbike to Bletchley, specifically Hut 6 and the Registration Rooms. It would, I was told, be my job to help sort and list the messages. Once that was done the process would begin on decoding them. This was done by those who were further up the chain, the elite in Hut 6.

I was warned that the task before me had to be done with painstaking care and that it could be mind-numbingly tedious. But I didn't care; I was fascinated by everything I saw and heard.

That evening, as I located my newly assigned billet, a cottage some four miles away in a hamlet with little to offer other than a clutch of houses, an ivy-clad pub and a duck pond, Melstead St Mary felt a long way away. No more would I have to deal with Mother's histrionics that she was at death's door. Guiltily, I was even relieved that I now had something to distract me from worrying about Kit.

It was hard to admit this, even to myself, and despite having encouraged Kit, I had been jealous of him joining the ATA. I envied his and Romily's contribution to the war effort. I had fought my jealousy by telling myself that I was doing essential work in teaching the young children of the village, as well as the influx of evacuees, like Stanley. But as fulfilling as my job at the school was, I didn't consider it enough. I felt I could be doing so much more.

With the light beginning to fade on that warm summer's evening, the sweat pooling between my shoulderblades as I trudged along the dusty road with my suitcase and handbag, I suspected I was lost. I plonked my suitcase down on the ground and referred to the small map I'd been given. It was no more than a sketch which I'd been told was not to scale. I concluded that I must have taken a wrong turn half a mile back, so picking up my case, I retraced my steps. When I eventually found my destination, at the end of a rutted track and knocked on the front door, I was ready to drop. It had been a long day.

Wayside Cottage was a modest red-brick Victorian dwelling which would win few prizes in a beauty contest. But the front garden was a much better proposition. Where flowers had very likely once grown, the patch was currently laid out with rows of vegetables. There were onions and potatoes, and peas and runner beans winding themselves up sticks fashioned into wigwams. With rationing making life so hard, everybody was digging for victory these days.

From the other side of the door, I heard a key being turned and then the door creaked open, but only by an inch. A girl wearing nothing but a towel and a shower cap peered cautiously back at me through the gap.

'I'm Evelyn Flowerday,' I said, 'I believe you were expecting me.' I smiled. 'I certainly hope you are at any rate.'

The girl smiled too and opened the door further. 'Come on

in,' she said, 'give me five minutes and I'll give you a proper welcome.'

She pointed towards a room off the narrow hall, and clutching the towel around her, she dodged upstairs.

I did as she said and went through to what I discovered was a decent-sized sitting room. The furniture was well-worn, but at least it appeared to be clean. A table covered in a gingham cloth was placed beneath a window looking out onto the front garden. I wondered if that was where I would eat.

On the opposite wall was another window and this gave a view of the back garden. I went to have a look and saw a long thin strip of a garden where chickens were pecking at the grass. To one side, jammed against a brick wall was an Anderson shelter. It seemed unlikely that the Luftwaffe would drop a bomb here, but as we were frequently told, better safe than sorry. The rest of the garden was given over to fruit trees and at the farthest end was an old timber-framed greenhouse.

The girl who'd opened the door to me now reappeared, dressed in a pair of dark green high-waisted trousers and a cream short-sleeved blouse with a bow at the neck. Her feet were encased in a pair of peep-toe wedged sandals. Her blonde hair was stylishly pinned up on her head with several decorative combs. She wore no make-up but still looked exquisite.

'Gosh,' she exclaimed, 'what a frightful first impression I must have given you opening the door like that when I was practically starkers! I do hope I can make amends. How about a drink? No, better still, why don't I show you where you'll be bedding down? I'll warn you now, sleep will be your best friend after a few weeks of being at the Park. Here, let me take your case for you. What did you say your name was?'

'Evelyn. Evelyn Flowerday.'

As effervescent as a glass of champagne, the girl thrust out her hand and shook mine vigorously. 'I'm Tally; short for

Natalia. Come on, let me take you upstairs. I do hope you're the kind of gal who can rough it, because there's nothing grand about Wayside Cottage.'

'I'm sure I'll be perfectly comfortable,' I said.

We were at the top of the stairs on the small landing when I asked if there was anybody else billeted here.

Tally turned to me with a shake of her head. 'There are only two small bedrooms, so it's just us.'

'Have you been here alone, then?'

'No. Until a few days ago Diana was here.'

'What happened to her?'

'The poor girl got herself into a bit of a fix, if you know what I mean.' As though to make sure I did know what she meant, Tally patted her stomach.

'No danger of that happening to me,' I said with a breezy laugh, thinking of Kit and that with still no sign of an engagement in sight as he came to terms with his injuries, we were resolutely chaste.

Tally looked at me, an expressive eyebrow raised. 'People are falling in love all the time at the Park. And if not love, then . . . well, I'm sure I don't have to explain. It's an outlet for the pressure we're under. That's what happened to Diana.'

They were words that would come back to haunt me.

Chapter Twenty

Meadow Lodge, Melstead St Mary
October 1962
Evelyn

'*Tick-tock-tick-tock*, I can literally hear your brain ticking.'

Startled, Evelyn spun round from where she was sitting in front of her dressing table and mirror. 'Em,' she said, 'how long have you been standing there?'

'Long enough to know that your mind is elsewhere.' She came over and sat on the corner of the bed. 'Everything all right?' she asked.

Evelyn smiled brightly at her daughter. But then it was easy to smile when she looked at Emily; she was such a delightful girl. Her heart-shaped face radiated a naturally caring and happy disposition that drew people to her. 'Oh, I'm perfectly all right,' she said, 'I was just taking a few minutes to catch my breath. It feels as though we've been preparing for this party for ever.'

Her daughter's expression instantly changed. Whenever she was concerned, two little lines appeared between her eyebrows. She had been the same as a small child. Like a barometer reflecting a change in the weather, she had always been sensitive to someone else's feelings, or a sudden change in atmosphere. In contrast, her brother, more often than not with his head in the clouds, could blunder into an almighty row and not have a clue that two people had been on the verge of throttling each other.

'That sounds like you'll be glad when it's over.'

'Heavens no!' Evelyn lied. 'I'm looking forward to it.'

'Good,' said Em, rising from the bed and kissing her mother's cheek. 'You deserve this party.'

Did she? thought Evelyn when Em had left her. Did she really?

Unable to look at herself in the dressing table mirror, she turned towards Kit's side of the bed and took in the precise way he had laid out his clothes ready to put on. He had planned everything like a military exercise, leaving nothing to chance. When he had first suggested they should celebrate their twentieth wedding anniversary, she had imagined a low-key family affair. But he had said two decades of putting up with him warranted more than that. 'And don't worry about arranging things,' he'd assured her, 'I shall do it all.'

Most husbands would happily come up with the proposition to throw a party and then immediately hand the responsibility over to their wives. Not Kit. Once he had a thing in his head, there was no stopping him. He had spent an age putting together the guest list and on a daily basis the list grew and grew. 'Is there anybody in the village you haven't invited?' she had teased him.

'We know so many people,' he'd replied, 'and there are some we simply can't *not* invite. Imagine how offended they would be not to receive an invitation.'

That was Kit all over; he hated to disappoint or upset anybody.

'Not dressed yet?'

Again Evelyn was startled out of her thoughts. This time by Kit.

'Just about to make myself presentable,' she said cheerily. 'Although I fear it's going to take more spit and polish than usual. I should have gone to the hairdressers and had my hair set.'

'Nonsense, you'll look your usual beautiful self.'

'Dear God, Kit, you do say the sweetest of things.'

'Only when it's true,' he said, coming over to her. 'I've brought you a cup of tea.' He placed it on the dressing table. 'I thought you might like one before the cocktails start to flow.'

'Thank you,' she said, thinking that she couldn't wait for a proper drink. Something to take the edge off her anxiety.

'Shall I leave you to get ready?' he asked.

'No,' she said. 'Stay with me for a while and then we'll get dressed together. For now, let's have a moment of calm before the storm.'

He sat on the corner of the bed where earlier Em had perched, then turned towards the door as a crescendo of laughter, male and female, could be heard, followed by the sound of somebody giving a rendition of a popular tune. Evelyn didn't know what it was, but it was rather catchy.

'It's fun having the children home with their friends, isn't it?' Kit said, facing her again.

'Yes,' she answered, 'they bring the house to life, don't they? When Edmund and I were growing up here, there was very little laughter. Mother would affect a fainting fit if there was so much as a whisper to shatter the peace and quiet.' She sipped her tea. Kit had made it just the way she liked, strong and with only a splash of milk.

'There was very little to laugh over at Island House either when I was a child,' he said. 'When I think about it, that's what stands out the most for me. Not my brother Arthur's sadistic cruelty, or Allegra arguing with Hope, or Dad always being away, but the lack of joy. That to me now, having experienced the happiness of being married to you and having Pip and Em, seems such a profound shame. Love, and making others happy, is all that counts if you ask me.'

He looked so earnest as he spoke, and Evelyn was struck, as she so often was, by seeing beyond his scars, beyond the moustache and the flecks of grey in his hair, and seeing the handsome young man he'd once been.

'Do you ever wish you could turn back the clock?' she asked.

'To a specific time?' he replied. 'Or just back to being young again?' He paused. 'Or to a moment before doing something rash that one now regrets?'

Noting the careful way he had answered her, she said, 'A bit of all three, I suppose.'

'Do you want to turn back the clock?'

She smiled. 'I asked first.'

'The obvious answer would be to say I'd go back to when I was in Canada, and I'd make sure I booked my passage home on a different ship.'

'And the less obvious answer?'

'I wouldn't turn back the clock and change what happened to me. Who knows what might have happened if I'd returned later, or sooner? I could have made it home safe and sound, then flown with the RAF and been shot down and killed on my first mission. I count myself as one of the lucky ones.' He leaned forward and touched her hand. 'I've been the luckiest of men, Evelyn. In so many ways.'

She raised his misshapen hand, the fingers of which had never straightened after being burned, and turning it over, she kissed his palm. 'I've been lucky too.'

A moment passed while she gazed into the blueness of his eyes and she was suddenly taken back to the day, twenty years ago, when she had stood before him in church and uttered the words 'I do.'

It had been a classic wartime wedding, hastily thrown together. She had worn a day dress bought with clothing coupons, some of which had been donated to her by Romily and Hope, and the service had been attended by just a few close friends and family. From the church they had walked the short distance to Island House where Mrs Partridge had served sandwiches and Kit's favourite tomato soup in mugs. By pooling rations, enough ingredients had been collected in order for Mrs Partridge to make a small wedding cake complete with dried fruit.

When they cut the cake together, Kit had kissed Evelyn with such a look of adoration on his face, she had promised herself she would never do anything to hurt him.

Chapter Twenty-One

Quince Cottage, Melstead St Mary
October 1962
Florence

Florence was not the murdering kind. She really wasn't. But when it came to her mother-in-law, she was prepared to make an exception.

Over the years she had thought of many ways to get rid of Ruby Minton, but being the sensible person she was, sneaking up on the old bat with a heavy saucepan, or adding arsenic to her tea, or placing a tripwire at the top of the stairs, was clearly out of the question. And anyway, no matter how vile Ruby was, the woman wasn't worth going to prison for.

However, right now she would happily swing for the old witch.

'I said you look like a cheap whore in that dress.'

'I heard you the first time, Ruby,' Florence said pleasantly, then muttering to herself, 'I'm not the one who's deaf, but who refuses to accept it.'

'Speak up! How do you expect me to hear what you're saying when you mutter like that? And where's my tonic? You know I have to have it straight after I've eaten. Dr Flowerday was most insistent on that.'

'I'm just getting it for you,' said Florence. From the shelf in the kitchen where she kept the tea caddy and cannister of sugar, along with the tin in which she put the housekeeping money, she took down the glass tumbler which Ruby insisted nobody but she used. Into this Florence emptied a sachet of white granules which Dr Flowerday had prescribed Ruby for her dyspepsia, and then held the glass under the cold tap. Stirring vigorously, Florence imagined the granules were a fatal dose of strychnine, which would cure her mother-in-law of her flatulence once and for all.

Back in the front room where Ruby was sitting in the best armchair directly opposite the television set waiting for *Dixon of Dock Green* to start, Florence handed her the glass. 'Here you are,' she said with a dutiful smile.

The effort was lost on Ruby. The woman scowled and all but snatched the glass from her. 'Well, don't just stand there, put the television on. Or are you deliberately trying to make me miss my favourite programme?'

'Of course not.'

'And make sure you have the volume turned up. I know you always turn it down to spoil my enjoyment. And when are you going to change out of that awful dress? It's too tight and too short. Billy will be shamed to his boots to be seen with you looking like that.'

'Billy helped me choose it,' Florence said with some satisfaction. 'He said the colour really suited me.'

'I doubt that very much,' Ruby scoffed. 'Out of the way, then. How do you expect me to see the television with you standing in front of it?'

Perish the thought that the old witch would ever be grateful for anything Florence did for her.

Upstairs she heard George humming to himself in the bathroom and Rosie drying her hair in her old bedroom. She had left home six months ago to work as a receptionist at the Angel Hotel in Bury St Edmunds, and where she lived-in. It was good to have the children home, if only for the weekend.

Florence found Billy standing at the full-length mirror in their bedroom, an exasperated expression on his face.

'I can't do this wretched bow-tie,' he said. 'Do I have to wear it? I look like a bloody waiter dressed like this, and I bet there'll be folk there who'll treat me like one.'

'Of course they won't. They'll all think you look exceedingly handsome.'

He grunted and tried again with the tie, but ripped it from his neck in angry frustration.

'Let me do it for you,' offered Florence. She went over and within seconds had deftly tied the bow-tie for him. 'There,' she said, with a final adjustment, 'as handsome as Rock Hudson in *Pillow Talk*.'

'And you, Mrs Minton,' he said, his face suddenly breaking into a wolfish grin, 'look gorgeous in that dress. Very sexy.' His hands moved around to her bottom and pressed her against him. 'It hugs you in all the right places. I reckon I'll have trouble keeping my hands off you tonight.'

'Billy Minton, just you behave yourself,' she said sternly. 'Whatever would they say down at the Sally Army if they knew the way you carry on,' she added fondly, remembering the first time she'd heard him play in the band at the village fête when it was held on Clover Field. She had watched him playing his trumpet and thought how smart he'd looked in his uniform. She remembered too how he had winked at her. That was more than twenty years ago, yet it felt like only yesterday.

The word 'yesterday' brought to mind the anonymous letter that accused Billy of cheating on her. It had to be Ruby who had sent it. Who else hated Florence so much? No one as far as she knew. But why would Ruby accuse her own son – her blue-eyed boy – of such a terrible thing? Or was she so bitter and twisted she would resort to any trick to undermine their marriage?

Billy's hands were busy again with her bottom, kneading her buttocks with his strong sure fingers. Not for the first time, she said, 'I'm not a lump of bread dough, you know.'

He laughed. 'I warned you I wouldn't be able to keep my hands off you.'

'Well, perhaps this might cool your ardour. Your mother's just said I look like a cheap whore.'

He swore under his breath. 'I'll speak to her.'

'It won't do any good. After all these years she's not likely to change. If anything, she's getting worse.'

'I'll still speak to her. I won't have her talking to you like that. It's not on.'

'I'm used to it, love. Water and a duck's back.' Releasing herself from his hold, she sat down on the padded stool in front of the dressing table. She carefully removed the chiffon scarf, which she'd tied around her head after washing and drying her hair the minute she'd got back from helping at Meadow Lodge. With equal care she began taking out the pins and rollers.

Behind her Billy said, 'I'll go down and warn Mum that if she doesn't treat you better, I won't let her come here to watch our telly.'

Florence watched him go, knowing that whatever stern ticking off he gave his mother, following a few days of good behaviour Ruby would revert to her nasty old self.

Most evenings Ruby came here to eat supper with them and to watch television. Billy had offered to rent her a set from Radio Rentals so she could watch in the comfort of her own home next door, where she lived above the bakery. It had been her home, with Billy's father, and where Billy grew up, for over fifty years. Her response to Billy's generous offer was to tell him not to be such a spendthrift, she was happy enough watching their television. To Florence she'd said, 'I suppose that was your doing, wasn't it, trying to stop me from spending time with my only son?'

Florence hadn't wasted her breath in denying the truth Ruby had concocted; there was no point. Ruby hated her and that was all there was to it. Some things you just had to accept.

But Florence would not accept spite-filled anonymous letters from Ruby, that was most definitely a step too far. Just as soon as she had the chance, she planned to sneak next door when Ruby was watching the telly here and see if she could find evidence of her mother-in-law having snipped out letters from the pages of a newspaper.

The last of the pins and rollers now removed, she took up her hairbrush and with the lightest of strokes, gently brushed out each curl. When she'd finished, she reminded herself that she had used the last of her Amami setting lotion and must remember to buy some more.

Once she was happy with the effect and had sprayed her hair, she opened her make-up drawer. She wore very little make-up, just a dab or two of blusher, a touch of mascara and a shimmery coating of pale pink lipstick Rosie had given her. With Rosie's help she had experimented with false eyelashes but had hated the effect. She didn't hold with too much artifice; she preferred a more natural look.

Which was what Billy said he liked too. But what if he'd grown bored of that and fancied something on the side that was a bit more . . .

No! she told herself firmly. Under no circumstances was she to start thinking there was any truth in that anonymous letter. Do that and Ruby would have won.

Chapter Twenty-Two

La Vista, Palm Springs
October 1962
Romily

The sky was the clearest and strongest of blues; there was not a cloud to be seen. High above Romily's head, and hidden within the foliage of the palm trees, birdsong rang out.

From where she was standing on the paved terrace, she could hear Red speaking on the telephone inside the house. He'd taken the call just a few minutes after she'd arrived. He'd wanted to ignore the ringing, but Romily had insisted he answer the phone. His doing so gave her the chance to explore the garden, just as he had suggested she might like to do.

While driving her back to Casa Santa Rosa late last night, Red's invitation to visit him this morning had not surprised her. What did surprise her was what she was seeing now; this was unlike any garden she had seen before. It had none of the stiff manicured splendour of Casa Santa Rosa, but was instead a joyous blend of natural form and colour.

With a choice of gravel paths in front of her, she selected the one that led to the right. It took her through what felt like tropical vegetation, such was the density of trees and bushes. Majestic palm trees towered overhead, and oleanders showed off every shade of pink. In turn, she then came to an area that was more open and planted with cacti and succulents, some of which were in colourful bloom with jewel-like flowers.

Following the path yet further, it led her down a series of steps hewn out of rock with yucca trees either side. There were large prickly bushes too that she didn't recognise, then rounding a corner, she suddenly found herself in a clearing overlooking a long thin swimming pool. It looked the sort of pool that was designed for somebody intent on swimming lengths to keep fit, rather than for merely cooling off in. Beyond the pool was a spectacular view of the mountain range that seemed to be within touching distance. It was one of the most impressive views she had ever seen.

When the taxi had delivered her here and she'd commented to Red how much she liked the location – his nearest neighbour was half a mile away – he had explained that he preferred to be on the edge of things, rather than in the middle of the town that was becoming too built up for his liking. She suspected that being on the edge of things was his modus operandi.

Taking her time over retracing her steps in the arid heat, she had just reached the terrace when her host reappeared.

'Sorry I abandoned you like that,' he said. 'Now then, let me fix you a drink. How about some iced tea? Or being British, would you prefer hot tea? If you trust me to make it properly, that is.'

'I'll put you to the test another time,' she said with a smile, 'for now iced tea would suit me very well.'

He indicated a comfortable-looking sofa in front of a glass-topped coffee table in the covered area of the terrace that stretched the full width of the house.

Painted white and built on one level with large windows, the streamlined property was everything she might have supposed she wouldn't like. But she did like it. She approved greatly of the strong clean lines of the architecture, and the boldness of the progressive mind that had created it. Sitting down in the shade, glad to be out of the sun, her back resting against the downy softness of a plump cushion, she thought how Stanley would love to design something so modern.

The rattle of ice cubes heralded Red's return. When he was seated on the sofa next to her and had passed her a tall glass of iced tea with a sprig of mint, she said, 'Thank you for inviting me here, and for last night; it was fun.'

'It was my pleasure, I enjoyed sharing the desert with you. If it wasn't for this damned leg of mine right now, I'd be off for a hike, as well as camp out overnight. There's nothing better than waking up to watch the dawn break when you're in the desert. It's the best tonic I know.'

'Is your leg troubling you today?'

He shrugged. 'A new prosthetic always takes some getting used to. Give me a couple of weeks and I'll be fine. But never mind that, we need to talk about you.'

She groaned. 'Must we? I find myself so very dull.'

'I'll wager you're the only one who does. I, for one, find you extraordinarily interesting.' He raised his glass. 'Here's to you. One of the most fascinating women I've met in a long time.'

She tutted. 'I advise you not to waste your breath on smooth-talking me. You won't come out of it well.'

He tipped his head back and laughed. There was something so free and uninhibited about the way he laughed.

'Is that what you thought I was doing,' he asked, 'smooth-talking you? Now why on earth would I do that?'

'To convince me we should work together. It's why you've invited me here this morning to see your home and to—'

'Hey, you mean a guy can't show some *bona fide* all-American hospitality without there being an ulterior motive? Whatever is the world coming to?'

'You know exactly what I mean.'

'I do. But I believe the woman doth protest too much and really you just want me to cajole you some more, and then,' he clicked his thumb and forefinger together, 'we'll be in business!'

'Evidently I have not protested enough,' she said, amused at his chutzpah. 'As otherwise you will have given up trying to persuade me.'

He leaned against the back of the sofa and crossed one leg over the other. 'Something you should know. I never give up on what I believe in. I'm relentless in that respect.'

She turned to look at him and held his gaze. 'I'm sure you are.'

'I'm told it's one of my finer qualities.'

'And what of your less commendable qualities?'

'That would be telling.'

'It would. That's why I'm asking.'

He cocked his head. 'Are you flirting with me, Mrs Devereux-Temple?'

She continued to meet his gaze, determined not to blink or be the one to look away. 'Certainly not.'

'I think you are. I think we've been flirting with each other since the moment we met.'

'All I can say to that is that Americans must have a different idea of what constitutes flirting compared to us Brits.'

'Oh, I doubt that. But to be serious, and yes, I can be exceedingly serious, I've known you for,' he checked his watch, 'almost twenty-four hours, but I—'

She wagged a finger at him. 'Don't you dare say it. Don't you dare say you feel like you've known me all your life!'

'Hey kid, credit me with more savvy than that! I was going to say, I haven't had this much fun in quite some time. You're a real breath of fresh air.'

'You realise you just called me kid, don't you? I'm fifty-five years of age; I'm anything but a child.'

'But I'll bet inside you feel like a child who has so much more she wants to see and do. Am I right? Or have I got you wrong?

Are you itching to get home so you can put on your slippers and sit by the fireside in your rocking chair, content to let others have all the fun?'

'Don't forget the cat on my lap and a pair of knitting needles in my hands.'

'I was coming to those.'

'Along with a dozen more misguided clichés I don't doubt.'

He grinned. 'See, not even twenty-four hours and you know me so well already.'

Incorrigible. Absolutely incorrigible. Dangerously so. If she wasn't careful, Romily warned herself, she could easily succumb to this man's charm and wit. In that respect he was a lot like Jack – confident and not afraid to make fun of her. Or stand up to her, yet at the same time prepared to treat her as an equal.

After spending time in the desert with Red last night, she had acknowledged that her mistake yesterday had been to underestimate him. Her initial reaction had been to dismiss him as being shallow and patronising. God knew she had met plenty of men like that over the years, the type who treated her as an inferior little woman who needed to be put in her place. That had been especially true during and after the war. Thousands of women had shown their mettle in helping to fight the war against Germany, only then to be expected to don their aprons and return to the kitchen where supposedly they belonged.

'I've lost you, haven't I?'

Her attention swiftly brought back to the man sitting opposite her, she apologised. 'I'm sorry, I was—'

'Thinking about something entirely different? Care to tell me what?'

She smiled. 'You always want me to do the talking, don't you?'

'That's because you fascinate me.'

She rejected his words with a wave of her hand. 'Not true.

You've been instructed by Gabe and Melvyn to twist my arm and by any means. Which includes flattery and, if necessary, seduction.'

'You make me sound like a Soviet spy!' he said with another loud and uninhibited laugh. 'But I told you last night, not everything I ask you has previously been scripted by Gabe and Melvyn. I'm quite capable of thinking for myself and, for that matter, writing my own scripts. But the thing is, I just can't get it out of my head that we could make a good team together, you and me. And before you get any ideas, I'm talking about working together. However, I'm astute enough to know that you're like me, that unless your heart is in a project, it's a non-starter.' He rubbed his hand over his chin. 'Is there anything I could say or do to persuade you to take me seriously?'

'Why do you believe I don't already?'

He shook his head and put down his empty glass. 'I'd feel it if you did. But I'm not getting that vibe.'

'Then perhaps you need to relax and stop trying so hard. What are we going to do for lunch?' she asked, keen to change the subject.

He looked surprised at her question. 'Well, I could cook us lunch, if you'd like?'

'You can cook?'

'Sure I can. I'm a dab hand when it comes to grilling steaks. Would that be agreeable to you?'

'It certainly would. Will you let me help though?'

'I think I can allow that. But finish your drink first.'

She quickly drank what was left in her glass. 'Ready when you are,' she said.

Lunch turned out to be cooked in another part of the garden, and on a large grill that was housed in a solid brick-built affair with a chimney above it.

'I don't suppose you have this kind of thing back at home in England, do you?' he said, poking at the hot coals with a pair of long tongs.

'No,' she said, 'but I'm beginning to think I should like to have one built. It looks fun.'

'Everything in life should be fun, don't you think?'

'I wish it could be, but sadly it's not always the case.'

'Which means, and don't get me wrong,' he said through a cloud of smoke, 'I'm not trivialising the harsh realities we all have to face from time to time, but we have to make every effort we can to bring more fun into our lives, and for those we care about. Can you pass me those potatoes you so carefully wrapped in aluminum foil, please?'

She did as he said and watched him place the potatoes on the wire rack a few inches above the hot coals.

'Okay,' he said, 'while they cook, I'll fix us both a proper drink. How does a martini sound to you?'

'It sounds heavenly. But why don't I do it for us?'

He smiled. 'Not on your life, you're my guest. So sit down and relax.'

Instead of sitting down as he'd instructed, she went over to a lemon tree. She breathed in the delicious fragrance from the blossom. Perhaps when she was home, she would try growing a lemon tree in the garden, then in the winter move it into the glasshouse for protection.

Thinking of Island House and its pretty garden – the epitome of an English garden – she thought how very far away it suddenly seemed. Intriguingly she no longer felt the need to rush home.

She sat down in the shade of a vine-covered pergola and tilting her head right back, she closed her eyes. Birdsong was the only noise she could hear. *Paradise*, she thought. No wonder Red said he loved living here. She was beginning to understand why. She was also beginning to wonder if he was right and they could work together on turning her novel *Sister Grace Falls from Grace* into a film script. It might be fun. But could she trust him not to ride roughshod over her creation?

'Your martini, Madame,' he said from behind her. 'Shaken, not stirred, just how you like it.'

'Thank you,' she said, sitting up to take the glass from him. 'I could get used to this.'

'That's what I like to hear.'

He sat opposite her and clinked his glass against hers. 'Cheers.'

'Cheers,' she echoed. 'You make an excellent barman,' she said after she'd taken a sip and savoured the dryness of the liquor.

'What can I say? It's a job I pride myself in doing to the best of my ability. And now that I've mixed you a perfect drink, please do me the kindness of telling the rest of your story, about you and the burning Walrus.'

She tutted. 'I knew that was the real reason you invited me here.'

He smiled. 'You would have been disappointed in me if I hadn't asked you.'

'Very well,' she said softly, as once more the door to the past opened and she allowed herself to be taken back.

Chapter Twenty-Three

Tilbrook Hall, Norfolk
April 1944
Romily

To this day I have no recall of the impact. Knocked unconscious, I came round to find myself choking on smoke and being hauled unceremoniously from the cockpit. I was dragged to safety and when I looked back at the Walrus, I saw it was on fire, along with the barn. The heat from the flames was scorching my face. Another one of my lives gone, I thought vaguely as my head spun and my vision blurred to the point I was seeing multiple burning Walruses. I was trying to work out how many lives I was down to, when an almighty boom ripped my eardrums apart and the world exploded.

I was dead. I was convinced of it. The conviction filled me with the sweetest joy as in that moment of certainty I saw Jack right there before me. Hadn't I promised him that we would be re-united in the afterlife? Filled with euphoria, I stretched out my hand to touch his face. 'Oh, my darling,' I said, 'I've missed you so much.'

I saw his lips move, but no sound came out. There was a frown creasing his expression. I then realised that the face before me didn't belong to Jack. The euphoria that had filled me evaporated in an instant.

The frown on the man's face intensified. Once more his lips

moved, but for some inexplicable reason no sound came out. Was he mute? I tried to battle my way through the fog of confusion that was clouding my brain.

I had just recalled the moment when the cockpit had filled with smoke, when my lungs gave a spontaneous heave and I coughed violently. Pain shot through my body and the frowning man now looked at me with increased concern. He spoke again and as before, no words came out. It was then that I became aware of an acrid stench. I twisted my head to my right and saw a colossal inferno, flames reaching high into the sky, creating an angry black cloud of thick smoke. It was, I realised, the burning wreckage of the Walrus and the hay barn I had tried to avoid hitting.

With that understanding came the knowledge that I had been dragged to safety by this brave stranger, and just in time before the fuel in the tank of the Walrus had ignited. Moreover, I comprehended that a fire of that magnitude would make a thunderous roaring noise. But I could hear nothing. I had been rendered deaf as a result of the explosion.

Irrationally I felt proud of myself for reaching this conclusion. I pointed to my ears. 'I can't hear anything,' I said. Or perhaps I shouted the words, I couldn't tell. 'The blast.'

He nodded and I gave in to another bout of violent coughing. When it passed, I sat up. It was then I caught sight of my left leg which was twisted at an unfeasible angle. In registering this, I succumbed to a wave of nausea and thoroughly let the side down by being hideously sick.

From somewhere about his person, my brave rescuer produced a handkerchief and began mopping me up.

'You're most kind,' I said (or yelled), as though we were at a cocktail party and not in a field with the burning wreckage of an aeroplane behind us, and my leg pointing the wrong way.

He smiled and for the first time I saw that my knight in shining armour was an extraordinarily handsome man with straight white teeth and dark expressive eyes beneath a pair of thick eyebrows. He was about the same age as me and I'd wager he was not English. He reminded me of a wildly attractive French racing driver I had once known. 'What's your name?' I asked, 'seeing as we've been so intimately thrown together?'

His thick brows drawn together, he spoke his name, but I shook my head, unable to make it out. 'Spell it,' I said, indicating that he should draw the letters in the air.

'M . . . A . . . T . . . T . . . E . . . O.' I said, when his hand came to a stop. 'Italian?'

He nodded and smiled again.

'Well Matteo, would you help me to stand, please?'

He looked at me doubtfully, but with great care, he did as I asked. It was when I was upright and leaning heavily against him, wondering where he might take me to get help, and how far that might be, that I noticed he was wearing a uniform that had seen better days. But what was significant about it was that there were large patches sewn on to the jacket and trousers, indicating that he was a prisoner of war. Rather gruesomely the patches were meant as targets should the prisoner attempt to escape.

Without warning, he turned abruptly and scooped me up in his arms. He had gone about a hundred yards, with me fearing he might collapse with the effort, when I saw a number of men running towards us. They had come fortuitously prepared with a couple of stretchers, no doubt in anticipation of more than one casualty from the aircraft that had come down.

I was laid carefully onto a stretcher and transported not so carefully, at speed, across a field where sheep were grazing.

With the woods behind us, I strained my neck to see where we were going, hoping a doctor might be quickly despatched to deal with my broken leg. Frankly I'd be happy with an equine vet if he could administer sufficient morphine into me to numb the pain I was in.

My luck seemed to be continuing. Firstly, I'd been rescued by the handsome Matteo and now I discovered that I had been taken to Tilbrook Hall, a grand old house some five miles from RAF West Raynham. I'd seen it on the maps. It had been requisitioned by the MOD, and not only was it partly used to accommodate prisoners of war, but it was also being used as a hospital for wounded servicemen.

What was more, by the time I was transferred from the stretcher and onto an examination couch, my hearing had begun to return, accompanied with a whistling as though I were under water with a kettle boiling inside my head. But I could hear enough to catch the contemptuous tone of the doctor who was examining me.

He was a stout, flush-faced gentleman of advancing years with monstrously bushy eyebrows, a pince-nez perched on his supercilious nose, together with a disagreeable look of censure.

'Well, well, well, this is quite the mess you've got yourself into, young lady,' he said, addressing me as though I were a silly young schoolgirl. For good measure, he tutted. 'This is what comes of you women imagining you can do the work of a man.'

I did a rare thing; I kept my mouth firmly shut. After all, I wanted this man to mend my leg. If I antagonised him, he might not feel so inclined to make a good job of fixing me. Instead I cupped my hands around my ears and shook my head, pretending I couldn't hear him.

As it turned out he instructed a younger doctor to operate

on my leg and some hours later, I came round from the general anaesthetic to find myself in a small room on my own. Presumably the wards were all full of servicemen. I was told by a pretty young nurse who, believing I was still deaf, spoke slowly and with exaggerated care in pronouncing each word, plainly hoping I might be able to lip-read.

'The operation went like clockwork,' she said, pointing to my leg which was now in plaster and suspended from the ceiling by a contraption of wires and pulleys. 'You'll soon be up on your feet and flying again,' she added with a smile.

I told her that my hearing had partially returned, and she went on to say that I was to take no notice of Dr Dorcas, that he was an old-fashioned stick-in-the-mud. 'If you feel well enough, there's somebody waiting to see you.'

'Really?' I asked. 'Who on earth could that be?' I didn't feel like seeing anybody, I was still feeling woozy from the anaesthetic, and was sure I could benefit from a dash of lipstick and a brush through my hair. But curiosity had the better of me.

The nurse grinned. 'I'll send him in. But don't tell Dr Dorcas I let you have a visitor so soon or he'll have my guts for garters.'

I promised it would be our secret and was surprised, and delighted, when minutes later she brought in my handsome rescuer, Matteo. He looked at me anxiously with his dark eyes, which I discerned now were clouded with what I recognised as sadness.

'I thought you might like these' he said with a shy smile, while holding out a small bunch of wildflowers.

'How thoughtful of you,' I replied.

'I'll fetch a vase,' the nurse said brightly, leaving us alone, but not before winking at me. Her expression suggested that she considered me exceptionally lucky to have a 'real looker' like Matteo standing by the side of my bed.

I was inclined to agree with her, and whether or not it was the lingering effect of the anaesthetic, I had a strange feeling deep inside me – like an unfurling of something that had been locked tight for a long time – that this handsome Italian POW with his sad eyes was going to be somebody I would never forget. And not just because he had saved my life.

Chapter Twenty-Four

La Vista, Palm Springs
October 1962
Red

What was it about this woman that she could hold his attention the way she did?

Had it not been necessary for him to fetch the steaks to put on the grill and to mix another round of martinis, Red would gladly have gone on listening to Romily for the rest of the day. But his stomach had begun to rumble with all the subtlety of a jet engine taking off, and she'd laughed, saying that she had better be quiet or they would never eat.

Pouring the vodka into the shaker with the vermouth, adding ice cubes and then shaking vigorously, he smiled to himself. When Gabe and Melvyn had started up about him collaborating with an acclaimed novelist from England, he'd visualised a wrinkled grande dame in tweeds with a face like an old boot. Never did he imagine a captivating woman who had the power to stop him in his tracks. Maybe even make him consider the improbable, that he could fall in love with her.

He shook his head in disbelief at such an idea. He was not the type of man who believed in love at first sight. Sure there had to be some kind of initial spark of attraction, but that was as far as he was prepared to go. He had always believed that to love – to love heart, body and soul – one had to dig down deep to find that particular buried treasure.

With most women he held himself in check, giving only of himself that which he was prepared to offer. That was why nothing ever lasted. The relationships he'd experienced had always been flawed for the simple reason the women wanted more than he would provide. He never blamed them for wanting more, it was entirely his fault he couldn't give them what they wanted, and he made a point of saying so.

But along had come Romily Devereux-Temple, and in twenty-four hours of knowing her, he was inexplicably thinking he might give more of himself to her than he had with any woman before. It was as if she had taken a knife to the locked-down shell of him and was prising it open to get at his heart.

To prevent that happening, he had no choice but to deploy his tried and tested old techniques of heavy-handed flirtation, knowing that she was not the kind of woman who would fall for it. But with each archly disapproving look she gave him, he felt that damned shell of his opening a tiny crack more.

To snap the shell shut again, to keep things entirely superficial, his tactic was to force her to keep talking about herself. While she spoke, he could observe her and figure out why he was reacting the way he was.

It was the damndest thing, but he could imagine that in another lifetime – when they'd both been young and carefree – she would have been the real deal for him. The whole enchilada, and some.

Had that Italian prisoner of war, Matteo, thought the same? Had he fallen under Romily's spell the moment he set his so-called sad eyes on her? Irrationally Red felt jealous of the guy having the chance to save Romily, to prove himself a hero and capture her heart. Because it sure as hell sounded like that was exactly what had happened. And had she deliberately told Red that story to say, 'Look buster, you stand no chance against the memory of my perfect husband, and what's more you, old-timer with your artificial leg, you are certainly not in the same league as a sexy Italian man who rescued me from a blazing inferno!'

He pulled himself up short. What the hell was this! What was he doing writing himself off as some old-timer? God damn it; he was a successful Hollywood scriptwriter, a bloody war hero who had bedded more women than he could remember, even with half his leg missing! So why now should he doubt himself?

Because this particular woman could see right through him.

And because there came a time when a person had to accept the obvious, that life lived on a superficial level was no longer enough. And at the age of fifty-six, he had reached that point.

Gabe and Melvyn had said much the same to him only a few weeks ago.

'Don't you get tired of being the eternal playboy?' Gabe had said.

'Haven't you ever wanted to settle down?' Melvyn had asked.

They were both devout family men, which was unusual for Hollywood, where affairs were all part of the crazy merry-go-round.

He'd indulged in affairs with a few married women himself, a couple of actresses too, seeing that as an easy way to avoid having to get too serious. Such was the strict rules laid down by the studio bosses, no actress wanted her extracurricular activities made known, so they were as safe a bet as any for allowing him the pleasure of sex without commitment.

Put like that, he sounded just the lousy bum Romily Devereux-Temple would wholeheartedly despise. Come to think of it, there were definitely times when he despised himself.

He poured the drinks into the cocktail glasses, placed them on a tray along with the plate containing the steaks and went back outside.

She was where he'd left her, sitting in the shade, her sunglasses off, her eyes closed in a tableau of perfect repose. She was so still he wondered if she were asleep. He wondered too what it would feel like to kiss those slightly parted lips of hers. No sooner had he thought this than she opened her eyes and for a guilty moment he could have sworn she'd read his mind and was about to rebuke him.

But she didn't. Her voice, silky smooth, she said, 'It's so peaceful and relaxing here. I was close to nodding off.'

'I'm glad you feel able to relax,' he said, lowering the tray onto the roughly hewn table he'd made himself, and which he was rather proud of. He liked nothing better than to take a hunk of discarded timber and turn it into something useful. 'How do you like your steak, rare or well done?'

'Nothing in between?' she asked, getting up to come and stand next to him.

'Nope, not with me there isn't,' he said, 'it's all or nothing.'

'Funnily enough I guessed that might be the case.'

'Yes ma'am, what you see is what you get.' He tone was upbeat and jokey.

'But that's not true, is it?' she said, after a meaningful pause.

Her question took him unawares. 'I assure you it is,' he replied.

She took a long sip of her drink, her gaze on his. 'It's not true of anyone,' she said at length. 'We all play a role we wish to convey, or believe others want of us. Seldom do we lower our guard and be our real selves.'

'Is that true of you also?'

'What? You think I'm exempt from normal behaviour?'

'I think most people regard themselves as the exception to the rule.'

'Is that what you do?'

'You betcha. I'm so shallow I've barely advanced from the amoeba stage.'

'And that's precisely the role you like to portray of yourself, isn't it? Which couldn't be further from the truth.'

He smiled. 'If you say so.'

For the next few minutes he busied himself with keeping an eye on the steaks. When he was satisfied they were ready, he arranged everything on their plates and sat down with her. He watched her take her first bite of her steak. 'Is it okay?' he asked.

'It's more than okay; it's delicious. You said you were a dab hand and you weren't exaggerating.'

'Oh, shucks, now you're embarrassing me.'

'As if!'

'You can never take anything I say at face value, can you?'

'When you say something I can take at face value, I'll let you know.'

Like he said, she could see right through him. 'Well then,' he said, 'in return for me cooking lunch, how about you continue with the story of your *bell' Italiano* who so touchingly brought you flowers?'

She shook her head. 'Not before you've talked some more about yourself. I want to know more about you.'

He tensed, his mouth suddenly dry. To moisten it, he reached for his glass and drained it in one long swallow. 'What do you want to know?' he asked as casually as he could.

'Has there ever been a Mrs St Clair?'

'Now why would you want to know a thing like that? Are you volunteering for the job?'

'You view the role of a wife as doing a job, do you?'

'It would be for any woman stupid enough to apply for the post of wife to me. It would be a pretty tough job at that.'

She tutted and gave him one of her dubious stares. 'Come on, Red, you can do better than that. What makes you so different from other men that you can't be husband material, even a poor husband?'

'Gee, you know how to make me feel special, don't you?'

128

'I suspect far too many women have thought you exceedingly special.'

'But you don't?'

She raised her chin and stared directly at him. 'I might do so if I could get to know the real you. The man behind the smart one-liners and self-effacing humour. Show me the genuine Red St Clair.' She leaned across the table and tapped his forehead with an elegant finger. 'Who's hiding in there.'

'But kiddo, take it from me,' he said, forcing himself not to rear back from the table so he was beyond her reach, 'that fella's not worth a dime.'

'Why not let me be the judge of that?'

'Why not drop the subject?' he said, slamming the brakes on the conversation. He felt she had a whip in one hand and a chair in the other and was backing him into a corner from which there was no escape.

She must have heard the terse warning in his voice and hesitated. 'I'm sorry,' she said. 'I didn't mean to—'

'Forget it,' he said, cutting her off. 'I've been insulted by better people than you.'

'I really didn't mean anything I said as an insult.'

'Accusing me of not being authentic, sounds pretty much like a put-down from where I'm sitting. You might go in for a lot of hokum self-analysis, but you can count me out. Just accept that I fall well short of your expectations.'

She sat perfectly still just staring at him until, and with great precision, she placed her knife and fork on the plate in front of her. 'Seeing as I've offended you so greatly, perhaps it would be better if I went.'

'Yeah, perhaps you're right.'

Chapter Twenty-Five

Meadow Lodge, Melstead St Mary
October 1962
Ralph

On arriving at Meadow Lodge for the party, the last thing Ralph wanted was to get stuck with his father and stepmother for the evening. He'd had enough of their company, in particular his father who had spent most of the day lecturing him about taking responsibility for himself.

'Good God, Ralph!' Arthur had spluttered into his kedgeree at breakfast that morning when Ralph had broached the subject of his father increasing his allowance. 'Can you never come home without asking for money?'

Ralph had done his best to assure the old man that he'd soon be gainfully employed.

'What evidence do you have to support such an outlandish claim?' his father had demanded.

'Have you so little faith in me, Dad?'

'What else do you expect when you spend most of your time fecklessly enjoying yourself?'

'Didn't you when you were young?'

'When I was not much older than you there was a ruddy war on and nobody was enjoying themselves!'

God, the way the bloody old fool went on you'd think he'd taken on the Jerries singlehandedly. Whereas the nearest Arthur

Devereux had come to danger was giving himself a paper-cut at the War Office.

And it wasn't as if his father had actually worked for the vast wealth he now hugged tighter to himself than a boa constrictor squeezing the life out of its victim. Marriage had secured his fortune, not hard graft.

The trouble was the old man enjoyed making Ralph, and others, grovel. It gave him a pathetic sense of superiority knowing that he had the power to make others do what he wanted. He was a bully at heart. And no doubt he bullied Julia. Really the woman should get a backbone and stand up to her husband. When the time came for Ralph to marry, he'd be sure to choose a woman who had some spirit to her.

A woman more like Isabella, he thought as he looked across the dance floor to where she was dancing with that puppy-dog, George Minton. On impulse, and stubbing out his cigarette, then dumping his now empty wineglass, he decided it was time to start enjoying himself. He went over and tapped George on the shoulder. 'Mind if I cut in here?' he said.

George looked disappointed, but sensibly he didn't contest the challenge. There was a pecking order to these things after all.

'You shouldn't have done that,' Isabella said, once Ralph had taken her in his arms and was expertly leading her round the dance floor, and performing a nifty foxtrot.

'And you, sweetheart, should know better than to dance with the local baker's son. What will people think?'

'What a dreadful snob you are!'

'And what a tease you are leading that poor boy on.'

'I was doing no such thing.'

He tightened his hold on her and leaned in to kiss her cheek. 'Of course you weren't.'

Isabella tutted. 'You don't change, do you?'

'I should hope not.'

Holding her close, Ralph thought how much he'd always liked Isabella. She was very different to the girls he knew in London, mostly they were the well-finished sort who were on the hunt for an obscenely rich husband. Isabella had more ambition than that; she wanted to make something of herself and though he lacked ambition himself, he admired her for being so determined and independent. She wasn't one of those clingy girls who sucked the air out of him.

He had known her all his life, but always at a distance. He knew all about Isabella's mother, Allegra, being the illegitimate child of Harry Devereux, his father's uncle who had been the notorious black sheep of the family. He knew too that Arthur was considered something of a black sheep also, that few people, if any, in the family actually liked him.

'So what have you been doing since our paths last crossed?' he asked Isabella.

'I've been busy working.'

'You call acting *work?*'

'That's rich coming from you, Ralph. When are you going to put in an honest day's work?'

He groaned. 'You sound as bad as my father.'

'Don't you get bored with being an idle gentleman about town?'

'But I do it with such aplomb.'

She laughed. 'Nobody could argue with that.'

He spun her round and laughed too. 'Now why is it we never meet up in London when we both live there?'

'What on earth makes you think I'd want to spend any of my precious free time with you?'

He grinned. 'Because I'm irresistible, and astonishingly handsome. So come on, agree to have dinner with me when you're back in town. We could go to a lively little club I know in Soho and go dancing.'

'And how would your father feel about you seeing me for dinner when he hated my mother so much? And let's not forget my illegitimacy. I'm not the sort of friend he'd like for you.'

He shook his head. 'Who cares what he thinks? And besides, your surname might be Hartley, but you're a Devereux through and through.'

'What makes you say that?'

'Because you just are. You're one of the clan. Romily has seen to that. You know, I've often envied you.' He saw the surprise flicker on her face.

'Envied me?' she said. 'Why?'

'You've had so many looking out for you. The same is true of Annelise. Romily took you both under her wing; there wasn't anything she wouldn't have done for you.'

'Are you saying you feel you've missed out?'

He shrugged. 'Let's face it, my father does not excel when it comes to having a loving instinct. But then sociopaths don't, do they?'

'That's pretty harsh, calling your father a sociopath. Especially as he could not have spoiled you more as a young child. I remember one Christmas when you had more toys than Santa's grotto.'

'That was only to make up for the lack of love.'

'Is this when I'm supposed to start feeling sorry for you and agree to have dinner with you out of pity?'

He laughed. 'I'll try any trick I can. But seriously, the way I see it, the Devereux family is like a club, you're either in, or you're not, and even though I carry the name Devereux, I'm not a member like you.'

'What a strange thing to say.'

'Not at all. I carry the stigma of being Arthur Devereux's son, ergo I'm regarded as suspect.'

'He doesn't exactly go out of his way to endear himself to others, does he?'

'As I said before, he's a sociopath; he doesn't care what anyone thinks of him.'

'Do you feel nothing for him? Not even a scrap of affection?'

'If you want my honest opinion, I despise him. Sometimes I look at him and wish he'd just do us all a favour and die. Oh, don't look so shocked. I'm sure there are plenty of people here this evening who would wish the same thing.'

'Julia and your stepbrother might think differently.'

Ralph scoffed. 'Julia is nothing but a slave to him. Do you know, I found her this afternoon taking an inventory of all the food in the kitchen and pantry. Apparently, Dad makes her do that on a weekly basis to make sure nobody is stealing from him. What's more, she has to mend his clothes and iron his shirts. Have you ever heard of anything more demeaning?'

'The poor woman.'

They both looked across the crowded dance floor to where Julia was standing alone and glum-faced.

'I feel sorry for her,' said Isabella. 'So much so, I'm going over to talk to her, seeing as nobody else is.'

Ralph held onto Isabella. 'Not before you've promised to let me take you for dinner next week when we're back in London.'

'Tell you what,' she said after a moment's hesitation, 'if you agree to dance with Julia and put a smile on her face, you can.'

He frowned and was about to say Julia was the last woman he wanted to be seen dancing with when he thought of his Plan B. 'You're on,' he said.

Chapter Twenty-Six

Meadow Lodge, Melstead St Mary
October 1962
Julia

'Stop, Ralph, you're making me dizzy!'

'Stop when we're having so much fun, stepmother dearest? Nonsense!'

The band was playing a lively jive number and as Ralph spun Julia round again and again, she couldn't help but laugh out loud. How different to the way she had been feeling before, standing on the edge of the dance floor in the marquee with nobody to talk to. She had always been a wallflower when it came to these social occasions, and so she had been grateful to Ralph when he had asked her to dance. Even if it had been an offer made out of pity.

'See,' he said with a charming smile as they continued dancing, 'you didn't mean it when you told me to stop.'

'But I'm afraid I'll fall over and make a spectacle of myself,' she said with another giggle.

He winked. 'Then you'd better hold on tight so that doesn't happen!'

When the music did come to a stop, and with her head spinning, Ralph suggested he fetch them both another cooling drink. He led her off the dance floor and went in search of a waitress, leaving her to worry that the punch she had already drunk had gone to her head a little. While she waited for him to return, she caught her breath and tried to locate Arthur amongst the crowd.

She felt guilty that she was having such a good time without him, and he'd gone to so much trouble to buy her this new dress for the evening. It wasn't really to her liking – the colour was wrong for her pale complexion, and the style made her feel matronly compared to all the other women here. They must think her dreadfully plain and dowdy. She longed to wear something dazzling, or even daring like some of the young girls here, but then she never had before, so why did she think she could now? She had been brought up to dress and act modestly, never to draw attention to herself.

It was one of the things that Arthur said he liked about her, her natural propensity for humility. He said she was very different to his previous wives who he described as vain show-offs who cared for nothing but their appearance, an attitude he couldn't abide. It explained why he had such definite ideas on how she should dress.

'You're mistress of Melstead Hall,' he would say, 'so you need to dress appropriately, not like those young tarts in the village.'

This was why she knew there was no truth in that malicious rumour she'd once heard in the village, that Arthur had forced himself on one of their maids. He simply wasn't the type of man to chase after young girls. Probably it was the other way round, the maid had thrown herself at him and he'd firmly rebuffed her. Maybe it was the same girl who had sent Julia that anonymous letter.

'There you go,' Ralph said, back with her now and passing her a glass that was full to the brim. 'Bottoms up!'

'I mustn't monopolise you,' she said, after she'd taken a sip of the sweet liquid, taking care not to spill it down her new dress. 'Not when you should be dancing with girls your own age.'

'Time for that later,' he said. 'For now I want to make you

laugh some more. You know, I don't believe I've ever seen you this jolly. You always give the impression of being so serious.'

She blushed at his words, not knowing how to respond.

'Tell me,' he said, 'apart from dancing with your stepson, what else makes you laugh?'

'All sorts of things,' she replied.

'Such as?'

'Charles; he always—' she broke off, realising she was about to betray herself by saying he always cheered her up. To say that would make her sound as though she weren't happy. And she was happy. It was just that now Charles was away at school she was lonely at times.

'What does Charles always do?' Ralph prompted.

'Smile,' she said. 'He makes me smile.'

'Do you miss him?' he asked.

Surprised by the question, Julia said, 'What sort of a mother would I be if I didn't?'

'He's lucky to have you as his mother in that case. I doubt mine gave me a second thought once she left my father. She was glad to be shot of us both.'

'Don't say that.'

'Why not? It's the truth. Drink up, I'm going to claim another dance with you, so brace yourself!'

'Oh, I'd better not,' she said.

'What, better not drink up, or better not dance some more?'

'Both. I ought to find Arthur. He'll be wondering where I've got to.'

'Come on, Julia, let your hair down. You're not shackled to the old man. You're not afraid of him, are you?'

With a slight recoil, she frowned at the taunting tone in Ralph's voice. 'What makes you say that?' she said.

'You're like a timid little mouse when he's around.'

'Don't be silly, of course I'm not. I just don't like to antagonise him like you . . . ' her voice trailed off as she lost her nerve.

'As I do, you were going to say?'

'Well, you do seem to fall out with him such a lot. Can't you be nicer to your father?'

'I would if he were nicer to me.' He drained his glass and looked at her with his charming smile. 'I say, I don't suppose you could do me a huge favour, could you?'

'What sort of favour?'

'Put in a good word for me and see if you can get the old man to change his mind about increasing my allowance?'

'I'm not sure he'll listen to me,' she said, startled at his suggestion. Money was not something Arthur discussed apart from how to save it. He gave her housekeeping money and it was her job to make it cover all the bills. She took pride in doing that, because she knew it pleased him.

'Or perhaps you could—'

'Yes?' she said, when Ralph fell silent.

'No. I can't ask you what I was about to. It wouldn't be right.'

Ever since she had married Arthur, Julia had wanted to have a better relationship with Ralph. Until now she had believed he didn't much care for her, that he resented her for marrying his father. In fact, until this evening they had never had a proper conversation. Perhaps this was a turning point for them. She hoped so because then he might also want to be closer to Charles, his stepbrother.

'Just say what you were going to say, Ralph,' she said.

He breathed in, then exhaled. 'I wondered, rather than bother my father, if you couldn't help me out a little.'

'Me?'

'Yes. I wouldn't ask, only that things are getting a bit embarrassing for me. Of course, once I have a job, I'll be able to repay you whatever you've managed to spare me.'

She thought how accurately she had to account for every pound, shilling and penny Arthur gave her and couldn't see any way in which she could help Ralph. But she couldn't bring herself to disappoint him.

'You know,' he went on, 'you really are quite an amazing woman.'

'I am?'

'Oh yes. You've made my father happier than I've ever seen him before.'

'Really?'

'Don't sound so surprised, it's obvious the difference you've made to his life.'

'Well,' she said cautiously, 'I suppose he's had so much sadness in his life, hasn't he, what with his first wife leaving him and then his second wife dying?'

'Precisely! You're a ray of sunshine in what had been a dark world for him. Now what do you say? Could you help me out financially, just temporarily?'

Julia was not as stupid as some people thought she was. She knew that Ralph was using charm and flattery to twist her arm, but she was prepared to overlook that if it meant he became a better stepbrother to Charles. 'I'll see what I can do,' she murmured.

'Good girl,' he said, a rakish smile brightening his handsome face. 'I knew I could count on you. Come on, drink up and we'll take another turn around the dance floor.'

Chapter Twenty-Seven

Meadow Lodge, Melstead St Mary
October 1962
Hope

'Everything all right?'

Watching Edmund dance with his niece, Hope turned to find Kit standing next to her.

'Of course everything's all right,' she said, 'why wouldn't it be?'

'No reason. Although I haven't seen you dance yet.'

'Nobody's asked me. And I'm certainly not going to make a fool of myself the way Edmund is. Just look at him with Em.'

'It's called the Twist.'

Hope grimaced. 'You can call it what you want, but it's not for me. Where's the elegance?'

'I suspect elegance isn't part of the deal,' Kit said with a chuckle. 'I'm reliably informed by both Pip and Em that to do it properly one has to imagine drying one's bottom with a towel while grinding out a cigarette with a foot.'

'Is that so?'

'I could ask the band to play a nice gentle waltz, or a foxtrot, if you'd like.'

Hope shook her head. 'Just ignore me, I'm not at my best at parties.' Observing her husband again, as he loosened his tie and threw off his jacket, and tossed it to Evelyn, she said, 'Have you noticed a difference in Edmund lately?'

'What sort of difference?'

Seeing the concern in Kit's face, she thought better of pursuing the subject. 'Sorry, I'm being a bore and a damp squib.'

'No you're not. And I know you well enough to recognise the signs when something is worrying you. You have your anxious 'frowny' face on.'

She smiled ruefully. 'Some would say that's my every-day expression. Oh yes, I know what the children used to say about me, there she goes, Auntie Crabby.'

Kit laughed. 'I've never heard them describe you that way. And the millions of children around the world who read your books would never say that of you.'

'Dear sweet Kit, you've always been so loyal to me. What would I do without you?'

He put an arm around her. 'Tell me what's troubling you, big sis.'

Leaning into him, she said, 'Do you ever feel we're being left behind, that we're no longer relevant?'

'You sound like Evelyn. She was asking me earlier if I ever wanted to turn back the clock.'

'Maybe it's seeing the younger members of the family all grown up that's giving us both pause to reflect on our mortality.'

'The pair of you need to snap out of it. We all have plenty of good years ahead of us yet. This party tonight is not only a celebration of what's gone before for Evelyn and me, but what we'll all share in the future.'

Hope smiled. 'You're a lucky man always to feel so positive about life.'

He squeezed her shoulder gently. 'I know it's not easy for you sometimes, Hope, but don't ever lose sight of how loved you are.'

'You dear man. You're eternally thoughtful and caring.'

He laughed. 'That's not what Pip and Em say when I'm

asking them to turn down their music. Or when I'm questioning whether it is actually music. "Oh Dad," they say, "you're such an old square, you need to get with it!"'

She smiled, and knowing just how much her brother loved his children, she said, 'Family life really suits you, doesn't it?'

'Marrying Evelyn and having Pip and Em is the best thing I ever did. But you know, I sometimes wonder why Evelyn did marry me. She's beautiful and clever – much cleverer than me – and could have married anyone she wanted. She could—'

'She chose you, Kit,' Hope interrupted him. 'Don't ever lose sight of that.'

'And don't ever lose sight of how proud we all are of you, for everything you've achieved. You're amazing, you really are.'

For some reason his words filled her with an emotion she couldn't tolerate – self-pity. To her horror and disgust, tears pricked at the backs of her eyes.

'Hope, whatever is the matter?' asked Kit.

In a strangled sob, she said, 'I'm such a failure.'

Her brother stared at her, his poor badly scarred face clouded with disbelief. 'How can you say that?'

'I'm a failure as a wife,' she said, struggling to get a grip on her emotions. 'Edmund doesn't love me. Why would he?' She looked to where he was so clearly enjoying himself on the dance floor with Em and now one of her young college friends. The three of them were putting on a show of some magnitude as they gyrated in what to Hope's way of thinking was a most undignified manner.

'Of course he loves you!' Kit asserted. 'Edmund's devoted to you. How could you think otherwise?'

Taking a deep breath, she turned around to face Kit. 'If I confide in you, will you promise not to say anything to anybody else? Not even Evelyn. Do you promise?'

He frowned, but acquiesced with a small nod.

She then told him about the anonymous letter she had received and what it accused Edmund of doing.

'A poison pen letter?' Kit exclaimed, incredulously.

'*Shhh!*' she hissed. 'I don't want people to know.'

'But you can't possibly take it seriously? It's just someone being spiteful, wanting to make trouble. It'll be a spiteful old biddy with nothing better to do.'

'But why? And who would want to make trouble like that for me? What have I done?'

'Did the letter actually have your name on it?'

'Yes, on the envelope.'

'Was Edmund's name used?'

She was about to say yes again, when she visualised the letter in her hand, each horrible word jumping out at her. 'No,' she replied.

'So it might merely be an anonymous wild shot in the dark that could have been posted through anybody's letterbox?'

'But it had my name on the envelope.'

'True, but the nasty individual who penned the letter might just as easily picked any woman's name who lived in the village.' He shrugged. 'Evelyn's name for instance. Can you think of anything more absurd and less likely than for me to be accused of cheating on my wife? Trust me, Hope, throw the letter away and don't give it another thought. It's nothing more than village mischief-making.'

'Village mischief-making,' said a voice from behind them. 'That sounds interesting.'

As if by magic their brother Arthur had materialised out of thin air. He had an uncanny knack for doing that, in spite of his bulk.

'How long have you been lurking there listening in on our conversation?' demanded Hope.

'*Lurking,*' he repeated, his tone as supercilious as the

expression on his jowly face. 'What a thing to accuse me of. I'm hurt to the quick.'

'I'm quite sure you're not,' she muttered, thinking it would take more than a few words to penetrate the layers of blubber Arthur had acquired with each passing year.

'I must say,' she went on, arming herself for the inevitable round of sparring that accompanied any exchange with Arthur, and which always resulted in trading insults. 'I'm surprised to see you here.'

He regarded her with a disdainful look. 'Why?'

'You spend so little time at the Hall these days. I wonder you can tear yourself away from the lure of the fleshpots of London. Poor Julia must get dreadfully lonely rattling around in that ghastly mausoleum all on her own.'

'What a jolly hoot you are, Hope. You know, nothing quite prepares me for seeing you again after an extended time apart. But you should know by now that it's a fool's game to bait me.'

'Come on you two,' remarked Kit genially, 'play nicely. I trust you're well, Arthur?'

'You find me in fine fettle,' he replied, lighting up an ostentatiously large cigar.

'How's Charles getting on with being away at school?' asked Kit. 'Julia must miss him terribly.'

'Boys need to have the apron strings cut early on,' asserted Arthur, 'the last thing they need is to be mollycoddled by an over-protective mother.' He puffed expansively on his cigar. 'You look a bit off the pace, little sis,' he remarked to Hope. 'Something on your mind? Apart from your husband making a fool of himself on the dance floor. Somebody should tell him that the twist is strictly for the young. There again, how can he resist dancing with two attractive young girls when his wife looks so miserable? Now what was this village mischief you were talking about?'

Suddenly gripped with sickening certainty, Hope stared at Arthur with loathing. It was him! It was her brother who had sent her the letter!

Chapter Twenty-Eight

Meadow Lodge, Melstead St Mary
October 1962
Stanley

'You seem subdued this evening, Annelise,' remarked Stanley. He kept his voice light, which wasn't easy given the volume of the band.

'Do I?' she said, turning her gaze away from the dance floor to look at him. 'I'm sorry.'

'Don't apologise. I was just concerned that you were feeling unwell.'

What really concerned him was that she might be bored in his company. On social occasions like this, when the great and the good from the county were gathered, he could never quite rid himself of the deep-seated anxiety that he didn't belong. Despite all his outward success at having reinvented himself, deep inside he was still Stanley Nettles, the illiterate kid from the East End.

But determined not to give in to those old insecurities of his, and reminding himself how much he had been looking forward to this weekend and seeing Annelise again, he smiled brightly. 'Would you like to dance?' he asked.

'Would you think me very boring if I said no?'

Disappointed, he shook his head. 'Not at all. And if I'm honest, I'm not really in the mood for dancing myself. Besides, you know I'm in possession of two of the clumsiest left feet.'

She smiled. 'That's so typical of you, Stanley, offering to dance with me in spite of not wanting to yourself. You're so sweet,' she added, placing her hand on his forearm.

Wishing she could consider him more than sweet, he accepted the compliment with good grace. 'In that case, how about something to eat?'

They cruised the trestle tables that were laden with food – venison pies, sausage rolls, coronation chicken, prawn vol-au-vents, cocktail sausages, cheese straws, bacon wrapped around dates, mini quiches, devilled eggs, celery with cream cheese, wedges of melon, and whole salmons poached and covered in wafer-thin slices of cucumber to resemble scales. It seemed only yesterday to him that a spread like this would have been inconceivable, and not just during the war, but for years afterwards when rationing was still in place.

'There's enough here for a very large army,' commented Annelise.

Stanley laughed. 'I can assure you we didn't have anything like this when I was in the army doing my National Service.'

She laughed too. 'I remember how handsome you looked in your uniform when you came home on leave.'

'And I remember you running out to meet me in the garden one day. You'd been helping Romily to pick raspberries and your mouth and fingers were ruby-pink with all the fruit you'd eaten.'

He remembered too how he'd swaggered along with his kit bag thrown over his shoulder wanting to impress her. He'd felt so grown up at the time, but looking back on it, he'd been nothing but a naïve child pretending to be an adult.

In a way he still felt much the same: pretending to be something he wasn't. Perhaps being here in the village where so many people knew him was a mistake. Would he be better off moving away to reinvent himself, somewhere completely new?

147

But would he feel even more of an outsider somewhere new and strange? Was that what he was destined always to be, an outsider?

'You suddenly look very serious,' Annelise said. 'What are you thinking?'

He frowned. 'About identity.'

'Ah, that old chestnut.'

She gave the words an airy tone which he knew she did not feel when it came to discussing *this old chestnut*. It was something they had in common, this longing to fill in the blanks. Not that Stanley wanted to rekindle any sort of relationship with his mother.

'Do you think we'll go through the whole of our lives with a question mark hanging over us?' he asked.

'I don't know if I'm honest,' she said. 'I want to believe I can accept what I do know as being enough and not worry about what I don't know. I doubt it can ever be as easy as that. But at least you do know where you're from, Stanley.'

'I do, and I don't,' he replied. 'I know I'm from the East End of London and lived in a terraced house in Halifax Road, but that's just bricks and mortar. What does that tell me about my place in life?'

She regarded him sceptically. 'Perhaps you should look at it differently. What does that house really have to do with the person you've become and what you've achieved for yourself?'

The advice was much the same as Romily had once given him and which he'd tried, but failed to heed.

Not a soul had he told that whenever he was in London he would go to Halifax Road and take in where No.5 had once stood, before it was bombed to a pile of rubble. Sometimes he thought that if the Germans hadn't bombed the house, he would have done so himself. Eventually the houses that remained were torn down and a die-cast works was built in their place.

Time and time again he would stare at the spot where he was convinced No.5 had been, trying to summon up just one memory that didn't make him quake inside. The stupid thing was he didn't know why he did it, why he should want to cling on to the hope that it hadn't all been a miserable existence before he'd been put on a train for Suffolk as a nine-year-old boy. Sometimes he thought he was trying to punish himself by reliving those days of terror inflicted on him by a vicious and sadistic woman. It was as if he still wanted her to torture him.

If he closed his eyes he could hear the hatred in her voice as she screamed at him. He could also feel the pain of her stubbing out her cigarette on his skin and telling him it was what he deserved for being such a wicked son.

What had terrified him initially, being locked in the cellar while she spent the weekend with her latest boyfriend, soon became a respite from the worst of his mother's violent mood swings. With only a candle for light, he would have to fend off the mice that tried to eat what little food she had given him.

He never knew how long he would be locked in the cellar, so he had to eke out what he had to eat and drink. What he hated most was the bucket she would leave for him to relieve himself into. More than once she returned and was so disgusted by the stench of the cellar, she called him every name under the sun and tipped the bucket over his head and locked him in there for another day.

'You're worse than an animal,' his mother would say. 'Is it any wonder that I have to treat you like a dog?'

His stomach churning at the memory, he looked around at the assembled guests in their finery and was suddenly consumed with the need to hide. To hide his guilty shame and dirty secrets. If they knew the ugly truth of him, they wouldn't want him in their midst. He wasn't worthy to be here. How could anyone love him? He wasn't worthy of being loved. That was what his mother always said. He was nothing better than something she'd stepped in.

No one knew the extent of what had gone on inside No.5 Halifax Road, not even Romily or Florence, both of whom had seen the bruises and burn marks on his body when he'd run away from his mother. During his time of being evacuated from London, his mother had turned up at Island House to take him back home. He hadn't wanted to go with her, knowing what it would be like all over again. But Romily had been unable to stop his mother from insisting that it was her right to have him with her. Some weeks later he had managed to run away in the middle of the night, and by hiding on a train he had found his way back to Melstead St Mary. For a long time he lived in fear of his mother showing up again to reclaim him, but she never did.

He suddenly shuddered and as his body began to shake with familiar dread, he gave in to the sensation of detaching himself from his surroundings, just as he had when his mother had beaten him. Squeezing his eyes shut and imagining that he was invisible had been his way of pretending she couldn't hurt him.

Feeling something touching him, he started violently.

'What is it, Stanley?' Annelise asked, her hand on his arm where it had been before, her beautiful face wreathed in concern. The sheer loveliness of her made him recoil.

'Nothing's wrong,' he said roughly.

How could she bear to look at him? How could she even contemplate being in his presence when she was so pure and perfect, and he was so disgusting?

He fought hard to stop the nausea in his stomach from rising up, to quell the shaking that was building. He swallowed hard and stepped away from Annelise.

He needed to get away. Out of this marquee. He needed fresh air.

'Stanley,' she said, her eyes wide with alarm, 'whatever is it? Are you unwell?'

Unable to speak, his palms sweaty, his heart thundering in his chest, he fled.

Chapter Twenty-Nine

Meadow Lodge, Melstead St Mary
October 1962
Annelise

Annelise chased after Stanley, convinced she had said something wrong, but not knowing what. She was appalled that she could have inadvertently upset him. She had just been on the verge of telling him about Harry, when she realised he wasn't listening to her.

She went in the direction she thought he'd gone, adjusting her eyes to the darkness of the garden which was prettily illuminated with fairy lights. But there was no sign of him.

Reluctant to go back inside the marquee, she decided to go for a stroll. She had just rounded the far side of the marquee and was moving in the direction of the orchard, the music fading into the background, when she heard voices.

Peering in the darkness to see who was there, she realised it was Evelyn standing on the verandah of the summerhouse. With her was the guest who had arrived well after the party had started. An arrestingly handsome man with a smattering of grey at the temples and a cream silk scarf tired artfully around his neck, he had stuck out for Annelise because he had the same polished manner as Harry. He had carried himself with an easy assurance, as though he knew everybody would be observing him. Another showman, she had thought as she'd watched him greet Evelyn, kissing her flamboyantly on both cheeks.

'I had no idea that Kit had invited you,' Annelise heard Evelyn say now. 'Why didn't you tell me you were coming?'

'Your husband said it was meant to be a surprise. You know the kind of thing, a gang of your old chums crawling out of the woodwork to help celebrate your many years of wedded bliss.'

'Surprise doesn't cover the half of it; I had the shock of my life when I saw you.'

'You make it sound like it's an unwelcome surprise.'

'It is, Max. You shouldn't have come.'

'But why, Evelyn? After all this time I thought you'd be pleased. Certainly Kit thought so. I say hats off to him turning detective and finding me.'

'You're being deliberately obtuse; something I recall you found contemptible in others. And in the circumstances—' her voice broke off.

'What circumstances?' the man called Max demanded.

There was a pause. Then Evelyn said: 'I don't like coincidences.'

'Back at the Park, that's what we counted on.'

'That was different; that was our job, to look for patterns.'

'So what are you getting at? What coincidence has my presence here tonight created?'

'I've received a letter.'

'What letter?'

'A vile poison pen letter insinuating that Kit isn't Pip and Em's father.'

'Good God! Do you know who wrote it?'

'No I don't. It wasn't you, was it, Max, wanting to stir up trouble? Because I'd happily kill you if that's the case.' Evelyn's voice was fierce. Annelise had never heard her sound so severe.

'Evelyn darling, how could you say such a thing after what we meant to each other?'

'Don't say that. *Not ever*. And don't call me darling! Swear to me, Max, that you didn't send that letter. Swear on whatever you hold sacred.'

'Evelyn, I swear I wouldn't do anything of the kind. For what purpose would I behave so dishonourably?'

Annelise didn't want to hear any more. She should have walked away the moment she heard the voices, knowing that it was a private conversation, but shameful curiosity had rooted her to the spot. Now she forced herself to move, to retrace her steps back to the marquee. But such was her shock at what she'd heard, she blundered into the low branch of a tree and let out a small cry.

'Who's there?' Evelyn called out.

Annelise didn't know what to do. Whether to show herself and pretend she hadn't known anyone else was nearby, or slip away into the darkness.

She chose the latter, but instead of going the way she had come, she went in the opposite direction, hoping that she wouldn't miss her footing in the dark.

No good ever came of eavesdropping, everyone knew that, and she wished with all her heart she could erase the conversation she'd overheard from her memory. Kit not Pip and Em's father? It couldn't be true. And just who was this Max character? A wartime lover?

Annelise knew that Evelyn's war work had been what was commonly referred to as 'hush-hush'. In Oxford she frequently came across dons and fellows who had been similarly employed in the fight against Germany. They never spoke directly to her of what they had done, but there were always hints and rumours. College life was like that, an endless cycle of gossip, some of it quite malicious. Annelise's biggest fear was that there might be rumours circulating about her and Harry. Harry maintained that if he caught anyone gossiping about him, he'd fight back. 'I'd make it known,' he once said, 'that, just as there was in

Cambridge, a KGB spy ring is at work in Oxford recruiting ideological students with Communist inclinations. That would really put the cat amongst the pigeons!'

Here in Melstead St Mary, the Cold War could not feel less of a threat, even with the Cuban missile crisis hanging over them. But in Oxford, where debates raged constantly, it seemed much more of a reality.

In April of this year Annelise had gone with Rebecca to Hyde Park with thousands of ban-the-bomb protesters. She had never done anything like that before. She had wanted Harry to go with her, to march together arm in arm, but of course something like that was out of the question. They couldn't be seen in public together. Not until he was a single man.

Not really knowing where she was going, just that she had been intent on putting as much distance between herself and the summerhouse, Annelise realised she was now on the path that lead to the vegetable garden. And just as the bank of clouds that had been hiding the moon parted, she saw Stanley sitting on a bench.

'Stanley, are you all right?' she asked.

'Please don't come any nearer,' he murmured.

'Why ever not?'

'I'm not fit to be in decent company.'

Ignoring his answer, she went and sat on the bench with him. He immediately made as if to get to his feet. She put her hand out to stop him. 'Don't go,' she said. 'Tell me what's wrong.'

'I stink,' he said bluntly. 'I've been sick.'

She could smell that he had. 'Would you like a glass of water?'

'No.'

'Shall I fetch Edmund?'

'I don't need a doctor.'

'Then what do you need?'

'To be left alone.'

'That's the saddest thing you've ever said to me. Have I done something wrong? Or said something to offend you?'

He shook his head.

'Then what happened back there in the marquee? One minute we were chatting, and the next you rushed off as though you couldn't get away from me fast enough.'

He turned to look at her and in the shadowy gloom his face looked eerily gaunt and contorted with something she couldn't name. 'Stanley,' she said softly, 'you look terrible; I'm worried about you. Are you sure you're not ill?'

'I told you I'm not. And please don't worry about me, I'm not worth worrying over.'

'Why would you think that?'

He sighed and hung his head. 'Just ignore me. Go back and enjoy the party.'

'I can't,' she said, 'not now. Something's troubling you, won't you share it with me?' She sensed him hesitate. 'Please, Stanley,' she pressed. 'There's never been any awkwardness between us before. Don't let that change.'

He didn't respond. She let the silence continue, waited patiently for him to talk.

'I can't explain it,' he said finally.

'Try.'

He slowly raised his head. 'It comes over me when I'm least expecting it. This . . . sickening horror that I'm back where I was as a child, before I arrived at Island House.'

'With your mother?'

He nodded.

'The past can't keep you hostage for ever,' she said. 'You mustn't let it. You deserve so much more.'

'Do I?'

'Of course you do! Whatever that despicable woman made

you believe as a child, it wasn't true. Just look at the success you've made of your life.'

'Most of the time that's what I believe. But then from nowhere it's as if she's here with me, filling my head with her poison, convincing me I'm worthless.'

Annelise frowned. 'When did this start happening?'

He shrugged. 'Earlier this year, after I'd been to her funeral.'

'Her funeral?' Annelise was stunned. 'You never said that you went to her funeral, or that you even knew she had died?'

'I didn't tell anyone. I didn't want anyone to think that she meant something to me. I thought everyone here who had helped me might feel I was being disloyal.'

'That's madness, Stanley. Why would anyone think that?'

He sighed again. 'Like I said before, I can't really explain it. None of it makes sense. All I know is that the fear, once it gets a hold of me, is so real it makes me believe what she used to say. It churns me up so much that I'm physically sick.'

'I hate to state the obvious, but you should see somebody about this.'

'A trick cyclist?'

She gave him a tentative smile. 'A doctor who can get inside your head and sort it all out for you.'

'But it won't change who I am, will it?'

'It's not about change, Stanley; it's about acceptance.'

'I still wouldn't be good enough for you, would I, not compared to your clever friends in Oxford?'

She stared at her dearest friend in horror. 'Oh, Stanley, you've got it all wrong. I've loved you like a brother all my life. You're as dear to me as anyone ever could be. Truly you are.'

'I'm sorry,' he muttered. 'I shouldn't have said anything. Forget it. I'm not myself.'

No, you're not, she thought. But then perhaps that was the point. Who were any of them beneath the outer layers with which they equipped themselves?

Chapter Thirty

Casa Santa Rosa, Palm Springs
October 1962
Romily

Just who the devil did he think he was?

Her arms slicing through the water, her legs kicking with concentrated intent, Romily had been asking herself this question since returning from the aborted lunch with Red St Clair.

What really infuriated her was that he had made no attempt to stop her from leaving. She had been calling his bluff by suggesting she leave, and he'd let her do just that. He had plainly known what she was doing and had called her bluff in return. Seldom did she meet anyone who got under her skin, but in this case Red St Clair had done exactly that.

Deftly turning at the end of the pool, she commenced another length. The only conclusion she could reach about what had happened with Red, was that she must have been too direct with him when asking about the *real* Red St Clair. It was funny how people went on about wanting others to be straight with them, but when they were confronted with even a mild dose of it themselves, rarely was it to their liking.

Obviously Red didn't feel comfortable with anyone being direct with him. He wanted to dictate the terms of any conversation and in the process ensure he revealed nothing of himself. Question was, why? What did he have to hide?

Well, one thing was for certain, she had put the kibosh on

their working together. She would telephone Gabe and Melvyn to explain, as well as apologise, and then book her flight home.

Home. Where she should have gone in the first place. She shouldn't be here. She should be at Meadow Lodge celebrating Kit and Evelyn's wedding anniversary. She hoped the party was the success Kit had so badly wanted it to be.

'I'd like to do something special for Evelyn,' he'd confided to Romily. 'It's the least I can do after everything she's done for me.'

Kit had always seen his marriage to Evelyn in those terms, as though he couldn't quite believe his luck. Often the consequence of that was the belief that good fortune was transitory, that any day it would come to an end.

Out of the swimming pool now, Romily dried herself vigorously, then lay back on one of the comfortable poolside loungers. She would miss this when she left. The sensation of hot rays of sunshine caressing her body felt good on what she ruefully called her 'old bones'. The leg she broke when she crash-landed the Walrus occasionally played up with a stiffness on a cold damp morning. Not surprisingly it hadn't bothered her while she had been here.

Looking at her leg now, she ran a finger the length of the six-inch scar. Despite the fashion for shorter hemlines, she always wore her skirts and dresses well below the knee to hide the imperfection. It was a poignant reminder of the crash which she had been lucky to survive, and of the man who had pulled her from the burning wreckage: Matteo Fontana.

Chapter Thirty-One

Tilbrook Hall, Norfolk
April 1944
Romily

Matteo visited me every day. With nothing to do but stay in bed with my leg in traction, his visits were all I had to look forward to.

He told me that he had learned English from an excellent teacher at school, and that he had been an officer in the Italian army and had been captured in North Africa. As a POW here at Tilbrook Hall, he helped in the infirmary as well as worked on the nearby farm with the land girls. He was considered to be a 'white prisoner', which meant he was a low risk POW with no political motivation. As a consequence, he was given a certain amount of freedom, such as joining in with local events in the village.

I was perfectly capable of doing it myself, but he read to me, borrowing books from the library. The owners of Tilbrook Hall, who had decamped to their Belgravia house, had given permission for their library to be at the disposal of the medical staff, as well as the patients.

He was reading to me now and it amused and charmed me to hear *Great Expectations* read with a gorgeously seductive Italian accent. Never had Dickens sounded so good! It may have been the effect of the strong medication I was given, but I could have listened to Matteo reading the telephone book and it would still have had my mind wandering into dangerous waters.

He was the first man I had encountered since my husband's death with whom I had experienced an attraction. Until now I had been unable to imagine another man's touch, never mind the kind of passionate intimacy I had enjoyed with Jack. Everyone had told me that I would one day fall in love again, that it would just take time. Had sufficient time now passed?

'Would you prefer I stopped reading to you?'

I opened my eyes to see Matteo regarding me intently. 'Yes,' I said, 'why don't you put the book down and tell me some more about yourself and your life back in Italy?'

'What would you like to know?'

'What did you do before you became a soldier?'

'It is hard sometimes to remember that I had a life before the world went mad.'

'Please tell me about it. Unless,' I added tactfully, 'it will make you too homesick?'

He closed the book and placed it carefully on the cabinet beside my bed. 'I grew up on the Island of Ischia and it was expected that I would become a doctor just like my father. "People", my father would say, "will always need a doctor, so you will always be in work." I did what he wanted and studied medicine and became a doctor.'

'So that is the reason you help out here in the infirmary?'

'Yes. And for some years I enjoyed what I did, but all I had ever dreamt of doing was paint. I wanted to be an artist. I wanted that more than anything in the world.'

I nodded. 'But to defy your father would have been out of the question?' I said, taking in his sensitive face with its fine features and enviably long lashes, and the gentle cadence to his voice.

'Everyone thought I was crazy, but yes, I disappointed my

family by giving up medicine to go and study at the Accademia di Brera in Milan, then I went to Florence. I never felt so alive as I did during that time. It was as if I had been born again.'

'To be the person you were meant to be?' I suggested.

'Yes,' he said, his dark eyes opening wide, his expression brightening, 'that was just how I felt.'

'Were you then able to make a living from painting?'

'I did, I am happy to say. If that does not sound too ... too arrogant of me.'

'I would love to see something you've painted.'

'Do you mean that?'

'Of course. Do you have access to any painting materials here?' I was thinking that maybe I could arrange for that to happen. I was thinking also how much I would like to do something for this intense and quietly spoken man. If only so I could see the melancholy fade from his eyes.

'I do,' he said. 'In fact, I arrange a painting class here for the other POWs. It gives them something to do. Some of them are beginning to show some talent.'

I heard the pride in his voice and the poignancy of it touched me deeply. It made me more determined to do what I could for him, to help him feel less of a prisoner. I suppose that was when I began to fall in love with him.

Chapter Thirty-Two

La Vista, Palm Springs
October 1962
Red

'Just what the hell is going on there?'

'Nothing's going on, Gabe,' Red lied.

'The hell there isn't! I've just been talking to Romily and she says she's flying home tomorrow.'

'She's a grown woman who's perfectly entitled to fly home any time she chooses.'

'And what about the script?'

'There isn't going to be a script. Not if she's leaving.'

'Hey, don't you dare try laying this one on Romily. If she's going it's because you've made her go. What did you do?'

'Nothing. We just didn't rub along like you imagined we would.'

'Romily gets on with everyone. She's a professional in all respects, so don't give me any bunkum about her—'

'Gabe, it didn't work out, so just give it a rest, will you? You win some, you lose some.'

'Yeah, and guess what, Melvyn and I are the ones losing out here. And I'll tell you this for nothing, you won't get another God-damned chance to work with us again.'

'Go on, go the whole hog-roast with your threat. Tell me I won't work in this God-damned town ever again!'

'Don't tempt me!'

Gabe's rant went on for some minutes more and when he'd seemingly run dry of invective, and after Red had pointed out that the studio could easily find another writer to work with Romily, he put down the telephone and poured himself a large bourbon. It was one of many which he'd consumed in the hours since Romily had left. By rights he should be drunk, but he was stone cold sober. A little blurring around the edges would suit him plenty, if he were honest. But no such luck. He could see things all too clearly and he didn't like what he saw. No sir.

Some would say he was a flawed man who just needed to work things through, but he was beyond that. Well beyond putting right the many crimes he'd committed.

For some strange reason women liked flawed men. They liked nothing better than a wounded man, or a man with some inner conflict who was fighting his demons. Put the two together and it was jackpot time. Before losing his leg, he would have believed an injury of that nature would limit his options when it came to women, but not a bit of it; it was like catnip to them. He soon realised he could put the injury to good use and exploit women for his own ends. It was all an attempt to soothe his ego, and convince himself that he was still in the game. No matter that his actions were in danger of turning him into an arrogant and manipulative bastard.

Doubtless this was the opinion Romily now held of him after his behaviour today. He should have apologised straightaway and stopped her from leaving, but he hadn't been able to bring himself to do it. That would have been the decent thing to do, the polite way out. But he'd taken the coward's way. Just as he had once before in what felt like another life. But a life that would always haunt him.

Suspecting that Romily had seen through him and identified him for the fraud he was was one thing, but being confronted with the certainty of it, quite another.

Who's hiding in there?

Those were her words. And it was a question to which she would never know the answer. Because if she did, she would despise him even more than she did now. The *pretend him* was so much better than the *real him*.

Being a writer meant he could create characters who had far better qualities than he possessed, and it didn't take too much figuring out to conclude these were people he wished he could be. Brave, decent and genuine.

A genuine apology to Romily would have been all that was required of him and Gabe wouldn't be making threats. But no. He'd blown it. He'd bailed out just as he always did when things got too emotionally sticky.

Slumped in a chair, he stared at the mountain in the distance. Already the light was beginning to fade and Mount San Jacinto was taking on its familiar brooding presence. No matter the pain in his leg, he would fill a rucksack and take off for a few days. He'd lose himself in the desert and forget what a bastard he was.

He'd forget Romily too. And he'd erase forever that look of cool contempt on her face when he'd agreed that she should go. Another woman would have flown off the handle and said exactly what she thought of him – a state of affairs he'd encountered many a time, thereby making the job of getting rid of the woman so much easier. Nothing but a shrew, he would tell himself afterwards, thereby justifying his behaviour. But Romily, and without a word of admonishment, had left him feeling as worthless as a cockroach.

In the gathering dusk Mount San Jacinto glowered back at him as though the very spirit of the desert was questioning him. 'What are you staring at?' he felt like saying. 'Don't you go judging me. Not you as well.'

Chapter Thirty-Three

Melstead Hall, Melstead St Mary
October 1962
Julia

'What did you think you were doing?' Arthur demanded.

'I . . . I don't know what you mean,' stammered Julia as she fumbled to undo the buttons on her overcoat. Although she knew exactly what her husband meant. She should never have allowed Ralph to talk her into drinking a second and then a third glass of the fruit punch. Poor Arthur had every right to be angry with her.

All the way home from the party he had been ominously silent. Not a word did he utter, despite Julia's nervous attempts to make conversation. His jaw set as he drove the Rolls along the lanes in the dark, he had kept his gaze fixed ahead of him. It was as if he were deaf to her voice.

It would have been different had Ralph left the party with them, he would have made conversation with either his father or Julia. But Ralph had been having too good a time to leave. He'd told his father he would find his own way home, and that there was no need for anyone to wait up for him. Yet even as she had wished for Ralph's company in the car, Julia had known it would only have been putting off the reckoning she was in for. It was what she deserved after all. She had not been a good wife. She had neglected Arthur, had barely seen him all evening. Worse still, she had made an exhibition of herself. Was it any wonder he was cross with her?

Handing his coat to their housekeeper, who could not look down her nose at Julia with any more disapproval if she tried, Arthur said, 'Go to your room, Julia, I'll speak to you after I've poured myself a whisky.'

Still in her coat, and clutching her handbag to her, Julia did as she was told and climbed the stairs.

'How was the party, Mr Devereux?' she heard Miss Casey ask.

'It would have been better had my wife not embarrassed me.'

'Quite so,' murmured the housekeeper, and in a consoling tone that implied Arthur had her full sympathy.

Thoroughly humiliated, Julia closed the bedroom door behind her and after removing her coat, she began to undress, folding and hanging her clothes with care. Looking at the rip in her dress and hoping she would be able to mend it, tears welled in her eyes. She brushed them away. She must not cry. Arthur hated it when she did.

She must learn to be a better wife. *To do her duty.* Her father's voice echoed in her head. '*Duty, Julia, you must remember always to do your best and not let people down.*'

She was in her nightdress when the bedroom door opened and Arthur came in, glass of whisky in hand.

'I know you're angry with me,' Julia said, 'and I just want you to know that I'm sorry. Very sorry. I'll do whatever you want me to do to make amends. Just don't keep being annoyed with me.'

'I'm not annoyed with you,' he said, crossing the room towards her. 'I'm disappointed. You let me down this evening. You drank too much and made a spectacle of yourself. I expected better of you.'

'It won't happen again,' she said. 'I promise. It's just that

Ralph was very sweet and asked me to dance with him and I didn't realise how much punch I had drunk, and—' She broke off, unable to speak, tears filling her eyes and spilling down her cheeks.

'Don't cry!' he snapped. 'It only makes you look even more pathetic.'

At the harshness of his voice, she trembled.

'After all I've done for you,' he went on, 'this is how you repay me.'

The tears really flowed now.

'You disgust me,' he said. 'Just look at the state of you.' He shook his head. 'Go and wash your face and pull yourself together.'

Again she did as he said, desperate for him not to be angry with her. Standing at the basin in her bathroom, she splashed cold water onto her face, then dried herself with a towel, dabbing gently at her skin so as not to redden it further. She had annoyed Arthur enough, she mustn't add to his disappointment in her. She must remember to be a better wife. To please him. *To do her duty.*

She took a deep shuddering breath and reminded herself that her husband was a good man. He only wanted the best for her. Just as her father had. She had done everything wrong this evening, she had drunk too much and danced too much. It was when Ralph had grabbed hold of her and said he'd teach her how to do the twist that she had really misjudged things. That was her real mistake.

'Let yourself go, Julia!' he'd said above the band playing 'Let's Twist Again'.

The crowded dance floor was full of gyrating bodies and everywhere she looked, people were laughing happily, their faces bright and shining with the fun of what they were doing. Suddenly she wanted to be just like them and after a few hesitant twists, and at Ralph's encouragement, she threw herself into the dance with gay abandon. It felt wonderful to feel so free and alive, to let herself go, just as Ralph had urged her.

Disaster struck in her attempt to copy Ralph and twist down almost to the floor on one foot. She was giggling so much she lost her balance and before she knew it, she was lying on her back, her legs sticking up in the air, her knickers and stocking tops on show for all the world to see. Only when Ralph had helped her to her feet did she realise her dress was ripped at the back, exposing her yet more. Then she saw Arthur staring at her with a grim expression on his face. Seconds later he came over and said they were leaving.

Confident that she now had her emotions under control, Julia returned to the bedroom. Arthur was standing at the foot of the bed and was in the process of laying his trousers on top of the ottoman, smoothing out any wrinkles or creases. He was so fastidious with his clothing.

'Take off your nightdress,' he said matter of factly. 'Then show me how sorry you are.'

He pointed to where she was to kneel, directly in front of him at his feet, and she willingly followed his instructions.

Always do your duty . . . Always do as you're told . . . Never disobey me . . . And never tell anyone.

The next morning she slept in, and just as Arthur had explained would happen, she was left undisturbed by the household staff.

'You'll want to sleep off your hangover,' he had said in a reassuringly solicitous voice when he'd left her to go to his own room.

'You're probably right,' she said, shamefaced. Her head had indeed started to thump, and her stomach was churning querulously.

'Of course I'm right,' he'd replied. His hand on the door

handle, he'd added, 'I'll inform Miss Casey that you need peace and quiet and won't need any breakfast. And while you're re-covering, you might like to consider how inappropriate your behaviour has been and how you let not just me down, but yourself.'

'I'm so very sorry,' she'd said. 'I promise it won't ever happen again.'

'You must see that it doesn't.'

It was now gone midday and hunger had replaced the quea-siness in her stomach. What she wouldn't give for a cup of tea and a slice of toast and marmalade. Hearing the sound of a car on the driveway, she slipped out of bed and went to the window. She pulled back the curtains and saw the Rolls with Arthur at the wheel. She watched the car disappear down the drive, and with her stomach rumbling, she decided she was quite well enough now to go in search of something to eat. Never had she slept in so late and heaven only knew what Miss Casey and the other servants would think of her. Added to what they already thought about her. Doubtless she was now the talk of Melstead St Mary.

She hastily dressed, making sure to cover up the bruises on her arms, brushed her hair, and crossed the room to go downstairs.

At first she thought the door was stuck, but no matter how hard she pulled on the handle, or how vigorously she turned it, the door refused to open.

It was locked.

Chapter Thirty-Four

The Randolph Hotel, Oxford
November 1962
Annelise

As always when she was in Harry's company, Annelise kept the extent of her feelings for him in check. Instinct told her that it would be a mistake to talk about love to a man like Harry. Crowd him out with overt displays of adoration and he'd be off like a shot.

Watching him sleep in the bed beside her – he always slept after they made love – Annelise felt her heart twist to the point of pain. She would never have believed that such a thing was possible, that loving a man could have this extraordinary effect on her. There was no logic to it; he was, after all, no more than flesh and blood. Yet he could reduce her to an absurd state of greedy need for his touch, for his hands and mouth to caress her body. When he did, it was as though his fingertips had the power to scorch her skin. But there was pain, too.

None of which Annelise could make sense of. It baffled her. She didn't like how weak her love for Harry made her feel. Was uncertainty the reason for that, constantly wondering when, or if, he would ever be a free man?

Carefully, so as not to disturb him, she turned over to look out of the sash window. The late afternoon light was fading, and rain was now pattering against the glass. When she came back to Oxford following Kit and Evelyn's party, the Cuban missile crisis and the immediate threat of a nuclear war had passed. Diplomacy had won the day. She and Harry had celebrated the news with a bottle of champagne in bed. This very bed in fact. For some reason she had hoped he might then say he was going to leave his wife. But he hadn't.

'I can't possibly sleep with your mind working away like a pneumatic drill,' murmured Harry. 'What are you thinking of?'

'Nothing of any significance,' she lied, still facing the window.

He put a hand to her shoulder and turned her to look at him. 'That's one of the things I love about you, Annelise.'

'What's that?'

'The way you never reveal what you're really thinking. Most women are only too quick to unravel their minds to a man and bore them rigid in the process.'

'Perish the thought I'd ever do that to you,' she said with some acerbity.

He grinned. 'You could never do that to me. You're an enigma, you keep me puzzled and wanting more.'

Wanting more of what? She wanted to ask. But nothing on earth would have allowed her to stray into the no-go area of their relationship. To hint to Harry that she wanted more than to be his mistress would be the end. He would not want to escape the confines of his loveless marriage only to be imprisoned by another demanding woman.

She sat up abruptly. 'I have to go,' she said.

'But it's not yet four o'clock,' he said. 'What's the hurry?'

'My aunt is visiting. I told you I would have to leave early.'

'Did you? It must have slipped my mind.' And then he smiled again and ran his hand down her neck and to her breast. 'I had better things to think of than your aunt paying you a visit.' He stroked her nipple lightly, then more firmly, twisting it skilfully so that from nowhere she was fully aroused. He raised himself to kiss her, his lips hovering so close, but not quite touching, his breath mingled with hers. 'Are you sure you can't stay?' he murmured, his bluey-grey eyes challenging her to say no. 'Just a little longer?'

With the heat of her arousal flaring from her core and fanning out through her body, right to her fingertips, she kissed him intensely. It was this visceral need in her that she was powerless to disguise. The raw baseness of her desire thrilled her, made her believe that if she had only these moments in her life, it would be enough. It would sustain her.

It was dark when she left the Randolph Hotel to go back to her rooms at St Gertrude's. With the rain coming down harder now, she hurried along St Giles in the glare of the headlamps and then on to the Woodstock Road. Luckily she had brought an umbrella with her.

Roberts the porter greeted her at the lodge with a cheery smile. 'Your guest has arrived. I hope it was all right, miss, but I took her up to your rooms.'

'That was absolutely the right thing to do, thank you.'

A shy smile on his face, Roberts went on. 'I also took the liberty of giving Mrs Devereux-Temple a cup of tea here in the lodge by the fire.'

'Oh, you needn't have gone to all that trouble.'

'It was no trouble. I'm a big fan of her books so it was an honour to have her company for twenty minutes. I told her she's welcome to join me for a cuppa any time she likes.'

Annelise left the man glowing in his appreciation for her aunt. Romily might not be a blood-relation, but Annelise had always regarded her as such, and the best of aunts at that. Crossing the front quad, she passed the chapel on her right, its stained-glass windows lit up from within where a choir practice was taking place. Annelise would have loved to join the choir, but alas she was as good as tone deaf. 'You look like an angel,' Hope once told her, 'but let's face it, dear, you sing like a harpy.'

Annelise had been eleven years old when Hope made the comment and all these years on, she could still feel the sting of the criticism. Silly really to be bothered by something so trivial when there were far bigger issues in the world to deal with.

She had received a letter from Stanley yesterday inviting her to join him on a protest march organised by CND. If she could spare the time from work, she would go. Before she'd left Island House to return to Oxford, Stanley had apologised for his behaviour that night at Meadow Lodge and while she was still saddened at what he'd said, she had promised him it changed nothing between them. She would do all she could to ensure that he didn't feel awkward around her. It would be awful if they couldn't retain the closeness they'd always enjoyed.

She reasoned that it was not unusual for those who grew up closely together to develop strong emotional attachments to each other; perhaps it was to be expected. She herself had had a crush on Stanley as a young girl, but had eventually grown out of it. She couldn't remember exactly when it happened; certainly there had been no conscious decision on her part. Maybe it was no more than growing up.

There had been nothing in Stanley's behaviour towards her to indicate that he viewed himself as any more than a devoted big brother. Not once during any of his visits to see her in Oxford had he betrayed himself.

Stanley hadn't been the only person on her mind since the night of the party at Meadow Lodge. Evelyn had been a source of concern too. Annelise had told no one of what she'd overheard in the garden. How could she, when she had been blatantly eavesdropping?

At the top of the stairs on the landing outside her rooms, Annelise breathed in the familiar scent of Romily's favourite perfume – Joy by Jean Patou.

'Romily!' she exclaimed happily when she let herself in and threw off her rain-soaked woollen coat, which smelt of an old dog in contrast to the delightfully floral air she had walked into. 'I'm so sorry to keep you waiting.'

Dressed in a stylish and perfectly fitting two-piece suit – probably Chanel – Romily rose elegantly from the armchair by the gas fire and hugged her. 'Don't give it another thought. I've been thoroughly entertained by your wonderful porter who took pity on a poor bedraggled old woman.'

'What a preposterous thing to say! You're incapable of looking bedraggled and you most certainly are not old. And for the record, Roberts is completely smitten by you. If you want someone to walk on hot coals for you, he's your man.'

'I'll bear that in mind. Now then, sit down and warm yourself by the fire and tell me all your news, and then I shall take you for dinner. It's been ages since we had the chance for a proper chat.'

'I agree. I still haven't heard in any detail about your time in Hollywood and Palm Springs, other than,' she added as she made herself comfortable in the armchair opposite Romily and kicked off her shoes, 'you were approached to have your first Sister Grace novel made into a film.'

'An idea that came to nothing in the end,' Romily said dismissively.

'You know Isabella is furious you didn't pursue the idea; she says she would have been perfect to play Sister Grace.'

'Lord yes, she has made her feelings very vocal on that account!'

'It's a shame though that things didn't work out. What was the reason?'

'An incompatibility issue with the scriptwriter the studio wanted me to work alongside. The whole thing would have been a disaster.'

'That's unlike you. You usually find a way to get on with people.'

'There's a first time for everything. Anyway, that's of no consequence, I'm much more interested in making amends for neglecting you these last few months. Isabella too. Now tell me all your news.'

Where to start? thought Annelise, staring into the fire and listening to the gentle hiss of the gas. More than anything she wanted to talk about Harry, to confide in Romily and pour out her heart. Instead she settled on raising her concern about Mums and asked if Romily had noticed anything wrong.

Drawing her brows together, Romily rested her chin on her thumb and forefinger and nodded thoughtfully. 'I'd only been home a few hours when I became aware of some kind of friction between Hope and Edmund. I've tried asking Hope several times if there's anything worrying her, but you know of old what she's like. Rather than deal with a problem she buries herself in her work. They move into their new house at the weekend, and so I'm hoping that will ease the situation. Maybe that's all that is at the bottom of the problem, Hope's impatience to be settled at Fairview.'

Not entirely convinced, Annelise said, 'Have you been to see the house?'

'Not yet, I haven't had time. But I hear Stanley has made a fine job of it. Just as I knew he would.'

It was during dinner that Annelise decided to be brave and broach the subject of Harry with Romily. 'Do you suppose love is ever a truly happy state of affairs?' she asked.

Romily put down her wineglass. 'My dear girl, what on earth makes you say a thing like that?'

'Because I'm in love with somebody and if I'm honest, at times the pain of it far outweighs the pleasure.'

'Are you saying it doesn't make you happy? Because if so, take it from me, that's not love.'

Chapter Thirty-Five

Early the next morning Romily greeted the day with drained relief.

All night she had drifted like the tide in and out of sleep, one hectic dream following another. But the most unnerving dream was the one that saw her back in Palm Springs. She was lost in the desert and with the light fading she caught the sound of her name being called. It was no more than a faint whisper carried on the cool evening breeze. But she recognised it instantly. Yet rather than be pleased that Red had come to rescue her, she hid behind a large rock until he was gone, and she was again alone in the dark and rapidly dropping night temperature. Shivering with cold, she had suddenly felt unutterably bereft. The feeling was with her still, giving her the sensation that she had lost something of great value. What irked her more was the irrational feeling that she was entirely to blame for getting herself lost in the desert.

It was only a dream, she told herself as she slipped out of bed and went to run herself a bath in the adjoining bathroom. But adding some scented bubble bath to the water before stepping in, she reluctantly acknowledged that, as Freud and Jung would say, there was no such thing as *just* a dream.

Logically she could work it all out. What had gone on between her and Red was that on a subconscious level there had been a spontaneous and mutual attraction, which, when reluctantly realised, had surprised and rattled them both, and for differing reasons. Or maybe for similar reasons. Perhaps they each had become too used to being autonomous and doing things their own way without ever being challenged.

She could go on theorising ad infinitum, but her time in Palm Springs was of no matter now. She had more important things with which to occupy herself following dinner with Annelise last night. It would appear that a lot had gone on in her absence from Island House. Which only came to light when, and as if opening the floodgates, Annelise had let it all pour out.

Firstly there had been Annelise's worry about Hope, which Romily felt was not misplaced. After what she had witnessed herself, she had been tempted to speak in private to Edmund, but had decided against it. What went on between a husband and wife was nobody's business but their own.

Stanley had his problems too, it now transpired, and that upset Romily hugely. More shocking though was what Annelise had told her about Evelyn, that she had received an anonymous letter implying Kit wasn't Pip and Em's father. Not only that, somebody with whom Evelyn had clearly been close had shown up at the party – and that somebody just happened to be called Max who had worked with Evelyn during the war.

Max Blythe-Jones. It had to be. Romily just knew it. And could it really be possible that Evelyn had had a relationship with Max, a man who had what could be politely called a colourful reputation when it came to women?

Before Romily met Jack, Max had flirted outrageously with her whenever their paths crossed at some party or other in London. It went without saying he was an attractive man, and Romily, even though she was a few years older, had enjoyed flirting back with him. But after the war she never came across him again. Last night, when Annelise had confided in her, was the first time in years she had thought of Max Blythe-Jones.

Romily had always suspected that the work Evelyn did during the war was not of the straightforward clerical variety, as she had claimed. With Evelyn's fine mathematician's brain, she would have been put to far better use than merely shuffling papers. Romily's closest friend, Sarah, had a cousin who worked at Bletchley and he had dropped a number of hints at what went on there, that it was a hothouse of top-secret activity. It would have suited Evelyn and Max perfectly.

Just as she had considered speaking to Edmund about Hope, Romily now wanted to talk to Evelyn as soon as she left Oxford and returned to Island House. But again, was it any of her business?

But what concerned Romily most about everything Annelise had told her last night was her being involved with a college professor. She had clearly fallen for him badly and had shyly taken out a photograph from her handbag to show Romily.

'His name's Harry,' Annelise had said, 'and I'm afraid I'm very much in love with him, despite him being married.'

The full story told, every protective instinct in her made Romily want to confront the man. She would guarantee he had no intention of leaving his wife – he would have done so by now if he was serious about Annelise. The sooner she realised that, the better. No wonder the poor girl spoke of the pain of being in love.

Much as Romily wanted to intervene, she knew she had to leave well alone. But it was hard not to throw herself into the fray and fight Annelise's battles for her. She was not, as she often had to remind herself, some kind of saviour. It was not her job to fix everyone else's problems. But a wily voice inside Romily's head whispered that it did stop her from thinking too deeply about her own mistakes.

Seldom did she waste her emotions on worrying about doubts and regrets, seeing it as futile. Which was what she had kept telling herself during the journey home from Palm Springs. What was done, was done. In her parting conversation with Gabe and Melvyn she had made a point of not blaming Red in any way for her declining the offer to collaborate on a film script.

'What if we found another writer?' they had suggested. She had refused that too, because otherwise it would look as if Red was the problem.

She was very much of the opinion that there was a lot more going on inside his head than he cared to reveal. Perversely she almost wished she had stuck around to dig a little deeper, to find out what he was hiding.

There she went again, always trying to fix things! When would she ever stop meddling and take a moment to consider that Red St Clair was not the only one to be hiding something?

She took a modest breakfast with Annelise in Hall, then leaving her to prepare for a tutorial, Romily returned to her own room to go over the notes she'd made for the talk she was giving that evening in Blackwells on the Broad.

The event had only been arranged a couple of days ago when her agent was approached to beg a favour of her. Could Romily, *always such a good stick*, be persuaded to step into the shoes of Ngaio Marsh who had been forced to cut short her book tour and return to New Zealand due to a family emergency? Romily had readily agreed to fill in, seeing it as a chance to spend some valuble time with Annelise.

She was currently between novels, having finished one before her trip to America, and was now playing around with a few ideas before knuckling down to work. She wasn't like Hope who hardly drew breath between finishing one book and starting another. They were very different in their writing habits. Romily had a more relaxed attitude, perhaps because she enjoyed the creative process so much and didn't like to rush it. Hope wrote as though her life depended on it.

Satisfied now that she was sufficiently prepared for her talk that evening, and looking out of the window and seeing that it wasn't raining, she decided to go for a walk in the park.

She had only made it to the far side of Chapel Quad when the lodge porter, Roberts, came towards her. 'I have a message for you, Mrs Devereux-Temple. The Dean wondered if you'd like to join her, and a few others, in the Senior Common Room for coffee.'

'I'd be delighted,' she said brightly, despite preferring the idea of going for a walk, followed by an hour of shopping before meeting Annelise for lunch.

The Dean greeted her warmly. She was a stately woman of ample girth with a head of grizzled curls. Her name was Dr Drusilla Spriggs, otherwise known as Spriggsy according to Annelise. While pouring Romily a cup of coffee from an urn on a white-clothed table, she set about introducing her to the college bursar, Dr Daphne Mallow, and a gaggle of Fellows and Tutors, whose names Romily forgot in seconds flat.

Predictably the conversation turned to novel writing.

'Please do tell us about your excellent mysteries,' the Dean said. 'I'm sure we'd all love to hear how you go about writing your Sister Grace novels.'

No sooner had Romily embarked on a brief description of the process, than through the window she saw Annelise hurrying across the quad towards the porter's lodge. She stopped short when a man carrying a briefcase appeared. Romily had the distinct impression that he had been waiting for Annelise. Was this the man with whom she was having a secret affair?

Summoning to memory the photograph which Annelise had shown her last night, Romily was sure it was. It took all of her willpower to remain where she was and continue talking, and not rush outside to give the man a hefty piece of her mind.

Chapter Thirty-Six

Chelstead Preparatory School for Girls, Chelstead
November 1962
Evelyn

Evelyn stood at her office window watching Miss Gillespie, Head of Latin and Classics, chastising Camilla Stewart and Lorna Fairfax for some playtime misdemeanour.

It was a cold blustery day, the sort of day that brought out the worst in the girls. For some reason the gusting winds made them high-spirited and prone to doing silly things, like letting off stink bombs, painting red dots on their skin to feign illness, or flicking ink at each other during lessons. The tomfoolery would escalate as the end of term drew to a close for the Christmas holiday, and by the last week of term the girls would be at the height of giddiness and the teachers at their wits' end.

Evelyn raised the mug in her hands to her lips and pulled a face. The coffee was stone cold, and the milk had formed a disagreeable skin on the surface. How long had she been standing here lost in thought? Too long was the answer. And it would never do. She had to pull herself together.

Since receiving that first anonymous letter and then Max turning up out of the blue the night of the party just over a week ago, she had been thrown off balance; the equilibrium of each day thoroughly destroyed.

Some mornings she woke with such a weight of dread

hanging over her she could hardly drag herself from her bed, the thought of driving to school to tackle the demands of two hundred and fifty lively girls and a staffroom of teachers too much for her. Many a time she found herself struggling to find the necessary patience and tact to deal with what she regarded as petty staffroom politics. Or the unruliness of a wilful child. Or an overly critical parent who could bore for England on the subject of how a school should be run.

In the past none of this would have taxed her in the slightest, but today it all felt too much. Which was why she was keeping a low profile by staying – *hiding* – in her office. Before setting off for Chelstead this morning, and thankfully after Kit had already left for a day of ground school teaching at the flying club, the postman had made his first delivery of the day. Amongst the mail was another vile letter accusing her of having been unfaithful to Kit.

Who was doing this to her?

Was it Max?

But he'd sworn it wasn't him. Who then? And why? Was it somebody from their Bletchley days? Somebody who had a score to settle?

The second letter was in her handbag, as was Max's card. He had been one of the last to leave the party and when he'd been saying goodbye he had given her his card with his telephone number. 'Come and meet me in London,' he'd said, 'let's have lunch. Or dinner if you'd prefer. For old time's sake.'

Despite keeping his card, she had no intention of telephoning him. She had promised herself a very long time ago that she would never contact him again and she wasn't about to break that promise.

Nor was she going to compromise the vows she made the

day she stood in front of the altar with Kit and married him. Saying the words *I do* had banished Max to the past.

Just as those same words had pushed Bletchley Park out of her life, including everything that had happened there.

Chapter Thirty-Seven

Bletchley Park
January 1942
Evelyn

Max Blythe-Jones made his appearance at Bletchley at the end of January in 1942.

He immediately attracted an above average rate of interest amongst the women at the Park because of his exotically good looks (his mother was half French and half Hungarian), and for being so charming. Within a short space of time, not only was he causing hearts to flutter at a considerable rate, but he had gained a reputation for being one of the best of the elite in Hut 6. It was widely understood that these codebreakers were of a superior breed of intellect and ability. Max was perfectly at home amongst them.

By this time my own ability for spotting patterns amongst the 'quatsch' – as we referred to the relentless chatter by enemy operators – had been recognised and I took pleasure in knowing that I was now of genuine use at the Park.

I first met Max in the canteen late one night when our shifts coincided. It was the day after I had found an important message secreted within the apparently innocent stream of chit chat. 'You're the girl who discovered that German sub tracking the convoy in the Atlantic yesterday, aren't you?' he said to me.

'I might be,' I replied in a low voice, conscious that secrecy, even amongst one's colleagues, was vital to security. I was conscious also that he probably thought, as did quite a lot of men, that I had got above myself and should get back to the more menial work of filing and indexing.

'That was good work on your part,' he said. 'How does it feel to know that you are personally responsible for saving all those lives?'

'I was just doing my job,' I said, certain now that he was patronising me. Under no circumstances was I going to admit that I was proud of what I had done, although, of course, I was. Especially as the officer with whom I had shared my discovery later informed me that as a consequence of what I'd spotted, the convoy had been alerted and straightaway changed course with wireless silence. It pleased me to picture the German U-boat arriving at the coordinates where it believed there to be a convoy of merchant shipping and finding nothing.

The next night Max approached me again in the canteen and setting down his tray on the table opposite me, said, 'I believe we have a mutual friend: Romily Temple.'

'You mean Romily Devereux-Temple?' I answered absently, turning the page of a book I was reading, and which was taking my mind off the awful food that was served up to us.

'Ah yes, I keep forgetting that she married. What was her husband like? Quite the roué in his day, I believe.'

I was clearly not going to get any peace to read, so closed the book with a meaningful gesture and looked him squarely in the face. 'How did you know that I was familiar with Romily?' I asked.

He tapped his nose. 'Careless talk costs lives.'

'I couldn't agree more.' I promptly opened my book again to make the point that he was disturbing me and that unlike just about every other female at the Park, his looks cut no ice with me. Somewhat arrogantly I wanted him to know that I was above such things, that I was immune to his brand of charm and attractiveness. But the thing was, I wasn't, which made it imperative that I gave no hint that I did indeed find him extraordinarily handsome. He was the sort of man who would age well, I found myself thinking.

'What are you reading?' he asked, my bluntness appearing to have no effect on him.

'Do you really want to know, or are you simply determined to gain my attention?'

'Both, I suppose. Is that so awful? By the way, we haven't been introduced properly. I'm Max.'

'Yes,' I said, 'I'm well aware of who you are.'

He grinned. 'My reputation goes before me, does it?'

'You're Max Blythe-Jones, a Trinity College classicist from Cambridge with a double first. You're also fluent in German, French and Hungarian, and you're a rowing blue, and you've been here scarcely a month and have bedded more women than—'

He held up a hand to stop me. 'You've been snooping in the files, Miss Flowerday,' he said with a wag of his finger. 'Miss Evelyn Flowerday, that is. She of the first class honours degree in mathematics from Lady Margaret Hall, Oxford and teacher of privileged girls at St Agatha's School, Kent. Followed by teaching less privileged boys and girls in Melstead St Mary. Something of a comedown for a person of your calibre, I'd say. Current boyfriend is Christopher Devereux, youngest stepson to our mutual friend Romily Devereux-Temple.'

'And now that we're properly introduced,' I said, 'you can eat your meal and I can read my book.'

'You still haven't told me what it is you're reading.'

I held it up for him, so he could see the dust jacket.

'*Murder at Midnight*' he read aloud, and then laughed. 'By none other than Romily Temple. Now there's a coincidence.'

Coincidence after coincidence followed from that evening

onwards. Or so Max liked to claim. The truth was he made it his business to know which clubs I had joined at the Park – the chess club, the choral and music societies, the Scrabble club and the Scottish country dancing club. It came to be that I didn't pass a day without encountering him in one way or another. I made it very clear that I would not be added to his roll call of conquests and in accepting the situation, we became friends.

I enjoyed his company. His erudite and lively mind appealed to me greatly and by the time spring arrived, bringing with it warmer weather, we took regular walks and cycle rides together during our precious time off.

I believed he valued my friendship because it was entirely uncomplicated, free of all ambiguity. With me he didn't have to resort to his usual tricks, which he still employed with regularity on other women at the Park. In the days before Easter he took up with a pretty and vivacious Wren, one of the many who operated the Bombe machines, but by the time the cherry blossom was being shaken from the trees he was bored of her slavish devotion.

'It's the thrill of the chase with you, isn't it?' I remarked one day when we were having lunch in a quiet country pub. We had cycled the nineteen miles to the Plough, an old-fashioned watering hole well off the beaten track and which served a decent plate of egg and gammon. Compared to the questionable food served in the canteen at the Park, it was manna from heaven. There was only so much whale meat one could stomach.

The other thing about the pub which I liked was that few others from the Park ventured there. It wasn't that I felt I had anything to hide in being seen with Max, but such was the hothouse environment in which we worked, tongues had a tendency to wag. I would hate for Kit ever to get wind of some piece of malicious tittle-tattle. For the most part, I was accepted as Max's friend, as 'one of the boys'. I would be a liar if I said I

191

didn't enjoy the feeling of being within his inner circle and that he considered me his intellectual equal.

'How shallow you make me feel,' Max said in response to my observation.

'Not as shallow as you probably make yourself feel,' I responded.

'Ouch. You have such a poor opinion of me, I wonder why you want to spend any time in my company.'

'I see it as my job to reform you.'

He raised an eyebrow. 'Do you indeed?'

'By the time I'm finished with you I might have fashioned you into a half decent human being. House-trained even.'

He laughed loudly. Over at the bar the woman serving behind it looked our way and smiled. His laugh had the ability to do that, to attract attention. But then he had only to walk into a room and people noticed him. I often thought that it was like being out with a film star whenever we went somewhere – heads turned and eyes lingered, as though they were working out if he was famous.

Some minutes later, and while we were racing through the crossword together, he said, 'Is that how you regard your boy-friend, Kit?'

'You've lost me,' I said, glancing up from the anagram I was focusing on.

'Do you view Kit in the way you do me; a work in progress, somebody to fix?'

I felt a twitch of unease, recalling something I had once said to Kit, when I had used the exact same words, describing him as a work in progress. It may have been a throwaway comment I had made in a light-hearted moment, but the truth was, this was what I did. I did it instinctively as a teacher.

'A habitual need to play God and recreate the world,' Romily called this character trait we had in common. It was one of the reasons we got on so well, we both wanted to bring out the best in those we cared about.

'Do you think you're in need of fixing?' I deflected.

'Most assuredly. If I weren't such a brute and a cad I wouldn't treat women the way I do. But isn't everyone in need of fixing?' He smiled and squared his gaze on mine. 'Apart from you, that is. You're unique.'

'I'm no such thing,' I remonstrated. 'I'm as flawed as the next person.'

He shook his head. 'I disagree. You're a woman of extraordinary ability and self-belief. I don't think I've ever known a woman like you before.'

'That's because you've never bothered to get to know one before. Other than in the biblical sense.'

His smile widened. 'And you're going to cure me of that.'

'Am I?'

'You know you are. Why else do you tolerate my wayward ways? And for the record, I can think of nobody finer than you to fix me.'

There it was. The gauntlet thrown down. A seductively irresistible challenge that was impossible for me not to accept.

I should have walked away. But I didn't. Max had found my Achilles heel – my arrogant self-belief that I could make him a better man – and I willingly allowed him to lead me to make the biggest mistake of my life. For which I would never forgive myself.

Chapter Thirty-Eight

Island House, Melstead St Mary
November 1962
Florence

It was Mrs Collings's day off and while Beatty was upstairs vacuuming, Florence was in the kitchen preparing supper for Romily when she arrived back. She would be eating alone tonight as Hope was down in London and Edmund was going over to Meadow Lodge to spend the evening with Kit and Evelyn.

Originally Romily had planned to come home two days ago, but she had telephoned Florence from Oxford to say she had decided to take a detour for a couple of days to go and see her old friend Sarah and her husband, Tony.

Florence moved about the kitchen with the ease and familiarity as though it were her own. Not surprising, given that it had been a second home to her for more than twenty years. She had spent more time in it than her own kitchen, which was very cramped in comparison.

One day she would have her dream kitchen – modern, bright and airy and full of the latest equipment, including a freezer. She wanted a breakfast bar where she and Billy could sit together on stools and look out over a pretty garden while eating their meals. A detached bungalow was what she wanted, with nice straight walls and central heating. She would have built-in kitchen cupboards and formica counter tops. In the garden she would have a patio made with that jolly crazy paving that was so popular.

Billy thought she was as crazy as that paving! He couldn't see anything wrong in staying right where they were. 'Living next door to the bakery couldn't be more convenient,' he would say whenever she brought up the subject of moving. 'If we lived anywhere else, I'd have to get up even earlier,' he'd grumble.

'I'm not talking any distance away,' Florence would say, 'we'd still be in the village, or on the outskirts. Wouldn't you like a bit more space around you? A bit more privacy?'

'I'm not moving into one of those houses on the Clover Green estate,' he'd say. 'You can forget that!'

Florence was reasonable enough to accept that very likely they wouldn't move until Billy decided to retire from running the bakery. Which was a long way off. But at least by then her mother-in-law wouldn't be around. Though it would be just Florence's luck that the old woman proved to be indestructible. The Soviet Union could drop a nuclear bomb directly on Britain and Melstead St Mary could be blown to kingdom come, but Ruby Minton would be the sole survivor. Out she'd crawl from the wreckage demanding to know what all the noise was about, and who the hell had made all this mess!

Florence had drawn a blank when searching next door for proof that Ruby was the anonymous letter writer. In haste, while her mother-in-law was watching the television with Billy, Florence had hunted through every cupboard and drawer, but not a single piece of evidence had she found. Not a hint of anything that might suggest Ruby's hatred for Florence had taken a more malicious turn. But maybe the nasty old woman had a hiding place that Florence hadn't found. Or she could have simply got rid of the evidence.

To Florence's dismay she had started watching Billy in a way she never had before. She had sworn she wouldn't allow any seed of suspicion to be sown as a result of receiving the anonymous letter, but she simply couldn't stop herself from wondering if Billy was messing around behind her back.

To her shame she had been checking his shirts before washing them – sniffing the collars for strange perfume or searching for smudges of lipstick. She had gone through his pockets too, dreading what she might find – a scribbled down telephone number, or a lover's keepsake.

Oh, how she wished she could talk to Romily about all this! She had wanted to when Romily returned home from America, but the moment had never seemed right. Also Romily had seemed, well, sort of unsettled. Perhaps it was having Hope and Edmund living in the house with her.

After Beatty had finished vacuuming and Florence had left everything ready for Romily, the two of them walked home in the dusk. They parted in the main street where Beatty waited at the stop for her bus, and Florence went on up to the Market Square.

The bakery was closed and assuming Billy was already home, she went next door to Quince Cottage and let herself in. There were no lights on, but even so she called out to Billy.

'I'm home,' she said, taking off her coat and hanging it on the row of hooks by the front door.

There was no answer.

Deciding he was probably with his mother, she switched on the hall lamp and bent down to pick up the mail from the doormat. That was when she saw the envelope with her name on it. It was just like the one she had received before.

She ripped it open and immediately wished she hadn't.

NOT MUCH OF A WIFE ARE YOU?
NO WONDER YOUR HUSBAND GOES
ELSEWHERE.

Chapter Thirty-Nine

The Athena Theatre, Covent Garden, London
November 1962
Isabella

'You know, if you're going to point that rotten little peashooter at me, you might just as well do it with more conviction.'

'Oh, so suddenly you're an expert on firearms, are you?'

Isabella sighed and turned to the director, Mallory Carlisle, for backup. 'He was pointing the gun over my shoulder,' she complained.

'Isabella, sweetie, it's only a dress rehearsal.'

'Correct me if I'm wrong, but isn't the whole point of a dress rehearsal to get things right in order to be ready for the actual performance?'

'And correct me if I'm wrong,' boomed the old goat at her side, 'I am the one with more theatrical experience under my belt than this . . .' he waved his hand dismissively in her direction, 'than this nobody has had hot dinners.'

'Judging by that paunch of yours,' Isabella muttered under her breath, 'you've also had plenty of experience when it comes to hot dinners.'

'I beg your pardon?'

From the front row of the stalls, Mallory clapped his hands. 'Let's take a short break, shall we?'

Isabella had a dramatic flounce down to a fine art, but as she marched off the stage in a marked manner, she had to admit

Hugo Gerrard gave an impressive performance himself.

Isabella had wanted to do a more modern play after *The Importance of Being Ernest*, but when her agent had received a call asking specifically for Isabella to join the cast for *The Broken Vow*, and with nothing else on the horizon, she accepted the role. She was told that the leading lady she was taking over from had walked out on the production, and Hugo Gerrard, the leading man, had refused to continue with the understudy. Opening night was in four days and Isabella had had less than a fortnight to learn her part.

She was always up for a challenge, but Hugo Gerrard was a challenge she hadn't bargained on. She could quite understand why the actress she had replaced had thrown in the towel. Having done very little in the way of acting for the last decade, other than a few minor parts on the television, and a cigar advertisement, Hugo's return to the stage was being billed as 'long awaited' and something the theatre-going public shouldn't miss. Nobody in the cast was allowed to utter the word 'comeback', not without risking a dressing down of monumental proportions, and they spent most of the time walking on eggshells around Hugo, the so-called star of the play.

'I never went away!' Isabella heard him roar at some poor stage hand yesterday.

Hugo was older than Isabella by thirty years and in playing her jealous lover it was a laughable piece of miscasting. As a romantic lead he was about as convincing as a coal-scuttle making advances on her. The scenes when he was supposed to be making ardent love to her were pure torture.

Two hours later, and when the rehearsal was finally over, and Isabella had changed out of her costume, she made her way to the box office where she had agreed to meet Ralph. She was keeping the promise she had made the night of the party at Meadow Lodge and was having dinner with him. After what had happened to Julia that night, Isabella regretted encouraging Ralph to dance with the poor woman. He claimed at the time that he hadn't meant to get his stepmother tipsy, but Isabella wasn't so sure.

She found him already waiting for her. Leaning nonchalantly against the wall and dressed in a smart suit and an overcoat with the collar turned up as he smoked a cigarette, he looked very rakish. He gave her a languid smile and kissed her cheek.

'Cousin Isabella,' he said, 'you look positively divine.'

She rolled her eyes. 'Well, I feel like hell after a day spent with that dreadful lush, Hugo Gerrard. He's such an old ham of an actor. Where are you taking me for dinner? I'm starving.'

'I've booked us a table at Rules. But first I suggest we have a couple of cocktails in the bar. Hopefully that will smooth your ruffled feathers.'

'You know I'm still quite cross with you,' she said, when they had walked the short distance from the theatre to the restaurant and were seated on padded stools at the bar.

'Why? What have I done?'

'You know jolly well what I'm talking about. You got your poor stepmother into so much trouble the night of Kit and Evelyn's party.'

'Am I to be held responsible for her inability to hold her drink?'

'You knew exactly what you were doing, and what the consequences would be. You did it to annoy your father, I shouldn't wonder.'

He frowned. 'Are you going to be like this all evening?'

'Like what exactly?'

'So boringly tetchy.'

'Would you rather I was more like your stepmother, then?'

'Not at all, but I'd prefer you didn't bite my head off every time I opened my mouth.' He took a gulp of his drink. Then appeared to think about it before draining his glass in one long swallow.

Seeing the way his face had darkened, Isabella thought how easily his mood slipped – gone was the easy-going insouciance of before; in place now was sulky annoyance. But then she had just deliberately riled him by taking him to task over Julia. Observing the taut expression on his face, she suddenly thought how similar he looked to his father. Not for the first time she wondered if, like his father, Ralph had his own darker side, and how that might manifest itself. She sipped her drink in silence, letting him stew in his own petulance.

Eventually, and after he'd lit a cigarette, he spoke. 'I wonder if the real reason you're so cross is because it was your idea that I charmed and flattered Julia. Perhaps you feel guilty?'

'Perhaps I do,' she conceded.

As though the admission had mollified him, he offered up a smile. 'You have to admit, though, it was quite funny when she fell over, wasn't it?'

Isabella shook her head. 'No. It was horrible. Like watching a car crash.'

'Then you shouldn't have made me dance with her.'

'I wanted you to make her happy, not get her punished by your bully of a father. It's common knowledge back at home that he locked her in her room the next day, and with nothing to eat.'

Ralph frowned. 'How would anyone know that?'

'Come off it, Ralph, you can't sneeze in the village without everybody knowing about it.'

'Well, they got it wrong. Julia was simply off-colour with a hangover and needed to rest.'

'And who told you that?'

'My father and Miss Casey.'

'You don't think that's exactly what he would tell you to hide what a monster he is?'

Viciously stubbing out his cigarette, he said, 'You know what, I'm sick of this conversation. I used to think you were fun.'

'You mean you thought I was as shallow as you,' she fired back.

He glared at her, then getting to his feet and whipping out his wallet from the inside pocket of his suit jacket, he threw down a handful of money on the bar. 'I'm not sticking around for any more criticism from you. I'm off someplace where the girls know how to enjoy themselves, and where they don't feel the need to put a fellow down.'

Quick as a flash, she scooped up the money and threw it at him. 'Then you'd better take this with you as you'll need to pay those girls, won't you?'

What happened next took no more than a split second. First, Isabella saw Ralph raise his hand to strike her across the face, then the man sitting at the bar on the stool behind Ralph snatched hold of his arm. 'That, sir,' he said, 'is no way to treat a lady.' Wrenching himself free, Ralph looked ready to strike the stranger who had intervened.

The stranger was now on his feet. 'Apologise to your friend this instant,' he said. 'And do it before I feel the need to take you outside and teach you how to be a gentleman.'

With people looking on, including the bar staff, Isabella saw the reluctance in Ralph's face to do as he was being asked. She didn't think she could feel more disgusted or disappointed in a person. 'You truly are your father's son, aren't you?' she said.

The change of expression on Ralph's face told Isabella that her words had hit home. 'I'm sorry,' he muttered.

'Try saying it like you mean it,' the other man said.

'It's all right,' Isabella said, not wanting the ugly scene to become any uglier. She was embarrassed enough as it was. 'He's said he's sorry.'

The man shrugged, but then jabbed Ralph's shoulder with a finger. 'Time you went, I think.'

For a moment Ralph looked as if he might disagree, and in the strongest terms. But then without glancing back at Isabella, he strode away, his head up, brazenly defying the stares of those who had witnessed the altercation.

Another theatrical exit, thought Isabella, watching him go.

'Are you all right?' the man standing in front of her asked.

'I'm fine,' she said. 'There was no need for you to involve yourself, but thank you for stepping in.' Studying his face closely, she suddenly had the strangest feeling that she recognised him, but couldn't think from where. He was rather handsome, for a man of his age, in his late forties, possibly early fifties. He had thick dark hair shot through with grey, and his equally dark intelligent eyes were fixed on hers.

'May I buy you a drink?' he asked, 'something to take away the unpleasantness of—' He broke off and stared hard at her with a peculiar look on his face. 'I'm experiencing the oddest sensation,' he said. 'Do I know you?'

Growing used to being recognised, she said nonchalantly, 'You might have seen me in a film, or on the stage in a play.'

'You're an actress?'

She nodded. 'I'm about to appear in a play at the Athena Theatre, alongside Hugo Gerrard.' She guessed a man of his age would probably remember Hugo from his heyday years.

He smiled, but looked puzzled. 'I really do feel that we've met before.'

'Funnily enough, you seem familiar to me too. Perhaps we met at a party?'

'I seldom go to parties these days; they bore me rigid.

Although I did go to one recently, up in Suffolk. It was for an old friend of mine and her husband who were—'

'Would that be Evelyn and Kit Devereux?' she cut in.

'Yes,' he said, surprise showing on his handsome face. 'Were you there? At Meadow Lodge?'

'I certainly was.'

His smile widened. 'Now isn't that a coincidence?'

'It is,' she said. 'But we weren't actually introduced. But I do remember you now.' She gave a small laugh. 'Mostly because of the look of astonishment on Evelyn's face when she clapped eyes on you.'

'I tend to have that effect on women,' he said with a small laugh of his own. Then making himself comfortable on the stool next to Isabella, he said, 'Now about that drink, what would you like? Or better still, how would you like to have dinner with me?'

Chapter Forty

'Look here, Hope, I can't help being called out, it is my job after all to care for my patients.'

'I'm just saying that it's not always necessary for you to drop everything and go tearing off. You've said yourself how people often take advantage of your good nature. Or how they cry wolf at the drop of a hat.'

'I'd hardly call poor old Fred Tucket falling down the stairs and breaking his elbow crying wolf.'

'You know what I mean!' snapped Hope, straining to move a heavy tea-chest.

They had finally moved in to Fairview four days ago but they were a long way from unpacking everything. Just in this room where they were standing – the library – there had to be at least twenty boxes full of books waiting to be unpacked. She had been here for the last two hours while Edmund was out. So much for his promise to help her. As he had promised yesterday, and the day before that. Three promises, all of which he'd failed to keep. What other more important promises had he broken?

He'd returned a few minutes ago full of talk about having received a telephone call at the surgery from some old colleague or other with whom he'd studied medicine. His jovial mood could not have vexed her more. It was during his absence that a second letter had arrived in the afternoon post. Heather, their housemaid, had brought it to Hope.

I WARNED YOU BEFORE ABOUT NEGLECTING YOUR HUSBAND. YOU'LL PAY THE PRICE ONE OF THESE DAYS.

The nasty tone of the letter – again compiled by words cut from a newspaper – made her suspect even more that it was Arthur who was behind it. But she knew that was wishful thinking, because if it was her brother, she could dismiss the letters as nothing more than spite on his part. But if it wasn't Arthur, and she had to consider that possibility very seriously, then she had to accept that there was some truth in what the letters said about Edmund.

Whoever had sent the second letter knew that Hope and Edmund had moved to Fairview, just as he or she had known they had been staying at Island House before. The handwriting on the envelope was not her brother's, that was just about all she could be sure of. She would recognise his scrawl anywhere. Holding the letter and reading it a second time, then a third and a fourth, Hope had shaken with angry shock.

To her shame she had wept, choking tears of misery rolling unbidden down her cheeks. But terrified Heather might hear her sobbing, she had pulled herself together and methodically folded the letter, put it back inside the envelope and slipped it into her skirt pocket. By the time Edmund returned she had taken out the worst of her wretchedness in the library unpacking boxes at a furious rate. But she didn't trust herself to look at him. She couldn't bear to see the duplicity in his face. A face she had always found so reassuring. Now she wanted to slap it hard. *How dare you betray me! How could you do it?*

'Hope, are you listening to me?'

Unable to speak, and blinking hard to stop hot stinging tears from spilling over again, she ignored his question and instead tried to move the heavy tea chest.

'For God's sake!' stormed Edmund, roughly snatching the box out of her hands and banging it down on the ground between them. Both his words and his actions made her jump. He so rarely raised his voice or lost his temper.

'Hope,' he said more reasonably, 'I know you're cross with me, but please, tell me what's wrong. What have I done that makes you want to find fault with everything I say and do?'

'I don't know what you're talking about,' she managed to say.

'Yes you do. You haven't been yourself for some weeks.' He hesitated. 'I've noticed you've been smoking more too. You're not . . . it's not a recurrence of—'

Despite the softness of his tone now, or maybe because of it and what it implied, fury pulsed through her. 'Do not patronise me, Edmund,' she retorted peevishly. 'Don't ever treat me like one of your simpering hypochondriac female patients! And so what if I am smoking more? Do not presume to lecture me!'

His eyebrows shot up. 'I'm only asking if—'

'If I'm having one of my *episodes*? I assure you I'm not.'

He shook his head with a weariness that added to her infuriation. He didn't believe her. Didn't believe that she could be perfectly all right. In his opinion, if she was behaving 'oddly', it could be only one thing, that she was succumbing to the dreaded 'black dog'.

That was the trouble with being married to a doctor; they always thought they knew best. She saw it all the time in the village, all those pathetically needy women putting their beloved Dr Flowerday on a pedestal, hanging on his every word.

Time was she had been proud of the adoration he instilled in his patients, proud too of the way everyone spoke so highly of him. But since that first letter had arrived, and now a second, she viewed the devotion of his patients as cloying. Now if she heard anyone saying what a truly special doctor he was, or how lucky she was to be married to such an exceptional man, she wanted to scream at them that he was nothing of the sort. He was a lying cheating husband!

'Hope,' he said, cutting short the flow of her thoughts, 'it's been a tiring time for us recently, what with selling our old home, staying at Island House and then moving here. It's a lot of upheaval and I know you don't like change, not when all you want to do is focus your energy on your writing. I know how important that is to you. I really do.'

'I told you I'm fine,' she said flatly.

'Why then is it that I can't open my mouth without you criticising me?'

'Maybe you should take a look at yourself and wonder why that might be. Now please, are you going to help with these books, or are you going to continue standing there hindering me?'

He stared at her. 'You clearly have something in mind that I've done, or not done, so why not do the decent thing and just tell me what it is?'

She wanted to. She really did. But what was the point? He would only deny it. Or worse, admit what he'd been doing. To hear him confess his deceit would be too much to bear.

The ringing of the telephone out in the hall called a halt to their conversation. 'Answer it then,' snapped Hope as he continued to stare at her. 'It'll be for you. It's always for you.'

With a sigh, Edmund left the room, closing the door after him. Seconds later it opened, and he poked his head around the door. 'I have to go. That was Miss Gant saying Miss Treadmill is having chest pains. Can we talk later, when I'm back?'

She gave an indifferent shrug of her shoulders, not caring

how he might interpret it. When he'd gone and she heard his car driving away, she hurled the book in her hands across the room. It was only a few months ago, while still living in their old house, that on a bright and sunny day she had taken Edmund outside, telling him to keep his eyes closed until she said he could open them. Handing him the keys to a new Jaguar Mk 2, the very model he had said he'd love to own, she'd said, 'Take it for a spin, to be sure that it lives up to your expectations.'

'Of course it will!' he'd said delightedly, his face wreathed in boyish pleasure. 'But I don't deserve it.'

No, she thought now, *you don't deserve it, Edmund, you bloody well don't!*

To stop herself crying again as she remembered so vividly her happiness at buying something she had known Edmund wanted, she clenched her fists and rammed them against her eyes.

When did it all go wrong? They'd been happy once, hadn't they? Or had their relationship been a mistake from the start? Had Edmund only ever felt sorry for her? Had he regarded her as a grieving widow to whom he could minister and make whole again?

Despite the cold of the day and the fading light, she went out to the hall, then along the corridor to the boot room where she threw on her old mackintosh. Pushing her feet into her rubber boots and then searching for a headscarf, she called to Heather in the kitchen that she was going for a walk.

She needed to think. She needed to decide what she was going to do. If she confronted Edmund, she had to accept that he might confess the truth to her. And if he did, she had to know what her reaction would be. Could she forgive him if he promised never to betray her again, or would it always be there between them, an impenetrable barrier? Could she ever trust him again? And was it her fault he had strayed? Was she simply too dull for Edmund?

Stomping along the lane, the wind whipping the leaves from the trees, and her hair working itself loose from the headscarf she'd tied under her chin, she thought back to the night of the party at Meadow Lodge. She recalled the way Edmund had enjoyed himself dancing that absurd dance called the twist. He had been so uninhibited, the exact opposite to her. She could never dance that way.

Her brother Kit had been his usual sweet self to her that night and, in his customary easy-going manner, had dismissed the idea that the poison pen letter she had been sent was anything but a case of village mischief-making. He'd told her not to give it another thought, which was so typical of him. He always did tend to put his head in the sand.

Had she done something similar during the years she had been married to Edmund? Had she subconsciously known something was wrong, but refused to face it by burying herself in her work?

The accusation in the letter that she had neglected her husband bit deep. But the truth always did hurt. She had told Kit the night of the party that she believed herself to be a failure as a wife, and while at the time she had made the comment out of self-pity, she now had to accept that she had indeed been a failure. Why else had Edmund gone elsewhere to satisfy himself?

It was almost dark, she suddenly realised, her eyes having grown accustomed to the gathering dusk. The presence of lights softly glowing from the cottages ahead of her brought about this awareness. She ought to turn around and go home, but she couldn't face it. Not yet. Not even to what was meant to be their dream home. Instead, and pushing her hands deep into the pockets of her coat, she trudged on in the gloom, the cold wind slicing through her.

She passed the turning in the road that led to the entrance for Melstead Hall, and for a moment was tempted to march all the way up the long drive to have it out with her brother. *'Is it you sending me these hateful letters?'* But if it was him, he would only deny it and would somehow end up with the upper hand. Just as he always did. Never would she give him the satisfaction of knowing he had successfully rattled her, or that somebody else had.

It amazed Hope that Arthur had found three women stupid enough to marry him. She was not so heartless that she didn't feel sorry for Julia, and she had, along with Romily and Evelyn, tried to extend the hand of friendship to her sister-in-law and nephew, seeing as they were members of the family. But they had never received more than a lukewarm response from Julia. Undoubtedly that was Arthur's doing, actively discouraging her from mixing with the rest of the family too often, especially without him there. He was probably worried they would tell her what her husband was really like.

It was completely dark now and with the wind gathering strength, and rain beginning to fall, Hope decided she had no choice but to retrace her steps and make her way back to Fairview. She had gone only a few yards along the narrow road when she heard the sound of a vehicle approaching. She turned around and saw the bright headlamps of a car travelling at speed towards her. Shielding her eyes from the dazzle of the car's lights, she waited for it to pass by. Too late, and with terrifying certainty, she realised the driver mustn't have seen her. And before she had time to step out of the way, the car slammed into her. For a moment she felt weightless as her body flew through the air. Then she landed with a heavy and painful thud that knocked the air out of her.

In the panicked confusion of her thoughts, she let out a small cry, no more than a whimper, and lay very still in what felt like a deep black hole waiting for the driver to come and help.

But with the taste of blood in her mouth, and sickening pain throbbing through her, she heard not the sound of hurried footsteps and a concerned voice, just the sound of the car continuing on with its journey.

Chapter Forty-One

Island House, Melstead St Mary
November 1962
Romily

Romily watched Stanley put a large log onto the fire in the grate, carefully pushing it into place with the poker, before adding another.

She remembered him as a boy doing the same thing. He used to love making up the fire for her, and always with his faithful dog Bobby at his side. Now he had Tucker, who was equally devoted. Like Romily, the dog was keenly observing Stanley's every move, no doubt waiting for him to get out of the way so he could resume his place on the hearth rug and enjoy the warmth from the fire.

The weather had suddenly turned quite wintry – a strong cold wind was blowing in from the North Sea and rain was lashing at the windows. Romily was glad to be in the warm, hunkering down in the drawing room with tea and crumpets.

It had been a strange day. She had woken with a debilitating headache and she hadn't surfaced properly from her room until nearly midday. By the time she had settled at her desk to get on with some work, the telephone had sprung into life and didn't stop interrupting her until gone four o'clock. On two different occasions Florence had come to Romily asking if she could talk to her, but each time the wretched telephone had put paid to that. Florence had left for home, along with Mrs Collings and Beatty, before Romily had a chance to go in search of her to ask what she wanted to discuss.

For now, though, Romily's priority was Stanley. She had invited him to join her for tea so she could find out more of what had passed between him and Annelise. Romily had always suspected that his feelings for Annelise went deeper than he made out, but she hadn't appreciated just how deep.

Pouring their tea, she waited for him to put down the poker and return to the armchair opposite her before resuming the conversation. So far it had been something of a stop–start affair, which was unlike both of them. Normally they had no end of things to say to each other. It was as if Stanley sensed why she had invited him here and was on his guard.

'You seem uncharacteristically quiet, Romily,' he said, when he was seated and had taken his cup and saucer from her.

'I was thinking the same of you.'

He pursed his lips. Then: 'In that case, I suppose we'd better cut to the chase, hadn't we? What has Annelise told you?'

'That you were unwell the night of the party,' Romily said, glad that he was prepared to be so direct.

He carefully put down his cup and saucer. 'Is that all?'

'No.'

He sighed and slumped forward, his hands hanging between his knees, his head low.

'Stanley, she told me what she did because she cares about you.'

'Yes,' he said, straightening up and meeting Romily's gaze. 'She does care for me. I know that. Just not in the way I've always wanted.'

'*Always?*' Romily repeated questioningly.

'For as long as it counts.'

'Why did you never make your feelings known before?'

'That's disingenuous of you. I've never been her equal, not socially or intellectually.'

'That's a terrible thing to say.'

'Let's face it, it's what Hope believes, even if she never says it aloud. You and I both know that she was happy to let me design her new house, but God forbid I should have designs on Annelise. Which is ironic, given how she used to go on about the classless society during the war.'

Romily knew that Stanley was right. There was a time when Hope had indeed been a great advocate of an egalitarian society, just as Romily had been. But whereas Romily still was, Hope's principles, and for whatever reason, had perhaps not stayed the course. And certainly not when it came to Annelise and the man she might one day marry. Heaven only knew what she would have to say about Annelise having an affair with a married man!

'Annelise said you were physically sick at the party.'

He frowned, plainly embarrassed. 'I'd drunk too much. That was all.'

Romily gave him a direct stare. 'Not according to Annelise. She seemed to think that it was talking about your childhood that made you ill. She mentioned also that you'd attended your mother's funeral earlier in the year and—'

She got no further as the telephone rang shrilly, causing Tucker to stir from his slumbering in front of the fire. Pointing to the plate of buttery crumpets on the table and indicating that Stanley should help himself, Romily went over to the telephone on the *secretaire* and picked up the receiver.

'Romily, it's me, Edmund.'

'Hello, Edmund. How's it going with the new house?'

'Is Hope with you?' he asked, ignoring her question.

'No. Did she say she was coming to see me?'

There was a silence down the line.

'Edmund, are you still there?'

'Yes.'

'What's wrong?'

'I . . . I don't know, to be honest.'

Thinking how odd he sounded, and aware that Hope had definitely seemed more on edge recently, Romily pressed for more information. 'I can hear in your voice that you're worried, Edmund. Please tell me if there's anything I can do to help.'

It was a few seconds before he answered. 'The thing is,' he said, 'we had an almighty row earlier and when I came back from being called out to a patient, Hope was gone. Heather, our maid, says she went for a walk. But that was hours ago.'

'Perhaps she went to see your sister?'

'I've just spoken with Evelyn and Hope hasn't been there. I can't think of anybody else she would go and see when, well, you know, when she's not feeling herself.'

Again Romily could hear the concern in Edmund's voice, as well as the storm that was building outside. 'We should go and look for her,' she said decisively. In a lighter tone, so as not to alarm Edmund any further, she added, 'Probably all that's happened is that Hope is sheltering somewhere until the worst of the weather has passed.'

Chapter Forty-Two

Melstead St Mary
November 1962
Stanley

The rain was icy cold, yet it pricked at his face like hot burning needles. The storm was making the tree branches creak and saw, and each time he tried to say anything to Romily, or called out Hope's name, his voice was snatched from his mouth and lost on the wind.

With Tucker accompanying them, they had set off in Romily's Lagonda to find Hope. They had only reached as far as the end of the drive when their way was suddenly, and terrifyingly, barred. A massive branch was ripped from the old oak tree in the gale and crashed to the ground just a few feet from the bonnet of the car.

With nothing else for it, they had taken the torch which Romily kept in the glove compartment and continued on foot. They were drenched in no time. Stanley hoped to God they hadn't embarked on a wild goose chase. These were not the conditions to be out on a fool's errand. He really wouldn't be surprised if Hope was somewhere warm and dry, and deliberately paying Edmund back for something.

To be honest, Hope wasn't Stanley's favourite person right now. Ever since moving into Fairview, she had been in constant touch with him to complain about one thing or another. He had tried explaining that there were always teething problems with

a new house and the contractors would happily resolve what-
ever needed putting right. But there had been no mollifying her.
He had made the mistake of talking to Edmund in private, but
Hope had found out and torn a strip off him.

During his years of training to be an architect, he had been
warned that even the most easy-going of clients could turn on
a sixpence. When he had accepted the commission from Hope
and Edmund to build them a new house, he had accepted the
inevitably of Hope keeping a close eye on every step of the
design and build process. What he hadn't anticipated was how
irrational or bad-tempered she would become.

Annelise once said the pressure Hope put on herself was mer-
ciless. Anybody could see that she lived a tightrope existence
and that those around her had to dance to her tune. Stanley
wondered how Edmund put up with it. He must love her an
awful lot was the only conclusion he could reach.

'Over there, Stanley!' Romily suddenly shouted, making him
start. He looked to where she was directing the beam of light
from the torch and then they hurried to where Tucker was peering into the ditch at the side of the road. His ears were pinned
back and his tail low and between his legs. He was giving off
alternate growls and whimpers. Pushing the dog aside, Stanley
saw what Tucker had found.

With Romily's help, they lifted Hope out of the ditch and
on to the road. It wasn't easy; her body was a deadweight, wet
and slippery, mostly from the rain, but there was blood too. He
fumbled to feel for a pulse at her neck. He couldn't find one.
Next he tried her wrists, first one, then the other. Still nothing.

He shook his head at Romily.

Romily stared back at him, her eyes wide with disbelief. 'She
can't be,' she said, wiping the rain from her face. 'Let me try.'

He watched Romily do the same as he had just done. An eternity seemed to pass as he silently watched, numb with shock.

Only minutes ago he had been thinking less than kindly about Hope, now she was dead. With Tucker at his side, shivering with the rain and cold, he knelt on the ground willing Romily to do the impossible, to bring Hope back to life.

'I've found a pulse!' she blurted out, her fingers pressed against Hope's neck. 'It's faint, but it's there. Just. Can you run and fetch help? I'll stay here and try to get some warmth back into her. She's frozen.'

Stanley shook his head. 'Better still, why don't I carry her back to Island House?'

Romily looked doubtful. 'Do you think you can?'

He nodded. 'If you think it's safe to move her, that is?'

'We've already moved her once, so let's risk it again,' said Romily.

Taking off his coat, Stanley wrapped it around Hope and had just lifted her when, in the light cast from the torch, he noticed something white drop to the ground and land in a puddle at his feet. It looked like a letter.

Romily noticed it too and bent to pick it up before stuffing it into the pocket of her raincoat.

Chapter Forty-Three

Chelstead Cottage Hospital, Chelstead
November 1962
Romily

'How is she, Edmund?' asked Romily. She and Stanley had been waiting anxiously for more than an hour at the small cottage hospital.

They had been making slow progress returning to Island House with Stanley carrying Hope when they'd been caught in the headlamps of a car coming towards them in the rain. Flagging it down for help, relief had flooded through Romily when she'd recognised it as Edmund's Jaguar.

'Not good,' he murmured in answer to her question. 'She has a serious head injury and is still unconscious. On top of that, she has three cracked ribs, a broken wrist and a whole range of cuts and bruises.'

'Oh, Edmund,' murmured Romily. 'I'm so sorry.'

'The car that hit her,' he went on, 'and I can't think of anything else that would have produced the level of injury she's suffered, must have been going at a hell of a speed.'

'The driver had to have known he'd hit something or someone,' said Stanley.

'Whoever the bastard is,' Edmund said furiously, 'he left Hope to die.' He ran a hand through his hair, which was already sticking up as though he'd been repeatedly tugging at it. 'What sort of person would do that?' he demanded, his voice

220

breaking. Then, and as if all the energy had now drained out of him, he took a step back and slumped against the wall of the corridor in which they were standing. Lowering his head, he rubbed his eyes. 'I just can't believe this is happening,' he groaned. 'And the worst of it is, that bloody row we had. What if those are the last words we—'

'Don't say it, Edmund,' Romily said firmly. 'Don't even think it. You have to believe Hope is going to pull through.'

'I wish I had your confidence.'

In the silence that followed, Stanley said, 'I did as you asked and telephoned Annelise. I didn't actually speak to her, but left a message with one of the college porters. I told him it was urgent and that Annelise should ring the hospital as soon as she could.'

Edmund straightened up and stood away from the wall. 'Thank you. And thank you both for finding my wife. Now if you'll excuse me, I want to be with her.'

'Is there anything we can fetch for you, or Hope?' asked Romily.

He shook his head. 'You've done all that you can. You should both go home and get out of those wet clothes.'

Sensing he no longer wanted, or needed, the strain of talking to them, Romily hugged Edmund goodbye. 'You know where I am if there's anything I can do,' she said softly. 'And I mean *anything.*'

She and Stanley had started to walk away down the length of the corridor when Edmund called after them. 'Perhaps you could tell Evelyn and Kit what's happened.'

'We'll go straight to Meadow Lodge,' Romily assured him.

Using the payphone by the main entrance, which was where they'd left Tucker, they called for Jim Trent, their local taxi driver. He was with them within twenty minutes and was a welcome sight.

'You two look like you've fair been in the wars,' he remarked, when they climbed into the back of the Ford Popular and apologised for their dishevelled state. Stanley's clothes were covered in Hope's blood. 'You been in an accident?'

'Helping at the scene of one,' Romily said cagily out of respect for Edmund, and knowing that Hope would hate to be at the centre of any gossip. 'Could you take us to Meadow Lodge, please, Jim?'

'I'll have you there in two shakes of a lamb's tail. So long as we don't come across any more fallen trees. It's a filthy old night, isn't it?'

'It certainly is,' she agreed, staring grimly out of the car window as the rain continued to beat down and the windscreen wipers swept ineffectually back and forth. She was thinking of Jack and how all those years ago he had entrusted her with the task of taking care of his family. She knew it wasn't her fault that his daughter, Hope, was now lying in a hospital bed, but her heart ached with sadness and the feeling she should somehow have stopped the accident from happening. Had Hope not been so wound up and cross with Edmund she might not have gone for a walk this afternoon. Why hadn't Romily paid more attention to her stepdaughter's mental state?

'*You cannot save everyone,*' a gentle voice from the past whispered to her, '*it is not possible. God does not expect you to do it all on your own.*'

It was Matteo's voice, reasoning with her that she had to accept her limitations, something she had never been able to do, as she'd told him.

The conversation had taken place at Tilbrook Hall when she had been grumbling that she needed to be back at Hamble, ferrying aircraft about the country. She had been stuck in bed with her leg in traction for over three weeks and by then it was May. She had heard the awful news the day before that one of her colleagues had crash-landed in a Mosquito and had not been as lucky as she had been when the Walrus had dropped out of the sky. Poor Mildred had died on impact.

'I'm needed,' she'd said when Matteo had tried to reason with her that she was in no state to fly. 'Look at your leg,' he'd said. 'You are not going anywhere. *Sei pazza!* You are mad to think you can!'

His diagnosis had not been far off the mark. She had indeed gone slightly mad, having succumbed to a fever because the wound to her leg had become infected. Only later did she know that Matteo had been instructed to sit by her bedside to keep an eye on her while the fever had raged. She was told it had caused her to hallucinate that she was back in the Walrus trying desperately to land the aircraft.

'Here you go, then,' said Jim, bringing the taxi to a stop in front of Meadow Lodge.

'Oh Lord!' exclaimed Romily when she reached for her handbag and realised she didn't have it.

'That's all right, Mrs Devereux-Temple, I'll put it on account.'

His hand inside his sodden overcoat, Stanley pulled out his wallet. 'I'll deal with this, you go and ring the doorbell,' he said to Romily.

He'd caught her up just as Jim drove off and Evelyn opened the door. 'What on earth are you two doing out in this weather?' she greeted them, ushering them inside and into the hallway.

When her comment didn't receive the light-hearted response she probably expected, her face turned serious. 'What is it? What's happened? It's not Kit, is it? Or the children?'

'No,' replied Romily. 'It's not Kit, or Pip and Em, it's Hope. I'm afraid there's been an accident and she was hit by a car. At least that's what we think has happened. We've just come from the hospital. Edmund is with her. He wanted us to tell you. Is Kit here?'

'No, he's been in London for the day. I have no idea if he'll manage to get back if this storm keeps up. How badly hurt is Hope?'

But before Romily had a chance to reply, Evelyn said, 'What am I thinking? Give me your wet things and come into the drawing room and warm yourselves in front of the fire. Then tell me everything you know. You both look like you could do with a stiff drink.'

'We won't say no to that, will we, Stanley?' said Romily.

He nodded his agreement and handed his coat over to Evelyn. Romily was about to do the same when the soggy envelope she'd earlier stuffed into her coat pocket slipped out and fell to the floor. She'd forgotten all about it, and stooping to pick it up, and curious to see if it was important or not, she looked at it more closely. The flap of the envelope was open and just as she pulled out what was inside and unfolded it, she heard a sharp intake of breath at her side.

She looked up and saw what could only be described as an expression of stunned confusion on Evelyn's face. But something else. If Romily didn't know better, she would say it was recognition.

'Evelyn,' she said, holding out the letter, 'do you know something about this?'

Evelyn said nothing, just stared at the jumble of cut-out letters, some of which were beginning to come unglued.

'What is it?' asked Stanley, leaning over to take a look. 'Good God,' he then said, reading the words aloud. '"*I warned you before about neglecting your husband. You'll pay the price one of these days.*" It's a poison pen letter!'

'It would appear so,' said Romily, once more regarding the other woman's face closely. 'And judging by your reaction, Evelyn, I suspect you do know something about it. Am I right?'

Evelyn hesitated, her eyes flicking between the piece of paper and Romily's gaze. 'How did you come by it?' she asked.

'Hope had it,' said Romily. 'It must have been in her pocket when she was run over.'

Evelyn swallowed. 'Let's go into the drawing room and I'll pour us all a very large drink.'

Chapter Forty-Four

La Vista, Palm Springs
November 1962
Red

'Red, I'm not going to beat about the bush; you look like hell.'

'Gee, thanks, little sis. Did you make a special trip to come and insult me?'

Patsy smiled. 'Chuck and I were in Bel Air last night for a charity gala dinner and ran into Gabe and Melvyn.'

So that was why she was here. Red might have guessed. 'I bet they were singing my praises,' he said.

'And some.' Patsy gave him a meaningful glance, which he chose to disregard. Except his sister, a power-house of outspoken frankness, was hard to ignore. Her speciality was showing up when he least expected it to make a nuisance of herself.

One minute he'd been sitting out here in the shade of the verandah bashing away at his typewriter, and the next, a localised tornado hit town in the form of his flame-haired sister. Twelve years his junior, she always managed to make him feel about a hundred and ten. From the age of eighteen Patsy had been a determined socialite. She had dated not one but two of the Kennedy brothers, and had been proposed to numerous times, including by an Italian count. She had turned them all down and on her twenty-seventh birthday married Chuck Seymour III, a decorated war hero and Ambassador to the United Nations. He was now a senator with designs on the highest office in the land. Their marriage had always been something of a mystery to Red. On the face of it they were polar opposites, but they were two of the happiest people he knew.

'Orange juice?' he said.

'Thank you. And neat, please.'

From the jug on the table, he poured a glass of the freshly squeezed orange juice his maid, Conchita, had prepared for him. 'I presume by *neat*, you mean without ice,' he said.

'What else could I possibly mean?' she replied archly, while taking the glass and peering at him over the top of her sunglasses.

'What else indeed?' he muttered, wishing he could splash a large measure of vodka into his own drink.

'I had wondered if you might show your handsome mug at the gala dinner last night,' she said.

'Patsy, you know I have no interest in showing my handsome mug at events like that.'

'But now,' she said, as though he hadn't spoken, 'I can see why you didn't go, you'd have been turned away as a hobo. Lost your razor, have you?'

'My dearest little sister,' he said, giving his stubbly chin a rub, 'oh how I love your jesting ways.'

'I know you do, which is why I'm here to cheer you up and put some pep back into your humdrum life.'

'Who says I need cheering up? And what the devil do you mean by my "humdrum" life?'

She lowered her sunglasses and gave him the benefit of one of her most scrutinising stares. 'When was the last time you went out and had fun?'

Her question brought him up short. It was too reminiscent of the charge he'd made against Romily.

'I've been out every night this week,' he lied.

'I'm not talking about propping up a bar and bringing some young blonde piece back to your bed and then sleeping off a hangover. That's not proper fun. That's just shallow distraction.'

He forced a grin to his face and lied again. 'It was fun to me.'

She gave him a pitying look. 'Oh, Red, you're so much better than that.'

'No, I'm not. You've always overestimated my competence. That's your trouble, Patsy, you want everyone to be as smart and as content as you.'

'I just want everybody to be happy. Is that so wrong?'

He shook his head. 'It's not realistic. As I've told you before; just because you were born with a relentlessly happy disposition, it doesn't mean the rest of us have to be like you. Take it from me, I'm happy enough when I'm working.'

'So what are you currently working on?'

'A new film script, if you must know.'

'A commissioned script?'

'No, something *I* want to write.'

'And?'

'And nothing. You know I hate to share anything until it's finished.'

She drained her glass of orange juice. 'Tell me about this English woman called Romily.'

He kept his expression frozen in neutral. 'Presumably Gabe and Melvyn brought her name up in conversation at your swanky dinner?'

'They might have,' she said carelessly. 'Now why don't you give yourself a break from your typewriter and take me for lunch. And then you can explain why you deliberately sabotaged the project Gabe and Melvyn wanted you to do.'

'I didn't sabotage the project,' he said with heat. 'If that's what they told you, then they're way out of line. It was Romily who walked away. She was the one who flew back to England in a state of high dudgeon.'

'Did you try to stop her?'

'Trust me, there's no stopping a woman like Romily Devereux-Temple; she's a law unto herself.'

'As are you, brother dear. As are you.'

Following lunch and his sister's departure to rejoin her husband and fly home to Washington, Red sat in quiet contemplation outside on the verandah watching the setting sun.

Never one to pull her punches, Patsy had seen fit to put him straight. 'You're drinking too much and making yourself maudlin because some clever English dame got one over you,' she'd said. 'Personally, I'd like to shake her by the hand. God knows it's high time your ego was given a good working over. Does it really matter so much to you that she outsmarted you?'

'I never said she did!' he'd remonstrated.

'You didn't need to. I know you, Red. I know how pig-headed you are when your pride has been dealt a blow. I also know that when somebody gets under your skin you deliberately push them away.'

'How the devil you've reached that conclusion is beyond me.'

'It's based on what you're *not* telling me.'

For all his sister thought she knew him, and she probably knew him better than most, she didn't know the whole of him. No one did.

In the distance Mount San Jacinto shimmered with a vibrant roseate hue as the setting sun smouldered and dipped yet further in the sky. The sight of it made him wish he could paint. But stick a paintbrush in his hand and he could do no more than produce a childish daub. Words were what he painted with.

But as his frustrated attempts to write that morning before Patsy had arrived had proved, he wasn't exactly scoring any bullseyes on that particular target. He gave the typewriter on the table in front of him a reproachful look. Then with sudden resolve, he pulled it towards him and putting in a fresh piece of paper, he took a deep breath.

An hour later, and in the light of several candles on the table, and with the ground around him covered in balls of screwed up paper, he took what he'd finally managed to write from the typewriter. He laid the single sheet of paper flat on the table and scrutinised every word he'd typed.

He then signed his name at the bottom of the page. First thing in the morning he would post it.

Chapter Forty-Five

Melstead Hall, Melstead St Mary
November 1962
Julia

Julia was a bundle of nerves. Sick with fear and dread, she had been unable to eat **any breakfast**. In the dining room, and at the other end of the table, hidden by that morning's *Times*, Arthur was calmly drinking his third cup of coffee after eating devilled kidneys, followed by several pieces of toast and marmalade.

All night she had lain awake in bed, reliving what had happened when they'd been driving home yesterday evening. Again and again she heard and felt the awful thump when the car had made contact with what Arthur maintained was a deer in the road. Julia had been sure it was no such thing, but when she'd voiced her belief and urged him to go back and see if she was right, he'd told her not to be so stupid, that she was imagining things. 'I'm the one who's behind the steering wheel,' he'd said, driving even faster now, 'and I know exactly what I saw and hit, so keep your highly impressionable imagination under control.'

'But it would do no harm to turn around and check,' she'd pleaded.

'Please do not contradict me,' he'd said, 'it doesn't become you.'

'But darling, I'm sure I wasn't imagining—'

'Don't but-darling me anything. Now put it out of your

mind; it was just a deer. Count yourself lucky it didn't cause us to drive off the road and crash.'

Julia had tried to do as he said, but she couldn't stop picturing what she was sure she'd seen in the light of the headlamps: a woman in a headscarf. To put her mind at rest, she planned to go for a walk later that morning. She wanted to go to that spot in the road where Arthur was so sure he'd hit a deer. It stood to reason that if he had, the body of the animal would still be there. Unless, of course, it had only been hurt and managed to get away.

As if reading her thoughts, Arthur said, 'What plans do you have for the day?'

'Erm . . . I thought . . . if you didn't need me for anything, I thought I'd—'

He lowered his newspaper with a display of annoyance. 'Don't dither, Julia, you know how it irritates me. Get to the point. What did you think you would do?'

'Sorry,' she said weakly. 'I thought I might write to Charles and then go . . . go for a walk.'

'Your inventory of the kitchen is overdue, so perhaps you should concentrate on that. And then I'd like you to redo the shirt you mended for me last week; the stitching wasn't up to your usual standard.'

'Yes, of course, darling,' she said as he raised the newspaper and disappeared behind it once more. Thereby ending the exchange. It was one of his rules that when he was reading the paper he wasn't to be disturbed.

In the silence of the dining room, Julia listened to the ticking of the ormolu clock on the mantelpiece and stared out of the window. The storm last night had wreaked havoc in the garden. The lawn was strewn with twigs and branches, along with the last of the leaves that had clung on so tenaciously.

November was her least favourite month. It brought back

too many painful memories. Of being a child and walking in the local park with her mother. She could see them now, hand in hand, the path covered with slippery wet leaves beneath their feet, the air dense with the earthy smell of decomposing vegetation. Julia knew that her mother was not well as they lingered in the park that cold afternoon, but she didn't realise just how ill. That was the last walk they ever took together. The next day the doctor was summoned and a week later, after being confined to bed, her mother died.

To this day Julia never knew what her mother died from. Her father refused to tell her, refused even to talk about her mother ever again. Overnight, life became very different. Her father couldn't bear any noise. Laughter, in particular, was banned. Not that Julia had anything to laugh about then. There were no more happy walks to the park, no more bedtime stories, and no more treats. She tiptoed round the house, afraid of upsetting her father. She did all that she could to please him, in the way that her mother had. She was a poor substitute, she knew. But she did her best. She did her duty, just as her father said her mother would have wanted . . .

A knock at the door made her blink and sit up straight.

'Enter!' Arthur responded without lowering his newspaper.

It was Miss Casey. The housekeeper looked as formidable as ever and without so much as glancing at Julia she addressed Arthur. 'I'm sorry to disturb you, sir, but the delivery boy from the butcher's has called and—'

'I'm sure I couldn't care less whether the butcher's boy has called or not,' interrupted Arthur.

'Yes, sir, of course. But he told me something I thought you might like to know. There was an accident last night.'

The newspaper lowered a few inches and Arthur peered over the top of it. 'What sort of accident?'

'It's your sister, sir. She's in the cottage hospital in Chelstead.

It seems she was hit by a car on the Melstead Road last night.'

Julia gasped. Arthur shot her a look. 'Did the boy tell you how badly hurt my sister is?' he demanded.

'No, sir. Those are all the details I have. Would you like me to organise for some flowers to be sent to the hospital?'

'No. My wife can see to that.'

'Very well, sir.'

Miss Casey quietly closed the door behind her and not caring if the woman was standing the other side of it, Julia said: 'I told you it wasn't a deer you hit.'

'Don't be so absurd. It's a coincidence.'

'How can it be? It's the same road. We should tell the police what happened. That you thought you'd hit a deer. It could have happened to anyone in that dreadful weather. They'll understand. I'm sure they will.'

Arthur cast aside the newspaper and cleared his throat. 'The only person who needs to understand what happened last night is you, Julia. I hit a deer, and that's an end to the matter.'

Julia was trembling now. She didn't understand how her husband could be so adamant that he'd done nothing wrong. 'But it's your sister,' she said.

He slowly rose to his feet and came towards her, his expression as hard as granite. 'Hope may well have been involved in an accident last night, but it has nothing to do with *us*.'

'What if she dies?'

'What if she does?'

Julia was appalled. 'Don't you care about her?'

'I care as much as she would care about my demise.'

'But Arthur, if she dies, it . . . it will be murder.'

'Don't be so melodramatic. And if her death was to be classed as murder, or perhaps manslaughter, it would still not have anything to do with me. For the simple reason, I didn't hit her. I hit a deer. Do I have to keep reminding you of that? But if you persist with this nonsense, you will risk sending me to prison for something I did not do. Is that what you want? Is it?'

'Of . . . of course not,' she stammered.

'Then you need to stop talking such gibberish. Or you'll get us both into a lot of trouble. Because, maybe I might become as confused as you and remember things differently. That it was you who drove us home and that I begged you to stop when you hit something in the road, but you refused.'

Julia stared at him, horror-struck. 'Why would you do that?'

'Darling,' he said with a laugh, 'I wouldn't. Why would I want you to be sent to prison? It would be too awful. Especially for Charles. Think what it would do to the boy.' He shook his head and sighed. 'But if you made the situation so difficult, well, then you would leave me no choice. Now why don't you be a good girl and go and organise those flowers for Hope?'

He was at the door, his fingers on the handle, when he turned around. 'By the way, don't forget the kitchen and pantry inventory, will you? Oh, and I've decided to go up to London for a few days.'

In a state of bewildered shock, Julia stared at him. 'When will you be back?'

'I don't know.'

Chapter Forty-Six

St Gertrude's College, Oxford
November 1962
Annelise

'I wish you could come with me.'

'I wish I could too,' Harry said.

'I've never asked you for anything before, can you not do this one thing for me?'

'Annelise, I'd do anything to be with you. You know I would.'

'Not quite anything.'

The words were out before she could stop them. They were words she had never wanted to utter; they were too loaded with need, the desperate need she had never wanted to reveal. But now she had, and with an unavoidable edge of scolding sarcasm that made her squirm.

'Don't be like that,' he said softly in her ear. 'You know I can't suddenly drop everything and leave Oxford. I'm not a free agent like you.'

Sitting at her desk, Annelise gripped the telephone hard, and held her tongue, not trusting herself to continue. A free agent, was that what she was?

'Darling?'

'Will you ever leave your wife?' she asked bluntly.

'Now is not the time to discuss my marriage.'

'It never is,' she muttered. Then: 'I must go.'

'Not like this.'

'I have a train to catch.'

'I know you do. But I don't want you so far away feeling badly towards me.'

'I'm going to Suffolk, not the ends of the earth.'

'It might just as well be.'

'Then do as I ask and drop everything and come with me.'

'This is family time for you,' he said, 'I'd be in the way.'

'You'd be there to support me.' She cringed. There she went again, showing her shameful need.

'Hope will be fine. And so will you. You're one of the strongest people I know.'

'How do you know she'll be fine?' Annelise snapped. 'You have no idea how badly hurt she is. And for God's sake, stop treating me as if I were a child!'

'Then stop acting like one!'

There. Finally she had provoked him into saying something that wasn't a worthless platitude.

'I'm sorry,' he said. 'I didn't mean that.'

'I think you did. I think that's the first thing you've said in a long time that you've truly meant.'

'Annelise, you're upset. It's understandable. You've had a terrible shock. Let's not argue. Catch your train and we'll talk when you're back in Oxford.'

'What would be the point?' she said. Before he had a chance to reply, she hung up.

The train journey felt interminable.

Every mile covered of clackety-clack track made her throbbing head ache all the more. It had started in the taxi ride from St Gertrude's to the station and worsened tenfold once she was on the train out of the city. Since changing trains on the last leg of the journey, a large man who had taken the seat next to her kept falling asleep and leaning into her. Several times she'd had to shove him back into his seat, inciting a loud snore from his gaping mouth.

The heating was turned up too high – the source of it was coming from the metal heating grille beneath her seat – and she longed to open the window, but daren't. It had started to rain earlier and a ruddy-cheeked woman in a thick tweed coat had slammed it shut, and with a defiance that challenged anyone to open it again.

After stopping at yet another train station, an elderly man now joined them in the carriage, and tipping his hat with a smile, stowing his umbrella and loosening his scarf and coat, he revealed himself to be a man of the cloth. He then proceeded to light up a pipe, drawing on it with zeal.

Within minutes the fug of smoke was making Annelise nauseous. Oh, how she bitterly regretted that she had not received the news about Mums earlier so she could have travelled home last night. But she had been at a formal dinner at St Hilda's and hadn't returned to her rooms in college until nearly midnight. Had she not gone out, she would have received Stanley's message in time to travel home at once. All she could do at that time of night was ring the hospital and speak to Edmund. The grave concern in his voice had meant she hadn't slept a wink all night. At two in the morning, and unable to speak to the one person she wanted to – Harry – she had rung Stanley. 'I couldn't sleep either,' he had said when she apologised for disturbing him. It had felt good to hear his voice and comforted by it, she had thanked him for finding Hope. 'It's Tucker who deserves the credit,' he'd said.

'But had you and Romily not braved the storm to look for her, Mums may well have died in that ditch.' Annelise was determined he should accept her gratitude.

As soon as she was up and dressed, and too sick with worry to eat breakfast, she had gone in search of the Dean to request compassionate leave. Dr Spriggs was kindness itself and told her it was almost the end of term anyway, so she was to take as much leave as she required.

The fug of smoke in the confined space was now causing Annelise's head to throb all the more. And with bile rising in her throat and desperate for some fresh air, she stood up, took down her suitcase from the overhead rack and slid open the compartment door and escaped.

Moving along the corridor, and finding most of the other carriages full, she gave up looking for a seat. With only twenty minutes of the journey left, she set her case down on the floor and stood next to a grimy window. The glass was so filthy she could only just see out of it at the passing scenery, the rain blurring the fields and houses. But at least she could open it and breathe in the damp cold air.

She closed her eyes and as the nausea and bile receded, she tried to focus on Hope, on willing her to regain consciousness, and for her injuries not to be life-threatening. But every time she attempted to corral her thoughts, Harry's voice intruded, his words echoing the rhythm of the train tracks.

I'd do anything to be with you . . . I'd do anything to be with you . . . I'd do anything to be with you . . .

He had said a variation on the theme of this many times since their relationship had begun. Since *their affair* had begun, Annelise corrected herself.

He was never going to leave his wife, was he? She'd been a fool to think he would. A blind fool. Why had it taken so long for her to wake up and realise that? Why had she wanted so badly to believe in his lies?

For God's sake, she was an intelligent woman, so she thought, but she had behaved as naïvely and as stupidly as the child he had accused her of being.

What had made her think she was so special that Harry

would divorce his wife for her? Arrogance, that's what it was! She had imagined herself to be infinitely better than that poor woman to whom he was married. She wasn't better. She was so much worse. She had cheapened herself by allowing herself to become his mistress.

His bit on the side.

The other woman.

The homewrecker.

Seeing her actions for what they really were, for the first time ever she felt guilty. Moreover she felt sorry for the woman she had never met, but whom she had turned into an inferior being. In her love for Harry, Annelise had convinced herself that his wife didn't deserve him, that she wasn't capable of making Harry truly happy. Only Annelise could do that, she had believed.

It was a pity she had not followed the advice she gave her students, that there was always more than one way of looking at something, that it was a mistake to limit one's potential by narrowing one's perspective. If she had heeded her own counsel, she might have seen through Harry's tissue of lies and seen him for what he was – a selfish man intent on having his cake and eating it.

Find what will make you happy. That's what Romily always used to say to her. She had convinced herself that Harry was what made her happy, but the reality was, he had drained the joy out of her with her constant battle to disguise just how much she loved him.

Love. Was that what she'd felt for him?

If it was, it had been the wrong sort of love, she now acknowledged; it was a destructive love.

Romily had not warned her off when Annelise had confided in her, that was not her style. Instead, she had said that love was an adventure, and nobody ever knew how or where it would end up, no matter the strength of the emotions involved.

With a deep sigh, Annelise accepted that Romily had probably known exactly how this particular adventure would end.

Staring at the passing scenery, and realising that she was nearly home, she felt cross that she had allowed herself to be consumed with thoughts of Harry when it was Hope who should be uppermost in her mind. And Edmund.

When the train finally pulled into the station at Melstead St Mary with a last puff of steam, Annelise couldn't step down onto the platform fast enough.

Stanley was there to meet her. She all but fell into his welcome embrace.

Chapter Forty-Seven

Island House, Melstead St Mary
December 1962
Florence

'Florence, do you have a moment to talk?'

In the laundry room, and hearing the serious tone to Romily's voice as she stood in the doorway looking in at her, Florence said, 'It's not bad news from the hospital, is it?'

Hope had been unconscious now for two weeks. The longer it went on, the more they all feared she might never regain consciousness. During that time Romily had been away on a ten-day tour of speaking engagements in Scandinavia and only returned late last night. She had wanted to cancel the tour, but Edmund had insisted she go, that everyone back at home would keep her up to date. Every day the news had been the same: Hope showed no sign of improvement.

Romily shook her head. 'There's been no word today from Edmund or Annelise. Would you come into the library, please, there's something I want to discuss with you?'

Putting the basket of washing on the floor, Florence wondered what Romily wanted to discuss. Was she unhappy with her work? Florence knew that she had been distracted recently, worrying about those poison pen letters, so maybe she had forgotten something important she was supposed to have arranged. She hoped not.

In the library, Romily invited her to sit in the comfortable armchair to one side of the fire. 'If you don't mind,' she said, 'I need to ask you something personal.'

'Goodness, that sounds ominous.'

Romily sat in the chair opposite. 'I'm afraid it is. We've always been very honest with each other, haven't we?'

Puzzled, Florence nodded.

'In the past when you've had any worries, you've shared them with me, and I with you. I've always valued that between us. It's made us the friends we are.'

'That's true,' said Florence.

'Yet, and I don't think I'm imagining this,' Romily went on, 'you haven't been yourself lately, have you? You've had something on your mind, and I've been a poor friend in that until now I haven't made the time to find out what was wrong.'

'You don't need to apologise to me, Romily, I know how busy you are. And then, what with Hope being in hospital and you being away, it didn't seem right to bother you.'

'My work schedule, no matter how busy, is no excuse. A while ago you tried to talk to me. In fact, you tried on several occasions, and for various reasons, for which I can only apologise, I didn't pursue the matter with you. It didn't, by any chance, have something to do with receiving an anonymous letter, did it?'

Florence's jaw dropped. 'How do you know about that?'

'It was a guess. You see, Hope received one, and Evelyn has had two sent to her. They both had struck me as being out of sorts recently, and the letters would explain their behaviour.'

'So you thought I was in the same boat?'

'Yes. It came to me while I was away. What did your letter say?'

'I've had two, both accusing Billy of cheating on me. Rubbish, of course. Billy's not like that. He really isn't. But—'

'But the letters sowed the seed of doubt,' said Romily, 'and now you can't stop wondering if it might be true.'

'Yes,' murmured Florence. It shamed her to admit that she could doubt her husband. 'It's been driving me mad. I've even begun snooping through his things. Can you believe that?'

'If it reassures you, the letter Hope received implied that Edmund was being unfaithful to her.'

Again Florence was shocked. 'Dr Flowerday would never do that!'

'I agree. No more than your Billy would. But to sow the seed of distrust in a wife's head about her husband is a particularly malicious act.'

'What about Evelyn's letters?'

Romily hesitated before saying, 'A variation on the same theme, but slightly different. Evelyn wondered if the sender of the letters was somebody with whom she worked during the war. But I think we can discount that theory now. Do you have any suspicions who it might be?'

'Only that it could be Ruby, you know how she hates me. I was so sure it was her I searched her cottage for any sign of glue and bits of newspaper.' Florence gave a hesitant smile. 'You would have been proud of me, I was just like your Sister Grace, looking for evidence. I didn't find anything though.' She paused and considered for a moment what she now knew. 'But it doesn't make sense that my mother-in-law would be sending anonymous letters to Evelyn and Hope, does it? Ruby doesn't have a grievance with them, only me for marrying Billy.'

Romily looked thoughtful. 'You're right,' she said. 'Would you show me your letters? There might be a clue in the wording that could give away who's doing this.'

'I'm sorry, but I've got rid of them. Do you suppose the three of us are not the only ones to be targeted, that there might be others in the village who have received letters?'

'Possibly.' Romily smiled. 'Who knows, I might be next on the list of recipients?'

'They wouldn't dare, not to you.'

'To a twisted mind nobody is immune.'

Florence knew Romily was right. Ruby was a perfect example of somebody whose mind was so twisted against her, she would stop at nothing to make life as difficult as she could for her.

Sensing there was nothing more to be said on the subject for now, Florence rose from her chair. 'I'd better get on,' she said.

She was at the door when she turned around. 'We won't have to go to the police about this, will we?'

'I'd like to think not,' Romily replied, 'but if the situation escalates it would be the sensible thing to do. We'll cross that bridge if we need to. Over the years, you and I have solved many a problem together, so let's see if we can resolve this one too. Oh, and I meant to say earlier, don't leave it too late going home this afternoon. By all accounts the smog in London is getting worse and heading our way. And knowing how you worry about George, why don't you try telephoning him before you go to make sure he's all right?'

'Thank you, Romily, I will.'

Chapter Forty-Eight

London
December 1962
Ralph

The smog was so thick visibility was reduced to less than a few yards. With a handkerchief pressed to his mouth and nose, Ralph had lost count how many times he'd bumped into another person or building, or stumbled off the pavement very nearly into the path of an oncoming car crawling along in the dark. It was unnervingly disorientating, and he supposed this was how it had been during the blackout in the war. Just without the choking air.

Everyone in London was hoping it wouldn't be as bad as the smog that killed thousands ten years ago. He'd been a boy back then and could remember receiving a rare letter from his mother – from the safety of the south of France – advising him to stay indoors. The letter had been sent to the prep school he attended in North London and he'd opened it with a mixture of emotions. He hated the slapdash nature of her communications – nothing for six months, then suddenly a rambling letter telling him how much she loved him and how she wished he could be with her. Initially he had made the mistake of believing her, but when he replied saying he would like to spend the school holidays with her, there was a lengthy silence. His father hated him to have any contact with his mother, and so he kept her letters secret. He had enjoyed keeping secrets. But didn't everybody?

More than once he had thrown a letter from his mother straight into the bin, not bothering to read it. She had abandoned him, after all. What kind of mother did that? But as the years went by, he reasoned that any woman in her right mind wouldn't stick around for long with a husband like Arthur Devereux. For the life of him, Ralph couldn't understand how any woman would want to attach themselves to his father in the first place.

Women were unfathomable creatures. Take Isabella for example. One minute she was fine with him, the next she was criticising him and making out she was so much better. He really shouldn't have raised his hand to slap her, but then she shouldn't have provoked him.

She was spoiled, that was her trouble. Just like Annelise. And that was Romily's doing. Why hadn't the woman shown him a fraction of the attention she'd lavished on those two girls when they'd all been growing up?

It was a rhetorical question. He knew jolly well why Romily had kept her distance. Why they all did. It was because of his father. They despised Arthur Devereux. When Ralph had been old enough to realise this, and wanting to dissociate himself from the old man, he'd tried his best to be affable and charming in order to gain acceptance into the inner circle, as he saw it.

In some small measure, he had achieved a degree of approval, but he would never be granted full membership to the clan. It was laughable, that he, a true-blooded Devereux – unlike Isabella, the bastard child of a mother who'd been a bastard child herself, and Annelise, a German and not even a blood relation – was made to feel he was a stranger on the outside looking in.

He let out a loud curse as he missed his footing on the kerb of the pavement and breathed in a lungful of foul sulphurous air. Where the hell was he, he suddenly thought? *Damn this smog!*

He'd been so preoccupied he'd taken a wrong turning. As he often did, he blamed his father. Had Arthur not insisted they meet for dinner at his club in St James's Square this evening, doubtless to check up on his employment status, he'd be enjoying a quiet night in.

His eyes itching and his mouth and the back of his throat burning with the poisonous cold air, he stood still and peered through the opaqueness to locate himself.

He arrived forty-five minutes late, as his father, already seated in the dining room with a half-empty bottle of wine, was only too quick to point out.

'As ever, your punctuality is not what it could be,' he said.

Ralph rolled his eyes. Could the old man sound any more pompous? 'I presume you have looked out of the window today from the comfort of your leather armchair and seen how awful the smog is?'

'Don't be smart with me, Ralph. Of course I know what it's like out there.' He moved the bottle of wine towards Ralph so he could fill his glass. 'I've already ordered for us,' he added.

Annoyed that he was denied the right to choose his own meal, Ralph wilfully filled his glass to the top and drank deeply from it. 'So what brings you to town?' he then said. 'The usual things, boredom and a desire to have your lungs poisoned with noxious smog? Or perhaps your visit was entirely for my benefit, an opportunity once again to tell me what a failure of a son I am to you?'

His father stared at him across the white-clothed table. 'I've been here for several weeks if you must know. But I would advise you not to engage in battle with me.'

'Why? What will you do, lock me in my room like you did with Julia? You're aware, aren't you, that people in the village know that you punished her for drinking too much at Meadow Lodge?'

'And whose fault was it that she drank too much?'

'I couldn't say,' Ralph responded with a detached air.

'I'm pleased to say that the severity of Julia's hangover has insured she'll never again drink or make a disgusting display of herself.'

Ralph took a long sip of his wine. 'You never have denied yourself the pleasure a good reprimand gives you, have you? You know, if you'd bestowed half as much love and affection on me as you did the belt or the cane, who knows, I might have turned out to be the perfect son. Imagine that.'

His father looked back at him unmoved. 'Frankly, I can't. At last, here's our soup.'

The waiter now gone, a silence settled on the table as they each picked up their spoons. The soup was thick and too salty, not at all what Ralph would have ordered. While his father gave it his full concentration, tearing at a bread roll and slathering butter on to each piece, before dipping them into the soup. Ralph shuddered with revulsion. He may well have inherited a number of his father's characteristics, but gluttony would never be one of them.

It hadn't always been this way between the two of them. Ralph could recall a time when his father had appeared to care about him. That all changed when Arthur discovered that not only had Ralph been receiving letters from his mother, but had kept some of them and written in return.

It had been one of the masters at school who had informed Arthur. From that day their relationship was different. Arthur made it clear he considered Ralph had betrayed him. Where there had once been pride in Ralph's achievements at school, and reward for doing well, there was now harsh criticism. Nothing he did was good enough, and the harder Ralph tried to win back his father's approval, the more he failed to do so. In the end he simply gave up. Would the same fate befall his stepbrother?

'How's Charlie?' Ralph asked, when he'd had enough of the disagreeable soup and sat back to drink his wine in preference. His father had all but licked his dish clean. The doddery old waiter immediately appeared at the table and shuffled off with the dishes.

'I've told you before,' Arthur intoned, 'it's Charles. And according to his letters, he's well.'

Poor devil, thought Ralph, remembering the Herculean task of trying to think of something to say in those tedious letters home when he'd been away at school.

'I suppose he'll be looking forward to Christmas, won't he?' Ralph said, remembering also how he came to dread the end of the school term. How he'd prayed that he could spend the holidays with one of his friends, or even remain at school in the care of matron.

Arthur's reply was halted by their waiter reappearing with a trolley laden with food. Removing a large silver dome, he commenced to carve slices of meat from a colossal joint of beef. When all was served, Arthur requesting extra potatoes and another Yorkshire pudding, plus a second bottle of Châteauneuf-du-Pape, he said, 'By the way, it's unlikely your aunt Hope will see Christmas, she's been in a coma for the last two weeks. Or perhaps you'd heard via the family jungle drums?'

'No,' Ralph said, 'no I haven't seen or spoken with anyone for some weeks. What's wrong with her?'

'I just said. She's in a coma.'

'But how?'

Arthur shovelled a forkful of beef and potato into his mouth. 'I don't know the full details,' he said at length, 'but somewhat carelessly she managed to get herself hit by a car. She always did have her mind elsewhere. Probably so lost in thought, she never heard the car coming.'

Only his father could sound so cavalier about another person's misfortune. 'Is there nothing that can be done?' asked Ralph.

Arthur chomped on another forkful of beef. 'Not my bailiwick, medical know-how,' he said, not bothering to finish what was in his mouth before speaking.

Ralph put down his knife and fork and reached for his wineglass. He was surprisingly shocked by the news that Hope might die, and by the callous manner in which his father spoke of his sister. Did nothing penetrate that thick blubbery skin of his?

'Was this the reason you invited me to join you for dinner this evening?' Ralph asked.

'Do I need a reason to see my eldest son?'

'You usually do.'

'As opposed to your only reason for ever wanting to see me: money.'

'That's not true,' Ralph lied. 'I enjoy our wrangling get-togethers. I think you do, too.'

Ignoring the comment, Arthur added more mustard to his plate. 'Perhaps you could tell me how your search to become gainfully employed is progressing?'

'I have a number of interesting avenues which I'm following,' Ralph lied again. He still hadn't given the matter much serious consideration; he'd been too busy enjoying himself.

'I'm glad to hear it,' Arthur said. 'Anything remotely promising?'

'Time will tell.'

'Meanwhile, I suppose you'd like me to help you out some more until you've secured a position that befits your particular skills?'

Surprised that his father seemed in such a generous frame of mind, he said, 'Well, if you could see your way to—'

'How much help would you require?' Arthur interrupted him.

Ralph resumed eating and weighed up his options. Ask for too much and his father would laugh at him. Ask for too little and he'd regret not asking for more. 'A thousand would go a long way to easing my situation.'

'And what situation would that be? Skid Row? Tight Spot Alley? Destitute Avenue? Beam End Road? Down on Your Uppers Street?' The old man was smirking. 'Or maybe Impoverished Cul de Sac?'

'There's no need to rub it in,' Ralph said.

'Why shouldn't I? Since I'm the one expected to bail you out.'

'Some of us haven't been as lucky as you. After all, when you were not much older than I am your father died and left you a sizeable inheritance.'

'Yes, yes, yes, I can quite see how my demise would be of the utmost convenience to you. But I assure you, I have no intention of popping my clogs any time soon.'

Ralph willed himself not to snatch up the plate in front of him and grind it into his father's insufferable gloating face. The old man couldn't help himself, could he? He couldn't just write out a cheque and be done with it. Oh no, he had to make Ralph squirm and reduce him to begging. But beg he would if he had to.

'Look, Dad, I know you have my best interests at heart—'

'You know, I'd have more respect for you if you showed some strength of character and told me to bugger off,' his father interrupted him. 'But there you sit, like a pitiful dog desperate to obey its master. Have you really no self-respect?'

At his father's question, combined with the sneering contempt in his voice, something deep inside Ralph shifted. All at once he saw himself in his father's face; it was as though he were looking in a mirror, and he didn't like what he saw.

You truly are your father's son, aren't you?

That was what Isabella had said to him that night at Rules when things had become so heated between them. The thought that he could ever be as abhorrent as Arthur Devereux filled him with disgust. *It's not too late*, he found himself thinking. Not too late to change, to be a better man. Because God forbid he would end up a carbon copy of the man sitting opposite him.

Very slowly, Ralph put down his knife and fork, then just as slowly, he rose to his feet.

'Sit down, Ralph,' warned Arthur. 'I haven't finished with you yet.'

It was all he could do not to grab hold of his father by the lapels of his jacket and shake him hard. But with the greatest of restraint, he said, 'I'm about to prove to you that not only do I have some strength of character, but I still have a modicum of self-respect. I'll bid you goodnight.'

He collected his coat together with his scarf and gloves from the cloakroom and seconds later he was back on the street in the dark, groping his way through the choking smog.

Yet however bad it was, it was better than staying a moment longer in his father's poisonous presence.

Chapter Forty-Nine

Charing Cross Mansions, London
December 1962
Isabella

Isabella was feeling immensely sorry for herself.

She had never missed a performance or rehearsal before. Nor had she ever turned up late for filming. She counted herself as a pro. But there was no way she could work, not unless the role called for a lingering death scene. That she could manage with considerable ease, and a great deal of conviction.

Never before had she felt so ill. She had started coughing a few days before the smog had descended, but once London was fully enveloped in the freezing cold fog that was a dirty grey-brown colour, she had succumbed to a debilitating chest infection. She shouldn't have gone out in the smog, the doctor had scolded her when she'd queued for more than an hour at the surgery yesterday morning. The cramped waiting room had been full of people coughing, their chests heaving, just like hers, with the effort to breathe.

The girl with whom she shared her flat had packed a case yesterday afternoon and fled to the country. Why hadn't Isabella thought to do the same and escape to Suffolk? Especially as Romily had telephoned to suggest the very same thing. But no, she had made light of how ill she was and cast herself in the role of trooper – the show must go on!

Her throat as parched as the Sahara, she ran her tongue over her dry lips and tried to swallow. Drink plenty of fluids, the doctor had told her, and seeing that the water jug by the side of her bed was empty, she tried to summon the energy to go and fill it. She had one foot on the floor when she was seized by a violent coughing fit. Reaching for a handkerchief, she covered her mouth in an attempt to contain the worst of the cough that racked through her body. When it eventually subsided, and she removed the hanky, she saw it was spotted with blood. Not good, she thought. Not good at all.

Drained of all energy, her body bathed in a disgustingly fever-ish sweat, she sank back against the pillows and headboard. She closed her eyes and a soothing image of Island House washed over her; it was of the garden in late spring when the lilac trees were in full bloom and the cherry blossom was at its best. It was an image that inevitably led her to think of her father, Elijah, who, as Romily's gardener, had worked so tirelessly to make the garden one of the finest in the area.

Some of Isabella's fondest memories were of the simple garden at the cottage where she lived with Elijah. He had given her an area in which she could grow whatever she wanted. She had been so proud of herself when she'd dug up her first potato. She had cradled it in her grubby hands as though it were the most precious of jewels. She had run to the back door to show her father. But in her excitement, she had tripped over a water-ing can and hurt her knees on the brick path.

She hadn't cried though. She had wanted to be strong for Elijah. He had suffered enough as it was, what with losing the woman he loved as well as what he'd experienced in the war. On seeing her bloody knees, Elijah had held her to him, then lifting her up, he'd carried her through to the small kitchen and sat her on the wooden draining board. With tender hands, he'd cleaned her grazed knees with TCP, found a plaster, and then wrapped her in his arms to give her another hug.

'What a brave girl you are,' he'd said. 'Just like your mother.'

It wasn't often he spoke of Allegra, but when he did, it was with loving admiration. She was a woman of great spirit, he would say, wild at times, fickle too, as difficult to pin down as quicksilver. It was her courage that Elijah often referred to, particularly her courage as an unmarried young woman to keep the baby she was expecting.

Isabella wished she had more of her mother's spirit right now and that she didn't feel so hopelessly feeble. Or so maudlin, fearing that she might die here all alone, her emaciated corpse undiscovered for days on end.

With these thoughts of death spinning around inside her head, Isabella suddenly remembered poor Hope. The last she'd heard from Romily was that Hope still hadn't regained consciousness. Her delirious mind as clouded as the smog outside, Isabella tried to remember when that last update was. It seemed an age away. Was it before London became shrouded in smog? No, it was after and when she'd received that unexpected letter of apology from Ralph. She couldn't believe how contrite he'd sounded as he asked for her forgiveness. She wanted to believe it was genuine. But with Ralph you never could tell.

Another painful coughing fit took hold of her, and when she'd recovered from the convulsion that tore at her chest, she closed her eyes and immediately fell into a deep sleep. But not for long. She was woken by the sound of knocking.

Knocking at Death's door, she thought woozily as the noise continued, growing in volume and persistence. She opened her eyes and realised that the knocking was at the door of her flat. Still half asleep, she dragged herself from her bed and went to see who it was, grabbing her dressing gown as she went. Perhaps it was a fellow member of the cast, or even the director, bringing her grapes and sympathy.

She placed her eye against the peephole of the door and jumped away in shock.

'Isabella, it's me: Max. Are you all right?'

'I'm really not fit company,' she croaked, her voice strained and hoarse.

'I've come bearing gifts to make you feel better,' he said.

'How did you know I was ill?'

'How about we have this conversation on your side of the door?'

She hesitated. If there was one person she didn't want to see her, it was Max. Suave and handsome, and very different to the usual men she dated, Max was a dangerous temptation. So far she had resisted his allure, telling herself he was too old – he was twice her age for heaven's sake! But on the several occasions he had taken her for dinner, each time after watching the play she was in, he had stirred within her the strongest of desires. He dazzled her with his charm and wit. He spoke of art and books, and a world of travel to places she had never imagined visiting – South America, India, deserted islands of the Polynesian coast. Afterwards he would see her home and linger on the doorstep outside the mansion building where her flat was. It had taken a lot of willpower not to invite him up, settling instead for a kiss on the cheek.

'Isabella?'

'I can't let you in,' she croaked, 'not when I look so dreadful.'

'Put your vanity aside and let me in, you silly girl. I've come to mop your brow, not seduce you.'

Accepting that it would be churlish to send him away, she tied the belt of her dressing gown around her waist, as though for protection, and unlocked the door.

And there he stood, a vision of dreamy perfection in his charcoal-grey overcoat, a burgundy coloured woollen scarf around his neck, and smelling divinely of cologne. In one hand he held a bouquet of flowers and in the other, a basket of what appeared to be fruit. He stepped inside and pushed the door shut behind him.

'They told me at the theatre you were unwell,' he said, 'that this bloody smog had knocked you for six. And I can see they weren't exaggerating. You poor, poor thing.'

His sympathy was too much. 'Don't,' she said, 'I'm not in any condition to be on the receiving end of kindness. I shall start blubbing like a baby.'

'I have seen a person cry before, you know. Now then,' he said all business-like, 'point me in the direction of the kitchen and I shall put this lot in there, and then I shall settle you back in bed. After that, I shall make you something to eat. When was the last time you ate?'

'I . . . I don't remember. And I'm not really hungry.'

He tutted. 'Don't fight me, Isabella, you don't have the energy.'

What resistance she still possessed vanished under his firmness, and before she knew it, she was sitting up in bed, the sheets and blankets straightened, and the pillows plumped and positioned for maximum comfort.

'There now,' he said, a short while later and placing a tray on her lap. 'A mug of tomato soup and a round of cucumber sandwiches cut into tempting triangles, the crusts removed. The best remedy I know for reviving an ailing patient.'

'How did you manage all this,' she asked, staring at the tray, while he put a fresh jug of water and a clean glass on the bedside table. As muddle-headed as the fever had made her, she could have sworn he'd have had as much chance of finding gold bars in the kitchen as anything fresh and wholesome to eat.

'I came prepared,' he said, 'like Little Red Riding Hood with a basket of nourishment.'

'More like the Big Bad Wolf,' she said.

He dragged the velvet-covered stool over from her dressing

table and placed it next to the bed. 'Is that how you see me?' he asked, when he was seated.

'I'm not sure how I should see you,' she replied. 'Or how you want me to consider you?'

He smiled, causing starbursts of lines to deepen around his eyes. 'Drink your soup while it's hot,' he said. 'We'll discuss weightier matters when you're better.'

She lifted the mug of soup, put it against her dry lips and took a cautious sip. 'Shouldn't you be at work?' she asked, not really knowing what he did, other than he said he was just a boring civil servant.

'How can I work when there's a medical emergency to deal with?'

'I'm hardly that.'

'I remember all too well the smog of 1952. So let me determine what is, and what isn't an emergency. Okay?'

She nodded and drank some more of the soup, then nibbled on a sandwich. Although she had claimed not to have any appetite, she was now glad of something to eat. All the while she ate, Max's eyes never wavered from her face. 'Stop watching me,' she said, 'you're making me nervous.'

'That makes two of us.'

'What do you mean?'

'Later,' he said. 'Weightier matters for when you're feeling stronger.'

Not daring to wonder what he meant, she said, 'Tell me about you and Evelyn.' Ever since they'd met, she had been curious about him knowing Evelyn. To Isabella's knowledge her aunt had never once mentioned the handsome and charismatic man sitting here by the side of her bed. To her surprise, Max suddenly looked awkward.

'What do you want to know?'

'How did you two meet?'

'War work,' he said.

'The hush-hush variety?'

'Yes.' He smiled again and put a finger to his lips. 'So hush and concentrate on eating.'

She drank some more soup. 'Were you close friends?' she asked.

'Everyone was a close friend in the environment we worked in,' he said. 'Intense relationships were forged in the fire of the pressure we were under. It was the nature of the beast.'

'Were you more than friends with Evelyn?'

'I've never been a monk, Isabella. I've always enjoyed the company of women. I flirt as unconsciously as I breathe.'

'That's not exactly an answer to my question, is it?'

'Yes, I flirted with Evelyn. She was a beautiful young girl with the kind of intelligence I admired. There was a time when I thought she was just the sort of woman with whom I could spend my life. But she loved another. I was no match for Kit.'

At his candour, and feeling as though a dark cloud had passed across the sun, Isabella wished now that she hadn't asked him about Evelyn. That's what you get for poking your nose in where you shouldn't, she thought. Then, and as if to teach her a further lesson, a racking cough took hold of her. With her shoulders heaving, it felt like her lungs were threatening to burst through her aching ribs.

On his feet, Max removed the tray from her lap and placed a hand to her back as she doubled over with the pain her chest was in.

When the coughing fit had run its course, she sank back against the pillows, exhausted and again bathed in sweat. 'I'd like to sleep now,' she murmured.

Once more he straightened the sheet and blankets, smoothing and patting them into place. Such was the care he took, it made Isabella think of her father doing the same for her when she'd been a child.

When he was standing at the door, Max said, 'I want you to know something important, Isabella. What I said before about Evelyn, that was then. This is now. This is you and me. And it's altogether different.'

Weightier matters, she thought as she drifted off to sleep.

Chapter Fifty

Chelstead Cottage Hospital, Chelstead
December 1962
Evelyn

It had been a particularly trying day for Evelyn.

A large part of her morning had been devoted to reasoning with an indignant parent who refused to believe her daughter might be dyslexic. The way the mother reacted to Evelyn's carefully worded proposal that the girl be referred to a specialist for testing, anyone would think she had recommended seeking help from a witch doctor.

No sooner had Mrs Bridgewater taken her leave and Evelyn had eaten a hurried lunch, than she had received a telephone call from a furious school governor. He had just learned of the existence of a well-thumbed copy of *Lady Chatterley's Lover* in the school library – the full unexpurgated version, no less. The book had been discovered by the librarian, Mrs Woods, and the general consensus was that it had been put there as a prank by one of the girls. Evelyn had read the novel shortly after the ruling two years ago that it could be published here in Britain, and had not found it half as salacious as the press and the Church of England had made out.

The school day now over, Evelyn was on her way to the hospital to visit Hope. She remained in a coma and the police still had no idea who had run her over.

Darkness had fallen early this evening, due in part to the

smog; it had spread out of London and across the country. Those who suffered with weak chests and heart complaints were advised to stay indoors. Evelyn had begged Kit not to go out when she'd kissed him goodbye this morning. Every year he succumbed to a shocking chest infection, just as he had as a boy, and subjecting his battered lungs to the current foul air was to be avoided at all costs. She suspected he would have ignored her advice and gone to see his sister anyway.

With her gloved hand, Evelyn wiped at the windscreen. The heater, such as it was, wasn't working and it was so cold inside the car her breath was misting the glass. She kept wriggling her toes in a vain attempt to keep them warm. Bill Noakes – the school caretaker, and general seer and clairvoyant – claimed the weather was set to take a turn for the worse. No doubt he knew this by conferring with a shrivelled-up piece of seaweed.

At the hospital, Evelyn parked alongside Romily's Lagonda. Switching off the engine, she took a moment to collect her thoughts. She hadn't seen Romily since the night of Hope's awful accident, and when Evelyn had learned that her sister-in-law had received an anonymous letter just as she had. Knowing that she wasn't alone in being singled out had initially given her a sense of relief.

Finding it impossible to be entirely truthful with Romily, especially with Stanley present, Evelyn had made vague noises about some person with whom she had worked during the war being the culprit. She had not revealed the true nature of the accusation made either, only that she was accused of betraying Kit.

If Romily had doubted any of what Evelyn had shared, she had not pressed for more details. Romily had then been away on yet another tour of speaking engagements, and for a while Evelyn had felt as though she were off the hook. Which was nothing but a display of short-sighted and cowardly behaviour on her part.

Out of the car, and covering her mouth and nose with her scarf, she made a dash for the entrance to the hospital and the private room Hope had occupied since being admitted. As she thought she would, Evelyn found Romily sitting by the side of Hope's bed. She was reading to her.

'The latest Ngaio Marsh mystery,' Romily said, holding up the book for Evelyn to see. 'Hope's always been rather fond of Roderick Alleyn.'

'I must confess that I have a weakness for him too,' said Evelyn. Removing her coat, scarf and gloves, she sat on the other side of the bed. 'How was your trip?'

'In a word: cold. It's good to be home. Even with this smog.'

Evelyn smiled. 'It's good to see you again.' Then taking hold of one of her sister-in-law's hands, she said softly, 'Hello Hope, it's me, Evelyn, here to bother you again. Apologies for interrupting Romily reading to you. Do you remember the two of us once discussing who would make the better dining companion?' she went on. 'Hercule Poirot, Lord Peter Wimsey or Roderick Alleyn? And we both said Roderick because he would be so quietly attentive to one's needs, whereas Wimsey would be a little too full of himself, and Poirot irritatingly pedantic, questioning the precise way the food was cooked.' She forced a small laugh, trying hard to keep her voice light and upbeat.

Edmund, along with the rest of the nursing staff, had told the family that they should talk to Hope as normally as possible. 'There's every chance she can hear what you say,' Edmund had explained, 'so keep the chatter going at all times.'

To begin with Evelyn had felt self-conscious talking to Hope this way, but it gradually became perfectly natural. She talked to her about work, about the children and how it would soon

264

be Christmas and that before too long Hope would be back with them, right as rain.

'Keep what you say light and positive,' Edmund had further instructed. Which was not easy, given that Hope was neither of these things and conversation with her had always tended to be on the serious side. Hope had never been interested in the mundane, so why bore her with it now when she couldn't escape the grinding tedium of it?

Edmund had stressed that he didn't want his wife knowing that her condition had now been reported in the national press, following the story being plastered over the front page of the local paper. Many column inches had been devoted to the bestselling children's author who had been *'mown down by a callous hit and run driver'*. Local and Fleet Street hacks had tried to talk their way into the hospital to get the inside story, but thanks to the smog, that was suddenly of more interest and now dominated the newspapers.

Sack-loads of letters and cards written by children from all around the world, wishing their favourite author a speedy recovery, had been delivered to Fairview. Evelyn had read just a handful of them with Edmund and had been reduced to tears. Hope was adored by her young fans and for the first time, Evelyn pondered what that pressure must have been like for a woman who was essentially so private and undemonstrative.

Romily had now closed the book she had been reading from and put it away in the locker. She then shut the door of the small room. 'I think it's time we put our heads together,' she said, coming back to her chair.

Evelyn looked at her. 'What do you mean?'

'I mean we have to turn detective and root out who has been sending the anonymous letters you've received. Florence has also been sent two.'

'Florence? But what could anyone accuse her or Billy of? A more blameless couple never walked this earth.'

'I don't think the letters are about blame, they're a means merely to cause trouble.'

Evelyn wanted to believe Romily was right, but she wasn't so sure. 'So that makes three of us who have received letters,' she said.

'Yes,' Romily responded with a small nod. 'There may be others, all of whom have kept quiet, just as you, Hope and Florence did. I think the person who sent the letters was perhaps banking on that. The letter we know Hope received was so obviously sent to undermine her confidence and make her suspect that Edmund was being unfaithful to her.'

'My brother would never cheat on Hope!'

'That's as maybe, but I think we should pool resources and see if that gets us anywhere.'

'By that, do you mean you want to know *exactly* what my letters accuse me of?'

'Only if you want to tell me. It might help us pin down the culprit.'

Before Evelyn could answer, the door opened and two nurses came in. Leaving them to tend to Hope, Evelyn beckoned Romily to continue the conversation in the corridor. If Hope could hear what was being said around her, Evelyn didn't want her to hear what she was going to tell Romily.

Alone in the corridor, her voice low, she said, 'The accusation in both letters I've received is that Kit isn't Pip and Em's father.'

Not missing a beat, Romily said, 'And is there any reason why somebody might think that?'

Evelyn steeled herself. 'There was a man where I worked during the war ... he and I ... well, it was a terrible mistake. A one-off moment of madness. You know him. Max Blythe-Jones.'

Again without missing a beat, Romily said, 'And I believe he came to your party when I was in Palm Springs?'

Evelyn nodded. 'Kit tracked him down, along with a group of other people I hadn't seen in years. He did it to surprise me.'

'And you'd had no contact with Max in the intervening years?'

'None at all. When I left the Park, that was an end to things with Max. Then when I saw him at the party after all this time, and when I had just received the first of the letters, I leapt to the conclusion that it was him who'd sent it. It was too much of a coincidence. I even challenged him, but he was adamant it wasn't him. And now that I know about Hope and Florence, I'm certain he was speaking the truth.'

'I think you're right.'

'Does Florence have any idea who it might be?'

'Her mother-in-law is her most likely candidate.'

Evelyn frowned. 'That would make sense if Florence was the only recipient of a letter, but I can't see a reason for Ruby Minton wanting to target me, it's not as if we've ever crossed swords.'

'I agree.'

Evelyn smiled ruefully. 'We need Roderick Alleyn, or better still, your Sister Grace to help us find the culprit.'

Romily smiled too. 'Life is seldom as straightforward or as tidy as it is in a crime novel.'

Yes, thought Evelyn, thinking back to the mess she had made of her time at Bletchley Park.

Chapter Fifty-One

Wayside Cottage, Buckinghamshire
September 1942
Evelyn

It was the discovery that Tally my housemate was a spy that led to my moral disgrace.

After a night-time shift at the Park, I cycled home in the early morning sunlight to our cottage and found that it had been burgled. There was no sign of Tally, but every room had been ransacked; the cupboards in the kitchen had been emptied and the paucity of furniture in the sitting room had been thoroughly upended.

Upstairs, my small collection of books had been swept from the shelf, the mattress had been removed from the bed, and the contents of the wardrobe, dressing table and chest of drawers lay strewn about the place. It was when I saw my framed photograph of Kit on the floor, the glass smashed and the back of the frame prised off, that I suspected that this was not a straightforward burglary: somebody had been searching for something specific.

I stared at the mess in bewilderment and dismay. Who could have done this? And why? Worried that whoever had been here might not have found what they were looking for and return, I cycled to the nearest telephone box, some two miles away. I rang Max's number at the house in Bletchley where he lodged. It was an age before anybody answered. His landlady informed me that Mr Blythe-Jones was asleep, but after I insisted it was imperative I spoke to him, that it was an emergency, she reluctantly went to knock on his door.

'Who the devil wants me?' he demanded when he picked up the receiver.

'It's me,' I said, and hurriedly explained the situation.

'Why haven't you called the police?' he asked when he arrived within thirty minutes on his Norton motorbike.

'Because I don't think it's an ordinary burglary. See for yourself,' I added.

'You're right,' he said when he'd looked around. 'What do you know about your housemate?'

He had clearly leapt to the conclusion I had. 'If I'm honest,' I said, 'I don't really know that much about her.'

It seemed so implausible, given that we shared a house, but it was true. I knew her name and her age and that in her free time she loved to be in the garden, but that was about it.

'What does she do at the Park?' Max asked.

'I don't know. We never talk about work, we're not supposed to. You know that as well as I do.'

'But you must have some idea, surely?'

'I honestly couldn't tell you.'

'Has she ever asked you about your work? Or behaved in a manner you thought odd?'

I shook my head. But then I recalled her recently joking about her duties at the Park, how none of her friends would ever guess that she had access to such important information regarding the war effort. Another time I had found her looking through my books. 'I hope you don't mind, but I'm desperate for something to read,' she'd said, a copy of *Murder at Midnight* in her hands. At the time I hadn't thought anything of it, but now I couldn't help but think she had been snooping. But what had she thought she would find in my bedroom?

I had just shared this with Max when there was a loud hammering at the front door.

'I suspect you're about to be interrogated,' he said.

He was right. When I opened the front door, two sombre-faced men dressed in suits stared back at me. Without introducing themselves, they barged their way into the narrow hallway, then into the sitting room. 'Are you Miss Evelyn Flowerday?' one of them asked.

'Yes,' I said nervously, glad that Max was standing next to me.

'We'd like to ask you a few questions about the woman with whom you share this house.'

'Before Miss Flowerday answers any questions you have,' Max said, 'I think it a reasonable request that you show us some identification.'

'And who would you be, sir?'

'I asked first,' he said firmly.

It was then, as I looked at the two men, and the window behind them, that something caught my eye in the back garden. At first I thought it was one of Tally's dresses drying on the washing line. But then I realised what it really was and let out an ungodly scream. Her neck in a noose, Tally was hanging from a branch of the apple tree.

What happened then, and to this day, was a nightmarish blur. After being taken to London, I was thoroughly interrogated – just as Max had predicted – and on being found to be innocent of any crime, it transpired that unwittingly I had been sharing a house with a spy who had been passing information on to the Germans. In the garden, and hidden in a tin box behind a patch of nettles and brambles, was evidence of ciphers which she had somehow stolen from the Park. A small case containing a radio device was found in an old potato sack in the greenhouse. It had been well hidden beneath an assortment of garden tools and pots.

More disturbing than any of this was that the official line on Tally's death was that she had killed herself out of remorse for betraying her country. But how could it have been suicide? I asked, when there was nothing beneath her on which she could have climbed to attach the noose to the branch. I was told that she had simply climbed the tree and I was not to ask any more questions; the matter was closed. I had no way of knowing whether it was MI5 or MI6 who had interrogated me, but I was under no illusion that whatever was going on was deadly serious. As to who had killed Tally, I would never know.

When I was released from London and allowed to resume my duties back at the Park, Max insisted that he stayed with me at the cottage. I knew it was a mistake, but frankly I was so unnerved by the whole episode, and a little fearful that whoever had murdered Tally might return, I allowed myself to believe that no harm would come of Max sleeping in what had been Tally's room.

How naïve I was!

That night, unable to sleep – the slightest noise putting me into a terrible state of alarm – I lay in the dark staring up at the ceiling. Just a few feet away from me, the other side of the wall, was Max. I tried not to imagine what it might feel like to have his reassuring presence with me on this side of the wall. But the more I tried not to think of him, the stronger the urge became to lie within his embrace, to feel what all those other girls had experienced with him.

Don't be a fool, I told myself. Think of Kit.

But Kit was as far from my thoughts as he could be. For once in my life I wanted to be rash, to forget about the sensible woman everybody took me to be. If I died tomorrow – found hanging from the branch of a tree just like Tally – what did it matter how rational and loyal I'd been?

A faint knock at the door made me start.

'It's me, Max. Can I come in?'

God knows I should have said no, but I didn't. At my affirmative reply, he entered the room. 'I can't sleep,' he murmured in the shadowy darkness.

'Me neither,' I replied.

'I can't stop thinking about you,' he said, approaching my bed. 'I keep thinking how I'd feel if anything happened to you.'

'How would you feel?' I asked. Under any other circumstances, I would have deemed the remark wholly coquettish and beneath me, but holding my breath, I waited for his reply.

By the side of my bed now, he got down on his knees. 'I'd be devastated,' he said.

'Is that what you say to all the women you've slept with?'

'Must you always regard me so sceptically, Evelyn? Why not trust me, just once?'

'Only once?' I asked, gripped with the desire to slip my hands around his shoulders and pull him into bed with me.

Leaning in close, he ran a finger along the length of my jaw, then brushed it against my lips. Any restraint that had kept my longing for him in check now deserted me, and I raised myself up so that my mouth touched his. I kissed him in a way I had never kissed Kit, driven by a passion that left Max in no doubt that I wanted him to make love to me.

He must have known that he was my first lover, and he took me to him with a tenderness I would never have expected. Afterwards, and without a trace of shame, I slept in his arms. We both woke some hours later, and with still no shame in me, we made love again, this time he was less cautious.

We slept once more, and after the deepest of sleeps, I woke to the sound of birds singing. The innocence of that dawn chorus made me think of Kit and suddenly, as Max stirred beside me in the narrow bed, shame now made itself known.

Later that day, and mortified at what I had done, I sought out the powers that be at the Park and claimed ill-health as a result of Tally's death. Rarely was such a request granted, there was a war on, after all, but I must have caught the administrative officer in charge in a sympathetic mood. My tearful entreaty was convincing enough for me to be granted a fortnight's leave.

I left no word of explanation for Max, but packed my case and fled to Bletchley station to catch the first available train to Suffolk.

As luck would have it, Kit was home on leave and, taking me by surprise, he made it clear that he felt we had waited long enough to commit ourselves to each other. I'll never know what made him decide this, but that night we made love in my old childhood bed at Meadow Lodge. (Thank God my mother was bedridden and her hearing had deteriorated to the extent it had!)

It was the first time I had seen him entirely unclothed and the sight of his badly scarred body filled me with a fiercely protective love for him. Full of remorse for my betrayal of him, I swore to myself there and then that I would be the best wife I could to this man I had known nearly all my life. I would never do anything to hurt him.

We were married within the month, which brought an end to my work at Bletchley Park, and my association with Max Blythe-Jones. I never saw or heard from him again.

Not until the night of the party twenty years later.

Chapter Fifty-Two

Chelstead Cottage Hospital, Chelstead
December 1962
Hope

No matter how hard Hope tried to open her mouth to speak, not a muscle moved. In her head she was screaming at the top of her voice that she knew who was sending the anonymous letters – it was Arthur, she was sure! But not a word would come out. She was as inert as stone.

She had overheard enough from the whispered comments amongst the medical staff to know that the worst of her injuries was a bleed on the brain, and that while they knew her brain was showing signs of activity, it was if the wires had disconnected and it could no longer instruct her body to move.

She constantly willed her limbs to do her bidding; just an inch would be enough, or a flicker of an eyelid, but her body refused point blank to obey her. Sometimes she felt her body was deliberately mocking her, teasing her into believing she had succeeded in regaining mastery of it and that her hand or foot had moved.

Listening to Romily and Evelyn she had been so sure that she had managed to twitch her fingers in response to what they were saying, but when they hadn't reacted, she was forced to accept that any movement she believed she was making was nothing more than wishful thinking.

There had been a moment when she had been lying in that

ditch with only the wind and rain for company, that she had been certain she was about to meet her maker. With the acceptance that her life was over, she had felt herself slipping away, as though falling over the edge of a cliff. Down and down she fell. Weightless. Not a terrified scream-filled hurtle towards the end, but a slow descent, like a piece of delicate blossom caught on a spring breeze floating gracefully to the soft pillowy ground.

With that sensation came the relief that no more would she have to carry the weight of the world on her shoulders. No more would she have the worry of Edmund no longer loving her. Of him loving another. Of him leaving her. *She* was leaving him. He would now be free to be with whomever he wanted. This, like the car with which she had surprised him, was her gift to Edmund. Her final gift.

In the endlessly long days she had been lying here in a state of purgatory – with a tube down her throat to help her breathe and a drip feeding God knows what into her – her mood had swung from one end of the pendulum to the other. To live or not to live. As if she had any choice in it!

Some days when Edmund was with her, when her mood was so low and she saw this permanent vegetative state as her future, she willed him to do the decent thing and put a pillow over her face. 'Just do it!' she longed to say. 'Put us both out of our misery.'

Other times when he was with her and holding her hand, telling her how everyone was rooting for her to get better, she pictured his face. His caring compassionate face. And it made her want to weep and beg him to put his arms around her. He repeatedly apologised for arguing with her, that he wished he could turn back time and make everything right again.

'I'm sorry I've been such a poor husband to you,' he'd said, 'that I don't seem able to make you happy in the way I once did.'

She could have wept when he told her he loved her. But was that remorse in his voice she could hear? Remorse for also loving another? Evelyn had just said her brother would never have an affair behind Hope's back. Was she right?

The silence in the room told her that she was now alone. The nurses had finished doing whatever they came to do and had gone. Where were Romily and Evelyn? Why hadn't they returned? She wanted to hear more of what they had to say about the anonymous letters. She wanted somehow to point them towards Arthur. He was just the sort of person who would enjoy stirring up trouble for the sheer hell of it.

Tormenting people was what he did best. He had done it as a child when he'd pulled the wings off butterflies. Or the time one hot summer's day during the school holidays when he trapped a field mouse under a jam jar and put it in the sun so he could watch the animal slowly die.

Beyond the quiet confines of her room, Hope could hear the sound of a trolley being pushed along the corridor. It was the trolley with the irritating wheel that needed oiling. Was she the only one who could hear it squeak, the only one to be annoyed by it?

On the whole the nursing staff were competent and did their job well. She wished though they wouldn't prattle on so much, telling her how much they'd enjoyed her books when growing up. They were familiar with Edmund in his capacity as a doctor, of course, and fussed over him whenever he visited, bringing him tea and shortbread.

It was all a far cry from her many dealings with the hospital in the past. For years she had helped with much-needed fund raising and every Christmas she would attend the children's parties to give out free copies of her books. For the children too sick to get out of bed, she would go to them with a book and a pat on the head. What she never told anyone, not even

Edmund, was that immediately afterwards she would have to wash her hands thoroughly, then rush home to change out of her clothes. She had a horror of germs, of catching something from a sick child which would prevent her from working.

Edmund had read out a letter from her agent, as well as several cards from her various publishers. They all wished her well. Flowers had been sent, too. She hadn't been able to see them, but their cloying perfume had been too much. It was a relief when they died and were removed from her room.

Thinking of her agent and her publishers, she supposed they were already totting up the loss of future sales from her. The golden goose that stopped laying. Was somebody also writing her obituary?

She remembered reading her father's obituary in *The Times* and the *Telegraph*. It had made impressive reading, but hardly reflected the man she had known. Would that be true of her? Probably. After all, the face she showed to the world as the renowned children's author was not the real Hope.

Lying here she'd had a lot of time to reflect on her life. It wasn't her achievements she dwelt on, but her failings. She had failed as a wife and as a mother to Annelise.

Annelise visited her every day. Sometimes she barely spoke; she just sat very still and held Hope's hand. The silence was oddly comforting. It was a rare moment of calm when Hope didn't have to listen, or think of something else to block out the flow of banal chatter.

Once more she heard the sound of the trolley with the squeaking wheel passing the door to her room. This time it was accompanied by the laughter of a couple of nurses.

She suddenly thought of something. Kit knew about the first letter she had received! She had told him about it the night of the party at Meadow Lodge. How had she forgotten that? Romily and Evelyn believed Hope had received only the one letter, but she'd had two. But then what did it matter how many letters she had been sent? Or that she'd told Kit and sworn him to secrecy?

Just as her head began to ache with the effort of trying to make sense of it all, she heard the door open followed by the sound of someone coming into the room. Listening hard, she could make out the noise of a coat being taken off. At the same time the distinctive sharp smell of a cold winter's day mixed with a slightly sulphurous odour permeated the sterile air of the room. The same smell had met her nostrils when Romily and Evelyn arrived.

'Hello Mums, it's me, Annelise.'

In her head, and listening to Annelise make herself comfortable in the chair to her right, she said hello back to her. In her head she also began to say how sorry she was for her every act of neglect and disapproval. For working when she should have been—

Mid thought, she stopped listing all the things for which she needed to apologise, and concentrated on what Annelise was saying. But she couldn't believe what she was hearing. Not from Annelise. *No!*

Chapter Fifty-Three

Melstead Hall, Melstead St Mary
December 1962
Julia

'Going out, Mrs Devereux?'

Julia nearly jumped out of her skin. She felt her cheeks flush and a quake of fear gripped at her insides. 'Yes, Miss Casey,' she said with as much authority as she could summon.

'Are you sure that's wise, madam?'

Grasping the handles of her handbag while standing in the large hallway, a couple of yards from the front door, Julia said, 'What do you mean?'

'I'm surprised to see you up and dressed, madam, that's all, let alone venturing out into the fog. It might not be good for you, given how unwell you've been of late. And you know how Mr Devereux worries about you.'

The quaking to Julia's insides intensified. But she was determined to go out. 'With Christmas around the corner,' she said, trying to stick to the script she had written for herself, 'I want to buy some Christmas cards.'

'But the car, madam. It's in London with Mr Devereux.'

'I'm quite capable of walking. It will do me good. Is that all, Miss Casey?' She forced a note of dismissal to her tone and the other woman, her face perpetually inscrutable, blinked, then looked steadily back at her with her cold blue eyes. Never before had Julia challenged her and she could see that it had taken the housekeeper off guard. Doubtless there would be consequences. *Toe the line or face the consequences.* That was another instruction from her father's rule book.

Shutting the front door after her, she set off down the driveway in the damp cold at a brisk pace. Not once did she turn around and look back.

The fog had finally begun to lift. When Julia had opened the curtains in her bedroom this morning and seen that for the first time in days the end of the driveway was clearly visible, she had made up her mind that she would dress and walk into the village. And nothing would stop her.

Until this morning, she could not have contemplated the journey. She blamed the tonic and the sleeping pills the doctor from London had prescribed her. 'He's the best in Harley Street,' Arthur had said when she had rung him one evening to say she needed him to come home, that she was sick with worry.

'For goodness sake, whatever are you babbling on about?' he'd demanded.

'It's Hope. Surely you've read about her in the newspapers. She's still in a coma. Arthur, we have to say something'

'And what do you suggest we say?'

'The truth! I can't go on like this. I can't sleep and I can't eat. My nerves are shot to pieces. What if she dies?'

'For God's sake, pull yourself together, Julia! You don't know what you're saying. You're overwrought and making yourself ill.'

'But the car, Arthur.'

'What about the car?'

'It must have been damaged in the accident. What if—'

'Now listen to me very carefully. What little damage the deer made, the car has been repaired while I've been here in London. And do I have to remind you that if you say anything contrary to the fact that I hit a deer, you know what will happen, don't

280

you? Prison. Not for me, but for *you*. Is that what you want? Is it what you want for Charles?'

She had been crying by this stage of the conversation and only stopped when Arthur's tone became more conciliatory. 'Come on old thing,' he said soothingly. 'Don't cry, that won't help anyone. Now I want you to promise me something. I want you to see this excellent nerve doctor I know. I'll send him up to you and he'll give you a thorough once over. But you must promise you'll take what he prescribes you. Will you do that for me?'

'I'd sooner you came home,' she'd said.

'I'll be home very soon. I have business matters here to deal with. Now will you promise you'll do as Dr Monk says? After all, you want to be well for when Charles comes home for the Christmas holiday, don't you?'

'Why go to all the bother of sending a doctor from London to see me?' she'd then asked. 'I'll see Dr Flowerday.'

'I want the best for you, Julia, not some country quack. Why bother Edmund when he's so worried about Hope right now?'

Julia had promised Arthur she would do exactly as he said. He was probably right; her nerves had got the better of her. And if this specialist from London was able to ensure she slept at night, that the nightmares of Arthur's car hitting his sister would stop, she would take whatever medicine she was offered.

Following Dr Monk's visit, and after several days of taking the medicine he prescribed, Julia was convinced it disagreed with her. As a former nurse she knew that not all drugs suited all patients, and while it was true that she slept at night – she was knocked out cold minutes after swallowing the tablets – the nightmares continued. In fact, they were worse, and during the day she felt sluggish, as though her body was weighted with concrete. She also had the sensation of viewing everything through the wrong end of a telescope. Her sense of balance was affected, too and had kept her in bed. It was most disconcerting.

As convinced as she was that the tonic and tablets disagreed with her, she began to wonder if Miss Casey might be adding something to the dishes of food she put before her and which she insisted Julia ate. But was that paranoia making her suspect Miss Casey was poisoning her?

That was the trouble with paranoia, one could never tell what was really happening and what was going on inside one's head. One thing she grew certain of was that she had to go out, if only to the village. Cooped up as she was, she was beginning to feel as mad as Rochester's lunatic wife in the attic. And to go out, she had to break the promise she had made to Arthur. So she pretended to take the prescribed medication, but secretly poured the twice-daily dose of tonic down the plughole of the basin in her bathroom, and crushed the tablets so they too could be washed away.

Since then Julia's head had cleared and the need to do what she considered the right thing became ever more vital to her. She wanted to visit Hope in hospital. What must the rest of the family be thinking that neither Arthur nor she had gone to see his sister?

While she had been out of her mind with worry, she had received another anonymous letter.

AFTER SHAMING YOUR HUSBAND YOU WON'T
BE MRS ARTHUR DEVEREUX FOR MUCH LONGER!

She supposed it was referring to her being drunk the night of the party at Meadow Lodge, but if she were honest, a spiteful village busybody was the least of her concerns right now.

With every step that took her further away from the Hall, Julia felt a mixture of emotion: pride that she had defied Miss Casey, and trepidation at what she planned to do. Her consternation wasn't helped by feeling lightheaded, together with the tiredness that was creeping into her legs. This was the most active she had been in days. She should have eaten some breakfast, but she hadn't wanted to risk eating anything Miss Casey brought to her. Not today.

In the centre of the village, she crossed the market square and went over to the bus stop. After checking the timetable, she saw that she had half an hour to wait. On the other side of the square, she spotted the Cobbles Tea Room. Or what used to be the Cobbles before new management took it over and renamed it the Bluebird Café.

A cup of tea and a scone would help pass the time. But she hesitated. Arthur had said she wasn't to frequent the establishment. 'Nothing but a parochial fleapit for the hoi polloi and gossiping old crones of Melstead St Mary,' he said of it.

Her stomach fluttering again with nerves that she was being so daring, she walked towards the tearoom and pushed open the door. It was invitingly warm inside and rather jolly with a prettily decorated Christmas tree in one corner, and paper chains strung up between the oak beams. It didn't look at all like a fleapit.

'A table for one, please,' she said when a waitress approached. Taking her seat, and picking up the menu, she was aware of people staring at her. Her head down as she looked at the menu, she wondered if the person who was sending her the anonymous letters was here.

'What'll it be, Mrs Devereux?'

Startled at the use of her name, Julia looked up to see an attractive young girl with a pencil poised over a pad of paper to take her order. It wasn't until the waitress returned some minutes later with a pot of tea and a toasted teacake as well as a mince pie – she really was ravenous – that Julia realised why the girl had known who she was. She used to work at the Hall but left unexpectedly and without a word of explanation. Julia had been disappointed because the girl had always been so polite to her. She racked her brains to remember her name. *Josie . . . Pam . . .* No, it was Pat, that was it!

'How are you, Pat?' she asked, pleased with herself for recalling the name.

'You remember me, then?' the girl replied.

'Of course I do. I was sorry you left.'

'No disrespect to you, but nothing would have made me stay a moment longer.'

Taken aback, Julia watched the girl walk away to serve another customer.

It was while she was buttering her toasted teacake that she heard giggling from behind the screen that separated her table from the kitchen area. When the giggling stopped, she heard a girl's voice. 'I'll tell you this for nothing, that Mr Devereux was like a bleeding octopus; he couldn't keep his disgusting hands off me.'

'Do you suppose his wife knows what he's like?'

'If she does, she's too much under his thumb to do anything about it.'

It was all lies! Julia wanted to shout. *Nothing but lies! Arthur wasn't like that!* She forced herself to stay calm. She must remember who she was. She was Mrs Arthur Devereux.

But maybe not for much longer . . .

She delved into her handbag for her purse, counted out the money to pay the bill, and tugging on her coat, she left.

Her heart racing, her breath short, she blindly crossed the cobbled square, just as the bus she had wanted to catch appeared. For a moment she hesitated, then suddenly guided by a force so strong it swept away any doubts, she boarded the bus and took a window seat at the front. It took her some minutes to compose herself – *to pull herself together*, as Arthur would say – and when she had, everything was frighteningly clear to her.

And just as clear was the decision that she must not lose her nerve when she reached the hospital.

She was used to hospitals and seeing very sick patients. She had nursed many to the end, right to their death rattle last breath. Yet for all her previous experience, Julia was shocked at the sight of her sister-in-law. But slowly removing her coat, she reverted to her old self, a trained nurse with a patient to take care of. She read the medical notes at the foot the bed, and then assessed the equipment that was helping to keep Hope alive. Satisfied that all was as it should be, she sat in the chair beside the bed.

Under normal circumstances Julia would never have dared to do what she did next, but she reached out for Hope's right hand – her left was partially hidden beneath the plaster cast that covered her forearm. Reassuring patients had been a forte of Julia's when she had been a nurse, that and listening. She had been taught to understand that these two things were a crucial part of being a good nurse. 'Hold their hand,' she was told, 'and listen to whatever it is they have to say. It's a great comfort to them.'

It was listening to Arthur when he'd been ill with pneumonia that had brought them together. He'd told her one day that he'd never before been treated with such kind compassion. 'You're a very special person,' he'd said, 'and I want to find a way to thank you for all that you've done for me.'

She had believed him. Every word. But now she didn't. Now she was about to betray him, despite the risk involved.

'Hope,' she said in a low voice, 'it's me, Julia. I should have come to see you sooner, but I didn't dare. You see, the thing is, I know who was driving the car that hit you. It was your brother, Arthur. He didn't mean to. It was an accident. But it was very wrong of him not to stop and help you.'

There, she'd said it. She had done her duty. Just not in the way her father or husband would have wanted.

Chapter Fifty-Four

Melstead St Mary, Suffolk
December 1962
Stanley

'I've been such a fool, Stanley.'

'Nobody, least of all me, would ever accuse you of being a fool,' said Stanley, trudging along next to Annelise.

'You'll think differently when you know the truth. You see, in common with all self-sufficient people when I did lose my self-control, I lost it comprehensively.'

It was difficult for Stanley to picture Annelise losing control and he said so.

A rueful smile flickered across her face, which until then had been intensely sad and pale, and with what anybody else would assume was worry for Hope. But for some days he'd felt Annelise had something else on her mind.

'And that's part of the problem,' she said. 'Perhaps deep down I had been longing to do just that; to defy expectations of me and rebel. To kick over the traces.' She came to a stop and stared out across the valley.

They had been walking across the fields at the back of Fairview and were now on the crest of the rise looking down towards the village, which was just discernible through the thinning fog. Scampering on ahead, Tucker was on the trail of something, probably a rabbit. It was Sunday morning and in the distance the bells were being rung, calling the faithful to church. Regular worship was an aspect of village life that had passed Stanley by. He never felt quite good enough – *clean enough* – to be there.

'There's something I want to tell you,' Annelise said.

'Sounds like you want to make a confession,' he said lightly, which belied how he felt. Filled with a sense of dread, he had the strongest sensation that he wasn't going to like what she was about to say.

But then the sense of dread had been with him since yesterday evening when he had driven her home from the hospital. He knew that she found visiting Hope upsetting, but last night she had been particularly upset. To cheer her up he had suggested they go for a drink, but with tears in her eyes, she had said she wouldn't be good company.

When Stanley had stopped the car in front of Fairview, she had sat very still, her hand resting on the door handle as if trying to decide something.

'I know Romily's invited us all for lunch tomorrow, but will you come for a walk with me in the morning?' she'd said finally. 'Fog or no fog, would ten o'clock be all right for you to meet me here?'

'I'll be here,' he'd said, hugging her goodnight. He'd driven home wondering what was wrong. Did she want to discuss how awkward she now felt around him, knowing what his true feelings for her were?

'I tried to tell you about Harry the night of the party at Meadow Lodge,' Annelise said now, her gaze fixed on some faraway point, 'but I'd only said a few words when you were suddenly ill.'

Harry . . .? 'Go on,' Stanley murmured, remembering how revoltingly ill he'd been, but he had no recall of anyone called Harry.

'I'm afraid I rather lost my head over him,' she continued.

'That's you rebelling, is it?' he quipped, forcing a levity to his voice he didn't feel.

'I thought he loved me,' she said, still staring into the distance. 'I thought . . . I thought everything he said was true, that his marriage really was on the rocks and he was planning to divorce his wife so he could be with me. But everything that came out of his mouth was a lie. I can see that now.'

'He's *married?*'

At last she turned to face Stanley. 'Have I shocked and disappointed you?'

He *was* shocked. He was hugely shocked that Annelise could be so credulous, but he tried to hide it. 'Of course not,' he lied. 'If we could choose who we fall in love with, and vice versa, life would be a lot easier.' And wasn't that the truth? he thought. 'Was it love at first sight?' he asked, despite the pain the question caused him.

She shook her head. 'No. But when it hit me, it was a *colpo di fulmine.*'

'Sorry?'

'It means I was hit by a thunderbolt. Which is nothing compared to what I feel I've been hit with now. Will you promise me something?' she asked. Her face was so earnest it hurt him.

'Anything.' He meant it, too. He would do anything for Annelise. He had always felt that way about her.

'You mustn't tell anyone what I'm about to share with you. Do you promise?'

'You have my word.'

'I'm pregnant.'

Seconds passed while Stanley floundered, trying to find the right words.

'Say something,' she said.

'Does he know?'

She shook her head. 'I've only just guessed at the truth myself.'

'You mean you don't know for sure?'

'I don't need a test to tell me what I already know. I've been feeling sick every morning since I arrived home.'

'But you might have a stomach virus, or— '

'No, Stanley, it's a baby growing inside my body that's causing me to have morning sickness. There's no point in pretending otherwise. I may have fooled myself into believing everything Harry told me, but I'm now level-headed enough to know that the folly of my actions has to be confronted.'

Listening to her calmly blaming herself for the predicament she found herself in filled Stanley with the need to get into his car and drive to Oxford to kill the man who had done this to her.

'What will you do?' he asked, when he trusted himself to speak as calmly as Annelise had.

'Will I keep the baby? Is that what you're asking?'

'Yes.'

She sighed. 'The thought of giving the baby up for adoption appals me, but if I keep the child, how would I be able to carry on with my work in Oxford? There's not a hope of St Gertrude's wanting to keep me on as an unmarried mother. My career would be over.'

Stanley took his hands out of his jacket pocket and wrapped them around Annelise's cold fingers. 'There's one very easy solution to the problem,' he said. 'Marry me. I'll help you raise the child. For all intents and purposes, it will be ours. Together. Nobody need ever know that it wasn't our child.'

Chapter Fifty-Five

St Mary's, Melstead St Mary
December 1962
Florence

Billy and his parents had always been members of the Salvation Army, and while Florence often attended the services with her husband, she didn't always. This particular Sunday morning she had fancied a change – and time away from her mother-in-law – and had come to St Mary's. If she had stayed at home, even on the pretext of writing Christmas cards and cooking lunch, Ruby would accuse her of being godless and bound for hell. Who wasn't in Ruby's eyes? Apart from Billy, that was.

The Reverend Allsop had now drawn his rather long-winded sermon to a close, and the organist started playing 'Thine Be the Glory'. With everyone rising to their feet, Florence glanced around at the congregation, wondering if it was one of them who was sending the anonymous letters. No one struck her as a likely candidate, but what did she expect the person to look like? Another thought then occurred to her. Who else here had received a letter? And was it only women who had been singled out?

When the hymn came to an end and they once again sat down to bow their heads in readiness for prayer, Florence spotted Julia Devereux amongst the worshippers. She was alone, which never happened. If she came at all, it was with her husband and invariably only for the special occasion services, such as Easter and Christmas.

When eventually the service was over and Florence was buttoning up her coat and pulling on her gloves, she joined the queue to get out of the church. While the vicar was engaged in conversation with a couple Florence only knew by sight and who had recently moved to the village, she found herself standing next to Julia.

'Good morning, Mrs Devereux,' Florence said politely.

The woman started violently and dropped one of her gloves, along with her prayer book. Florence picked them up for her.

'Thank you,' she said, giving Florence a puzzled look, as if trying to place her.

'Florence Minton,' she said helpfully. 'I work at Island House, and my Billy runs the bread shop.'

'Yes. Yes, of course.' Clutching her handbag to her, the woman looked a regular bundle of nerves and appeared desperate to get away from Florence, as though she might catch something from her.

'Ah, hello Mrs Devereux!' chimed the vicar, as they moved forward, 'what a pleasure to see you; it's good of you to join us this morning. Mr Devereux not with you?'

'He . . . he's in London. Business matters . . . he's always so busy.'

'I hope he's not suffered any ill-effects from the smog while there. It was bad enough what drifted our way here in dear old Melstead St Mary. We must give thanks that it's now dissipated. Will you and Mr Devereux be here for Christmas? And your young son, Charles?'

Whatever her answer was, Florence didn't hear the woman as she seemed intent on escaping as quickly as possible. Florence followed soon after and caught up with her on the gravel pathway where she was blowing her nose. But just as Florence was about to pass by, she realised Julia was crying. She slowed her step.

'Everything all right, Mrs Devereux?'

Again Julia started. The woman was as nervous as a rabbit! 'I'm . . . fine,' she stuttered, fumbling with the handkerchief. 'It's the cold, it always gets in my eyes like this.'

Florence wasn't convinced, but it wasn't her place to press the point. Even so, she couldn't just walk away. The woman looked so distressed. To Florence's knowledge she had no friends in the village. Romily had often invited Julia to join them at Island House for lunch or dinner when Arthur was away, as he often was, but the invitations were always declined.

'If there's anything you need, Mrs Devereux,' Florence said, 'you only have to ask.'

The comment drew a stifled sob from her, much like the sound Florence had heard when the vicar had announced they should pray for Hope.

'Excuse me,' Julia muttered, 'I need to get home before—' her words ground to a halt as she pressed the handkerchief against her mouth.

Her misery was horrible to see. 'Before what?' Florence said gently. Before Julia broke down completely? Before that unpleasant housekeeper could look down her snooty nose at Julia?

In the last twelve months since Miss Casey had started working at the Hall, she had gained herself a reputation for being rude and stand-offish. Nobody in the village had warmed to her.

But without answering Florence, Julia wheeled away sharply and set off down the road. Florence watched her go. She couldn't help but feel sorry for her going back to that great mausoleum of a house. It must be a lonely life there for her.

Chapter Fifty-Six

Island House, Melstead St Mary
December 1962
Romily

Conscious that Edmund was at the end of his tether worrying about Hope, Romily had invited him and Annelise for Sunday lunch, along with Kit and Evelyn, and Stanley. Had Pip and Em not been away in Lincolnshire for a house party to celebrate a friend's birthday, the invitation would have included them too.

The meal of roast pork now served, and with plates and glasses filled, the talk around the table turned to the ever-reliable topic – when the mood was awkward – of the weather.

'They say it's going to become a lot colder,' said Evelyn.

'I read in the newspaper it's going to snow,' agreed Kit.

'I read that too,' remarked Romily.

'A white Christmas is on the cards,' said Stanley.

The stilted conversation moved on to snatches of village gossip, but it was desperately forced and through it all Edmund remained tight-lipped, his expression impassive. But was it any wonder when there was still no improvement in Hope's condition and optimism was fast running out? Annelise was also quieter than usual, and to Romily's eye, the girl didn't look well. There were dark shadows beneath her eyes which emphasised just how pale she was.

'Evelyn and I saw Julia walking home on our way here,' said Kit, when the conversation ran dry and a jarring silence had fallen on them. 'I stopped the car to say hello, but she behaved most oddly.'

'It was quite extraordinary,' Evelyn said, perhaps glad of something to say, 'but she as good as ignored us. Just carried on walking. Almost at a run.'

'I know we've always had our difficulties with Arthur,' Kit said, 'but I had hoped we were on better terms with Julia, and young Charles too.'

'Do you suppose she's all right?' asked Romily. 'I'd heard that Arthur was away in London and I telephoned this morning to invite her to join us for lunch today.'

'What did she say?' asked Kit.

'She didn't say anything. Miss Casey answered the telephone and told me Mrs Devereux had left instructions not to be disturbed.'

'Well,' said Kit, 'she was most assuredly out and about this morning.'

Romily made a mental note to contact Julia again. Since her return from America she had heard a number of unpleasant rumours flying around the village about the way Arthur treated his wife, but what with one thing and another, she hadn't found the time to find out if there was any truth in the stories.

'Pip and Em have expressed a wish to see Hope when they're back from Stamford, Edmund, would that be okay with you?' asked Evelyn.

'I'll have to check with the hospital,' her brother said. 'Some days it's like Piccadilly Circus there with the number of visitors coming and going.'

'If you'd rather they didn't see her,' said Evelyn softly, 'I'm sure they'd understand.'

'Well, they'd understand a darned sight more than I do, in that case!' Edmund's voice was unexpectedly loud and caused everyone to stare at him.

'I'm sorry,' he said, 'it's just that I can't make sense of what's happened to Hope.'

'We none of us can,' said Romily gently.

'The worst of it is, the last words Hope and I spoke were in the heat of a row. I'd give anything to take back those words. Anything.'

'What did you argue about?' asked Evelyn.

Edmund put down his knife and fork. 'That's the devil of it; I don't know exactly. I was trying to provoke some sense out of Hope, because for weeks it was as if she was accusing me of something, but she wouldn't come right out and say what it was.'

'Did you think she was depressed again?' This was from Annelise.

Edmund puffed out his cheeks with a long exhalation of breath. 'Yes and no. I can't put my finger on it, but I just felt this was different. I felt that I was the cause of her unhappiness, that I couldn't do anything right for her.'

Romily exchanged a look with Evelyn. They had agreed not to say anything to Edmund about the anonymous letters until they knew more, and also because they didn't want to burden him with anything else. Evelyn had her own reason for keeping quiet; she didn't want Kit to know about the letters she had received.

'But it's obvious, isn't it, it was the letter Hope was sent that was making her feel so unhappy?'

Both Romily and Evelyn looked at Stanley in alarm.

He stared back at them and then, as if realising his blunder, that he wasn't supposed to mention any letters, he frowned and reached for his glass of wine. But the harm was done.

'What letter?' demanded Edmund.

After another exchange of anxious glances with Evelyn, and an imperceptible nod from her, Romily outlined what they knew. But without being too specific in Evelyn's case.

'And now you know as much as we do,' she said when she came to the end of her explanation. 'That Hope, Florence and Evelyn have all been on the receiving end of these spiteful letters. They may well not be the only ones.'

'This is monstrous!' exclaimed Edmund, banging his fist on the table. 'Of course I haven't been having an affair! Oh my God, that Hope had been taunted into believing I had! No wonder she was so cross with me. I just wish she'd said something.'

Seeing his distress, Annelise reached over to squeeze his hand. 'It explains so much,' she said softly. Then to Stanley, she said, 'Why didn't you tell me?'

'Don't be cross with Stanley,' Romily said before he had a chance to reply. 'We agreed to keep it to ourselves until we'd discovered who the perpetrator was.'

'What did your letters say, Evelyn?' asked Kit. There was no mistaking the concern in his voice, or face.

'Just some vindictive tosh,' Evelyn said airily. 'Nothing that made any sense.'

'I haven't been accused of being unfaithful, have I?' he asked.

'No,' she said. 'Nothing like that.'

'What then?'

'Oh, that I was a harlot, the usual stuff that a person who enjoys sending poison pen letters would say of a woman they don't like.'

Kit was aghast. 'Why didn't you tell me?'

'Because I didn't want to give the silly letters any credence. Or upset you. And you are now, aren't you?'

'As would any husband be upset when his wife is being attacked like this. It's not on. It's . . .' He faltered and then slapped a hand to his forehead. 'Oh my God,' he cried, 'I've just remembered something!'

'What?' asked Evelyn.

'She told me . . . well, it was in confidence. Hope made me promise I wouldn't say anything and so I didn't. It was the night of our party. She told me she'd received a poison pen letter, but I'm afraid I didn't take it seriously.'

'Why on earth not?' demanded Edmund.

'I'm sorry, Edmund, but I thought it was no more than some silly old biddy in the village up to mischief. I advised Hope to ignore it.'

'And look where that's got us. You should have told me!'

'Edmund, that's not fair,' intervened Evelyn. 'If Hope swore Kit to secrecy, what else was he to do?'

As the voices around the table became more heated, Romily noticed that Annelise had barely touched what was on her plate. 'Are you all right, Annelise?' she asked quietly. 'Can I fetch you something else to eat if the pork isn't to your liking?'

'I'm sorry,' the girl murmured, her pallor now the colour of putty, 'but I'm not very hungry. It must be the shock of hearing about these awful letters.'

'That's my fault,' said Stanley. 'I shouldn't have said anything.'

'I disagree,' retorted Edmund, turning towards him, his tone uncharacteristically harsh. 'You should have spoken up before. So should Kit. Maybe then Hope and I wouldn't have had that dreadful row and she wouldn't have gone out for a walk. And then,' he went on, his voice rising, 'she wouldn't have been hit by some bloody reckless driver and now be fighting for her—' He broke off as Annelise suddenly pushed back her chair and stood up.

'Please excuse me,' she murmured before bolting from the room.

Watching her go, Romily was visited by the strongest sense of déjà vu. In a flash she was transported back in time to a day more than twenty years ago when a similar scene had taken place in this very dining room. The memory, along with another that was much more painful, propelled her to her feet.

'If you'll excuse me, I'll go and see if Annelise needs anything,' she said, gesturing to Edmund that he should leave this to her. 'The dear girl is obviously upset.'

Chapter Fifty-Seven

Island House, Melstead St Mary
December 1962
Annelise

Annelise made it upstairs to the nearest bathroom just in time. She flushed away the small amount she had just eaten, then went over to the basin to wash her face. Running the taps, she shuddered at the blotchy-faced woman staring back at her in the mirror. Who was she? Who was the idiotic person who had got herself into this mess?

Pregnant.

The word alone was enough to make her feel sick all over again.

There was a discreet knock at the door, followed by Romily's voice. 'Annelise, can I get you anything?'

'I'm fine,' she answered. 'I'll be down in a moment.' How long had Romily been standing there? Had she heard Annelise being sick? If she had, she would know that Annelise wasn't fine. But then anyone sitting around the table would have reached the same conclusion.

'Annelise, I know you probably want your privacy,' said Romily, 'but I'd like to help if I may.'

How could anyone help her? She was beyond help. She had brought this on herself and somehow, she would have to live with the consequences.

She did her best to tidy herself up, then opened the door,

all set to make light of feeling 'a little under the weather'. But seeing the look on Romily's face was too much and she had to bite on her lower lip to keep it from wobbling and betraying her.

'Come with me,' Romily said, taking her by the hand.

Annelise did as she said and allowed herself to be led along the carpeted landing to Romily's bedroom. Again at Romily's instruction, she sat on the window seat. 'I used to love sitting here listening to you reading to me when I was little,' she said absently.

'It seems like only yesterday,' Romily responded, sitting next to her.

'Life is so much easier when you're a child, isn't it?' Annelise said.

'It doesn't seem that way at the time, but it is. When's the baby due?'

'You never did beat about the bush, did you?'

'I've never seen the point. I'm assuming nobody knows about it?'

'Stanley knows.' Then before Annelise could stop them, tears filled her eyes. Romily magically produced a handkerchief. Annelise blew her nose and took a steadying breath. 'Nothing ever shocks you, does it?' she said.

'Very little.'

'How did you guess? What gave me away?'

'Let's just put it down to a sixth sense. When *is* the baby due?'

'July. I think.'

'And the father, Harry, does he know?'

Annelise shook her head. 'I only realised, or rather, I only accepted that I was pregnant when I came here and started feeling so queasy. I can't help but wonder if subconsciously I already knew that I was pregnant the morning I spoke to

Harry shortly before I caught the train to come home. I so badly wanted him to come with me and I suppose I was testing him. If he agreed to drop everything I would know then that he . . .'

'That he would what?' asked Romily when she hesitated.

Annelise sighed and dabbed at her eyes with the handkerchief. 'That he really did care for me. That there wasn't anything he wouldn't do for me.'

'But he failed the test?' suggested Romily. 'Is that what happened?'

'Yes, and in an instant the scales fell away from my eyes. I knew then that I didn't matter sufficiently for him to leave his wife and commit himself to me.'

'Would he seek a divorce if he knew you were pregnant?'

Such had been Annelise's complete turnaround in her feelings towards Harry, she had not asked herself this question. 'I've seen him for what he actually is,' she said, 'a liar and a cheat. I could never trust him. And I'm appalled with myself that I fell for him the way I did.'

'Did you love him very much?'

'I did, to the point of pain. But now I hate him. Truly I do. And I've never felt that way about anyone before.'

Romily put a hand on her shoulder and squeezed it gently. 'My advice is don't waste your energy on hating him. You have far more important things to think about.'

'Yes,' Annelise said with a heartfelt sigh. 'My life at Oxford is now over. St Gertrude's likes to be regarded as a progressive college, but a pregnant unmarried junior fellow would be considered a reformist step too far. It would be a wholly inappropriate example to the undergraduates.'

'Let's not get ahead of ourselves,' said Romily. 'It might be too soon for you to answer this, but do you plan to keep the baby?'

'Or give it up for adoption, you mean? Because the third option just isn't an option for me. I couldn't do that.'

'That's not what I'm asking you to do. But how do you feel about adoption?'

Fresh tears pricked at the backs of Annelise's eyes. Every time she thought she had decided what she would do, she lost her nerve. It was a constant battle between her brain and her heart. Her brain said she should give the child up, but her heart pleaded to keep it.

Her throat thick with emotion, she said, 'I don't know what to do, Romily, that's my honest answer. If I give the baby away, how could I ever live with myself having cast it aside? What would my parents have thought of me doing that? Giving away their grandchild? They gave me life, not once, but twice. First when I was conceived and born, and then again when they handed me over to Hope to bring me here to safety. If they hadn't done that, I would have been murdered just like them. And then there's what Hope is going to think of me. I told her yesterday. I . . . I felt I had to confess to her while I still could. Now I wish I hadn't. It was selfish of me. Why couldn't I have left well alone; if she's not going to make it I should have let her die thinking well of me. Or if she pulls through she's going to say I've carelessly thrown away every chance she's given me. She and Edmund will be so disappointed in what I've done.'

Romily tutted. 'Don't write Hope off too soon; she's a fighter, and if anyone is going to survive what she's gone through, it's her. And I implore you to stop worrying about what others may or may not think of you. This is your life, nobody else's.'

'That's easier said than done.'

'I've always had a golden rule,' Romily said, 'and that's never to give a damn what others think of me. You're a person in your own right, and you're allowed to make whatever decisions and mistakes you want to. What other people think of that is up to them. Those who truly love you will continue to love you no matter what.'

'This might sound odd, but part of me, the cowardly bit, was glad that Hope wasn't able to respond to my confession. But another part of me hoped that if she really could hear, like Edmund says she can, that she would be so shocked it would jolt her out of the coma.'

'That would certainly have been worth the pain of confessing,' Romily said with a faint smile. 'And who knows, it may yet happen. Maybe the thought of a grandchild might spur her to pull through. Wouldn't that be wonderful?'

'That's a nice idea, but you and I both know that Hope may devote her life to writing for children, but the actual human specimen is not entirely to her liking.'

'It's always possible she may regain consciousness with a new perspective on life.'

Somehow Annelise couldn't imagine that. But then she couldn't imagine so many things, like how she had managed to get herself into such a mess. Well, she knew the reason for her being pregnant, of course she did, but it was the sheer wanton carelessness of her behaviour that she couldn't comprehend. Loving Harry had made her reckless, something nobody in the family would have predicted of her.

'I mean no disrespect to my cousin,' she said, 'but if it had been Isabella who had got herself into this fix, nobody would have been very much surprised. Actresses lead such rackety lives, they would say, but academics are supposed to know better.'

'Goodness me,' Romily said with a shake of her head, 'you must feel so giddy up there on that pedestal.'

'What do you mean?' asked Annelise with a frown.

'I mean stop imagining that you're not as flawed as the next person. Nobody is immune from falling in love. Or getting something wrong.'

'I know one person who has put me on a pedestal,' she said quietly.

'Ah, that would be Stanley, wouldn't it?'

'Yes.'

'He's adored you all his life, but I wouldn't say he's put you on a pedestal.'

'Aren't the two one and the same?'

'Absolutely not. Adoring a person means you love them with all their flaws.'

'Do you know what he said this morning, while we were out walking and I told him about the baby? '

'Go on.'

Once more tears filled Annelise's eyes. 'He said I should marry him so that the baby would have a father and I could continue with my work. Can you believe he would say that?'

'I can. Stanley is a decent man who always believes in doing the right thing.'

'But this wouldn't be doing the right thing for him.'

'Why not? And I'd like to point out that Elijah did much the same in marrying Isabella's mother, Allegra. They had very little in common on the face of it, but they made each other happy.'

'That was different. Allegra loved Elijah.'

'There are many shades of love. What you felt for Harry in Oxford was one variation, and the feelings you have for Stanley, another. With the benefit of hindsight, which do you trust more? Passion for a man prepared to cheat on his wife and lie to you, or—'

'But Stanley is like a brother to me,' she interrupted.

'Could you regard him differently, in time?'

When Annelise didn't answer her, Romily continued. 'I've known you both since you were children and I've never known the two of you to fall out.'

'Is compatibility enough reason to marry?'

'Marriages work on many levels and for all sorts of reasons.'

'Maybe so, but I won't saddle Stanley this way. It wouldn't be right. I would be using him, and one day he would realise that and end up hating me. And I'd rather face my predicament alone than do that.'

Romily wagged a finger at her. 'One thing of which I can assure you, whatever you decide to do, you will not be facing the future alone. If you keep the baby, he or she will be a part of our family, and I for one shall do all I can to help.'

Annelise turned and hugged Romily. 'You've already helped by talking with me,' she said. 'But I want you to promise that you won't breathe a word to anyone else. I don't want Edmund knowing while he's worrying about Hope. It's a distraction he doesn't need.'

'I promise. And now, if you can face it, I think we should go back downstairs and join the others. If Edmund asks, you can pass this off as a tiresome monthly issue. That should keep the father and doctor within him from pressing for any more details.'

They stood up together and once more Annelise hugged Romily. 'Thank you,' she said, 'for being you. For always being so practical and reassuring. What would I ever do without you?'

'Oh, you'd manage very well. Now come on, best foot forward and let's put Stanley's mind at rest. Knowing what he knows, out of everyone he will be the most anxious about you.'

'Yes, I'm afraid he will.'

'Let him worry about you, Annelise. And in return for the promise I made you, I want you to promise me you won't shut him out. It would break his heart if you did.'

'All right. I promise.'

'Good girl.'

But when they were downstairs and were entering the dining room, and Annelise saw the troubled expression on Stanley's face – his obvious concern for her – she felt her own heart break a little.

Chapter Fifty-Eight

Island House, Melstead St Mary
December 1962
Romily

That night in bed Romily lay awake unable to sleep. It had become a regular occurrence since her return from America. Initially she blamed it on the time difference, and while it was true that may have contributed to her inability to sleep well, there was more to it than that. It grieved her immensely to admit it, if only to herself, but Red St Clair was at the heart of the problem.

She had hoped, perhaps somewhat arrogantly, that he might write. But there had been nothing from him. Did she really think she had made that big an impression on him? Heavens, the man would simply have moved on to the next woman! And why on earth shouldn't he?

The image of him that came to her, and far too frequently for her liking, was of him that night they'd gone out into the desert together. For the first time in his company she had begun to relax and enjoy being with him. It seemed a shame now that they had parted the way they had.

But what is done is done, she told herself firmly. No regrets. It was an echo of what she had whispered to Annelise when lunch was over and everybody was leaving, putting on their coats to brave the cold.

She had done her utmost to conceal her shock at Annelise's

news and had given the poor girl what she so badly needed: unconditional love and support.

People were always claiming that the times were changing, that so many of the old rules were being jettisoned. But times hadn't changed that much for women, not yet at any rate, not when the rules that applied to men did not apply to women. Why should Annelise have to lose her position at St Gertrude's, and very likely her reputation as a fine academic, while the man who had got her pregnant would carry on with his life as though nothing had happened?

For all her understanding of Annelise's plight, had Romily been too insistent in advocating so strongly that she should seriously consider marrying Stanley? An answer to a prayer was often no such thing. But what if, in this instance, it could be the perfect solution? Stanley would devote himself to making Annelise happy and in time, once the child was of a suitable age, Annelise, as a respectable married woman, would be able to pick up where she'd left off with her career.

But what of love? Stanley deserved to be truly loved, not just admired or cared for in the manner of a brother. Could, as time went on, Annelise's feelings for him develop into something deeper and more passionate?

In many ways Romily had to agree with Annelise when she'd said that if Isabella were to announce she was pregnant in the same circumstances, it would not come as so great a shock. Like mother, like daughter, some would take delight in saying, and very unfairly in Romily's opinion. It was never as simple as that; it was much more a case of *there but for the grace of God go I.*

Nobody knew the truth of those words more acutely than Romily. Had she remained alone with Annelise any longer, she may well have shared her most closely guarded secret with her.

Chapter Fifty-Nine

Tilbrook Hall, Norfolk
August 1944
Romily

I had been back at work for some weeks ferrying aircraft around the country when I was given a few days' leave. I took the opportunity to go home to Island House, and then drive over to Tilbrook Hall in Norfolk.

Since I had made a full recovery and been discharged from the medical care at Tilbrook Hall, Matteo and I had exchanged letters on a regular basis. The pages of his letters contained exquisite little drawings in the margins. Sometimes a whole page was devoted to a sketch of something that had caught his eye – a child flying a kite, a butterfly sunning itself on a wall, a squadron of bombers flying overhead, an old man leaning against a stile smoking a pipe. In comparison, I feared he found my letters rather ordinary. Although he said not. '*You cannot know the pleasure I experience,*' he wrote to me, '*when I see an envelope with your beautiful handwriting on it.*'

I had decided to keep my return visit to Tilbrook Hall a surprise. And having saved up valuable petrol coupons, I was enjoying the freedom of driving my beloved MG. With the top down, I drove at speed along the winding country lanes, the sun shining down from a clear blue sky, my heart soaring at the prospect of seeing Matteo again. Untying the scarf from around my head, I shook out my hair, letting it catch in the wind. I hadn't felt this carefree in a very long time. I began to sing at the top of my voice.

It was almost possible to believe there was no war raging, no bombs dropping, no rationing, no hardship, and no death. There was just this beautiful summer's day to enjoy, and the prospect of spending it with a man whom I had fallen in love with. In the five years since I had been widowed, I had been told repeatedly that I would one day find love again, and perhaps when I least expected it. I hadn't believed them. Or perhaps I hadn't wanted to because it would have seemed like a betrayal of my love for Jack. But Matteo had changed that.

Stuck behind a horse-drawn cart laden with milk churns, I was forced to drive the last mile at a snail's pace. I knew better than to roar past and unnerve the horse, so quelled my eagerness to reach my journey's end. When I entered the village of Tilbrook and parted company with the milk churns by taking the first turning to the left, I then pulled into the long driveway that led to the Hall. Part way along, and in the shade of a magnificent chestnut tree, I drew the car to a stop. Vanity prevailed, and I took out the necessary equipment from my handbag to make good the damage the drive had inflicted on my appearance. Hair combed and protected once again by the silk headscarf, perfume dabbed behind my ears, powder and lipstick reapplied. Make-up was in such short supply, all I had by way of lipstick was a measly stub of my favourite Chanel lip-colour. I used it only for special occasions, and today was just that.

Reporting in at the office, a delightful sun-filled south-facing room that had been the owners' informal sitting room, I was told that Matteo was out working in the woods.

Picnic basket in hand, I crossed the sun-drenched slope of lawn and followed the directions I'd been given. I found him stripped to the waist and wielding an axe. He was fully immersed in the task of chopping down a tree, and taking advantage of his absorption, I observed him for a few moments, shamelessly enjoying the sight of the muscles in his back and shoulders rippling in the dappled sunlight.

Some distance from Matteo, two lumberjills were tackling a felled tree with a cross-cut saw. It was one of the girls who saw me first.

'I'm guessing you haven't come here to help?' she said, weighing up the smart summer frock I had deliberated over first thing that morning. It contrasted forcibly with the uniform the two girls were both dressed in – sturdy dungarees with a beige short-sleeved shirt, and a green beret. The girl's tone was teasing, but not unfriendly. Her fellow member of the Women's Timber Corps turned to look, followed by Matteo, who promptly dropped the axe he was holding. He could not have looked more startled if the sky had parted and Moses had been standing before him, stone tablet at the ready.

'Why did you not tell me you were coming?' he asked, after the two lumberjills had given him permission to take a break, and not without a good deal of mischievous asides. 'Don't do anything I wouldn't do,' one of them called out to us as we walked away.

'I wanted to surprise you,' I said.

'You certainly did that,' he remarked, a shy smile covering his face. He had now smoothed back his dark hair and put on his shirt. I had to admit privately that I experienced a flicker of disappointment as he did up the buttons and snapped his braces into place over his shoulders. It also did not pass my notice that he was all fingers and thumbs and the buttons of his collarless shirt weren't correctly aligned.

'Is it a good surprise?' I asked, suddenly anxious that he

might be annoyed I had caught him in a state of partial undress. POW or not, he was Italian and Italian men were the vainest I had ever come across.

He stopped walking and turned to face me. 'Seeing you again is . . . is like the sun bursting through the clouds after many weeks of rain.'

'What a lovely thing to say,' I said.

He smiled and took the picnic basket from me. As we walked on, he slipped his free hand through mine and a spontaneous spark of electricity ran through me. It felt so real, I half expected my hair to stand on end.

'Where are we going?' I asked.

'To my favourite place. It is where I go when I want to think of you.'

'Do you think of me a lot?'

'More than I should say.'

'What if I said that ever since I left here, I haven't been able to get you out of my thoughts?'

'I would then have the courage to say that you are the first thing I think of when I wake in the morning, and the last when I go to sleep. And if I am lucky, I dream of you.'

Hand in hand, we walked on without another word, the air fragrant with haymaking, the hedgerows filled with the fluttering of birds and their sweet song. Overhead a lark swooped and dived in the crystalline sky; its distinctive call adding to the perfection of the day.

Our destination proved to be a secluded spot on the riverbank. Unfolding a tablecloth from the basket, I laid it on the bone-dry grass. 'I'm afraid it's not much,' I said, revealing the meagre picnic I had thrown together, 'it was the best I could manage in the circumstances.'

'For some reason I am not hungry,' he said, his soft dark brown eyes settling on mine. I held fast to his gaze and as the moment – potent with a pulsating energy – stretched between us for the longest time, I smiled.

'But it would be a shame for it to go to waste,' I said finally, passing him a precious bottle of champagne to open. 'And if you're going to be felling more trees, you'll need your strength.'

Having said he wasn't hungry, and doubting my own appetite being this close to him, we made short work of the half loaf of bread I'd brought, along with the lump of cheddar, the small jar of Mrs Partridge's homemade apple chutney, a clutch of pea pods, and the tomatoes I'd picked from the greenhouse. For dessert I produced the remains of an apple pie, again care of Mrs P.

As we ate and drank our fill, I thanked him for his letters, saying how much I had looked forward to reading them.

'I could not say all that I wanted to,' he said, lying on his side, his head propped up so he could look at me.

'Why not? Were you worried about our letters being censored?'

'No. I was afraid if I said too much . . . if I declared my feelings for you, it would ruin our friendship.'

'Is that what we have, a friendship?'

He traced his forefinger along the chequered pattern of the gingham tablecloth beneath us. 'I do not know what we have, Romily, only that it feels wonderful and I never want it to end.'

His hand moved towards mine so that our fingertips were touching. Once more that spark of electricity fizzed through me causing my heart to race and my mouth to turn as dry as the champagne we were drinking. My gaze locked with his, and with my body zinging with the kind of desire I hadn't felt since being with Jack, I didn't know how much longer I could continue in this virtuous manner. I tilted my head, just the slightest of movements, and it appeared to be all the signal he needed.

When our lips met, the passion between us ignited

spontaneously, putting us both in danger of self-combusting. Our hands, no longer tentatively touching, explored each other's bodies with an urgency that matched the fervour of our kissing. But when he entered me, he did so with a more measured tenderness. Impatient for that soaring moment of euphoric release that I knew I was seconds away from, I urged him on.

'Slowly,' he whispered, cupping my face in his hands, 'I want to remember this always.'

At the mercy of his self-control, he kept me teetering on the brink until finally in an explosion of mutual climax, we clung to each other as one complete body. Then with tears in our eyes, we stared at each other as though we couldn't quite believe what had just happened.

'*Ti amo*,' he murmured. 'I love you.'

I never thought to hear those words again, or utter them myself, but I wiped the tears from his eyes, and mine, and told him I loved him. '*Ti amo, Matteo.*'

We lay for some minutes in the warm sunshine, basking in the exquisite bliss of what we had just done. 'I can't believe you're really here in my arms' he said. 'I shall wake up in a minute and find it was just a beautiful dream.'

Thinking it would be wonderful to lie here for ever, I sighed like the most contented of cats who had got more than her share of cream.

'I'm so happy I could sing!' I suddenly exclaimed.

He lifted his head. 'And what would you sing, *mia cara?*'

I grinned. 'I don't know. But I'm sure I'll think of something.'

'I'm sure you could. You are, after all, the most beautiful and amazing woman I know.'

'Well, that's true, of course. I am incredibly beautiful, and fantastically amazing.'

He laughed. '*Dio mio,* how can I ever let you go now?'

'You don't have to let me go. Not if you don't want to.'

His expression changed, and he suddenly looked painfully solemn.

'What is it?' I said.

He sat up and like the gentleman he was, smoothed down my rumpled dress so that I looked a little less in disarray. 'It's this war,' he said quietly, his back to me as he faced the river. 'It is going to tear us apart.'

'Not necessarily,' I replied, raising myself up so that I was sitting next to him.

He twisted his head round to look at me and my heart missed a beat at the sadness in his eyes. 'I wish you didn't have to leave,' he murmured.

'I wish I didn't have to either, but I'll come again just as soon as I can.'

'You are a famous lady novelist and a pilot with the ATA, what do you see in a man like me?' he asked when we were retracing our steps back to where he was needed to help the lumberjills. 'I have nothing to offer you,' he continued, 'I'm just a prisoner of war who has to work like a peasant.'

'Oh Matteo,' I said, 'don't speak that way. That day when you pulled me from the wreckage of the Walrus, you saved my life. And in so many ways,' I added.

'So you love me out of gratitude?'

I stepped in front of him and pressed my finger to his lips. 'Shh . . . ' I said, 'don't spoil our brief time together. Just accept that fate brought us together.'

And fate might separate us, was the thought that kept me company during my lonely drive home to Island House.

True to my word, I returned to Tilbrook Hall the following month in September. On this occasion Matteo knew to expect me and had managed to request some time off from potato picking with the rest of the POWs.

Again we went for a walk and, as if guided by our very own North Star, we ended up on the riverbank where we'd made love before. We did so again, but this time Matteo came prepared, having acquired the necessary item through a source he was at pains not to reveal.

But it turned out that it was a case of shutting the stable door after the horse had bolted. I was already pregnant.

Chapter Sixty

Chelstead Cottage Hospital
December 1962
Hope

Pregnant . . . Pregnant . . . Pregnant . . . The word kept spinning around inside Hope's head.

But she must surely have dreamt Annelise telling her that she was pregnant? Annelise would never be so stupidly careless. She just wasn't that sort of a girl. But why then had Hope's brain seized hold of the notion that she was expecting a baby?

Every time Annelise visited, Hope tried desperately to speak, to ask the girl if it was true. But it was futile; Hope could do nothing but rage against the frustration of her useless body while listening to Annelise talk about it being almost Christmas. During her last visit she had read from *A Christmas Carol*, a book that Hope had loved as a child. Not a word did Annelise say about being pregnant. Did that mean Hope had dreamt it?

The longer she lay here, the more difficult it became for Hope to keep track of time, and of what was real or imagined. Edmund explaining that he now knew about the anonymous letter she had received felt very real. As did him saying he would never be unfaithful.

'The very idea that you could be persuaded of such a thing makes me sick to my stomach,' he had said. 'You have to believe me, Hope, I would never *ever* have an affair.'

She had cried inside at the intensity of his words, filled with happy relief that he hadn't been cheating on her.

But what if he was lying?

Or what if this was all going on in her head and was just another of the many dreams she had? Some of the dreams were terrifying and made her want to scream. The one about the nurses who were trying to kill her by injecting her with lethal poisons was particularly disturbing. Other times she dreamt she was out walking and being chased by a car. Sometimes the speed of the car was as fast as a bullet, coming at her out of nowhere, and other times it was menacingly slow, hunting her down. But always the driver was her brother, Arthur. Sitting behind the wheel, he would be laughing at her, then driving off into the darkness with a cheery wave.

There was something about those dreams that snagged on her brain. It was to do with Arthur's wife, Julia. A feeling that Julia had been sitting here by the side of Hope's bed saying she had something important to tell her. But was that just another dream?

Oh, if only her muddled brain could make sense of it all and discern what was real and unreal!

Chapter Sixty-One

Island House, Melstead St Mary
December 1962
Romily

It was the day before Christmas Eve and Romily should have been wrapping presents. But as the last of the afternoon light drained from the wintry sky, her mind simply would not settle to the task. Instead, she was in the cold and dusty attic clambering over old items of cobwebby furniture and rolled up rugs. She was hunting for what she had hidden up there many years ago. More than once she had considered throwing the contents of the box away, but she hadn't been able to bring herself to do it.

Perhaps this moment was always going to happen, that there would be a catalyst for her to revisit this particular episode in her life. Annelise's news that she was expecting a baby – and in similar circumstances – had been that unexpected catalyst. Romily had resisted the urge to do what she was now doing for more than a week, forcing herself to concentrate on the book she had started writing as well as preparing for Christmas. But this afternoon she had finally given in.

She found the wooden jewellery box inside a large travelling trunk, the sort that opened up like a mini wardrobe. The last time she had used the trunk was ten years ago when she had gone on a world cruise on board the illustrious RMS *Caronia*.

Back downstairs, and the house cloaked in silence – Florence, Beatty and Mrs Collings having gone home – Romily placed the old jewellery box on her desk in the library and sat down. She stared at the box, as though waiting for the lid magically to rise all on its own.

But when she tried to lift the lid, it refused to budge. It was locked. With no idea where the key was, she reached for the letter opener on her desk, and not caring about the damage she would be inflicting, she pushed the pointed blade into the lock and jiggled it around. When that didn't work, she forced the knife under the lid and pushed hard to prise it open. It was no match for her determination to gain access and with a splintering of wood, the lock gave way and she raised the lid. At once the air was fragrant with the poignant scent of summer. She had forgotten that before locking the box she had placed sprigs of lavender from the garden within the precious contents.

Putting the knife down, she lifted out the bundle that had lain as dormant as a seed in winter. A lilac-coloured ribbon was tied around the bundle and attached to it was a small card. Written in her own hand were the words: *Letters From the Past*.

As though it were only yesterday, she could remember writing those few poignant words and how heartbroken she had been. She had encountered heartbreak before, but this was different. Very different. She had lost an integral part of her that could never be replaced.

She untied the ribbon with a scattering of desiccated lavender, and one by one, she passed Matteo's letters from her left hand to her right. The postmark on each envelope revealed the letters were in date order. How typical of her that, even in the depths of despair, she should have been so organised.

While some memories were a comfort to revisit, others were too painful. It was why she had gone to the lengths she had to commit Matteo to the past. And yet she had been reluctant to let go entirely. If she had, these letters would not exist. Nor would his painting that was in the drawing room.

She sifted through the envelopes once more and selected one that was postmarked 20 October, 1944.

Carissima Romily,

You have brought such happiness into my life, but I do not deserve it. All this time in the days since we met – since that fateful day when your aeroplane crashed – I have kept something from you. I am ashamed of myself for my deception. I have become the type of man I never thought I would.

I said that this war would tear us apart and it will. For when the fighting is over and I am free to return to Italy, I will be reunited with my wife. There, at last I have admitted the truth to you. I am married. I never meant to deceive you, but I have and for that I know you have every right to hate me. Why would you not, when I hate myself so much? Before you rip this letter into many pieces, please let me try to explain. I had no intention of falling in love with you, but the more time I spent in your company, the stronger my feelings became, and then before I realised it, it was too late and I could not bring myself to tell you the truth. For I knew that once I confessed my sin and guilt to you, that would be the end of my happiness.

This is no justification for what I have done, but my marriage is not a happy one. My wife, just as my family did, wanted me to be someone I could never be. I have been a great disappointment to my wife. I have never matched the expectations Maria had for me. I believe that when we married, she had the strongest confidence in her ability to make me the man of her dreams. Instead, I am the man of her nightmares of whom she is ashamed. I am weak in her eyes. And perhaps I am.

But far worse, in her eyes, I have failed Maria in my duty to give her a child. In my heart I want to believe that God did not want us to have children, that it would have been wrong to bring a child into the world whose parents did not love each other in the way they should. For me this is both a blessing and a curse. Is it arrogant of me to think that I would be a good father? I believe I have lost the opportunity ever to know what it would feel like to hold the hand of my child. But I tell myself that it is better this way. Better that Maria could not manipulate a child against me. For surely as I breathe, I know that this is what would happen.

Why do we not divorce? you ask. Maria would never agree to that. When it suits her, she wears her faith in the Roman Catholic Church with fierce devotion. I have asked her before to free us both from our unhappy marriage, but she refuses to agree. She believes it is a far greater sin to divorce than it is to make another person miserable.

I now have to accept that in writing this letter I have made you as unhappy and angry as Maria. I will not waste my time in asking you to forgive me. It would be asking too much, and more than I deserve.

You have given me more joy in these few months than I have ever experienced in my life. It is a precious gift I will treasure always.

And now I must accept the inevitable, that I will not receive a reply to this letter. But how ever you feel about me, my dearest Romily, my feelings for you will never change.

With love and sincere regret
for causing you pain,
Matteo

Her eyes blurred with tears, the pain returned to Romily afresh of that day when she had read the letter for the first time.

Married . . . wife . . . Maria . . .

The words had leaped off the pages at her, like a knife repeatedly thrust through her heart. How had she not suspected he was married? Why hadn't it crossed her mind to ask outright if there was a wife or a girlfriend back in Italy waiting for him? Because she had assumed he would have mentioned one if such a person existed.

That's what she had told herself for a long time. Until she had eventually confronted her own part in his deception. She had deliberately chosen not to ask him if he were married because she hadn't wanted anything to burst the bubble of her happiness. In doing that she had deceived herself as much as he had lied to her through omission.

Now, in the soft light cast from the lamp on her desk, and thinking of what followed, she gave an involuntary shiver, as if a shadow had passed across her. Seeing that the fire had burned down to a faint glow, she stood up and carefully added some logs from the basket.

Perched on the soft leather of the fender, she waited impatiently for the fire to spring back into life and to warm the chill that had seeped into her bones. A biting cold easterly wind had blown in from the North Sea today, she could hear it still hurling itself against the windows, and the forecast was for a heavy fall of snow in the next twenty-four hours. With a wry smile, she thought how much she had enjoyed the more temperate climate of Palm Springs back in October, and how well it had made her feel.

The thought inevitably led her to think of Red. She wondered what he was doing right now. Counting the time difference in her head, she worked out that it would be late morning for him. She pictured him in his garden with the stunning mountain backdrop in the distance. But then just as vividly, she pictured the scene over lunch when she had offended him. She had touched a nerve and wished now that she hadn't. Everybody was entitled to their no-go areas and inadvertently she had trampled all over his.

She gave an exasperated sigh at the futility of her regret, and with the fire now burning brightly and its warmth spreading through her, she returned to her desk and the bundle of letters.

She selected the one dated 30 October, 1944. It had been in response to her carefully worded letter to him, a letter she had known would be read by the censors. Just as his to her would have been.

Carissima Romily,

I know I said before that I would accept that you do not want to see me again, but after reading your letter which arrived today, I would give anything for you to visit me so that we can talk properly, and in private. You say you are unwell, and that is of great concern to me. Please my darling, I know you are strong and resourceful, like no other woman I know, but I cannot bear the thought of you being unwell without me to help you.

You must believe me when I say that when this awful war is over, I will make my wife agree to a divorce. I will then return to you, I swear. Nothing will stop me! Not now!

You say that I have a duty to be with my wife, but I see it differently. I now have a bigger duty to be with you.

Please, I beg you, write to say that you have not given up on me. Or on us.

With all my love,
Matteo

With tears in her eyes once more, Romily carefully refolded the letter, and slid it back inside its envelope. She was about to return it to the wooden box when there was a ring at the doorbell. With nobody else in the house, she went to answer it.

Nothing could have prepared her for the bewildering shock of who was standing there on the doorstep.

Chapter Sixty-Two

Island House, Melstead St Mary
December 1962
Red

'Red! What on earth are you doing here?'

'I was just passing through and thought I'd say hi,' Red replied, cranking up the tone of his most light-hearted voice.

The stunned expression on Romily's face was definitely worth every minute of the time and effort it had taken for him to make the journey. Even that taxi ride from the station when he was worried to death what kind of reception awaited him. At every twist and turn in the road, he'd been ready to abandon the enterprise and head for home. But here he was, and who knew how it would play out?

'I don't remember it being this cold when I was last in merry old England,' he remarked, when she'd let him over the threshold and was shutting the door against the sub-zero air outside.

'Apparently there's a lot worse to come,' she said, still staring at him as though she couldn't quite believe her eyes.

'Hey, that's the story of my life,' he quipped, expecting Romily to smile. When she didn't, but continued to regard him steadily, he wondered if he'd made a mistake. Would turning up like this – a grand gesture if ever there was! – be considered just another example of crass behaviour for which she would condemn him?

With an imperceptible shake of her head, she said, 'I'm so

sorry. I seem to have completely forgotten my manners. Please, let me take your coat.'

Okay, so he wasn't being thrown out into the cold of the night straight off the bat. That was a good sign. Putting his suitcase on the floor and shrugging off the big woollen overcoat he'd had the sense to bring with him, along with a scarf, he passed it to her.

'Nice house,' he commented, when she showed him through to a large and very English-style drawing room. He watched her switching on a collection of silk-shaded lamps; at the same time he took in the tasteful décor of pretty rugs and chintz-covered sofas and armchairs. There was a large Christmas tree in one corner of the room, decorated with coloured glass balls and tinsel. Nothing in the room jarred. Apart from him, that was. He was a mass of jangling nerves.

'Thank you,' she replied, drawing the curtains across and blocking out the darkness. 'I'm afraid you've caught me on the hop somewhat, I was busy in my library and haven't lit a fire in here yet.'

The room was indeed on the chilly side. 'I could do that for you, if you like?' he offered.

'There's no need, I can manage.'

I'm sure you can, was on the tip of his tongue. But with great restraint he held his tongue. He had not come all this way to blow it within the first few minutes of his arrival. He also had the sense to realise that having a task to do gave Romily time to assemble her wits and self-possession. Something he guessed she would value highly.

He watched her strike a match and put it to the screwed-up balls of newspaper and kindling already placed in the grate. With her back to him, he took the opportunity to take in some more of the room. There was a console table behind a sofa that was home to an array of framed photographs, and he was tempted to go over and study them closely, to see if he could learn anything new about the extraordinary Romily Devereux-Temple.

For safety's sake – his own safety – he fixed his attention on a painting on the wall nearest to him. It was illuminated by a lamp positioned beneath it and, bending in for a closer look, he could see the strong fluid strokes the artist had employed to capture a group of men gathering in the harvest. The sun was low in the sky, casting a fiery glow of light across the field in which they toiled under the watchful eye of a man in a soldier's uniform. The men themselves were all similarly dressed in khaki-coloured trousers and shirts with the sleeves rolled up. On the backs of their shirts and trouser legs were large red circles. Prisoners of war, he guessed, put to work to ease the shortage of labour. He thought it an unusual choice of painting for an English drawing room. But remembering Romily telling him about the Italian POW who had rescued her from the burning wreckage of her crashed Walrus, he leaned in closer still to locate the artist's signature. He failed to find it though.

'There,' said Romily behind him, 'the room should soon start to warm up. May I offer you something to drink? And I expect you're hungry too.'

She had completely recovered her composure, he could see and was now the perfect hostess, graciously at ease with an unexpected guest. 'A drink would be great,' he said, 'thank you. But I don't want to put you to any unnecessary trouble.'

'It's the least I can do. What would you like, tea or coffee? Or perhaps something stronger?'

He'd sworn to go easy on the hooch, determined to keep a cool head on his shoulders while here. His sister had been right to say he'd started drinking too much. She had told him that the time before when it had got out of hand. 'I'll have some of your famous British tea, please,' he said. 'When in Rome and all that.' He winced at the cliché, but she merely smiled politely.

'Make yourself comfortable by the fire,' she said, 'I'll go and put the kettle on.'

In front of the fire that was satisfyingly ablaze now, the logs popping and crackling like a barrel of firecrackers, Red inspected the objects on the mantelpiece. There was an elegant carriage clock, two expensive-looking porcelain vases, and a number of Christmas ornaments. One of which was a glass snow globe with a wintry scene of trees and a snowman. He couldn't resist picking it up and giving it a shake, sending glittery snowflakes fluttering. It made a faint chiming sound and he realised it was a musical snow globe. A couple of twists of the metal winder underneath produced a tinkling rendition of 'Silent Night'.

Listening to it was like having a thousand tiny hammers tapping tacks into his skull. He could never hear the carol without thinking of hiding in a cold, damp cellar and hearing it sung in its original language, German. He promptly returned the globe to its position on the mantelpiece, the unwelcome tune playing on to its tinny and mawkish end.

Stille Nacht . . .

For as long as he lived, he would never fathom how soldiers could have sung the carol with such mellifluous harmony and feeling, but two days later carry out such inhuman acts of barbarism. Lining up the courageous men and women who had helped the Resistance, they had shot them in a torrent of gunfire, while forcing the rest of the villagers to watch.

Hidden on the back of a cart, Red had heard the shots and the screams of terror. The cries of the children too. It was a sound he would never forget. He sometimes dreamt he was back there in that small French village having rewound the clock so that innocent people weren't murdered because of him.

'Are you quite warm now?'

He spun round at the sound of Romily's voice, his hand

catching on the snow globe. It fell from the mantelpiece and crashed onto the stone hearth. The glass shattered on impact and liquid splashed into the fire with a hiss.

'I'm so sorry,' he said, bending to pick up the debris. 'I'll replace it for you. Of course.'

'You'll do no such thing,' she said, putting the tea tray down, then coming over to him. 'In fact, you've done me a favour by breaking the thing. I've never liked it, but out it comes each year because it was a gift and I've never had the heart to throw it away. Careful with that glass,' she added.

Her warning came too late and with a perversity that served him right for his clumsiness, a shard of glass sliced his thumb, drawing from him a muttered expletive.

'Here, let me see,' she said.

'It's okay, I'm not about to bleed to death all over your hearthrug.'

'I couldn't give a damn about the rug. Hold out your hand.'

He did as she said. What man wouldn't when confronted with those violet eyes? Goddammit, she was even more beautiful than he remembered!

After inspecting his hand, she took a linen napkin from the tray behind her, and deftly wound it tightly around his thumb.

'My surprise visit is not going well, is it?' he said. 'Should I just fetch my coat and leave you in peace? God knows what next I might break or inflict on you.'

'Curiosity makes me inclined to let you stay,' she said, 'if only so I can see what else you get up to. But you must warn me if there's a danger of you breaking anything of value.'

He held up his hand with its makeshift bandage applied. 'I knew there was something about you I liked. Your absolute commitment to making me look more foolish than I already am.'

'Nothing could be further from the truth. Now please, sit

down and have your tea and cake, then I'll find a proper dressing for your thumb, Mr St Clair.'

'Are we to be so formal now . . . Mrs Devereux-Temple?'

She placed the dainty cup and saucer and plate on the occasional table next to him. And then her face broke into a smile. It was the smile that had lured him thousands of miles across the Atlantic on a mission to win her over. As Rudyard Kipling said, 'Nothing is ever settled until it is settled right.' And he was here to do exactly that.

'I don't know why I said what I did,' she said, sitting down, 'it just came out.'

'It's probably because I have put you on the spot by arriving unannounced.'

'Was that your intention?'

'No. And this may come as a surprise to you, I came all this way because I wanted to apologise to you. I was unforgivably rude to you. Not to say, pig-headed too. You should speak to my sister on that particular subject; she's an expert on my manifold failings.'

'You could have simply written.'

He drank some of his tea, before saying: 'I did.'

'Oh? I haven't received a letter.'

'That's because I lost my nerve and didn't post it. And you know what? It was a masterpiece of writing. Possibly my best.'

She smiled. 'I'm disappointed I was denied the pleasure of reading it.'

He took another sip of his tea. 'And this is the bit when you say, but instead of a mere letter, you have the pleasure of seeing me in the flesh once more.'

'Red, it's a pleasure to see you again.'

He smiled. 'With a little more conviction, if you could manage it. You know, just to put me at ease.'

'Do you feel very ill at ease?'

'You bet I do!'

She too drank her tea, while he took a bite of the cake. Followed by another. It was delicious. And he was starving into the bargain. He settled back into the armchair and stretched out his legs in front of him.

'What are your plans?' she asked, as though warning him not to get too comfortable.

'For the rest of my life?'

A smile twitched at the corners of her lips. 'I was thinking more of the immediate future. Have you booked somewhere to stay tonight?'

'You afford me more common sense than I possess. Forward planning is not one of my strong suits. Half-baked schemes, that's more my line.'

'I'll bear that in mind. In the absence of a plan, you must stay here.'

'I couldn't possibly put you out. Well, no more than I have already.'

'Come, come now,' she said archly, 'don't be disingenuous. You know jolly well that I could no more turn you out into the cold, than I could accept your apology without giving you one of my own.'

'What do you have to be sorry for?' he asked, surprised.

'Something which has been on my mind since we last saw each other. I was inexcusably rude to you and overreached myself when we were talking. And if we're speaking of failings, that is one of mine. I've always been too meddlesome for my own good.'

'You did nothing wrong,' he said. 'I overreacted to a question which ... which scratched at a raw spot. As you doubtless suspected it would. Which is why you asked the question in the first place; you were trying to shake me out of my evasiveness.'

'I had no right to do that. You were perfectly entitled to be as evasive as you wanted. More cake?'

'Thank you.' He leaned forward and held out his plate with his injured hand.

'How's your thumb? Has it stopped bleeding?'

He gave it a cursory look. 'I believe it has. But I'm afraid your napkin may never be the same again.'

'A good soak overnight and it'll be as right as rain.'

'If only all life's problems could be so simply resolved,' he said with a smile.

'And what problems do you have that you wish you could be rid of?'

He fixed his gaze directly on hers. 'I have one very tricky problem and I'm darned if I know how to go about resolving it.'

'Can I help in any way?' she asked, relaxing into the cushions behind her on the sofa.

'I'd like to think you could. Perhaps we could discuss it over dinner? May I take you somewhere this evening?'

Her unwavering gaze still locked on his, she said, 'I have a better idea; I shall cook for us. Nothing fancy though.'

At the powerfully penetrating look she was giving him, he felt practically cooked himself!

Chapter Sixty-Three

Island House, Melstead St Mary
December 1962
Romily

At Red's suggestion, or rather his insistence that she didn't go to any trouble on his account, they ate in the kitchen. Romily often did, preferring it to the dining room, which was a beautiful room, but it felt much too grand to eat in when alone. When she'd told Red she would cook, what she'd actually meant was that she would put the ham and chicken pie Mrs Collings had made into the oven and boil the potatoes and carrots which had also been prepared. The meal eaten, Red further insisted that he would earn his keep by doing the dishes.

'You'll do no such thing,' she remonstrated.

'I think you'll find I will.'

He began rolling up his sleeves until she pointed to his thumb and the plaster which she had earlier applied. 'I'll wash, you dry,' she said by way of compromise, opening a drawer for a clean tea towel and giving it to him.

'You're used to doing things your way, aren't you?' he said.

'And you're not?' she replied, selecting a wooden-handled mop from the pot on the windowsill.

'I guess we're just two of a kind,' he replied with a small laugh.

They worked steadily together with Romily trying to kid herself that there was nothing out of the ordinary in them

335

performing this simple domestic chore together.

'We're like a married couple, aren't we?' he said when some minutes had passed. 'And yes, I'm well aware that that comment will strike an uncomfortable chord with you.'

He was right, but she chose to ignore it. 'Do you make a habit of flying halfway around the world to help with a person's washing up?' she asked.

'I do if the person is worth it.'

Her head down as she concentrated on scrubbing a pan, she smiled to herself. He had an answer for everything, didn't he? She had to admit, though, she couldn't help but admire his boldness and the impetuous spirit that had brought him here. It was a long time since anyone had gone to so much trouble to make an impression on her, and she would be lying if she didn't feel enormously flattered. Moreover, his arrival could not have been better timed; it had provided a welcome diversion from the sadness of reading Matteo's letters. The instant she had seen Red's handsome face staring back at her with his large frame filling the doorway, Matteo and the past was swept away.

With everything tidied and put back in its proper place – Mrs Collings would play merry hell tomorrow morning if she found her domain with so much as a teaspoon in the wrong place – they returned to the drawing room. While Red dealt with building up the fire again, Romily poured two glasses of brandy.

'Only a very small one for me,' he said, 'I need to keep my head when I'm around you.'

As do I, she thought with growing awareness that, minute by minute, she was becoming increasingly susceptible to what she could only describe as Red's potent masculinity. He somehow seemed taller and broader here than he did in Palm Springs. Was it because the little time they had spent together there had been mostly outside, and here his large frame was confined by bricks and mortar? She smiled to herself, thinking that his presence was as incongruous as it would be if one of those enormous cacti she had seen in the desert with him were suddenly to pop up in her garden. It would be wildly out of place, but dramatically attractive all the same.

When he'd coaxed the fire back into life, and she'd given him his glass of brandy, they made themselves comfortable on the sofa, one at each end. Kicking off her shoes, she tucked her legs beneath her.

'Am I forgiven for storming your castle and intruding on your privacy?' he asked.

She swirled the brandy around in the large balloon glass and took a long and appreciative sip. 'What do you think?'

He raised an eyebrow. 'I think we'll never have a conversation that doesn't resemble a ping-pong ball being batted backwards and forwards.'

'Is that the way it feels to you?'

'There you go again, answering my question with one of your own.' He smiled. 'You're like a very beautiful butterfly, tantalisingly close, but always hovering beyond reach.'

'I've been described as many things, but never a butterfly. It makes me sound disagreeably flighty and insubstantial.'

His smile widened, deepening the lines around his dark eyes. His profile was brought into sharp relief by the flickering flames of the fire, accentuating his cheekbones and the lines either side of his mouth. *How would it feel to kiss that mouth?* a covetous voice whispered in her ear.

'Insubstantial is absolutely not the word that springs to mind when I think of you,' he said.

'I'm glad to hear it.'

He drank from his glass, tilting his head back, his neck and Adam's apple revealed in the soft light. How tempting it was to lean over and touch that patch of exposed smooth skin. To place her lips against his jawline and breathe in the scent of him. She cleared her throat and took a large mouthful of her drink, willing her scheming desire to get back in line.

'More brandy?' he asked. She stared at the glass in her hand, realising that it was empty. Before she could say no, he had taken it from her and was on his feet. He went over to the console table where the bottle of Rémy Martin was. It was only then, as he refilled her glass, and not his, that she registered he was barely limping. Until then she had forgotten all about his artificial leg.

When he sat down again, he had contrived to close the gap between them, brushing against her knees with his thigh. The fire popped and crackled, adding to the forcefield of static that was fizzing between them.

'You're limping less,' she said, grasping at something normal to say in a thoroughly abnormal situation.

'How very observant of you. And if I can be equally observant, you have the most bewitching eyes I have ever had the good fortune to gaze into.'

In danger of losing herself in his at such close proximity, she said, 'Your eyes aren't so bad either.'

He tapped his glass against hers. 'Well then, here's to our mutually appreciated eyes.'

'I have a confession to make,' he then said.

'Don't tell me you're here to resurrect Gabe and Melvyn's idea about us working together.'

He shook his head. 'No, I'm out of the picture on that project; they're looking for another writer who might tempt you to take up their offer.'

Her agent had told her much the same. 'I'm sorry if my decision to leave so suddenly made things difficult for you,' she said.

'Don't give it another thought. It was my fault for rubbing you up the wrong way.'

'So what is your confession?'

'Well, it's kinda weird, and you have to promise not to laugh, but I have a thing for English women; it's the accent. It makes me do crazy and improbable things.'

She worked hard to keep her face from breaking into a smile. 'Is that so?' she said. 'And how many English women have you known who have had this effect on you?'

'Do you really want to know?'

'Why else would I have asked?'

'You might not like the answer.'

'That's not a reason to avoid asking the question in the first place.'

'In that case I have no choice but to risk it. You see, it's just the one English woman, and the one English accent that drives me nuts. It's yours.'

Determined to keep her expression as neutral as she could, she said, 'How interesting. I wonder why that is?'

'I was hoping you'd put me straight, because I'm damned if I know why. I'm in uncharted territory here; I'm all at sea.'

'You don't strike me as a man all at sea,' she remarked. 'Far from it.'

'I hide it well. But then I hide so many things. As you pointed out to me that day when I behaved so badly.'

'We all hide things,' she said, thinking of Matteo's letters.

'Even you?'

'Oh yes. I have plenty of things I'd sooner not reveal.'

'Bad things?'

'Bad enough.'

For a few minutes neither of them spoke. Romily put down her glass and went to put another log on the fire. After nudging it into place with the poker, and seeing Red's empty glass on the table next to hers, she offered him a refill.

He shook his head. 'No thanks. I've cut back. I go through phases when I drink far too much.'

'Is there a reason for that?' She was surprised at his admission.

'There's a reason for everything.'

She sat down again, and once more tucked her legs beneath her.

His arm trailing along the back of the sofa, he said, 'Can we rewind to that moment when I said you had the most bewitching eyes?'

She turned so that she was facing him square on. 'Is that because you want to make a seductive move on me?'

'Would it be wholly unwelcome if I did?'

'What do you have in mind?'

His hand crept towards her shoulder, and then her neck, releasing a wave of spine-tingling desire within her. 'I'd like to kiss that delectable mouth of yours,' he said.

She grimaced. '*Delectable?*'

He smiled. 'Okay, way too clichéd. How about irresistible?'

'As bad,' she said. 'Definitely as bad.' Then putting a finger to his lips, she pressed ever so slightly against his teeth. His eyes blazed, and she felt a tremor run through him at her touch. 'How about you stop talking for two seconds?' she murmured.

'Why, what will you—'

She silenced him by removing her finger and kissing him lightly on the mouth. His lips were warm and soft, and tasted of Rémy Martin. She let her lips linger against his, until he tilted his head away from her. For a moment he gazed intently into her eyes, then he kissed her deeply, his hands firmly around her shoulders pulling her closer. Still kissing him, she somehow managed to slip her legs out from under her and he tilted her back so her head was resting on the arm of the sofa, his body on top of hers. It felt good to feel the weight of him against her.

His mouth moved slowly from her lips to her throat, and just as he reached the hollow above her collarbone, she let out a gasp of pleasure.

'Have I found your weak spot, Mrs Devereux-Temple?' he said, teasingly. Before she could reply, he had kissed her in the same place again and elicited another sigh from her. In turn she slid her hands to his chest and began unbuttoning his shirt. She had three buttons undone when he suddenly raised himself off from her.

'I think we need to stop,' he murmured.

His words were like the pricking of a balloon and at once she felt deflated and embarrassed. 'If you say so,' she said, not without a tinge of annoyance. Was this some kind of game for him?

'No,' he said, 'you don't understand. I don't want this. I mean, not like this.'

Confused, she said, 'You're right, I don't understand.'

'I don't want it to be a momentary loss of control. I don't want you to wake in the morning and think, "What the hell was that all about?" Or worse, think that I took what I could on a spur of the moment thing.'

'I assure you I can think for myself.'

He sat up. 'Now you're cross with me.'

She sat up beside him. 'Maybe I am. Because I really don't understand you, Red. Most men would have simply—'

'That's just my point,' he cut in. 'I don't want you to think of me in that way. Oh sure, I've behaved like that a hundred times. Hell, maybe more! But this time I want it to be different. Is that asking too much?'

His pained expression touched her, and taking hold of his hands, all her annoyance gone, she said, 'For it to be different, Red, we need to know each other a lot better.'

'That's what scares me.'

'Why?'

'It would mean I would have to be completely honest with you.'

'Would that be so awful?'

'There are things I've done that would shock you. Perhaps even make you hate me.'

'Have you thought that maybe I've done things that would shock you?'

He shook his head. 'I doubt what you've done comes close.'

'Then tell me. Tell me everything. Even if we have to be up all night.'

Chapter Sixty-Four

France
December 1943
Red

In early November of 1943 I was shipped over to England and stationed at what had been RAF Leiston, but now designated Station 373 (LI) after it was allocated to the Eighth Air Force of the United States Army Air Forces. After a brief settling in period, our missions began. I named my P-51 Mustang fighter airplane 'Patsy' after my sister, knowing that she'd get a kick out of it.

On a freezing cold day in December, I was part of a mission to attack targets in the Bordeaux area. All I knew about Bordeaux was that it produced excellent wine. I was thinking of that as I took up the tail-end-Charlie position of the four-plane flight. I was the oldest by quite a few years and we all had just over three months' experience in combat and between us had shot down seven enemy aircraft.

We had crossed the channel and were set on a course over Brittany then south towards our destination, a Luftwaffe airfield at Merignac, west of Bordeaux. When out on a mission we were under orders to strafe anything that moved, an order that didn't sit well with me. The only way I could rationalise it was to remind myself that this was the real deal – kill or be killed.

In common with many of my fellow pilots, I had my little rituals which I had to obey every time I climbed into the cockpit of my P-51. Such as reciting Psalm 23 – *Even though I walk through the valley of the shadow of death, I will fear no evil, for you are with me.* Another ritual was always to have the watch my father had given me on my twenty-first birthday. It had become a lucky talisman to me. And wouldn't you just know it, on this particular morning, I had forgotten to put it on. That had never happened before, and it was niggling away at me when I suddenly realised I was being shot at by two German aircraft. The pair of Fw 190s had appeared from nowhere.

Taking immediate evasive action by breaking position, I turned myself into a lone target. I had been in this position before and survived, so I rolled the dice and hoped for the best. Adrenaline pumping through me, I circled sharply back on myself and became the attacker. But I hadn't reckoned on a third Fw 190 joining the fray and within seconds, gunfire was pummelling my Mustang. An explosion from behind my seat spelled the end and so I had no choice but to bail out.

The Germans, however, had not yet finished with me, and as my parachute opened, one of them started firing at me. It was a miracle that only my leg was hit before the pilot dived away to rejoin the other Fw 190s. I hoped to God that Mike, Stevie and Pete who had set off from Leiston with me succeeded with our mission and made it safely back to the airbase.

I landed with an excruciating thud in a field that I knew to be enemy-occupied territory. The ground was rock hard and as cold as ice. In agony, I extricated myself from my parachute and after bundling it up and crawling to the relative safety of a hedge, I inspected my blood-soaked leg. I was not the squeamish sort, but the sight of my ripped-open flesh from the knee down was enough to make me roll over and be violently sick. I was contemplating my next move, doubtful that I would be able to walk any distance, if at all, when I saw an elderly woman coming towards me.

'American,' I said, when she was standing a scant few feet from me. 'American pilot.' I pointed to the sky, as though this would explain everything. I spoke no French, and she, it turned out, spoke no English. Within seconds she hurried away, leaving me to hope that she was pro-France and not an ardent supporter of the Third Reich. Would it be my second misfortune of the day to have been found by a collaborationist?

The pain in my leg was getting worse and my stomach was pitching again with the need to be sick. Shock, I supposed, as the blood continued to flow and I began to shiver, and not just from the cold. I was in the process of tearing up the silk parachute to make a bandage when I heard voices. This time coming towards me was a group of men who, one way or another, looked like they meant business, a number of them having a gun slung over a shoulder. I reached inside my leather jacket for the Smith & Wesson .38/44 with which I had been issued. But it was quickly apparent, as the men stood over me discussing something in hushed tones, and then hoisted me off the ground, that they were not the enemy. I had no idea where they were taking me, and to be honest, I was in so much pain, I didn't care.

I must have passed out because when I came round, I found myself lying in a bed, and sitting close by was a beautiful girl reading a book. She was as delicate and petite as a china doll, with dark curly hair tucked behind her ears.

'Hello,' she said, when she noticed I was awake, 'how are you feeling?' Her English was heavily accented.

'Better than before,' I said, my voice strained and croaky. In need of a drink, and noticing a full glass of water on the table beside me, I tried to sit up, but immediately regretted my attempt. At the pain shooting through me, I remembered my badly injured leg and looked down at it. I half expected it no longer to be there.

345

'You have lost a lot of blood,' the girl said, coming to my aid and passing me the glass of water. She held it against my dry lips. 'Not too much,' she said, 'or you will be sick again.'

'Where am I?'

'You are safe, that is all you need to know.'

'The men who brought me here, are they with the Resistance?' She nodded.

'Will they help me get back to England?'

'Yes. But you need to be stronger before that is possible.'

'My leg,' I said, 'will it be okay?'

'A doctor removed some bullets and stitched up the wound, so maybe yes, it will be okay.'

'I'm very grateful to you, and the doctor. May I know your name?'

She hesitated before telling me it was Sophie.

Two days later and after I had been moved to another hiding place, I discovered that Sophie was older than she looked. She was twenty-three and a kindergarten teacher. Both her brothers were in the Resistance.

I felt badly for my rescuers because I was stuck with them until my leg was well enough for me to walk on it. So far, the only movement I had managed was in going to the bathroom, and that was with help from a stocky young farmer. The following day Sophie presented me with a pair of crutches, which meant I could at least move about unaided. But such was the pain in my leg, and the foul smell coming from it, I suspected that it was infected. Sophie did her best to remove the existing bandages and apply fresh ones, but we both knew that things were going from bad to worse. Once more I was confined to bed as a fever took hold of me. I began to think that it would have been better if the German pilot who had shot at me had made a thorough job of it and finished me off good and proper.

Dipping in and out of consciousness, I woke in the middle of what I thought was the night in yet another hiding place. A wizened old man with wire-framed spectacles was doing something agonizingly painful to my leg. I screamed out in pain, only for my mouth to be stuffed with a wad of something to contain my screams. Terrified, I tried thrashing free, but I was pinned down.

Sophie informed me later that the man in the wire-framed spectacles had been the doctor tending to my leg, and with a small degree of success. While this gave rise to me hoping I would soon be in a fit state to be helped back to England, possibly via Spain, my hope was soon dashed. An informer in the village, Sophie explained, had passed on to the German troops who were stationed on the outskirts of the village that there was an American pilot hiding in their midst.

I already knew that my presence was putting the brave men and women who had helped to conceal me at considerable risk, and that if suspicion fell on them, they would be rounded up and sent off to a concentration camp. Or shot on the spot. I had seen a torn-down poster that had been nailed to a tree, warning that anyone caught harbouring Allied pilots would be executed.

Yet again I was moved under cover of darkness, this time to the crypt in the village church. Sophie came to visit me, bringing food and wine. I had grown fond of her, and she of me, but frightened for her safety, I told her not to come anymore.

'I don't want you involved,' I explained, 'it's too dangerous now. You have done enough already. Please don't put your life at risk for the sake of mine.'

'It is too late to worry about the risk,' she said. But I could see that she was scared. Already villagers had been taken away for questioning and had not returned. It was believed they had been taken to the nearby chateau occupied by the Nazis and where they would be tortured for information.

347

It was also believed that German soldiers who spoke excellent English would dress in RAF and American Eighth Airforce uniforms and wander the countryside pretending they had bailed out and needed help to return to England. Their job was to infiltrate the Resistance and report back to their superiors so that the culprits could be rounded up.

The following night I was moved across the road to the cellar beneath the village blacksmith's forge. It had just been searched so was, for the time being, considered a safe hiding place. Next door was a bar frequented by German soldiers. How I longed to take my pistol and go up and shoot the damned lot of them!

That was the night I heard the soldiers singing 'Stille Nacht'. Sophie was with me and we were eating a simple meal of bread and cheese which she had brought with her.

When the singing came to a stop, Sophie looked serious. 'I must go,' she said.

Despite my insistence that she should stay away from me, I couldn't help but want her to stay longer. 'Do you have to go so soon?'

'I must,' she said.

'Promise me you'll take care walking home.'

She merely nodded, as she so often did. But before she left, she came back to where I was sitting on an old olive-oil drum, and knelt before me. 'Will you do something for me?' she asked.

'Anything,' I murmured, not sure I could resist the temptation to kiss her if she remained there a moment longer. I was only flesh and blood, after all, and she was so lovely.

'I want you to promise to do something for me.'

'Go on,' I said.

'If I ask you to put a bullet in my head, will you do it?'

'No!' I exclaimed in horror.

'I would sooner you killed me than those animals take me

away to be tortured for information. I am afraid I am not strong enough to resist.'

'Then you must make sure you don't get caught.'

'But what if I am? Would you not want to save me from the brutality they would surely do to me?'

The thought of this beautiful young girl being harmed in any way made me take her in my arms. 'If it was in my power, I would keep you safe forever,' I said. 'But I can't agree to your request.'

She raised her head and with the most solemn expression on her face – so solemn it hurt to look at her – she kissed me on the mouth. She kissed me passionately and with the blood rising up within me, I kissed her back. We made love in that least romantic of places, and all the while I was haunted with the thought that it might be the last time I ever did.

The next morning, I was told that some time tomorrow I would be smuggled out of the village. My presence, it had been decided, was putting too many people at risk. I understood completely and if only my damned leg wasn't still such a mess, I would have struck out alone, but on crutches I knew I wouldn't get far.

Mid-afternoon the next day, two men came to the cellar and rolled me up inside a large rug, along with my crutches. They carried me outside and put me on the back of a cart, then proceeded to add barrow loads of rubble.

It was an hour or so later that the carnage started. Unable to see what was happening, I listened to the sound of boots marching close by, and then shouting as the German soldiers started rounding up men and women. I had no idea if they were selecting villagers at random, or whether it was based on information provided by their informant. Shots began to ring out and then the screaming started. It went on and on, a blood-curdling sound I knew I would never forget.

The horse that was harnessed to the cart began kicking up a row at the shots and cries, rocking the cart violently. Was Sophie amongst those who had been shot? I didn't know what to do, stay where I was as instructed, or prove my mettle and use what bullets I had in my pistol to exact revenge. *Strafe anything that moved . . .*

The answer was taken away from me by the cart slowly moving, the wheels grinding against the cobblestones. Was the horse moving the cart of its own accord? Or had someone come to get me out of the village? Would a German soldier notice that the cart was moving? All I could hope was this was planned, that all attention would be focused solely on those poor devils who were being shot.

Feeling every bump and pit in the road as the cart rolled on its way, I felt sure that we would be stopped.

After what felt like an eternity had passed, the cart finally came to a stop. I then felt a different kind of movement, a slight shifting of weight. Was it somebody climbing down from the cart seat? If so, when had they got up there? Or had they been so furtive I hadn't been aware of it?

A whispered voice called my name. 'Red, are you okay?'

I couldn't believe it; it was Sophie!

'Is it safe for me to show myself?'

'Yes.'

When I was free of the constraint of the rug, I saw that we were in a densely wooded area and it was dark. I couldn't stop myself from hugging Sophie. 'Thank God you're all right,' I said, grasping her tightly. Then letting her go, and leaning on my crutches, I asked what had happened back at the village.

'They chose people at random and shot them,' she said

gravely. 'When they were dead, the soldiers took more from the crowd. They made everyone watch what they were doing. Even children. It was to teach us a lesson.'

Rage burned deep inside me. 'I'm sorry,' I said. 'I brought this on your village. I shouldn't have stayed for so long. But how did you manage to move the cart without attracting attention to it?'

'I chose my moment when the soldiers were satisfying their lust for blood.'

I stared at her, wondering how this beautiful girl would ever get over what had happened today.

'You mustn't go back,' I said. 'I mean it. It's too dangerous for you there now. Come with me.'

She shook her head. 'I must go back,' she said. 'It is my duty. Just as it is your duty to return to England and get better so you can fly again. Germany has to be stopped.'

'I won't ever forget your help,' I said. Just then two figures emerged from the bushes behind us. Sophie spoke in French to them and they beckoned for me to join them.

'You must go now,' she said.

'Maybe one day we will meet again,' I said, 'in happier times.'

'Maybe. *Bon chance mon cherie,*' she said, with a ghost of a smile, and lapsing into French, something she seldom did with me.

I hugged her again and watched the cart disappear into the darkness. I felt like a chunk of my heart was disappearing too.

Two weeks later, when I was safely across the border in Spain, word reached me via the Resistance network that the soldiers had returned to the village and had taken Sophie away to the chateau. She was tortured, the one thing she was afraid of. Though it was counter to everything I believed I was capable of doing, I wished I had been able to spare her that by shooting her as she'd asked. But could I really have done it?

She died, so the Resistance said, bravely and without giving anything away.

She died because of me.

As did so many other villagers. How would I ever live with that on my conscience? If I had been paying better attention that day and spotted the Fw 190s on my tail sooner, I might not have been shot down. A better man would have blasted his own brains out rather than put an entire village at risk.

I let Sophie down in another way. I never got to fight again. When I finally made it back to England, my leg was in worse shape, having become reinfected, and I was shipped home to the US to have it amputated.

I lost my leg, but far worse, I lost the person I had once been. I was hollowed out. Haunted by the sacrifice that Sophie had made, I then spent the greater part of my life blaming myself for her death.

In comparison to what she had done with her life, mine wasn't worth a dime.

Chapter Sixty-Five

Island House, Melstead St Mary
December 1962
Romily

When Red finally fell silent, he slowly turned away from the fire to look at Romily. Not once had he looked at her while talking; his focus had been entirely on the flickering flames, as though seeing the past in them.

It didn't seem possible, but he suddenly looked ten years older. His face was ravaged by what she knew was guilt, and guilt of the very worst kind. She suspected it was a wound that ran so deep he probably believed the pain of it could never be healed. She knew from experience that by burying the pain deeper still with layers of self-recrimination, the wound only became more infected.

Everything he had told her explained so much about his behaviour. How his mood could turn on a sixpence if he sensed somebody was getting too close and might catch a glimpse of the darkness within him.

'I'm sorry,' she murmured. 'Truly I am.'

His eyes misted with emotion, he rose stiffly from the sofa. He stood for a moment in front of the fireplace, then pushed a hand roughly through his hair. 'I need some fresh air,' he blurted out. He looked about him as if searching for an escape route.

Romily stood up and went over to the French windows. She

yanked back the curtains, unlocked the doors and swung them wide open. Immediately a blast of glacial night air swept in. To her surprise, she saw that it was snowing. Red joined her in the open doorway and together, they watched the snowflakes, like hundreds of small white handkerchiefs, fall from the dark sky. In the light spilling out onto the garden, Romily could see that it was already covered with a thick blanket of snow. How long had it been snowing?

'I've told very few people what I've just shared with you,' he murmured, after breathing in the cold air, 'but you're the first person whose immediate response hasn't been to tell me it wasn't my fault, that Sophie and everyone else who was murdered in that village were just casualties of war.'

'Whoever said that to you, I'm sure they said it out of compassion,' Romily responded, 'but it's bound to hit a false note for you. How could it not? You were there to experience the horror; they weren't.'

It was some moments before he spoke. 'Thank you,' he said gruffly.

'What for?'

'For not patronising me. Or claiming that you know somebody who had gone through something similar. I've had that a couple of times. People rattling on as if they had any idea what I was feeling.'

'They doubtless did it to minimize and normalise what you've gone through, without ever considering what an insult it would be to you.'

'It was years before I told anyone what had happened. As you can see, it's something I still find it hard to talk about.'

'I expect you always will. But I'm glad you felt able to tell me.'

'I'm glad too,' he said quietly. He then lapsed into silence, his gaze steadfastly on the falling snow.

'You know,' he said at length, 'I think those are the biggest snowflakes I've ever seen. No wonder it's settling so fast.'

Noting the change of gear he'd made, Romily took her cue and wrapped her hand around his.

He slowly turned to face her. 'You're freezing,' he said, lifting her hand to his lips and kissing it. 'Had we better go inside?'

She shook her head, reluctant to break the spell of the moment. 'No, not yet.'

'You realise, don't you, that if we stay out here for too long the cold will make me say things that will embarrass us both?'

'Such as?'

'Such as you're one of the most extraordinary and beautiful women I know, and that you're worthy of so much more than I could ever offer you.'

'Doesn't the last part of that sentence depend on what you have in mind to offer me?'

'I think you know. I think you always know what I'm about to say or do when we're together.'

She tutted. 'You'll be crediting me with witchcraft skills next.'

He let go of her hand and put his arms around her. 'Well, you've thoroughly bewitched me.' He groaned. 'Geez, forget I said that. That was real bargain basement corn.'

'I'm beginning to think it's your default setting.'

'Only when I'm around you.'

'Is that so?' she said with a smile and tilting her head back so she could look into his eyes.

'Good God, do you have to do that?'

'What? What have I done?'

'Look so bloody gorgeous.'

'It's the snow, it would make a warthog look gorgeous.'

He lowered his hands to encircle her waist. 'Accept the compliment or pay the consequences.'

'I'm intrigued to know what the consequences might be.'

'You like to live dangerously, don't you?'

'Always.'

'Okay, here goes, and don't say I didn't warn you. You remember the day we met?'

'Of course. You kept me waiting for an age.'

'Are you never going to let me forget that?'

'I doubt it.'

He smiled. 'Be that as it might be, when I saw you sitting there in the garden of the restaurant, it was as if the tectonic plates had shifted. Before I'd even exchanged a word with you, I knew life was never going to be the same again. I fought it though. Boy, did I ever fight it! Especially when later I realised you could see through my every move. That was what pained me most and drove me to be so rude, your ability to know a fraud when you saw one.'

'You're no more of a fraud than the rest of us. We all have our weak spots which we try to protect.'

'Do you?'

'Of course. Why would I be any different?'

'Because you are, Romily. It's like there is this golden aura around you that makes you—'

'Enough,' she interrupted him. 'You warned me that the cold would start making you say things that would embarrass us, and you've gone well beyond that point.'

He smiled and with his hands still around her waist, he drew her close. 'In that case we'd better go inside and warm ourselves by the fire.'

'Good idea.'

'And then what shall we do?' No sooner had he asked the question, then he yawned hugely.

'Then you're going to go to bed,' she said firmly.

Chapter Sixty-Six

Melstead Hall, Melstead St Mary
December 1962
Ralph

His speed greatly reduced because of the snow, the journey was taking Ralph longer than usual. He hadn't expected it to snow tonight. That was the reason he had set off for Suffolk this evening – the day before Christmas Eve – to avoid the very thing he was now battling through: a blizzard. In places, where the snow was compacted down and already freezing, the roads were lethal.

Some might say it was masochistic of him to want to spend Christmas in Suffolk with his father, but with nowhere else to spend the holiday, Melstead Hall was the only option available to him. That, or be on his own. Which he didn't fancy. Still, it looked like they were in for a white Christmas, which oddly cheered him. Maybe because snow had a tendency to bring out the child in them all. Until one grew bored of the stuff and it turned to piles of dirty grey mush. A metaphor, if ever there was, for the relationship between him and his father. Where once Ralph had been the apple of his father's eye, now he was nothing but a thorn in his side.

Despite the hazardous nature of his journey, he was in a strangely mellow and repentant frame of mind. Christmas was, after all, a time of goodwill, and a host of other festive sentiment. Well, he wasn't exactly awash with goodwill, but like

Scrooge, he did have a number of regrets. Chiefly his behaviour towards Isabella.

He hadn't received a response to the letter he had sent her in which he had apologised for his appalling behaviour. He just hoped they would be able to smoothe things out over Christmas. Thinking about it, he really should have contacted Isabella to offer her a lift home for the holiday. That would have been a good olive branch on his part.

Since the evening he'd dined with his father in his club, and the revelatory moment when he realised how abhorrent it would be to go through life as unpopular as Arthur Devereux, Ralph had taken a long, hard look at himself. Changes were required, he'd concluded. Big changes. It was quite an epiphany, realising that he could actually reinvent himself.

The first thing he had vowed to do was to be a better brother to young Charlie-Boy. God knew the little nipper needed somebody to take an interest in him when he was home from school. Somebody who could stand up to his father for a start. Because there was no chance of Julia being brave enough to do that. Not when one wrong step from her would have her locked in her room!

And that was another thing he would put right. He wouldn't stand by and let his stepmother be treated no better than a slave.

As he drove through the entrance to Melstead Hall and travelled the length of the tree-lined driveway, he was relieved to see there was no sign of his father's Rolls.

He'd come prepared with presents and hauling them out of the car, along with his luggage, Ralph carried everything up the steps to the front door. He didn't bother pulling on the bell, he just tugged on the handle and let himself in.

The vast house was as quiet as the grave. And cold. It had all the makings of a horror-film set. His footsteps echoing on the black-and-white marble floor, he dumped his stuff on top of an oak chest and called to his stepmother. There was no reply. He called again, and this time he heard a sound coming from the other side of the door that led to the kitchen and to what had been the servants' quarters. Nowadays there was just Miss Casey and whichever girls from the village were desperate enough for money to work there.

The door opened and Miss Casey appeared. She looked as stern-faced as she always did, and not at all pleased to see him.

'Hello, Miss Casey,' he said cheerily. 'How are you?'

'I'm very well, Mr Devereux. Are you *expected?*'

The supercilious tone to her voice thoroughly riled him. 'It's Christmas,' he said, tossing her his coat to hang up, 'of course I'm expected! I'll have a whisky to warm me up, please. Make it a large one, that way I won't have to ring for you to bring me a second.'

The woman hesitated before saying, 'Where will you be?'

'I'll be with my stepmother and young Charlie-Boy. Wherever they are.'

'I'm afraid that won't be possible.'

'Why ever not?'

'It's nearly ten o'clock and master Charles has been in bed for some hours.'

'In that case I shall see Julia on her own.'

'Again, I'm afraid that's also out of the question. Mrs Devereux is in her parlour. She's not receiving guests.'

He laughed. 'I'm not a guest; I'm her stepson.'

The woman was not to be put off. 'Mrs Devereux left instructions that she wasn't to be disturbed.'

You mean Mr Devereux left instructions, more like it, thought Ralph.

Determined to have his way, he moved towards the stairs. 'I'm sure Julia will make an exception for me,' he said. 'You

359

can bring my whisky up there, Miss Casey. Oh, and I'll have a sandwich too. Ham, cheese, or whatever else is to hand. I'll have my usual room, please.'

He took the stairs swiftly, two at a time. When he was on the landing, he looked back the way he'd come and saw Miss Casey down in the hall picking up the telephone receiver. The telephone hadn't rung, so who was she ringing? His father? Alerting the old man that Ralph had shown up unexpectedly?

Having earlier thought the house would make an ideal set for a horror film, Ralph suddenly felt like he was in one of Hitchcock's psychological thrillers. His stepmother certainly had all the makings of a victim at the mercy of a cruel husband and a scheming housekeeper.

He knocked on her door. There was no reply, so he knocked again, this time louder.

'Julia. It's me, Ralph.'

'Ralph?'

'May I come in?'

'Is Arthur with you?'

'No. It's just me.'

He heard the handle turn and then the door slowly opened, but for no more than a couple of inches. Julia's eyes darted over his shoulder, then back to his face. 'Has your father sent you?'

'No. Why would he?'

She put a hand to her mouth. 'I've . . . I've done something which he won't like. He'll be furious with me. I had to do it, though. It was only right. But now I'm scared.'

With no idea what she was talking about, but seeing how anxious she was, Ralph looked over his shoulder to see if Miss Casey was on the warpath. She wasn't. 'Julia,' he then said, 'why don't you let me in and tell me what you've done. It can't be all that bad, surely?'

He had never before seen himself in the role of knight in

shining armour, but there was something about the despera-
tion in Julia's voice that stirred him to help. For once in his
life he was compelled to do something good. Perhaps it was
a guilty conscience from what he'd done the night of the
Meadow Lodge party. Or maybe it wasn't so much an act of
kindness he wanted to perform, but an act of revenge on his
father?

She opened the door just enough to let him in, then quickly
shut it.

'What are you so scared of?' he asked. 'And why the hell is
it so cold in here?' He looked at the empty grate where a fire
should have been burning.

'I'm used to the cold,' she said.

'Well, I'm not. I shall insist that Miss Casey provides you with
some coal and logs. Now sit down and tell me what's going
on.'

With the blind obedience of a dutiful child, she sat in an
armchair to one side of a table on which stood an open sewing
box. He sat opposite and gave her an encouraging smile.

'It's your aunt Hope,' she said.

'Hope? She hasn't died has she?'

Julia shook her head and fiddled with a pair of sharp pointed
scissors from the sewing box. 'Not that I know of.'

'So what does my aunt have to do with why you look so . . .
so fraught?'

Before she could get the words out, there was a knock at the
door and Julia, her eyes wide with fright, jumped to her feet
and dropped the scissors.

'Let me deal with this,' he said. 'It'll be Miss Casey, I asked
her to bring me something to eat and drink.'

'Don't let her in,' Julia whispered.

'I won't.'

True to his word, he opened the door just enough so that he

could take the tray the housekeeper had brought up for him. She tried to step into the room, but he deftly blocked her way. 'Thank you,' he said, 'that'll be all.'

She stood before him seemingly as resolute to defy him as he was to repel any advance on her part. 'It's colder than a morgue in here,' he said, 'will you bring up some logs and coal for my stepmother, please?'

'I'll see what I can do in the morning,' she replied stiffly.

Beginning to shut the door, he added, 'By the way, when is my father expected home? Presumably he is returning from London to spend Christmas in the bosom of his loving family?'

'He's due to arrive tomorrow afternoon.'

'I can't wait! Don't forget to make up my room, will you?'

Ralph decided to watch her walk away down the corridor before closing the door. When he was satisfied that she really had gone, he shut the door and placed the tray on the table. He urged Julia to stop pacing the room and sit down again. She looked a bag of nerves.

'Now start at the beginning and tell me what it is that's re-duced you to this state of . . . ' he wanted to say paranoia, but settled on, 'alarm.'

Her voice low, as though she feared Miss Casey was hover-ing outside with her ear pressed to the door, she said: 'It was your father who ran Hope over. It was dark and raining and he swears he did no such thing, that what he hit was a deer. But I know what I saw. I was in the car with him.'

Ralph couldn't believe his ears. His first thought was that Julia was quite mad, that his father had pushed her over the edge. But then he remembered the cold-blooded manner in which his father had informed him of Hope's accident. He had implied Hope had brought the accident on herself by being careless.

No, thought Ralph, Julia wasn't mad; she was speaking the truth. If anyone was mad, it was Arthur Devereux.

'Have you told anyone?' he asked. 'Like the police?'

'Yes. But not the police. I wanted to, to explain it was a terrible accident, but your father said if I so much as breathed a word of it to them, he'd say it was me driving and I'd go to prison and never see Charles again. And who would believe my word against his?'

'So who have you told?'

'I caught the bus in the village and went to the hospital, even though she's still unconscious. I told Hope. If she could hear what I was saying, I wanted her to know the truth.'

'Bloody hell, of all the people to tell! Why did you do that?'

'I had to tell someone, the secret was too much for me to keep to myself. And there's something else you should know; Arthur insisted a doctor from Harley Street came to see me. He claimed I was unwell, that I was suffering with a nervous disposition.'

That much was obvious, Ralph thought. But he kept quiet.

'The pills the doctor gave me made me feel worse,' she continued. 'I felt so awful I couldn't get out of bed. Which I now think was the plan. But I stopped taking them, although I've been pretending that I am still.' Her words tumbled out of her in a breathless rush, as though she couldn't contain them a second longer.

Ralph knew his father was capable of many things, but drugging his wife to keep her captive – to keep her from talking to anyone – well, that was beyond anything he might have imagined.

But what was he thinking? If his father was capable of running over his own sister and not stop to help her, drugging his wife was small potatoes!

He was mulling this over when it occurred to Ralph that

perhaps the reason his father had been in London for as long as he had was because he was having the car mended.

Another thought came to him. 'What about Charles in all of this?' he asked. 'Does he have any idea what's going on?'

'It's Charles I'm most worried about,' Julia said. 'Arthur insisted that I was too unwell to make the journey to fetch him home from school and so he sent Miss Casey to bring him back on the train. She's trying to keep him away from me, saying I need to rest. But I don't.'

Swallowing a large swig of whisky, Ralph contemplated everything Julia had told him. 'We need a plan,' he said thoughtfully.

'You believe me, then?'

Frankly he didn't think Julia had the cunning to come up with such a story. 'Yes,' he said. 'But what happens next depends on what you want to happen. If we tell the police the truth, all hell will break out. And worse still, with that scenario, if Hope dies, my father won't hesitate to insist it was you driving, and you'll go to prison. But if we're clever we can find another—'

'I just want Arthur to love me like he used to,' she wailed, interrupting him. 'He did once upon a time. I know he did.'

Ralph stared at her in astonishment. 'You can't mean that! You know what he's capable of, and yet you still want to be married to him?'

'But he'll take Charles away from me. I can't lose my son. He's all I have.'

'Julia, he'll try to do that anyway. He might even have that doctor from Harley Street – if indeed he was any such thing – certify you as being off your rocker, and you'll never see the light of day again, never mind your son. And to be honest, unless you do perform as though you're fully in charge of your faculties, nobody will believe your story.'

The sternness of his voice instantly calmed her. 'You really do believe me,' she said quietly, more to herself than him.

She was right, he did. But perhaps that was because he was his father's son and he could see a way to take full advantage of what Julia had shared with him. But he would have to find a way to ensure his stepmother and stepbrother didn't suffer as a result of what he was prepared to do.

'Julia, I want you to trust me,' he said. 'Can you do that?'

Wiping her eyes with the backs of her hands, she nodded.

Chapter Sixty-Seven

Meadow Lodge, Melstead St Mary
December 1962
Evelyn

In the early hours of Christmas Eve, and unable to sleep, Evelyn was downstairs in the semi-darkness of the kitchen, warming a saucepan of milk on the stove.

It was so cold in the kitchen she stood as close as she dared to the gas flame without running the risk of catching her dressing gown alight. The last time it had been this cold was back in 1947. The country had practically ground to a halt, with snow so deep the army had to be called out to clear it. There were fuel shortages too. It had been a miserable time, coming so soon after the war when rationing was still in place and people had hoped for life to be so much better. Pip and Em, who were only young, had thought it all a big adventure. Even sleeping under a weight of blankets and eiderdowns with a hot water bottle apiece had been a lark for them. 'Snug as bugs in a rug,' she would say when tucking them into bed at night.

Sleep, she thought. What wouldn't she give to sleep the night through? Every night was the same. Including this one when, following a scant few hours of sleep and after listening to Kit gently snoring, and the grandfather clock in the hall striking first two o'clock, then three, she had given in and slipped quietly out of bed.

How much longer would this go on for? Would there ever

be an end to the guilt and the gnawing fear that Kit himself would be sent a letter? In the days since they'd had lunch at Island House and she'd admitted to Kit that, along with Hope and Florence, she too had been sent anonymous letters, he had stood guard at the front door in anticipation of the postman's arrival. With the flying school closed now until mid January, he was able to perform this duty three times a day for each delivery. She knew he was doing it to protect her from any further unpleasantness, but as he methodically sorted through the Christmas post, it terrified her that he would indeed find a third poison pen letter for her. Or worse, one for himself.

She would sooner die than have Kit's happiness destroyed. Or that of the children. She thought of Pip and Em, home now and sleeping soundly in their beds upstairs, and felt a tremendous surge of protective love for them.

There had to be a way to find out who was behind the letters, and then stop them.

The milk now warm enough, she switched off the gas beneath the pan and filled the mug on the draining board.

'Any chance of a drink for me too?'

'Kit!' she said, so startled the pan nearly slipped from her grasp. 'I'm sorry, did I disturb you?'

'Not really, I was having one of those annoying dreams that take you round in ever decreasing circles.'

'I know exactly what you mean,' she said, passing him the mug of warm milk she'd made for herself. She went over to the ancient refrigerator that was buzzing like an angry hornet and took out the opened bottle. While she heated more milk, Kit sat at the table.

'It's still snowing,' he remarked.

'Is it?' She leaned over the sink, parted the cotton curtains with their pattern of lemons and oranges and peered into the darkness, cupping her hands around her eyes to block out what light there was in the kitchen. 'You're right,' she said, turning away from the window. 'No doubt about it being a white Christmas, then.'

He sipped his drink. 'It's not going to be a happy time this year, is it? Not with the way things are with Hope.'

Evelyn knew how desperately upset Kit was about his sister and looking at him in the shadowy light of the kitchen, she could see how his scarred face was ravaged by the gravest of concern.

'Yes,' she murmured, 'it will be a low-key Christmas this time. I doubt anyone will be in the mood to celebrate very much. Are you sure you still want us to spend tomorrow with Romily?'

'It would be rude to back out now,' he said. 'And Pip and Em always enjoy being with Romily. It will mean less work for you, too. Especially as you have so much on your mind.'

His comment brought her up short. 'What do you mean?' she asked, switching off the gas again and pouring the warmed milk into another mug. But it wasn't until she was sitting at the table opposite Kit that he answered her.

'I know receiving those awful letters must have been a terrible shock for you, but is there anything else troubling you?'

Her heart sank that he felt the need to ask her this. 'Oh, you know what it's like at this time of year,' she said, 'the end of the school term is always manic and it takes me a while to shake off the madness.'

He put down his mug and slid a hand across the table to her, palm upwards. It was his most badly burned hand, the one which didn't lie flat and with his little finger melded to the one next to it. Such was the turmoil of her emotions, she could have wept at the sight of that vulnerably upturned palm. She covered it with her own. 'You don't need to worry about me,' she said.

'But I do. You know I can't help worrying about you. Is it me? Have I done something?'

'Why ever would you think that?'

The heartbreaking answer to her question showed in his eye. 'Oh Kit, why, after all these years, do you have to doubt my love for you? What's brought all this on? Is it Hope? Has her accident unsettled you?'

He shook his head. 'It's not Hope. It's you, Evelyn. You haven't been yourself for some time now. You're awake most nights, aren't you?'

'I think I must be going through a phase of wakefulness,' she said lightly. 'Perhaps it's my age.'

He withdrew his hand from hers and placed it around his mug. But clearly he hadn't given up. 'You've seemed preoccupied ever since the night of the party. Has it anything to do with that old friend of yours showing up?'

'Which old friend? There were lots there who you'd dug up from way back when.' Again her tone was light in a bid to hide her reaction to what he was now hinting at.

'Max Blythe-Jones,' Kit said flatly.

'Well, it was certainly a surprise to see him after all this time. But he most assuredly hasn't been on my mind since that night,' she lied. 'Far from it.'

'He's a good-looking man,' Kit said. 'Charismatic too. And he seemed inordinately pleased to see you again. I wouldn't be surprised if he still carried a torch for you.'

'*Still?*' she repeated. 'What makes you think he ever did?'

'Just something he said to me. In fact, he said it several times at the party.'

'And what was that?'

'That I was a lucky man to have won the heart of such an exceptional woman.'

Furious with Max, Evelyn wanted to crash her fist down on the table. Instead she forced a smile to her lips. 'He always was such a flatterer.' She could have choked on the levity she was feigning. She hated the pretence, it was so dishonest.

'I wouldn't blame you,' Kit said quietly. 'I mean, he must have been good company back then when you knew him.'

'He was. And yes, he's still charming and handsome, but he's nothing but a tomcat. He was back then, and he always will be!' The volume of her voice had risen with exasperation. Just what did she have to do to prove to Kit that she loved him?

'I'm sorry,' he said.

His apology only added to her guilt and frustration. 'Kit, you've done nothing wrong. It's me. I'm just on edge knowing that there's somebody out there sending people nasty notes accusing them of God knows what. Now drink your milk and let's go back to bed, if only for a couple of hours.'

Disaster averted, she thought, with her conscience not so much pricked, as shredded. *Averted for now*, she then corrected herself as she gathered their empty mugs and put them in the sink.

Damn you, Max! she thought angrily. *Why did our paths ever have to cross?*

Chapter Sixty-Eight

Charing Cross Mansions, London
December 1962
Isabella

It was Christmas Eve morning, the fingers of a cold wintry dawn only just reaching through the curtains. They were both awake early and lying in bed with her head resting on Max's chest, Isabella let out a long and very contented sigh.

'I'm so glad our paths crossed that night at Rules,' she said, dreamily.

'Me too,' he murmured. 'And I'm glad you're feeling so much better.'

'I am, thanks to you and your sexy bedside manner.' She giggled. 'I shall have to call you Dr Max, from now on.'

His hand on her head, he stroked her hair. He had such gentle hands. 'You can call me anything you want.'

When Max had deemed her well enough, he had explained what he had meant by wanting to discuss *weightier matters* with her. His words had both thrilled and scared her. She had never dated anyone too seriously before; her preference was always to keep things as brief and as superficial as possible. The thought of being with someone on a permanent basis who might interfere with her acting career, or put a stop to it, chilled her to the marrow.

When Max had declared his feelings for her, that he didn't want an inconsequential fling with her, Isabella could not have

371

been more surprised. But perhaps she shouldn't have been; he had, after all, been so good to her when she'd been ill. Initially, while taking care of her, he had been the perfect gentleman and slept on the sofa at night, rather than leave her on her own. When she was over the worst, he slept in her bed with her. Fortunately her flatmate hadn't bothered to return once the smog had cleared, claiming that since it was nearly Christmas, she would stay in the country with her parents and return in the new year.

What would Isabella and Max do then with a flatmate playing gooseberry? Would Max invite her to stay at his place?

Of greater concern to Isabella was her extended absence from the theatre, but the doctor who Max had insisted make a house call to see her had said she was in no fit state to work, let alone perform nightly on stage.

'You may well regard yourself as a trooper, Miss Hartley,' he'd told her, 'but you'll be of no use to anybody if you go down with pneumonia as a result of not following my instructions. Complete bed rest and plenty of fluids.'

After an awkward telephone conversation with the director of the play, it was agreed the understudy would continue standing in for Isabella until the new year.

Yesterday morning she had gone out for the first time in weeks to do her Christmas shopping. She had returned home exhausted, her body limp and clammy, her chest rattling like a battered tin with a couple of coins in it.

Her ear pressed to Max's chest, Isabella listened to his heart thudding inside his ribcage. She lay like that for some time, thanking providence that they had met. Compared to her previous lovers, he was by far the most experienced and expert. He took his time, teasing her with his fingers and his mouth, keeping her deliciously on the brink before finally bringing her to climax. He seemed to care much more about her pleasure than his own, which heaven knew made a refreshing change.

In the quiet still of her own company while Max was at work, she was plagued by a small but insistent voice: Was he too good to be true? What was he doing when he wasn't with her? Who was he with? He rarely spoke of where he worked, or with whom he worked, just that he was a civil servant and worked in an office where nothing of any significance was done. But then come six forty-five, as regular as clockwork, he would appear with food to cook for her, and the doubts would vanish like steam on the bathroom mirror. *Be happy for the moment*, she would tell herself. And she was happy. Oh, she was blissfully happy! She was also, very much to her astonishment, most definitely in love.

'What are you thinking?' Max asked, his hand now stroking the nape of her neck.

'How happy I am.'

'What would make you happier?'

She raised her head and looked into his eyes. 'Right now, I don't think that's possible.'

He smiled. 'There must be something. Something I can do, or something I could give you?'

'What about you? Could I give you something that would make you happier?'

He breathed in deeply so that his chest rose beneath her. 'Yes,' he said, 'I want to spend Christmas Day with you.'

She was both pleased and disappointed. 'But I'm going up to Suffolk this afternoon. It's all arranged.'

'I know that. But I don't like the thought of you travelling alone on the train in this cold weather. You might have a relapse. Or far worse, the train might get stuck in a snowdrift and some heroic young man might come to your rescue and carry you off on his steed.'

She tapped his chin with a finger. 'And what makes you think

373

'I'd allow a complete stranger to carry me off on his steed?'

'You agreed to have dinner with a complete stranger the night we met.'

'Hmmm . . . so I did. What could I have been thinking?'

'And besides, you know perfectly well what I mean.' He moved his head down and clamped his teeth lightly around her finger.

She found the sensation of his teeth pressing against her skin hugely erotic. 'I'm not sure that I do, Dr Max.'

He now kissed her finger. 'Don't be disingenuous, my darling. I'm displaying all the classic signs of a jealous lover, so please do me the courtesy of not compounding my shameful agony.'

The admission sent a spark of pleasure running through her. 'Why should you be ashamed of your jealousy?'

'Because it's not something I've experienced in a long time.'

She smiled. 'Well, we'll have to do something about that, won't we?'

'Such as?'

'You must come to Suffolk and spend Christmas there with me.'

He looked doubtful. 'You wouldn't rather stay here in London and let me spoil you?'

She shook her head. 'I haven't ever missed Christmas at home. It's a tradition. Come with me,' she added, her mind running over the pros and cons. Romily wouldn't mind one more guest, surely? But how would the rest of the family greet Max, him being so much older than she was? And what would Evelyn think? There was also Hope's condition to consider. Would it be inappropriate to bring a stranger into the family at such a time? But then Max wasn't a total stranger, was he? Not from what he'd told her about knowing Romily and Evelyn from before and during the war.

'Won't that be a break in tradition, having somebody with

you?' he asked, while her mind was racing on ahead.

'It had to happen some time,' she said, 'it might just as well be now. And with you.'

'In that case, we ought to telephone Romily and make sure it's convenient for her to have an extra guest.'

But each time they tried ringing, there was no reply; the line was permanently engaged. 'I don't feel comfortable showing up without warning Romily,' he said.

'Don't worry, she'll be fine. Nothing ever fazes Romily.'

Isabella shivered and pulled her mink coat around her. The heater wasn't working in their compartment on the train, which explained why it was as cold as an iceberg and why they were the only ones occupying it. They had tried looking for two seats together in the other compartments, but despite catching an earlier train than planned in the hope they might avoid the worst of the crush of people going home for Christmas, there were none to be had. At least she had Max to help keep her warm.

'I'm intrigued,' he said, 'am I the first man you've taken home to meet your family?'

'Yes,' she said, trying to suppress a cough. Since leaving the cosy warmth of the flat, her chest had felt like hot daggers were being systematically pushed into it. Maybe Max had been right to say that she wasn't well enough to travel yet. But it was too late now to regret leaving London. Too late also to worry about the reception they might be given on arriving at Island House.

'I'm honoured,' he said.

'So you should be.'

'Does that mean I'm special to you?'

She nestled in closer to him, both for warmth and because she loved being wrapped in his arms. He made her feel cherished. And safe. No man other than Elijah had been able to do that.

'Max,' she said, 'what is it you're really trying to ask me?'

For a moment he didn't speak. Leaning forward slightly, he used his gloved hand to wipe the steamed-up window. Through the porthole-sized space he'd cleared, Isabella watched the snow falling on the already white landscape. It all looked so unreal and impossibly beautiful. She felt as though she were travelling through a land of make-believe, a wondrous and magical fairytale.

At last Max turned his gaze back to her. 'I know I'm much older than you,' he said, 'and we've known one another for so little time, but I want you to know that I'm serious about you.'

She returned his gaze. 'You've told me that before. And for the record, I like the fact that you're so much older than me.' It was true. Any reservations she'd initially held about the twenty-six-year gap between them had long since disappeared.

He smiled. 'Hey, you don't have to emphasise it quite that much, you know.'

'You were the one who brought up the age difference, not me. And I assume you're no stranger to dating younger women, so why let it trouble you now?'

'For the simple reason this is different. Being with *you* is different. I've never felt the way I do when I'm with you. Or when I'm not with you. You . . . you've done something to me that no other woman has.'

'What's that?' she murmured.

'You've made me question myself, and the way I've lived my life.'

'How have I done that?'

'By being entirely yourself. By not playing silly mind games with me or having an ulterior motive behind anything you say or do. You're so refreshingly open and honest, and so full of life.' He smiled. 'Even when you're unwell.' His expression suddenly turned serious again. 'But I need to know how you feel about me. If you genuinely feel the same as I do. Because if we're going to keep on seeing each other, and I hope to God we are, there are things you need to know about me.'

The quiet but persistent voice that had previously questioned whether Max was too good to be true was now bellowing for all it was worth that it had been right. 'If you're about to confess that you're married with a brood of children and have been playing me for a fool, you can get off at the next station,' she said, sitting up straight so that she was no longer wrapped in his arms.

As fiercely hard-headed and certain of herself as she sounded, Isabella could feel the thump of her pulse, and the unexpected pain of what she was about to lose. Without realising it, she had subconsciously allowed herself to dream of a future with Max. And now those dreams were to be snuffed out like the flame of a candle.

So much for travelling through a magical and wondrous fairytale! But then didn't bad things always happen in fairytales?

Chapter Sixty-Nine

Island House, Melstead St Mary
December 1962
Red

Red had surprised himself. No mean feat, given how predictable his behaviour could be when it came to women. As his sister would be only too quick to point out. But here he was, having flown across the Atlantic expressly to see Romily, lying in bed completely alone and as chaste as a monk.

It would have been the easiest thing in the world last night to take the obvious step of sleeping with her, but two things had happened to prevent him from doing so. Firstly, he hadn't wanted to rush things, just as he'd admitted, and secondly, the journey and time difference had caught up with him.

Once he'd started yawning he couldn't stop, and with a firmness that had brooked no argument, Romily had shown him upstairs. Within seconds of undressing, he had collapsed into bed and slept the sleep of the dead. He had woken a short while ago and after checking the time on his watch, he had been shocked to see that it was gone one o'clock in the afternoon.

A better guest might have leapt out of bed and rushed to dress in order to go downstairs, but he had wanted to continue lying here some more so he could take stock. If he were honest, everything about seeing Romily again scared him. Never before had he bared his soul to a woman as he had last night. To have shown such vulnerability was anathema to him.

For the best part of two decades, he'd had Sophie's death on his conscience. As well as the death of all those other villagers. It had been a heavy load, but one he was reluctant ever to lose. He believed that it would be a betrayal to forget Sophie and all those villagers who had sacrificed their lives in order to protect his. He should never have put them at risk. He should have been a better pilot. A better man . . .

He was well aware that he was not the only serviceman to make a mistake and end up in enemy territory and be helped by the Resistance. But they hadn't been with Sophie. They hadn't seen the fear in her eyes when she'd asked if he would shoot her to prevent the Nazis having the chance to torture her. That was what haunted him most: her fear. And yet she had still helped him escape. When had he ever displayed courage of that magnitude?

Why didn't she shoot herself? He had often wondered. Or asked somebody she knew from the village to do it? Was she frightened they would call her a coward? And when had she thought he would put a gun to her head to protect her? He had no answers to any of his questions. But whatever her reason for asking him, what he really blamed himself for, was failing to insist that she escape with him. He should not have let her return to the village when it was to her certain death. That was the crux of his guilt, and never, as long as he lived, would he forgive himself for not taking her with him.

For all the years since, he had successfully fooled people – apart from Patsy – that he was okay. Sure, he'd lost a leg. Sure, he had occasional nightmares of hearing guns firing and people screaming, and of a girl being dragged off to a chateau, but hey, that was war for you; it went with the territory. But along had come Romily and, as though she possessed X-ray vision, she had seen through the carefully applied veneer.

The irony was, in his film script for *Yesterday is Tomorrow*, in which Spencer Tracy and Ava Gardner had starred, he'd written: '*You cannot be close to another person unless you are mad enough to self-eviscerate and be cold-bloodedly honest with them.*'

Writers did it all the time, imbued their characters with a wisdom and valour they didn't have themselves. Or if they did have that acumen, they lacked the courage to act on it. For some writers – he was one of them – their characters were their alter ego.

Was that true of Romily, he pondered? Did she write the novels she did because she relished putting her protagonist, Sister Grace, into danger so that the author could recapture the sense of adventure she'd experienced during the war? From everything he had read about Romily, Red knew that she had been a thrill-seeker in her younger years. Did she hanker for those days?

Red had encountered many a decorated war hero who had found it impossible to readjust to civilian life. In much the same boat himself, he recognised the signs – a volatile temperament, a maudlin fondness for drinking too much, and needless risk-taking. One guy he knew blew his brains out playing Russian roulette with an old military issue pistol.

Had it not been for his reckless desire to lose himself in the arms of women, Red may well have done something equally stupid. Every time he bedded a woman, it was that moment with Sophie that he had wanted to evoke. It was like a drug for him. Over and over he repeated the pattern, the desperate and twisted need to resurrect Sophie. For a time, and when he moved to Los Angeles, he saw a shrink; after all, everybody there did. You weren't considered normal unless you paid somebody to whom you regularly spilled out your guts. The sessions were laughable and became a game to him. He took perverse pleasure in running rings around the so-called expert; an attractive woman with eyes the colour of cobalt. Inevitably he slept with her and having fully compromised her, that put paid to any more sessions. He had done it deliberately, of course. Sex was always his weapon of choice.

Question was, was he brave enough to admit that to Romily? Did he need to? Was she smart enough to figure that out already? Probably yes.

Pushing back the bedclothes, he placed his foot on the floor – his prosthetic leg was propped against the wall the other side of the nightstand. At home he used a crutch to get himself about until he was showered and dressed, but without one here, he used the furniture to assist him. He made it over to the window and pulled back the heavy drapes. The dazzling brightness of the snow-covered landscape made him blink, and leaning against the sill, he stood for a moment taking in the magnificence of the view, his gaze sweeping over the sculptured effect the snowstorm had created. It was a timeless and monochrome world he looked out onto. A magpie flew across the pewter-coloured sky, putting him in mind of a Brueghel painting. He watched the bird land on a tree branch, scattering a mini snowstorm with its movement and weight.

'Toto,' he murmured, thinking of Palm Springs and the desert, 'I've a feeling we're not in Kansas anymore.'

He was showered, shaved and fully dressed and with his prosthetic leg strapped on, and was whistling Bing Crosby's 'White Christmas', when there was a light tap at the door. He went to open it.

Dressed in black slacks and a red polo-neck sweater and wearing a pearl necklace, Romily stood before him with a tray of what looked and smelt like a pot of coffee. There was also a plate of toast on the tray with a small dish of butter, and another of what he guessed was marmalade.

'Sorry I'm such a lousy house guest,' he said, 'staying in bed so late. You should have banged on the door hours ago.'

'No need to apologise, your sleeping in gave me time to wrap some presents.' She stepped in and placed the tray on the table between the two armchairs in front of the window. 'I didn't expect you to surface before noon anyway, given how tired you were last night.'

'That's one way to describe me yawning my head off so rudely. Is there sufficient coffee in that pot for two?' he asked.

'Depends how much coffee you like to drink.'

'It would be nice to share. If it wouldn't be keeping you from something more important.'

She smiled. 'Now what could be more important than tending to my guest?'

She was back upstairs with another cup and saucer within minutes and the coffee poured.

'You need to be honest with me, Romily,' he said, biting hungrily on a triangle of toast. 'It's Christmas Eve and if I'm gatecrashing your perfectly orchestrated holiday, you must say so.'

'I assure you, you're not. And the arrangements I had in place for Christmas are already in tatters. My cook telephoned earlier to say she is snowbound and with reports on the wireless that there's more snow on the way, who knows who will make it for lunch tomorrow. If anybody.'

'Does that mean we might be snowed in together? I can't think of anything I'd like more.'

She laughed. 'It may come to that.'

'But seriously, if you need me to get out of Dodge, just say the word, I won't be offended.'

'I told you last night, you're welcome to stay, and in any case, just like in Bethlehem, there'll be no room at the inn around these parts. The only house guest I'm expecting, that's if she makes it up from London this afternoon, is Isabella. Everyone else is local.'

'If I stay, you must let me help you in the kitchen.'

'Offer of help accepted,' she said with alacrity. 'But before that happens, I need to go to the village to collect the turkey and the rest of the shopping.'

'Won't the shops deliver?'

'I suspect the roads will make that extremely difficult. Much easier, and more fun, if I go on foot.'

He took a sip of his coffee. It was good and strong, just how he liked it. 'Do you have a sledge?' he asked.

'Of course. Several in fact.'

'Then our problems are over. We can pile the shopping onto one and Bob will be our Uncle St Nicholas!' He saw her gaze flicker towards the lower part of his leg. 'Don't give it another thought,' he said. 'I can handle snow all right. I'm a pretty good skier, and not a bad skater, even if I say so myself.'

'I should have known,' she replied with a smile.

He shook his head and tutted. 'Do you mind not doing that?'

'Doing what precisely?'

'Smiling. I need to stay focused.'

'On anything in particular?'

'On behaving myself.'

'Please don't feel you have to.'

'Are you giving me permission to take liberties with you?'

She gave him one of her penetrating stares. The type that left him feeling thoroughly exposed. How the hell did she do it? For good measure the cup wobbled precariously on the saucer in his hand.

'I think we've danced around that particular question long enough, haven't we?' she said.

The cup wobbled some more and before it jumped clean out of his hand, he put it down on the table. He stood up and holding out his hands to Romily, he pulled her to her feet. He had her in his arms, his mouth hovering just a tantalising inch from hers, when there was an explosion of sound coming from downstairs.

'Whoever that is giving your doorbell hell, their timing is appalling.'

'I couldn't agree more.'

'Shall we pretend there's no one at home?'

She grazed his mouth with her lips. 'We'll continue this moment later,' she said, pulling away from him.

He hung on to her hands. 'Do you promise?'

'I promise.'

'You'd better be a woman of your word.'

'I assure you I am,' she said with a laugh.

He followed her downstairs. They were at the bottom of the stairs when the bell rang again, long and hard. Next thing, the letterbox flipped open and a pair of eyes peered in.

'Romily, let us in, we're freezing to death out here!'

Chapter Seventy

Island House, Melstead St Mary
December 1962
Romily

'I knew you wouldn't mind my bringing along an extra guest,' declared Isabella with a hacking cough while standing on the hall rug shivering. She resembled a bedraggled abominable snowman in her mink coat, which was covered from top to bottom with clumps of frozen snow. 'After all, what's Christmas without a few surprises?'

'What indeed?' Romily replied with a reticent smile. Her pleasure at seeing Isabella was severely marred by the presence of the man standing next to her with a case in each hand. What on earth was Isabella doing with Max Blythe-Jones? More to the point, what was he doing with Isabella? And what on earth would Evelyn have to say when she found out about this?

'Long time no see,' said Max, lowering the cases to the floor. 'I do hope this isn't too much of an imposition, me turning up out of the blue like this. It was very much a last minute decision. We did try telephoning this morning, but couldn't get through.'

'It's true,' said Isabella. 'We kept getting the engaged tone.'

Romily could believe it, she had spoken for some time with her old friend, Sarah, as they always did on Christmas Eve, and afterwards with Mrs Collings, and then Annelise.

'But I told Max nothing was ever an imposition to you, Romily,' chirped Isabella. 'Isn't that right?'

'We all have our limits,' said Romily mildly. Then more cordially, forcing herself to sound less aloof, she said, 'Now let's get you out of those wet things and warmed up. The pair of you look like you've trekked across the Siberian tundra! What were you thinking coming on foot from the station?'

'We had no choice,' said Max. 'The taxi we thought we were lucky to find at the station had only gone a short distance when it slid off the road and we ploughed into a snowdrift that could rival the White Cliffs of Dover.'

'We were lucky to escape with our lives,' said Isabella with a laugh. Her laughter gave way to another rattling cough. Frowning, Romily took her sodden coat, but not before noting the concern on Max's face.

'I knew we should have stayed in London,' he muttered, placing an arm – what looked to be a surprisingly protective arm – around Isabella's shoulders.

Like a sunflower turning towards the sun, Isabella leaned in to him. It was only then that she seemed to realise that Romily wasn't alone, that there was a fourth person standing in the hall with them. 'Oh,' she remarked, 'you have company.'

'This is Mr Red St Clair over from America,' Romily told her, 'I'll introduce you properly once you're in the drawing room sitting by the fire.' *And then you can tell me about you and Max*, she thought.

'How about I make your guests a drink?' volunteered Red. 'Maybe some hot chocolate? I'm a dab hand at that.'

Grateful for his offer of help, Romily told him hastily where to find everything. She then shooed Isabella and Max through to the drawing room, where she removed the guard from the fire and threw another couple of logs in the grate.

Isabella flopped into one of the armchairs nearest the fire. 'I don't think I've ever been so bone-numbingly cold,' she said, stretching out her stockinged feet and resting them on the fender to warm.

'I have to agree with Max on the wisdom of you making the journey,' said Romily, brushing the log dust off her hands by rubbing them lightly against the backs of her legs. 'That cough of yours sounds terrible. You told me on the telephone that you were better.'

'I thought I was,' she said, moving her feet so Max could perch on the corner of the fender next to her. 'But I'll soon be on top form again. You know how being at Island House always agrees with me.'

'I fear it's not going to be that jolly a Christmas, what with your aunt Hope still in hospital and now this weather.'

'How is poor Hope?'

'The same as before, I'm afraid.'

'No sign of improvement at all?'

Romily shook her head. 'So tell me how you two met,' she said, keeping her voice as casual as she could while glancing at Max.

'It was wonderfully romantic,' Isabella gushed, 'Max came to my rescue.'

Max scoffed. 'I'd hardly call it romantic, me stepping in after that churl raised his hand to you.'

'Heroic then. How does that sound?'

He smiled indulgently at her. 'A slight exaggeration, darling.'

'Who, I should like to know raised his hand to you, Isabella?' asked Romily.

'Oh, it's all history. He's since made an apology, which I've accepted, so water under the bridge now. I'm much more inter-ested in hearing about the delicious man shacked up here with you, and currently in the kitchen making us hot chocolate.'

With a roll of her eyes, Romily tutted. 'He's not *shacked up here* as you so vulgarly put it; he's a friend who is visiting.'

Isabella wriggled her toes on the fender. 'If you say so,' she said with a smile. 'Is he a souvenir from your trip to America?'

'Put your overactive imagination away, Isabella, and behave, or you'll find yourself back out in the snow.'

'And knowing Romily of old, as I do,' said Max with a laugh, 'I wouldn't put her threat to the test.'

Isabella smiled up at him. 'It's funny, isn't it, to think how you all know one another from yonks ago.'

'*All?*' repeated Romily.

'Well, you and Evelyn that is.'

An eyebrow raised, and knowing what Evelyn had told her about *a one-off moment of madness* that had occurred between her and Max at Bletchley, Romily looked askance at him.

In the silence that followed, as brief as it was, a log on the fire popped and spat. 'There are no secrets between Isabella and me,' he said. 'She knows that I had a bit of a thing for Evelyn all those years ago. And that it wasn't reciprocated in the way I would have liked at the time.'

'Be that as it may,' Romily said, surprised at his admission, 'it would be better that you never repeat that while you're here at Island House.'

'Of course,' he said. 'The last thing I would want to do is cause any trouble. I thought it might be prudent of me to give Evelyn a ring later, just to explain the situation.'

'Yes,' said Romily, 'that might be prudent. Do you have her number?'

'No. I was hoping you would give it to me.'

'Of course,' Romily said, turning to look at Isabella. The girl's face was now glowing radiantly from the heat of the fire, and it was obvious from the adoring expression in her twinkling eyes as she looked up at Max, that she was hopelessly in love with him.

Romily wanted to be happy for her, but to be in love with

a man like Max, how could that ever be a good thing? Short term, yes. But if Isabella was wanting something lasting and meaningful, Max could only disappoint her. Unless he had changed. Could he have done so? She reminded herself of that look of concern and the protective arm she had seen while out in the hall.

'I know what you're thinking, Romily,' said Isabella.

'You do?'

'Yes, that Max is frightfully old for me.'

'Is that what you imagine me to be thinking, Max?' Romily asked him directly.

'Oh, I wouldn't presume to trespass on that fine brain of yours,' he said smoothly.

'But, Romily,' continued Isabella, 'you can't possibly criticise me for doing exactly the same thing as you did? Jack Devereux was years and years older than you, wasn't he?'

'She has a point,' said Max.

Romily wanted to tell him to keep his opinions to himself, and that Jack had been the best of men and utterly devoted to her. Not once had she doubted his faithfulness in the short time they had shared together. Would Isabella ever know that peace of mind in a relationship with Max? In *loco parentis*, her every instinct was to take him aside and demand to know what his intentions were.

She was saved from doing just that, and embarrassing them all, by Red entering the room bearing a large tray.

'I took the liberty of commandeering some mince pies loitering in a tin in the pantry,' he said cheerfully. 'I hope that's all right with you, Romily?'

'A splendid idea,' she said, taking the tray from him and placing it on the console table behind the sofa, 'thank you so much.'

'I must say, you really are the perfect house guest,' said Isabella. 'Now come and sit down and tell me all about yourself.

389

Romily has been remarkably coy in sharing any information. If I didn't know better, I'd say she was hiding something.'

'Behave yourself, Isabella, don't think for one moment I won't carry out my threat.'

Every inch the actress, Isabella put a hand to her heart, 'Mr St Clair, can you believe what you're hearing, that my guardian would throw a poor sick waif out into the snow? It's like something out of a Dickens novel!'

Red smiled back at her. 'I suspect she'd do it in a heartbeat.'

Everybody laughed and Max went over to Red and shook hands with him. 'I'm Max, an old friend of Romily's from way back when, and . . . ' he hesitated before continuing, plainly unsure of what he should say.

'And he's my beau,' supplied Isabella. She extended her hand towards Red. 'I'm Isabella Hartley, the actress of the family.'

'As if he couldn't guess that for himself,' said Romily, while Red shook hands with her.

'Red is a scriptwriter and we met while I was in Palm Springs,' she explained, passing round the mugs of hot chocolate and mince pies.

'That's where I live,' Red joined in.

'Have you been to England before?' asked Max.

'Yes. During the war. I was stationed not that far away from here at a US airbase.'

'So a trip down memory lane for you?' said Isabella.

'Absolutely not,' he said, his gaze sliding towards Romily. 'From here on, it's all about the future. I've spent too much time dwelling on the past.'

Chapter Seventy-One

Minton's Bakery, Melstead St Mary
December 1962
Florence

Every Christmas Eve Minton's Bakery was one of the last shops to close, and every year, for much of the day, it was the same; the queue of customers was out of the door and almost to the butcher's shop where an equally long queue was formed.

Busy refilling the shelves of the window display with sausage rolls, mince pies and loaves of warm bread fresh out of the oven, Florence smiled at their loyal customers patiently waiting in line. Stamping their feet to keep the circulation going in their toes, their breath forming in the icy air, most of them clutched overflowing baskets of shopping, and one or two held Christmas trees in their gloved hands.

George had earlier cleared the pavement in front of the shop, but within minutes fresh snow had fallen and it was as bad as ever it was. He was now delivering orders on foot to their elderly customers who couldn't brave the treacherous conditions. Rosie was also pitching in on one of her rare days off and helping to serve behind the counter with her father. It was times like this, when they all pulled together as a family, that Florence felt sad that neither of their children wanted to continue the tradition of running Minton's Bakery. But she accepted that George and Rosie had their own lives to lead.

Across the market square, and in front of the tall Christmas tree which Billy and the other shopkeepers had erected, she saw a group of children breaking off from building a snowman to have a snowball fight. Their whoops of delight caused those in the queue outside to smile, and more so when a couple pulling a sledge stopped to join in.

It was a few seconds before Florence realised it was Romily with the sledge. But who was the man with her who appeared to be throwing himself into the snowball fight with such gusto? When he hurled a snowball at Romily, she didn't waste any time in retaliating. Everybody in the square began watching them with amusement. Funny how snow, as inconvenient as it could be, brought out a light-heartedness in people.

Florence had offered to extend her hours at Island House to help Romily in the run-up to the festive period, but she had said that with Hope in hospital she wouldn't be hosting Christmas in the grand way she normally did; she felt it wouldn't be appropriate. In place of her lavish Boxing Day party, she would be hosting just a small gathering for drinks. And as far as Florence knew for lunch tomorrow, Romily would be entertaining Isabella, Stanley, and Kit and Evelyn with the twins. Perhaps the mystery man who was now being pelted with a torrent of snowballs by Romily, and all the children, would also be there?

The shelves in the window display now replenished, Florence was about to turn away when she saw the housekeeper from Melstead Hall passing by. She was a miserable-looking woman who didn't mind who she offended, much like her employer, Arthur Devereux. She had on one occasion accused Billy of selling her a stale loaf of bread, something he would never do. The butcher had also come in for criticism on the quality of his meat, and the fishmonger was accused of overcharging her.

'Still doing your round?' Billy called over to Frank Bushy, the postman, as he came into the shop with what looked like a full sack of mail. 'I thought you'd be long since at home warming your feet in front of the fire with a bottle of beer in your hand.'

'Chance would be fine thing,' said Frank, puffing out his cheeks as he squeezed his way passed the customers. 'With this snow I doubt I'll be home before midnight.' To Florence he said, 'I thought I'd drop your post off here, seeing as there's a parcel for your George.' He handed her a small package tied up with string and three envelopes. Hardly daring to look at the envelopes, she put the post on the shelf beneath the counter. She then popped a couple of mince pies into a paper bag. 'Here you go, Frank,' she said, 'something to keep you going on your round. Happy Christmas to you and the family.'

'Thanks, love. You too.'

When he'd gone, wishing everyone in the queue a happy Christmas, Florence scooped up the post and pushed through the swing doors, telling Billy she would get the next batch of bread rolls out of the oven.

Only when she had placed the hot rolls on a wooden tray did she steel herself to open the envelopes. The first one, which was addressed to Mr and Mrs Minton, and to her relief, was just a Christmas card, as was the second. But the third – addressed only to her – had Florence's fingers fumbling.

WOMEN LIKE YOU ARE SO STUPID!
YOU HAVE ONLY YOURSELF TO BLAME
FOR YOUR HUSBAND LOOKING ELSEWHERE.

She knew that the accusation was rubbish. Of course it was! But there was something about seeing it in black and white that made it seem true.

'Flo, how are those rolls doing?' called Billy from the shop, 'we're clean out here!'

Stuffing the letter into her apron pocket, she grabbed the tray and pushed open the swing doors.

'I thought perhaps you'd fallen asleep back there,' he said with a laugh. At the front of the queue Gladys Turner laughed as well. A big-bosomed divorcée who wore too much make-up and her skirts too short and too tight, Gladys always had a lewd word to share with anyone who would listen. She winked at Billy. 'I'd be happy to take your old woman's place if she's not up to the job, you just say the word, lover-boy.' Her remark produced laughter from the queue.

'I'll bear that in mind,' Billy replied with a wink and a smile. He was merely entering into the spirit of the exchange, as he always did, but with this third letter in her apron pocket, Florence couldn't help but regard Gladys with suspicion. Had she done more than just flirt with Billy? And had that enormous bosom of hers lured him into her bed? Could she actually be the sender of the anonymous letters?

With no concern for the cold, her coat undone to reveal an expanse of wobbling cleavage that was trying to escape over the top of her low-neck dress, Gladys said, 'I'll have one of your special cream horns, Billy.' She let rip with a lusty cackle, which predictably set everybody else off.

'Sorry,' said Florence, barging Billy out of the way as she carried the tray of bread rolls over to the window, 'there's only four cream horns left and they're reserved.'

Billy gave her a quizzical look. 'Your mother,' lied Florence. 'She asked me to put them by for her. Rosie, when you've finished serving Mrs Turner, put them in a box, will you?'

'Yes, Mum.'

'You okay, Flo?' Billy asked quietly some minutes later when Gladys had taken her bosom off to flaunt under some other man's nose.

'I'm fine,' she said through gritted teeth, her back to the queue of customers. 'Why wouldn't I be fine when that trollop throws herself at you? I'm surprised she didn't haul you over the counter and have her way with you right there in front of all the customers!'

'You know what Gladys is like, she can't help herself,' Billy said. 'You've never complained about her before; why today?'

Because I'm sick of receiving these horrible letters, thought Florence miserably.

By the time Romily came into the shop to collect her bread order, the snow was coming down so heavily the buildings on the other side of the market square were hardly visible. George had returned from delivering orders and with the queue for the shop slowing down, he and Rosie had gone next door to see their grandmother.

'You two looked like you were having fun earlier,' Florence said to Romily, glancing at the man with her. He was very tall and had a commanding presence about him, even with the knitted hat that was jammed onto his head. It was red with a white pom-pom like a snowball perched on the top. Florence recognised it as one of Romily's skiing hats. It contrasted with the man's smart woollen overcoat and the dove-grey coloured scarf tied around his neck. She put him in his mid-fifties and most definitely in the category of 'extremely handsome'. He looked like a film star.

'You must be Florence,' he said with an instantly engaging smile. 'Romily tells me you're indispensable to her, and that you've been through thick and thin together.'

Blushing, and conscious that the other customers in the shop were as curious as she was and were blatantly listening, she said, 'Oh, I don't know about that. But I'm pleased to meet you.'

'Likewise,' he said, taking off a glove to shake her hand. 'Red St Clair is the name.'

'You're American, then?' she said, immediately feeling stupid for stating the obvious.

'Got me bang to rights,' he said with an expansive grin that revealed two rows of perfectly white and very straight teeth. 'How did I give myself away?'

'I can't think,' said Romily, exchanging a smile with Florence.

'And you, sir,' the handsome American said, turning to Billy, 'must be none other than Billy Minton. It's a pleasure to meet you.'

Billy shook hands with him. 'Are you staying in the village?'

'I sure am. I showed up unannounced and being the perfect English hostess, Romily has kindly invited me to stay for Christmas.'

'You might not think that after I've put you on potato peeling and washing-up duty for the duration of your stay,' said Romily.

He laughed and Florence said, 'How will Mrs Collings feel about that?'

'She won't know anything about it. She's snowed in, so I shall be in sole charge of the kitchen this year. You and the family will join us on Boxing Day for drinks, won't you? Snow permitting, that is.'

'Of course.'

From a large shopping bag, Romily pulled out four beautifully wrapped presents. 'Put these under your tree,' she said.

Taking them, Florence said, 'If you have a moment, could I have a word with you, alone, please?' She inclined her head towards the swing doors.

'I'll just be a few minutes,' Romily told her handsome friend.

'Take as long as you like. I'm going to enjoy choosing us a selection of these fine pastries. Billy, what do you recommend?'

'I'm sorry for dragging you away from your guest,' Florence said, when the swing doors closed behind them, 'but I wanted to tell you I've received another letter. It was delivered just a few minutes ago.'

'Presumably it wasn't to wish you season's greetings?'

'No, it wasn't.' Florence took the letter out of her apron pocket and gave it to Romily.

When she'd read it, Romily said, 'You know there's no truth in it, don't you, Florence? It's just spiteful meddling.'

'It's hard not to think the worst,' murmured Florence.

Romily stared at the piece of paper with its glued-on words cut from a newspaper. 'I'm still convinced these letters are nothing but wild shots in the dark. Nothing but somebody wanting to cause mischief in order to give themselves a feeling of superiority.'

'Wouldn't that person want to see the results of their spite, though? Otherwise, what's the point?'

'Sometimes it's enough for a twisted mind to stay in the shadows imagining the trouble being stirred up. A bit like playing God.'

'If it is random, why haven't more people received letters?'

'Unless the recipients of the letters are prepared to come forward, we have no way of knowing just who has received one.'

Taking the letter from Romily, Florence slipped it back into her apron pocket. 'I know we can't be sure, but it seems it's only women who have been targeted.'

'I agree, and would therefore surmise that it's because the person behind the letters sees women as weak and easily upset. And I think for your sanity, Florence, you should show this latest letter to Billy and tell him about the ones before. You'll feel better for having Billy knowing what's troubling you. And now I really ought to go and save Red from an excess of interrogation by the good ladies of the parish.'

Florence smiled. 'He is rather dishy. Like Gregory Peck, or Rock Hudson. Is he somebody . . . *special?*'

Romily smiled too. 'Strictly between you and me, I think he might be. But not a word to anybody else.'

'My lips are sealed.'

They hugged each other goodbye, wishing one another a happy Christmas.

Watching Romily and her handsome American friend leave the shop, their sledge loaded up with shopping, Florence thought they made an attractive couple. And since Christmas was a time for wishes, she wished that Mr Red St Clair might become a very special part of Romily's life.

She wished too that she didn't feel so nervous telling Billy about the letters. What if he was upset that she had doubted him?

Or worse still, what if guilt got the better of him and he admitted there was some truth in what he was accused of?

Chapter Seventy-Two

Melstead Hall, Melstead St Mary
December 1962
Julia

Breathless with laughter and exertion, Julia stood for a moment to watch Charles chase after Ralph with a snowball in his hand.

They had been out here in the garden for over an hour, the snow constantly falling. It had been Ralph's idea for Julia to have a go at sledging with him and Charles. To Ralph's disbelief, she had admitted that she had never been on a sledge before. Her father had been against such frivolity when she'd been a child, and Arthur had said it was not befitting of any wife of his to behave in so undignified a manner. 'Then you haven't lived, step-mama.' Ralph had said. 'And it's time you did! Isn't that so, Charlie-Boy?'

His eyes ablaze with delight, Charles had agreed. 'Come on, Mummy,' he'd said, 'it'll be fun. You can be on the sledge with me, that way you won't be scared. I'll look after you, I promise.'

Her heart had melted like the snow on his long lashes as he'd stared up at her. How had she and Arthur produced such a sweet and beautiful little boy?

Charles had been right; it had been fun racing down the slope, and even when they'd hit a bump and they'd both been thrown off the sledge, she had rolled over in the snow and laughed. She'd laughed and laughed, until her sides had ached. How free she had felt!

She smiled now as Ralph deliberately let Charles catch him up and then bombarded him with snow, making Charles yelp. Watching them play so happily together, Julia wished it could always be like this.

No Arthur.

That was what she meant. No Arthur telling her what to do and threatening to tell the police that she was the one who drove into Hope.

And no Miss Casey either, always looking down her nose at Julia, making her feel so insignificant.

Ralph had forced her to see her situation exactly for what it was. She was married to a man who couldn't possibly love her, not when he kept her virtually as a prisoner, and was prepared to lie so she would be sent to prison.

Could there be another way to live, just as Ralph said? But how would she manage? How would she care for Charles the way she would want to? She had no money of her own. Not a penny.

Guiltily, and through the falling snow, she turned to look up at the house behind them, as though it could somehow read her mind and betray her to Arthur. At the top of the house, in one of the windows where Miss Casey had her suite of rooms – a bedroom with her own private sitting room and kitchenette – stood the woman herself. Her arms folded across her chest, she stared back at Julia. At this distance, Julia couldn't make out her expression, but it was probably one of haughty disapproval.

'Don't let the old witch intimidate you,' said Ralph, coming over to Julia. 'Wave back at her with your cheeriest smile.'

To her amazement, Julia found herself doing as Ralph in-structed and when Miss Casey stepped away from the window, she felt a small sense of triumph.

'See,' said Ralph. 'Nothing to it. You just have to show her you're not scared of her.'

'Who was that you were waving to?' asked Charles, joining them. 'Was it Father?'

'It was Miss Casey,' said Julia.

'I don't like her very much,' said Charles, wrinkling up his nose.

'You're a boy of discerning taste,' said Ralph.

'What does discerning mean?'

'It means you have good taste and know a rotten apple when you see one.'

Julia frowned. 'You mustn't repeat what Ralph has just said, Charles.'

'Why not?'

'Your father wouldn't like it.'

'But Father's not here.'

'True. But he'll be home soon.'

'Maybe he'll get stuck in the snow somewhere,' said Ralph with a smile.

'I hope he does,' said Charles. 'It's a lot more fun without him.'

'Darling,' said Julia, 'that's not a nice thing to say.'

'Well, it's not nice some of the things Father says or does. I like it better when it's just us. I'm going sledging again!' And off he ran, happier than she had seen him in a long time.

'As I say,' muttered Ralph, 'the boy has discerning taste.'

'Ralph, please don't turn him against his father, it wouldn't be fair or right.'

'Strikes me that Charlie has made his mind up already. And if you don't mind me saying, you're looking and sounding a lot better today than you did last night when I arrived. You have some actual colour in your cheeks.'

'That's because of the cold.'

'No it's not. You're beginning to feel alive, aren't you? And more importantly, strong enough to stand up for yourself. You mustn't let my father push you around anymore.'

Ralph was right to say she was feeling better; she was. And that was down to him. Being able to tell him everything that had been going on, and him believing her, made all the difference. For days she had been out of her mind with worry, desperately trying to think what she was going to do. Had she made a terrible mistake visiting Hope in hospital and telling her the truth? She had gone to church desperately wanting the power of prayer to calm her nerves, but it had made her feel even worse.

But this morning, after talking late into the night with Ralph, she woke up feeling a lot clearer-headed. Somehow, she had to escape, just as Ralph said. But when she thought how Arthur might react, how angry he would be, a shiver of fear ran through her. It made her wonder if it wouldn't be easier to make more of an effort to be a better wife to Arthur. Surely she could do that for Charles's sake, couldn't she? If things could just be like they were in the beginning, because it hadn't been so bad then, had it?

'You mustn't lose your nerve, Julia,' said Ralph, as though picking up on her thoughts.

'But what if loving Arthur more could help change him?' she said. 'It's only when I do something wrong or annoy him that he becomes angry. It's . . . it's my fault he does what he does. If I just tried harder to please him, to be a more dutiful wife, maybe he—'

Ralph brought a stop to her words by clamping his hands down on her shoulders and making her face him head on. 'Listen to yourself! Can you not hear how crazy you sound? Your husband ran his own sister over and is prepared to blame you if it gets out. How will loving him more change that?'

'It's because deep down he's scared.'

'No, it's because deep down he's evil! And trust me, when he's had his fill of making your life hell, he'll move on to Charles, if he hasn't already.'

'He wouldn't! Not a defenceless child.'

Ralph removed his hands from her shoulders. 'Trust me,' he said, 'he would. He did it to me, so I know what I'm talking about. It's just a matter of time, I assure you. He'll never change.'

Her voice cracked as she asked, 'Did he hit you?'

Ralph looked at her incredulously. 'Did he hit me? My God, he thrashed me! And took too much pleasure in it, I swear. The man's a sadist. With a father like that, is it any wonder I've turned out the way I have; feckless and with a pathological loathing for him?'

'Mummy!' shouted Charles. 'Do you want to come on the sledge with me?'

Before she could answer, his tone urgent, Ralph said, 'You must leave him, Julia. Do it for your son's sake, if not your own. He's a good kid. It would be the best Christmas present you could give the boy.'

The thought of her precious son coming to harm, of him being thrashed, made Julia feel unimaginable pain. It strengthened her resolve. 'Will you really help me?' she asked.

'I told you last night I would. And I meant it.'

'But why? Until now you've never really liked me.'

He smiled. 'Call it a Road to Damascus change of heart.'

Her gaze wavering from his, she gave a small gasp.

'What is it?'

'He's home.'

Ralph twisted his head and followed her gaze. There at the upstairs landing window was Arthur Devereux staring down at them.

Chapter Seventy-Three

Melstead Hall, Melstead St Mary
December 1962
Ralph

His father's blatant displeasure at seeing him was matched only by his disapproval that Julia had so obviously been enjoying herself.

'My wife might at least have made more of an effort to welcome me home properly after the awful journey I endured to be here,' he complained, his temper simmering darkly in his eyes.

'We had no idea what time to expect you,' Ralph said.

'And I had no idea that you would be here,' his father snarled across the drawing room. 'I don't recall inviting you.'

'I invited him,' said Julia. In the dwindling light, and moving silently, almost invisibly, around the large drawing room, she was switching on lamps.

Arthur turned from where he was warming his enormous porcine backside in front of the fire. 'You?'

'Yes,' she murmured, now absently straightening a cushion in one of the armchairs. 'Christmas is a time for family, so I thought it would be nice for us all to be together.'

It was an audacious lie from Julia and impressed, Ralph went along with it. 'I accepted the invitation in the hope it would give me the opportunity to apologise to you, Father,' he said. 'I was rude to you that evening at your club. I'm sorry.'

His father regarded him with disdain. 'You can drop the act

of contrition; I'm not taken in by it. I've seen it too many times before. You can leave first thing in the morning.'

'But it's Christmas Day tomorrow,' said Julia, 'you can't make him go. And not in this weather.'

Arthur turned to look at her again. 'Since when have you started telling me what I can and cannot do?'

'I . . . I'm not telling you what to do,' she stammered.

'Bloody well sounds like it. This is my house and if I say Ralph goes, he goes. And that's an end to it. Do I make myself perfectly clear?'

'Yes, Arthur,' she said meekly.

Ralph could see Julia's courage draining out of her. It was all he could do not to step in and remind her that she had to stay strong, that she mustn't revert to the pathetically timid creature his father kept under his thumb. *Remember the happy woman out in the garden on the sledge*, he wanted to whisper in her ear, *the woman who rolled in the snow and laughed with her son*.

'Now leave me to talk to Ralph,' Arthur said with a dismissive wave of a hand. 'Well, don't just stand there, go and tidy yourself up. You look an embarrassing mess from all that cavorting in the snow. I don't know what you were thinking. And later, and only if Charles has put on clean clothes as I asked, you can send him down to me.'

Her head lowered, Julia dutifully left the room, quietly closing the door behind her.

Adopting his most nonchalant tone, Ralph said, 'You do realise, Dad, that it's 1962 and not an era when wives were chattels and treated like servants.'

'The way I treat my wife is my business. And don't think for one minute I don't know what you're up to.'

'What would that be precisely?'

'Encouraging Julia to disobey me. I watched you while you were in the garden and without hearing a word that passed between you, I could see that you were filling her head with nonsense.'

'To *disobey* you?' Ralph repeated. 'From which Victorian novel do you take your views on marriage?'

Arthur jabbed a finger in the air at him. 'You're skating on very thin ice, I suggest you don't say another word.'

'Why?' demanded Ralph, squaring up to his father. A good deal taller, he had the advantage and could easily look down on his grotesque blob of a father. 'What will you do, beat me like you did when I was a child?'

'Far worse than that,' the old man sneered. 'I shall cut off your allowance completely.'

'Go ahead,' retaliated Ralph. 'I couldn't give a damn about your money. It's been nothing but a millstone round my neck anyway.'

'Let's see if you're still saying that in however many weeks it takes for your funds to run dry. If they haven't already. Which I expect is the real reason you're here.'

'You couldn't be more wrong,' said Ralph. Turning away from his father, he went over to the drinks table and helped himself to a glass of whisky. 'I suppose this is still allowed, is it?'

'Help yourself while you still can. Because after tomorrow I don't want to see you here ever again. You're to leave Julia alone, too. And my son, Charles. I don't want you having any kind of influence over him.'

Ralph drank half the glass in one go, refilled it, then turned to look at the man before him. 'I wonder what made you the repellent monster you are?' he said. 'The psychologists would have a field day figuring you out. As for Charles, I can only fear what you'll turn him into.'

'In my opinion, so long as he doesn't turn out like you, he'll be fine.'

'You believe that, do you?' Ralph shook his head. 'The poor little sod doesn't stand a chance.'

He contemplated telling his father that he knew who was to blame for Hope being in hospital, but decided against it. He needed more ammunition up his sleeve before he was prepared to reveal that particular trump card. Moreover, to bring up the accident now would only leave Julia vulnerable to more punishment. She was probably going to be punished tonight anyway. Unless Ralph could intervene in some way.

He drained his glass of whisky. 'Well, it seems we've said all we need to say to each other. So I shall go and change out of these wet clothes. If that meets with your approval?'

Arthur tutted and went to pour himself a drink.

Upstairs, and going in search of Julia, before his father got to her first, he went to warn her to be on her guard.

'Will you really leave in the morning?' she asked.

He heard the despair in her voice. 'If I have to, I will.'

'Where will you go? Back to London?'

'No, I shall try my luck at Island House. Romily's a good sort, she'll take me in with a bit of luck. You should come with me. Charlie too.'

Julia visibly trembled.

It was then that he reminded her of what they'd discussed in the garden, that she had to stay strong.

'You can do this,' he said. 'Because you're doing it for your son's sake.'

'You're right,' she murmured. 'I must keep reminding myself of that.'

He left her and went to run himself a hot bath. His father being too tight with his money to install central heating, the house was bloody freezing, apart from the few rooms where fires were lit.

Lying in the bath with the water as hot as he could bear, Ralph thought of Julia asking him why he wanted to help her, and his answer about him having had a Road to Damascus change of heart. And who would have ever thought that would happen? But he was determined to do better with his life. He'd frittered away too much of it already. It was partly because he had devoted the last ten years or more to provoking his father. His every action had been calculated with revenge in mind, to get his own back on the bastard for the way he had treated Ralph as a child. And how he still enjoyed humiliating him.

The beatings began when his father discovered that Ralph had been secretly receiving letters from his mother in France. He had always known his father had a temper and a streak of cruelty running through him, but overnight it was transformed into something far more dangerous. A straightforward punishment of being whacked with a cane or shoe, like they were at school, wasn't enough for Arthur Devereux. For him it had to be more of a sadistic performance, a show of his strength and power. To this day, Ralph could still see the sick gleam in his father's eye when he summoned Ralph to his study, and then when he locked the door and opened the drawer of his desk where he kept the cat o' nine tails. The ordeal would last as long as it took for his father to satiate his appetite for violence. The look on his face afterwards would be one of iron-cold indifference.

Not a word did Ralph say to anyone about the punishments. Instead he vowed that one day he would pay his father back. And with what Julia had now told him, he was pretty sure he was close to doing just that.

But he wasn't doing it only for himself, to honour the promise he'd made. He now had a better cause: he wanted to save young Charlie-Boy from experiencing what he had. It made him feel physically ill to think of the boy going through what he had suffered.

Out of the bath now, he dried himself as quickly as he could and dressed even faster. Pulling on his warmest sweater, a black polo neck, he thought how much he'd enjoyed being around his little brother. In the past he had not wanted anything to do with him, which seemed petty now. But then nor had he been interested in getting to know Julia. He hadn't seen any point in doing so. But he could honestly say he enjoyed being around the kid; he was fun and full of childish innocence. Had Ralph been like that once upon a time? Before his father had crushed and poisoned him?

Miss Casey, her brooding presence casting a gloom over the proceedings and adding to the chill of the room, served dinner. The joyless atmosphere could not have been worse, and given how many excruciating meals Ralph had eaten with his father, that was saying something.

From the moment they sat down, Arthur kept up a steady barrage of reprimands for Charles, criticising him for eating too noisily or too quickly, or for putting his elbows on the table.

'Charles,' he said now, 'how many times do I have to tell you not to scrape your knife and fork against your plate?'

'Sorry Father.'

'If you can't behave like a gentleman, you'll have to eat in the kitchen with the servants. Is that what you want?'

'No Father.'

'Julia,' he snapped, turning his attention to her, 'what on earth is the matter with you? Why aren't you eating?'

'Sorry, Arthur, I don't seem to be very hungry.'

'Then I shall have to call for Dr Monk from London again. I'm sure he'll make a special visit on Boxing Day if I ask him to.'

'I doubt that,' muttered Ralph, 'not if this weather keeps up.'

'Did I ask for your opinion?'

'No, but you can have it for free. Miss Casey, I'll have another potato, please, if it's not too much trouble for you?'

The woman actually looked to Arthur for permission and after he'd acquiesced, she dropped a potato onto his plate.

After she'd left the room, and in a valiant attempt to jolly things along for his stepbrother's sake, Ralph suggested a game of cards after dinner. 'Or better still, how about a game of Monopoly?'

'Out of the question,' said Arthur before the boy had a chance to reply. 'Charles needs to go to bed early tonight. From what Miss Casey tells me, he's been having far too many late nights since coming home from school.'

'But it's Christmas Eve,' said Ralph. 'Let the lad have some fun.'

Arthur crashed his fists down on the table, making them all jump. 'Enough! You will not interfere in how this house is run. Charles, go to your room now.'

Julia's lower lip wobbled as the boy did as he was told. He was probably only too happy to escape.

'I think I'll go to my room as well,' Ralph said, tossing his napkin onto his plate.

Late that night, unable to sleep, and regretting he hadn't finished his dinner, Ralph went in search of something to eat from the larder. Wrapped in his dressing gown, his slippers on, he padded down the wide staircase as quietly as he could. The wall to his left was covered with heavy, gold-framed oil paintings of hunting and moorland scenes, grazing Highland cattle, and noble stags. His father had bought the paintings from country house sales, the owners no longer able to afford to run their once great houses. From the same sales Arthur had bought most of the furniture and rugs to furnish the Hall, along with a plethora of stuffed animals' heads and bronze statues. He would have taken enormous delight in every single purchase, gloating that he could afford to snap up these family heirlooms, as though they were cheap trinkets in a penny bazaar.

Ralph was back upstairs with a tray of cold meats and pickles as well as a bottle of wine from the cellar, when he heard noises coming from the floor above him – where Miss Casey had her rooms. Curious, he abandoned the tray and crept as stealthily as a cat burglar up the narrow flight of stairs.

On the top landing, he pressed his ear to the door of Miss Casey's room. Holding his breath, he quietly bent down to see if he could look through the keyhole. But he was out of luck; his view was obscured by the key in the lock.

But he didn't need to see what was going on inside the room. He knew. More importantly, he knew who was in there with Miss Casey.

His father.

Chapter Seventy-Four

Island House, Melstead St Mary
December 1962
Romily

Yet to go to bed, Romily was alone and sitting at her desk in the library. Behind her, the carriage clock on the mantelpiece chimed the half hour, signalling that it was half-past twelve and thirty minutes of Christmas Day had already passed.

Time was a strange phenomenon. As a child one thinks it passes with inexorable slowness and that there's simply too much of it wafting around. But as an adult, time is an altogether different commodity, there isn't enough of it and it slips away faster than water gushing down a plughole.

'I've spent too much time dwelling on the past . . .'

Those were the words Red had used this afternoon when he'd answered Isabella's question about his visit here not being a trip down memory lane. He had said what he did for Romily's benefit, giving her a clear message; why else the look he'd given her?

With a fire burning in the grate, she had been sitting here for the last forty-five minutes, long after everyone else had retired to bed. She had been reflecting on what Red had said, knowing that there was a part of her that remained locked in the past.

In front of her was the wooden box which for all these years had contained Matteo's letters. She lifted the lid, once more allowing the summery scent of lavender to escape. Was it now time to get rid of the letters? She would never be able to eradicate entirely that painful episode in her life, but would destroying them be a symbolic gesture, her way of finally laying that time to rest?

It was, she understood, part of the human condition to fall into the trap of looking back too much, no matter how hard one tried to look to the future. The trouble was, one was saddled with being the sum of one's parts. It meant that everything a person did or experienced was thrown into the mix and affected one's behaviour. But had Romily allowed the past, even unwittingly, to influence her too much?

Look how she had reacted at seeing Max with Isabella. The moment she set eyes on him, she had regarded him as the man she had known all those years ago; an inveterate womaniser. The thought of him playing fast and loose with Isabella's affections appalled her. But as Isabella had rightly pointed out, Romily's relationship with Jack proved that a person could change. The right person, as Jack had said, could actually change someone, so they became a better and happier person. She had done that for him, he had claimed. 'You have transformed me,' he'd said the day they married.

But how often did that happen? How many leopards were really capable of changing their spots? Was Max capable of undergoing such a transformation? Or was she doing him a disservice, had he already put his past behind him?

The bigger question she had to ask was far more difficult to answer – was *she* capable of changing? Could she shake off her own spots sufficiently in order to trust her feelings for Red?

If she thought only of the smaller picture, she could happily throw herself into a relationship with Red, but the moment she panned out to see the whole picture, she lost focus. Perhaps that was her mistake, trying too hard to gaze into the crystal ball of life. Why not simply enjoy the moment? It was what they had all done during the war. They had made whatever fun they could, and whenever they could.

There was no getting away from it, she had enjoyed herself immensely today going out into the village with Red and throwing herself into a snowball fight with him. Not since Isabella, Annelise, and Stanley had been children had she done anything like that. Nor, in a long time, had she kissed a man in the way she had Red.

They had been on their way to the village with the sledge when, and with no one else around, he had swept her up in his arms and kissed her, pressing her against the snow-covered tree. It had been the most delicious kiss, full of breathless passion, just as when they had kissed the night before. There was no mistaking the desire that existed between them. But could she trust it?

Since when had she been so distrustful of her feelings? Did it go back to that awful day – a day she had tried so hard to forget – when she lost her child?

Her mind instantly dodged answering the question by thinking of Annelise. Poor Annelise suffering just what Romily had all those years ago. What would she decide to do?

It was easy to think that in 1962 they lived in more enlightened times, but an illegitimate baby was still frowned upon. Just as it was when Romily discovered she was carrying a child who would never know its father.

She could have cast herself as a victim, but what good would that have done? It would only have been a lie. She had made love with Matteo with her eyes wide open, somehow believing that the worst couldn't happen. Not to her. Why would it, when she saw herself as practically invincible? She had survived the crash in the Walrus, and any number of near misses, before and after, why would her luck run out and she fall pregnant?

Hearing the library door creak open, she looked up and was

surprised to see Red peering in at her. He had gone to bed the same time as Isabella and Max, and she had assumed he would be out for the count like last night.

'Waiting for Santa to arrive?' he asked.

'Just thinking over a few things,' she said, closing the lid on the box.

'May I come in?'

'Of course.'

She motioned for him to sit in the comfortable chair to one side of the fire, which was still glowing and throwing out plenty of warmth.

'So why aren't you fast asleep?' she asked, moving away from the desk to sit opposite him.

'I was thinking about you and how much I'd enjoyed today.'

She smiled. 'I enjoyed it too.'

'That's good to know.'

'Is it?'

He leaned forward, his dressing gown opening slightly to reveal the blue silk of his pyjama top. 'And what sort of a question is that?'

'A fairly straightforward one, I'd say.'

'The hell it is,' he said with an easy laugh. 'Everything with you is loaded with complicated significance. Do you ever just trust your gut and act on impulse?'

'Not as much as I once did.' Without meaning to, her gaze slid towards the box on her desk. 'But since many years ago, it hasn't been so easy for me to be quite so impulsive.'

His own gaze followed hers. 'Did somebody let you down?' he asked.

She shook her head at the leap of thought he'd made. 'Yes. But I let myself down more. It's perhaps the only thing I've done in my life that I regret.'

'Do you want to tell me about it?'

She thought of all that he had shared with her about his time in France, and of Sophie. But she couldn't bring herself to be as honest in return. 'Another time maybe,' she said evasively.

He nodded thoughtfully. 'You look and sound like you have a lot on your mind,' he said.

'You're right,' she said, 'I do.'

'Are you very bothered about Isabella and that fellow, Max?'

She smiled. 'Does it show very much?'

'You don't approve of him, do you?'

'I have my reasons.'

His elbows resting on the arms of the chair, he laced his hands together in front of him. 'Were you and he, well . . . you know, an item some time ago?'

Her smile widened. 'No. Max loved to charm and flirt, but it was no more than a game between us.'

'No harm in that when you're young and the sap is rising. But you know, he seems sincere enough around Isabella. To a complete stranger, that is. And I don't regard myself as being too gullible when it comes to these things.'

'I agree with you, he does seem to be genuinely concerned about Isabella.'

The clock on the mantelpiece chimed the hour; it was one o'clock.

'It's late,' she said, 'I suppose we really should go up.'

'Suddenly I'm not in the least bit tired. Are you?'

'Not in the slightest,' she said. 'Why don't you put some more coal on the fire, and I'll pour us some brandy?'

'I shouldn't have anything to drink, not given my resolve to keep a cool head around you.'

'I'm prepared to risk the consequences if you are.'

He smiled. 'Go on then.'

She fetched two generous measures of brandy from the cabinet where she kept a selection of drinks. They stood in front of the fire and he raised his balloon glass to hers. 'Happy Christmas to you, Mrs Devereux-Temple,' he said softly.

'And a Happy Christmas to you, too, Mr St Clair.'

'I have a confession to make,' he said, after they'd both taken a long sip of their drinks.

She eyed him warily. 'You're full of confessions, aren't you?'

'I'm afraid I'm about to break another promise I made to myself.'

She looked at his face in the soft light cast from the lamp on her desk as well as the glow of the firelight. How handsome he was, and how mesmerising his brilliantly dark eyes were. She put a hand to his cheek, something she had longed to do all evening. But with Isabella and Max around, she had kept herself in check. Now though, just the two of them, her desire for him raged through her.

'What promise is that?' she asked. She could see a vein pulsing in his neck and feel the sudden tautness in his body.

He turned his head into the palm of her hand and kissed it, his soft lips against her skin making her heart thud. 'The one I made last night,' he said slowly, now taking hold of her hand in his. 'About not rushing things. But you see, I'd give anything to wake up in the morning with you by my side. It would be the perfect Christmas present. One I would always treasure.'

'The thing about some promises,' she said, transfixed by the yearning in his face, 'is they're just like parking meters.'

He raised an eyebrow and cocked his head. 'Whatever response I was expecting, or hoping for, it certainly wasn't that!'

She smiled. 'It's really quite simple,' she said. 'The promise you made was the sort that wasn't meant to last longer than twenty-four hours.'

'It was?'

'Oh yes. And,' she pointed to the carriage clock, 'by my reckoning it ran out a few hours ago.'

417

He stared at her, then threw back his head and laughed. 'Now she tells me!'

When he fell silent, he drank the rest of his brandy, as did Romily. They each placed their empty glasses on the mantelpiece, and then, as one, moved into each other's arms and kissed. Her hands pressed into his shoulder blades, he moved against her, strong and sure, his right hand holding the nape of her neck. Locked together, they kissed as they had before, passionate and with the need for more from the other.

At last they pulled apart, both breathing hard and gazing deep into each other's eyes. Without another word exchanged, Romily switched off the lamp on her desk and led Red from the room to go upstairs.

Chapter Seventy-Five

'I don't believe for one minute that story Romily gave us about her and Red being just friends. The sexual tension between them last night during dinner was akin to watching bacon sizzling in a pan!'

Max smiled. 'What a way with words you have, my darling. Does it bother you that they might be lovers?'

Wearing the shirt Max had worn yesterday, Isabella turned away from the window where she had been watching yet more snow fall from the leaden sky. 'Heavens no!' she said. 'I think it would be wonderful for Romily to have a man in her life after all this time on her own.'

'What about you, do you like having a man in your life?'

Isabella thought how much Max had come to mean to her. How he filled her heart in a way no man ever had before. People often spoke of finding a partner who was the missing piece they had never even realised was missing from their lives, but only now did she know how true that was.

'You'll know,' Elijah had once said to her when she'd been in her early teens and had asked him how she would know that she was in love with somebody. 'You'll just know with all your heart that you've found the right person.'

She went back to the bed where Max was lying on his side

looking at her. 'I rather think I do,' she said, slipping under the warm bedclothes to join him.

He contemplated her for a few seconds, then rolled over to lean on top of her. 'I hope it's this particular man you enjoy having around,' he said.

She placed her hands either side of his bristly unshaven face and kissed him. 'Do you really?'

'How can you ask that after everything I told you on the train yesterday?'

'Well,' she said, teasingly, 'put yourself in my shoes. Why should I believe I'm any different to all the many women you've had in your life before me? Including,' she said with extra emphasis, '*my aunt.*'

He frowned and suddenly looked serious. 'You will keep your promise never to say anything about that, won't you? I only told you because I meant it when I said I didn't want there to be any secrets between us.'

When he'd admitted to her that he had been somewhat economical with the truth in his explanation as to how well he knew Evelyn, she had greeted his confession with relief. She had been utterly convinced he was about to ruin everything by saying he was married. Compared to that, a brief affair with her aunt all those years ago didn't bother her in the slightest. 'Ancient history,' she had assured Max. 'I couldn't care a fig about it.' Perhaps it was her reaction – her fear that she was going to lose Max – that made her realise just how strongly she felt for him.

However, knowing what she now knew did make her review her opinion of her aunt. Evelyn had never struck her as the spontaneous sort to throw herself into a passionate fling. Certainly not when she was already seeing another man: Kit.

'Of course I won't say anything,' she said to Max. 'I'd hate to cause Evelyn any embarrassment. Or Kit. Although there are plainly going to be some awkward moments ahead for us, aren't there?'

'We'll ride them out,' he said firmly. 'My first hurdle is to convince Evelyn that I'm not the dirty dog she imagines me still to be. She didn't exactly sound full of the milk of human kindness towards me when I spoke to her on the telephone. But that wasn't really what I was referring to. What about the other thing I told you?'

'You mean your job?'

'No, the other and far more important thing. Are you sure that's not a problem? Have you given it any more thought? I would understand if it's—'

She kissed him again. 'Shh . . . not another word. I've given it all the thought I need to.'

'But it's important. You're so much younger than me and—'

She silenced him with another kiss. 'Stop looking for problems where there aren't any. It's Christmas Day and I don't want anything to spoil it.'

Then, on impulse, she said: 'And to prove to you that I don't care about any of the stuff you're worried about, there's something I want you to do for me.'

'Name it.'

They dressed in as many layers as they could put on, and in which they could still move. And with no sign of Romily up and about, or her guest, Isabella opened the back door and let them out.

They had only been trudging through the falling snow for a short distance when the bitterly cold air found its way to her chest. She started to cough.

'Is this such a good idea?' asked Max.

'I'll be fine,' she assured him. She loved it that he was always so concerned for her. Never would she forget him turning up that day during the smog, when she was stuck in bed feeling so ill.

He took hold of her gloved hand in his. 'But where are we going?' he asked.

'Somewhere that means a lot to me.'

Following the footpath that was so deep with powdery snow it was coming over the tops of the wellington boots they had found by the back door, and which they'd borrowed, they eventually emerged into a clearing. Ahead of them was St Mary's. It was too early for the Christmas morning service yet and Isabella wondered if it would be cancelled in view of the weather.

She led Max around the church, and when they had reached their destination, she bent down and with a gloved hand, swept away the pillow thickness of snow that covered her father's gravestone. She did the same for her mother's next to it.

'My parents, Elijah and Allegra Hartley,' she said, looking up at Max. 'I've never brought anyone here before. I promised myself that only the man I truly believed in would be worthy of making this visit with me.'

He hunkered down in the snow next to her, but didn't say anything. The muffled quiet that enveloped them was absolute. Not a bird chirped. Not even the crows and rooks that could usually be heard cawing in the tops of the trees stirred.

Her voice hushed, Isabella said, 'I told you before that I never knew my mother, but what I didn't tell you was that Elijah, the man I always regarded as my father, wasn't.' She turned to face Max. 'It's never bothered me that I was illegitimate, the same as my mother; not when Elijah raised me as his own. He loved Allegra so much; he promised her when they married, and she was pregnant with another man's child, that he would always take care of her. And me.'

'It takes a special kind of love to do that,' Max said softly, taking off a glove and brushing away the snowflakes that had settled on her nose and cheeks.

'Yes,' she murmured. 'You need to know that any man who professes to love me has a lot to live up to. I couldn't accept someone who wasn't prepared to love me in the way that Elijah loved my mother.'

'He was a rare man.'

'He was,' she said simply.

'Do you think he would have approved of me and the age difference between us?'

She smiled sadly. 'I never knew him to be anything but open-minded and fair. But I'm pretty sure he would have been wary of your motives until he knew you better. He would also have known that I'm just like my mother, so I'm told, headstrong and wildly impulsive, so . . .'

'So he would have known it would have been futile to inter-fere?' Max finished for her.

'More or less,' she said through frozen lips, her teeth beginning to chatter.

Rising slowly to his feet, and holding out his hands, he pulled Isabella up into his arms. 'We should go now. Before you perish from the cold.'

They walked back to Island House in sombre silence, the only sound to be heard in the still of the frozen morning, was the crunch of snow beneath their boots. What was he thinking? she wondered. That he couldn't live up to the expectations she had of him?

'Max,' she said, when the footpath was behind them and they were walking the length of the garden at Island House, following in the footsteps they had made earlier, 'if you feel, after what I've just shared with you, that this is a turning point for you, I will understand. There'll be no hard feelings, I promise. I'd just prefer to know.'

'You're right,' he said slowly, coming to a stop and staring straight ahead of him. 'It is a turning point. And not one I can pass over lightly.' He then swung round to stand directly in front of her.

At the intensely solemn expression on his face, Isabella's legs turned to jelly. Just as she had feared the worst on the train yesterday, she braced herself now.

Chapter Seventy-Six

Island House, Melstead St Mary
December 1962
Red

From the bedroom window, Red watched Max and Isabella in the garden. If he didn't know better, he'd say he was witnessing a proposal of marriage. Why else would Max be down on one knee in the snow?

The next thing he saw was Isabella clapping her hands together before dropping to her knees and flinging her arms around Max's neck. She must have thrown herself at him with some considerable force as Max then toppled backwards, taking her with him. Smiling to himself, Red watched them roll over in the snow like a couple of crazy kids. He didn't think he'd seen two happier people. Well, apart from him and Romily pelting each other with snowballs yesterday!

He wondered what Romily would make of the scene he was witnessing, given her reticent manner towards Max.

Unlike her manner towards him in bed last night, he thought with a grin. 'I ought to warn you,' she'd said, when they'd made it upstairs to her room and began undressing each other, 'I'm a little out of practice.'

'Me too,' he'd said.

She'd laughed and told him he was a shocking liar.

He had felt self-conscious when he had taken his pyjama bottoms off and had to remove his prosthetic leg. It was a

sensation he had not experienced before. Perhaps it was because he'd wanted the moment to be perfect, for Romily not
to be disappointed in him. As they explored their bodies and
found their rhythm, her every caress, her every kiss, and every
look, tipped him closer to the edge of losing himself in her.

Now, this morning, and already showered and dressed, he
moved away from the window. With some difficulty, he knelt
beside the bed and just drank in the face of the woman he had
travelled halfway around the world to be with. Everything with
Romily was new and magical to him, and completely unlike
how he'd felt with any woman before.

'What have you done to me?' he murmured. 'And where do
we go from here?'

At his softly spoken words, she stirred.

'Hello you,' he said as her eyes flickered open. 'Happy
Christmas.'

'Happy Christmas to you, too,' she said.

'You're beautiful when you sleep,' he said.

She smiled. 'You say the nicest things.'

'I do my best.'

She stretched her hands above her head. 'What time is it?'

'Half-past ten.'

All trace of sleepiness was instantly gone from her face. 'It
can't be! Not when I have so much to do.'

'Relax. I told you, I'll help you in the kitchen. If there's one
thing we Americans know how to cook, it's a turkey with all
the trimmings.'

She slid a hand round the back of his neck and pulled him
closer to kiss his mouth. 'Mmm . . . you smell nice. What's the
cologne you're wearing.'

'It's *eau de* love.'

She groaned and gave him a playful shove. 'That is the most
awful line I've ever heard.'

He laughed. 'It's so bad, even the toes on my prosthetic leg are curling up with embarrassment. To make amends, would you like your Christmas present now?'

She drew her shapely eyebrows together. 'But Red, I haven't bought you anything.'

'At the risk of distressing you with another corny line, waking up beside you this morning was your present to me.'

'Sweet man.'

'You didn't think that of me when we first met. You thought I was arrogant, conceited and self-absorbed, and full of a sense of misplaced entitlement. Yes?'

'They were your finer points,' she said with a smile. 'What did you think of me?'

'That you were beautiful and smart with a short fuse when it came to men who show up late for lunch. But boy did I get a kick out of being with you that day! So what's it to be, your present now, or later?'

'Later, please.'

'As you wish.'

Pushing himself to his feet, he moved to one side so Romily could get out of bed. Reaching for her apricot-coloured dressing gown, which matched her nightdress, she slipped it on and kissed him.

'I'm so very glad you came,' she said.

'Not as glad as I am.'

She smiled and went over to the window. 'I see it's still snowing,' she said. 'And judging from the footprints from one end of the garden to the other, two people have been out for a walk. Presumably Isabella and Max.'

He told her what he'd earlier observed.

'A proposal?' she said. 'Are you sure?'

'Looked like it from where I was standing. I can't think why else he'd be down on one knee.'

427

She tutted. 'I need to talk to Isabella. And Max.'

'I totally accept it's none of my business, but they both looked over the moon.'

'But Isabella's so young to marry. What will happen to her career as an actress if she marries?'

He frowned. 'Plenty of girls continue with their acting careers when they marry. It doesn't have to put a halt on things. And Isabella strikes me as a girl who knows her own mind.'

Romily shook her head. 'You don't know Max as I do.'

'No disagreement there, but we all change as we grow older. Jeez, I wouldn't want you to hold my past against me.'

'I believe you've done that to yourself,' she said, staring out of the window.

'You've lost me.' Although she hadn't. He knew what she meant, but was surprised at the way she'd said what she had.

She shook her head again. 'Forget it, I shouldn't have said anything. It was wrong of me.' She turned to face him. 'I'm sorry.'

'No, go on, tell me what you meant. Please.'

She sighed. 'You've held your past against yourself, Red, you admitted that the other night. It's why you've never given the whole of you to anyone, just the bits you're prepared to share.'

'Well, that's harsh, but also true, I don't deny that. Can I ask you something?'

'Yes.'

'Haven't you done the very same thing? You said last night that you weren't as impulsive as you used to be, that it was because of something that happened some years back. Whatever it was has affected how you trust people. Am I right?'

'You are,' she said, at length. 'And I'm sorry for sounding so negative; it's Max, he's thoroughly rattled me. I promised Elijah, Isabella's father, that I would do all I could to take care of her. I just don't want Isabella to be hurt. By Max, or any man for that matter.'

'If someone had tried to stop you marrying Jack, would you have listened?'

'Of course not. And everything you've said, I've thought myself already. I'd give anything to be able to trust Max.'

'You need to give him the chance to prove himself.'

'I know. But, and as if the situation isn't complicated enough, there's someone . . . someone nearby who once made the mistake of growing too close to Max, and if he becomes a member of the family, it's going to complicate matters horribly.'

'Life is complicated,' he said. He took her in his arms. 'Look at us. How are we going to continue seeing each other when we live so far apart?'

'That's a very good question,' she said with a long sigh, her head resting against his shoulder.

He kissed the top of her head and when she released herself from his arms and went to shower, he thought how committed she was to this beautiful house, and the extended family she had inherited through marrying Jack Devereux.

It seemed to Red, based on what she had shared with him, that she resided over the family like a generous-hearted matriarch. But had she sacrificed part of herself to do that? Did they, the Devereux clan, appreciate what she had done for them, he wondered? And could she ever give it up? Even partially?

Chapter Seventy-Seven

Woodend Cottage, Melstead St Mary
December 1962
Stanley

Christmas Day had got off to a terrible start for Stanley.

He'd been woken by Tucker barking and dragging himself from the warmth of his bed, he'd gone downstairs and discovered that the pipes had frozen in the night and burst. The kitchen floor was inches deep in a lake of icy cold water.

Stanley prided himself on having a practical nature, but he knew he'd be better to restrict his efforts to turning off the stopcock and baling out the kitchen, rather than attempt to mend the faulty pipe. Fortunately, the kitchen and scullery were a step down from the small sitting room, so the damage was limited to this lower level of the cottage. Odds on he wouldn't be the only person facing a burst pipe, not when the temperature had dropped well below zero. It was anybody's guess when a plumber would be available to fix the problem.

Now, having mopped away the last of the water and stoked up the Rayburn with coal to help dry out the place, he finally got around to making himself some breakfast.

While the kettle came to the boil on the hotplate, and too hungry to bother toasting the bread, he cut himself a thick slice and loaded it up with butter and jam. He was onto his second slice when the kettle boiled. His coffee made, he drank it while standing next to the Rayburn where Tucker was warming himself. Apart from the fireplace in the sitting room it was the only source of heat in the cottage.

'Happy bloody Christmas,' he toasted himself with the mug of coffee. Then looking around him, he suddenly thought of the absurdity of suggesting Annelise marry him as an answer to her problems. Why would she lower her standards to be with him?

Oh yes, some time in the future, he planned to have a bigger and better house, and one he would design himself, but that was a long way off. He needed to make a name for himself as an architect before that dream could ever be a reality. Fairview was the first really big commission he'd been given, and he'd always be grateful to Hope and Edmund for providing him with the chance to prove his ability. Very likely Annelise had had a hand in persuading them to appoint him, although when he asked her directly if she had, she denied it.

He sipped his coffee thoughtfully, wondering why love had to be so hard. Why did some people fall in love with the right person, and others the wrong? Look at Annelise, as smart as paint, but still she had fallen for a married man.

As for him, why did he have to love Annelise the way he did? She was unattainable, he knew that, he always had. But his feelings for her made it impossible for him to love any other woman. He was stuck in limbo, for ever wanting what he couldn't have.

Was the answer to get away from Melstead St Mary and everything connected to Annelise? To put as big a distance be-tween him and the village as was possible?

He thought of the Christmas card he'd received a few days ago; it had been sent from the other side of the world: Australia.

What if he went there?

The sender of the card had studied architecture with him and many a time they'd revised for exams late into the night together. Last year John had become a Ten Pound Pom and went to live in Sydney. According to the message in the card he was having the time of his life and earning a ton of money into the bargain.

Why shouldn't Stanley do the same? He was well qualified and certainly not afraid of hard work. What was more, there'd be no risk of any freezing pipes. He'd spend his free time on the beach, just as John boasted he did. Better still, from all that Stanley knew of Australia, it was a classless society, a place where he could reinvent himself to be whoever he wanted.

The more he thought about it, as he stood watching the snow fall outside, the more tempting the idea became. What if, putting all this behind him, he could shed his past like an unwanted coat? Maybe then he'd also be free of the nightmares and the debilitating self-loathing that still had the power to rip the guts out of him.

But what of the people who had shown him such kindness? Those who had given him a home as a child and helped educate him? Could he really walk away from Romily and Evelyn and the debt of gratitude he owed them? And could he really leave Annelise?

What if she came with him? She could easily find a job at a top university in Sydney. And she could pretend to be widowed and therefore perfectly respectable in having a child.

Just as he was getting carried away with the idea that they could each build an exciting new life in a far-off land, he saw the fatal flaw in his thinking. The whole idea of him going to Australia was to escape his problems, not take them with him. If seeing Annelise was too difficult for him, then it would be better to remove her from his life completely.

He briefly closed his eyes at the pain he knew that would cause him, but what choice did he have? He couldn't go on as he was. Something had to change, and it had to be him. He had to create a new existence for himself. A fresh start.

As if picking up on his thoughts, Tucker pressed his nose against one of Stanley's legs. *And what about me?* The dog seemed to ask. Oh God, thought Stanley bending down to him, how could he leave his beloved dog behind?

An hour later, his boots on and bundled up in his duffle coat, a woollen hat pulled down over his head and the hood of his coat up, Stanley was ready for the trek to Island House. On his back was a rucksack containing Christmas presents, and a pair of shoes with clean socks to change into. It was rare for him not to take Tucker out with him, but he decided the snow was just too deep. 'Best you stay here next to the Rayburn,' he told the dog.

He'd walked for about a mile and not a single car had passed him. Or anyone else on foot. It was as if he was entirely alone in the world. At a sharp bend in the road, he recognised Edmund's Mk 2 Jaguar sticking out of the hedge. The only reason he knew it was Edmund's car was because as he approached, a great drift of snow slid down the back of it and revealed the number plate. Worried, he brushed the snow away from a side window to make sure Edmund and Annelise weren't stuck inside. To his relief, they weren't.

From the direction the Jag was pointed, Stanley guessed that Edmund, and probably Annelise too, had been returning from seeing Hope. He pressed on, deciding to take a detour to Fairview to make sure they were okay.

Annelise opened the door to him.

'Stanley!' she said, ushering him over the threshold, 'what are you doing here? I thought you were having lunch at Island House?'

'I was on my way there when I saw Edmund's car and was worried.'

433

'That's so kind of you, and it's not as if we're on your way to Romily's.'

'It doesn't matter. How . . . how are you?' He forced his eyes to stay on her face and not travel down to where the baby was growing inside her.

'Still feeling hideously sick,' she answered quietly.

'Any decisions made? And I don't mean about marrying me,' he rushed to clarify. 'I know you can't do that. It was a mad idea on my part.'

'It wasn't mad, Stanley, and I'm too fond of you to want to lumber you with another man's child. That wouldn't be fair to you.'

Aren't I the best judge of what's fair for me? he wanted to say, but he knew there was no point.

'Will you stay for a drink to warm you up?' she asked. 'It is Christmas, after all.'

'I don't want to intrude.'

'Don't be silly. Since when have you ever intruded? To be honest, Edmund could do with being cheered up. He's upset that we can't spend the day at the hospital with Hope as we'd planned. We were on our way home last night when we skidded off the road.'

'You weren't hurt, were you?'

'No. It happened in slow motion, so not even a bump. But the car's stuck in the hedge and so there's no way we can get to the hospital now. Edmund started talking about walking, but it would take him the best part of the day to make it all the way to Chelstead.'

'Why don't you both come to Island House with me?' he said. 'I'm sure Romily wouldn't mind two extra for lunch; you know how she likes to gather everyone together.' He was about to add that it would be like the old days, when he stopped himself short. With Hope fighting for her life, and Annelise pregnant,

434

a comment like that was hopelessly inappropriate. How could anything be like it used to be?

'Why not telephone Romily to see if she has enough food to go around?' he said.

Annelise didn't look convinced. 'I'm not sure Edmund's in the mood for enjoying himself to that extent.'

'A change of scene might do you both good,' he suggested. Selfishly all he could think was that Christmas Day spent *with* Annelise would be better than without her.

Chapter Seventy-Eight

Chelstead Cottage Hospital, Chelstead
December 1962
Hope

Hope had the curious sensation of floating. It was as if whatever had been keeping her anchored had released its hold and her body, which had felt so leaden and inert, was now as light as air.

Was this death? Was she finally to be released from the cruel torture that had robbed her of all movement? She had a sense of her mind clearing too, as it did when a migraine passed. Or when she came through a period of time with the Black Dog. Was this what was meant about being made whole when entering the state of heaven?

Not by any means was she a regular churchgoer, but she knew her Bible, and if there was one quote that had been a comfort to her when Dieter died, it was Revelations 21:4.

'And God will wipe away every tear from their eyes; there shall be no more death, nor sorrow, nor crying. There shall be no more pain, for the former things have passed away.'

She had hung on to the belief – *the hope* – that it was true, that Dieter was in a better place. Such was her heartbreak at his death she had considered ending her own life to be with him. All that had really stopped her from doing so was the fear she would then be bound for hell and not heaven. Forever parted from Dieter.

There had been times when Hope had doubted the existence of heaven, but hell, oh yes, she knew that hell existed. So much of her life had been just that, and never more so than lying here in this bed powerless to move or speak.

Her body feeling yet lighter still, and ever more convinced the end was drawing near for her, she suddenly wanted Edmund and Annelise to be with her. She wanted to say goodbye to them. Where were they? Had they forgotten to come? Or had they grown bored of sitting here with her, constantly having to think of things to say?

She wanted to say sorry to Edmund for having been such a poor wife to him. And Annelise, the dear girl had not been given the love she deserved from Hope. And now it was too late to explain how desperately sorry she was that she had failed them. It was also too late to wallow in self-pity. What she had to do before she ran out of time was confess her sins and seek forgiveness. God loved a death-bed act of contrition, didn't he?

She was just marshalling her penitent thoughts when she heard singing. Was that the sound of angels she could hear?

As the singing grew louder and more distinct, she could clearly hear that it was 'Away in a Manger' being sung. Did angels sing Christmas carols?

Then she remembered that it was Christmas Day. The nurses had been chattering on about it last night, how it would definitely be a white Christmas. They had been worried about getting home and whether or not this morning's shift of nurses would make it in. Somebody had joked that if the snow kept up, they'd be snowed in and would have to spend Christmas here.

Was that why Edmund and Annelise weren't here? She remembered them saying they would spend the day with her. Edmund had said they would have their very own Christmas Day together, complete with decorations from home which Annelise had put up in her room.

The singing was much louder now, and 'Away in a Manger' had been replaced with the irritatingly jolly 'Jingle Bells'. She wished whoever was singing would go away. If she was about to die, she did not want 'Jingle Bells' to be the last thing she heard.

Stop it! she wanted to shout.

Go and annoy somebody else!

Leave me in peace!

To her surprise the singing immediately stopped, and she was rewarded with silence. Feeling a strange rasping sensation in her throat, there then followed a cacophony of voices. One of which was full of urgency.

'Quick, fetch Dr Carling, and then telephone Dr Flowerday.'

Another voice, and one that was much nearer to her, was softer. 'Mrs Flowerday ... Hope ... can you hear me?'

'Of course I can hear you!' Hope replied. It took her a moment to register that the ugly croaking sound she could hear had come from her own mouth, and wasn't confined to the inside of her head.

Very slowly, as though there were the heaviest of weights resting against them, she opened her eyes.

Chapter Seventy-Nine

Melstead Hall, Melstead St Mary
December 1962
Ralph

Ralph really shouldn't have polished off that bottle of wine last night, but one glass had led to another and such was the excellent quality of the claret that before he knew it, the bottle was empty, and he was spark out on the bed. As a consequence, he was dead to the world until lunchtime. Now, up and dressed, and ready to face his father, he went downstairs. It was time to prove his mettle and play his first move.

'I thought I'd told you to leave this house.'

Ralph regarded his father as he sat at the head of the dining-room table. A napkin tucked into the collar of his shirt, the grotesque man was tucking into his Christmas lunch. On one side of him sat Julia, a visible nervous wreck, and opposite her, and looking like he'd rather be anywhere but here, was Charles. The atmosphere could not have been less cheery had the threat of the Black Death been at the door.

'And a Happy Christmas to you, Father,' Ralph said brightly, pulling out the chair on which he had sat last night. There was no place setting for him today. Undeterred, his voice still as upbeat as he could make it, he said, 'Happy Christmas to you, Julia, and you too, Charlie-Boy. What did Santa bring you?'

'How many times have I told you not to refer to my son in that way? His name is Charles.'

'You don't mind me calling you Charlie-Boy, do you?' Ralph said to his half-brother. 'I bet you have any number of nick-names for me.'

The poor lad, his lips clamped together as if to keep him from bursting into tears, shook his head.

'What? Not one little name?'

Arthur glared at Ralph. 'He's been told not to speak to you. One word, and he won't receive a single present.'

Ralph looked across the table at his stepmother. 'And does the same go for you, Julia? Are you also under orders not to speak to me?'

Giving him the smallest of nods, she poked at a sprout on her plate.

'So what will you do to your wife, Father, if she dares to disobey you? Will you send for that quack of a doctor from London again? Or perhaps you'll just lock her in her room?'

'I suggest you keep your mouth shut and let the rest of us enjoy our lunch.'

'Well yes,' said Ralph, 'I can see that this is the merriest of Christmas lunches, isn't it? I doubt there's another household in the land enjoying themselves as much as we are this fine day.'

In the silence that followed, and after helping himself to a chipolata from the dish on the table, he said, 'By the way, Dad, how's Miss Casey this morning?'

'What sort of a question is that?' his father demanded. 'How should I know?'

Ralph shrugged. 'I could have sworn I heard her being ill in the night. Sounded very like she was having trouble breathing. Does she suffer from asthma?'

The expression on his father's face was priceless, his eyes bulged, and he looked ready to spit out whatever it was in his mouth. 'I have no idea what you're talking about,' he snarled.

'Oh, I think you do. What is more, I think you're going to let me stay for as long as I like. Won't that be nice?'

Arthur wrenched the napkin from the neck of his shirt. 'Julia and Charles,' he barked, 'kindly leave the room. I need to teach Ralph some manners.'

With not a word uttered, the two of them did as he said.

'Well, this should be fun,' said Ralph with a smirk when they were alone. For good measure he helped himself to another chipolata.

'I don't know what sort of game you think you're playing, Ralph, but I won't tolerate your insolence in front of Charles.'

'I don't give a damn what you will or won't tolerate. I know what you're up to with that Miss Casey, I heard the pair of you last night. At it like a couple of dogs. And guess what else I know?'

In the look he gave Ralph, his father managed somehow to convey both boredom and menace simultaneously. 'I can't imagine what sordid fantasies your mind has come up with,' he said.

'Oh, let me assure you, my mind is as pure as the driven snow that is currently deep and crisp and wonderfully even outside. You see, I know who is responsible for running over my poor Aunt Hope.'

There was a satisfying pause before Arthur spoke. 'I suppose that's what Julia told you, isn't it?' He leaned back in his chair, making it creak ominously. 'What can I say, that's the kind of woman to whom I'm married. A feeble liar who won't accept responsibility for what she's done.'

'That's right, and because you're such a loving and benevolent husband, you're covering for her, aren't you, instead of going to the police?'

Arthur narrowed his eyes. 'It might be unlawful, but any husband in my shoes would do the same. All I'm doing is trying to protect my wife, and my son.'

'And you know what, you almost sound convincing. But the thing is, there's not a member of the family who will believe you. They know what you're capable of. As do I.'

'You shouldn't give any credence to the stories my brother or sister have told in the past about me. Or Romily for that matter. They've always resented my success.'

Ralph snorted. 'For what possible reason could they think you've done better than they have? Hope and Romily are both celebrated authors and Kit is a war hero.'

'Hardly that. All he did was survive a fire.'

'And recover sufficiently to join the ATA. Whereas you did what exactly during the war, Father?'

'I'm bored with this conversation.'

'I'll bet you are! But I'm not. Tell me about you and Miss Casey. How long have the pair of you been indulging in late night sex together? Pretty steamy sex from what I heard. And please don't insult my intelligence by denying it.'

'What exactly is it that you want from me, Ralph?'

'Money.'

His father shook his head. 'What a surprise. Does nothing change with you?'

'Why should I change when I do so well out of it? After all, I am my father's son. I'm a regular chip off the old block. You should be proud of me.'

'And if I don't submit to your . . . your request, what then?'

Ralph laughed. 'Is that something you really want to put to the test?'

'You realise, don't you, that your accusations boil down to nothing more than your word against mine?'

'No smoke without fire, as they say, so that should be sufficient to blacken your name amongst the august folk of the county.'

'Do you really believe I give a damn about such things?'

'Oh, I think you give quite a damn about your social standing. Why else do you live here in this mausoleum? You love to lord it over the rest of the village, particularly your family. So how about it?'

Arthur tutted. 'How much are you hoping to extract from me.'

'Twenty-five thousand would suit me.' Ralph knew this was a staggering amount of money, but in for a penny, in for a pound.

'Twenty-five thousand pounds!' exploded Arthur. At his temple a thick ropy vein throbbed, and his chins wobbled; he looked on the verge of an apoplectic fit.

'I call that a bargain, given what I know.'

'I'd sooner call it daylight robbery. If I agree, will you then leave and never make the same demand of me?'

'Happily. But don't think for one moment of cancelling the cheque. Do that, and I shall do my worst. If we have an agreement, I'll go upstairs and pack. But not before saying goodbye to Julia and Charles.'

His father looked as if he were about to object, but then merely nodded.

Twenty minutes later, and with the requested cheque safely in his hand, Ralph went in search of Julia. He expected to find her in her parlour, but Charles was there alone reading a book. 'Charlie-Boy,' he said quietly, 'I want you to do something for me. Go and pack a small bag of your favourite things, and a few clothes. Can you do that?'

'Are we going somewhere?' the boy asked anxiously.

'Yes. But it's a surprise. A secret. So not a word to your father.'

'Is Mummy coming with us?'

'Of course.'

The boy nodded and slipped off the chair. 'If you're looking for Mummy, I think she went upstairs.'

Wondering what she was doing up there, Ralph climbed the stairs, just as he had last night. On the landing he saw that Miss Casey's door was ajar. He pushed it further open and saw Julia inside the room.

'What are you doing here?' he asked.

'After what you said about Miss Casey, I came up here to see if I could find any evidence of what you'd hinted at between her and Arthur.'

'I'm sorry I did that in front of you and Charles. I should have waited until I had my father on his own.'

'I don't care about that. But look what I've found.'

Standing in front of a dressing table, she pointed to an opened drawer. Going over to take a look, he frowned at what he saw. 'Is that what I think it is?' he said.

'Yes,' Julia murmured. 'And it all makes sense now.'

He had no idea what she meant, but he quickly told her what she had to do next.

Chapter Eighty

Island House, Melstead St Mary
December 1962
Evelyn

Evelyn had had half a mind to feign sickness and back out of Christmas lunch at Island House, but she knew it would have raised too many questions. In particular from Kit, who would have worried what had brought on the sudden illness.

So after they had tramped through the snow on foot to attend that morning's brief Christmas Day service at church, they had arrived at Island House where Evelyn was forced to make an enormous effort to behave as normally as possible.

The shock she had experienced on hearing Max's voice on the telephone yesterday explaining about him and Isabella had now been compounded by something even more unbelievable. With something of a dramatic flourish, Isabella had revealed over a glass of champagne in the drawing room that she and Max were to be married. The announcement had caused Evelyn very nearly to choke on her champagne. While everybody else had greeted the news with astonished delight, Evelyn had caught Romily's eye and detected a wary look of apprehension. And rightly so. What did Isabella think she was doing? And what was Max up to? Marriage? *Him?*

Thank God for Romily's other house guest. With a naturally affable way of chatting to everybody, Red St Clair brought a

445

breath of fresh air to the proceedings. Now as they ate lunch, which apparently Red had helped Romily prepare, he and Kit were engaged in a conversation about Kit's time spent in Canada learning to fly. It turned out that they had a mutual friend who had trained at the same flying school. What were the chances?

And what were the chances of Max being a faithful husband? Evelyn looked across the dining table to where he was sitting between Isabella and Em. He was amusing them with some tale about a puppy he'd been given as a child, and how the dog had been utterly devoted to him. It was on the tip of Evelyn's razor-sharp tongue to interrupt the conversation and say, 'Well, that's Max for you, he always could instil slavish devotion.' She wisely said nothing.

'You've always had a wonderful way with dogs, haven't you?' said Isabella to Stanley.

Before he could reply, Em said, 'I'd have loved to have a dog, but Mum wouldn't let me.'

'And with good reason,' responded Evelyn. 'It would have been left to me to house-train and take care of it while you were away at school.'

'But wouldn't you like a dog now?' continued Em.

'Why now?'

'Well, because it won't be long before Pip and I won't be spending anywhere near as much time at home and it would be nice for you and Dad to have one. You know, for company. Don't you think?'

Evelyn frowned, but Kit laughed. 'Careful, Em, you're making us sound as if we're dangerously close to slipping into our dotage.'

Glancing further down the table, Evelyn thought how tired Annelise looked. Like Edmund, she was unusually quiet. The most Edmund had said since arriving was to say how awful he felt at not being at the hospital with Hope.

More food was passed around, and then Kit brought up a subject Evelyn would have preferred he hadn't. Not with Max at the table.

'Edmund,' said Kit, 'have you discovered if anyone else has received an anonymous letter like the ones Hope and Evelyn have been sent?'

Before he had a chance to reply, Isabella let out a hoot of laughter. 'Anonymous letters,' she repeated, 'what's all this about?'

Pip laughed too. 'Don't tell me there's some frustrated old biddy in the village with nothing better to do than write poison pen letters!'

'Who's the suspect?' joined in Em. 'And why didn't you say anything, Mum? Oh, this is straight out of a murder mystery novel, isn't it, Romily? What a lark!'

'Hardly a lark, I'm afraid,' replied Romily.

'No,' agreed Evelyn. 'I'm afraid it's not as funny as you youngsters seem to think it is.' Across the table she felt Max's eyes on her. She hoped to goodness he would keep his mouth shut and not let on that she had already spoken to him about the first letter she received.

'Evelyn's right,' asserted Edmund. 'I'm convinced that if it weren't for the letter Hope was sent, she wouldn't be where she is now.'

'You mean the two things are connected?' asked Red. 'Her accident and the letter? Hell, what kind of village is this?'

'The same as any other,' said Romily with a sigh. She was about to say something else, when from the hall came the sound of the telephone ringing.

She was gone no more than a few seconds before she returned. 'Edmund,' she said. 'That was the hospital. They've been trying to ring you at Fairview for the last hour.'

The colour drained from his face. 'But I rang them to say I'd be here.'

'Somehow the message was mislaid. But it's wonderful news. Hope is awake and asking for you.'

Chapter Eighty-One

It was anybody's guess how long it would take them to reach the hospital, but nothing was going to stop Romily from making the journey.

Firstly, she telephoned her nearest neighbour, Reggie Potters of Holmewood Farm, to ask if she could borrow his Land Rover. As soon as he knew the reason why, he was only too keen to agree. She gave Edmund no choice in the matter as to who would drive, telling him he would be too agitated to get them to the hospital safely. It was better that she be the one to do it.

The Land Rover had three seats and a rear canvas hood, under which Kit and Evelyn, along with Red, and wrapped in blankets to keep warm, were hunkered down as best they could. Twisting her head round to check that they were okay, Romily saw Red grinning back at her through the smudged glass. He gave her a thumbs-up sign.

Red had been keen to accompany them on the basis that some extra muscle-power wouldn't go amiss if they were to find themselves stuck in a snowdrift. They'd loaded the Land Rover up with blankets, turkey sandwiches, mince pies, and thermos flasks of coffee, as well as spades and shovels to dig themselves out if needs be.

Not since the war had Romily driven a vehicle of this sort, and gripping the steering wheel with her gloved hands, the wipers only just keeping up with clearing the windscreen of snow, she was determined not to be defeated by the treacherous conditions. With each hazardous snowdrift they pushed through, she experienced a thrill of exhilaration.

Crammed against the passenger door, and constantly fidgeting, Edmund alternated between leaning forward, as though urging Romily to go faster, and throwing himself against the back of the seat. When he wasn't doing that, he was wiping the steamed-up windscreen.

Next to Romily, Annelise was sitting perfectly still, her mittened hands resting on her lap. Had they been alone, Romily would have asked how she was feeling and whether or not she had reached a decision about the baby.

They saw no other traffic, not until they were about a mile from the hospital. Coming towards them in the blizzard was a tractor; it was towing a small car with its front caved in. Very carefully, Romily slowed her speed to a stop, then wound down the side window. The driver of the tractor stopped also. 'We're trying to get to the hospital,' she said, 'what do you reckon to our chances?'

'Now that I've cleared the road of this abandoned car you should make it. Be sure to keep your speed low. And don't hang about for your return journey, the forecast is for the temperature to drop dramatically. Happy Christmas to you,' he added with a smile.

'And to you too,' she replied, winding the window back up. 'That's a stroke of luck for us,' she said, when she had the Land Rover into gear and was moving again.

'Yes,' said Annelise, 'it was good of that man to help clear the road.'

Edmund's only response was to give the windscreen another wipe.

When they reached their destination, and before Romily had switched off the engine, Edmund was out of the Land Rover and all but running across the snow-covered parking area. Annelise stayed where she was.

'What's wrong?' asked Romily.

'What if Hope remembers my confession and asks me about the baby in front of everyone?'

'I suggest we cross that bridge if we need to,' Romily replied.

'Nice driving from you,' said Red, after he and the others had clambered out of the back of the Land Rover and Kit, Evelyn and Annelise went on ahead. 'I hardly felt a skid or a bump.'

'I'm relieved to hear it,' she said. 'It couldn't have been very comfortable for you. How's your leg?'

'Hey,' he said, putting a hand on her arm just as they reached the shelter of the entrance porch to the old Victorian hospital. 'You've gotta stop worrying about me.'

'I ask because I care, is that so very wrong?'

'It's wrong if you think I'm a has-been who needs fussing over.'

'I don't fuss,' she said indignantly.

'Yes you do. I've been here less than forty-eight hours and I've seen first-hand how you fuss over your family.'

She frowned at his perception. 'Is that such a bad thing?'

'The only fussing I want from you is when you're lying next to me in bed. Then you can do all the fussing you like!'

Smiling, she shook her head at him. 'You Americans are all the same, only ever happy when dishing out the orders.'

'Like you Brits are never slow to do the same thing.'

'But we always ask so politely.'

He laughed. 'We're gonna drive each other nuts, aren't we?'

'You're certainly giving it your best shot,' she said. Then:

'Come on, let's catch up with the others and hear what the latest is on Hope.'

'Before we do,' he said, 'I think you should know that things were getting pretty intense on the way here.'

'What do you mean?'

'Kit asked Evelyn several times what she thought about Isabella and Max marrying.'

'And?'

'Let's just say to begin with she was tight-lipped, very reluctant to give her opinion. But when she did, boy, the floodgates opened. It was quite something. Is there some kind of history between them?'

Romily knew what Red was really asking and saw no reason not to be honest with him. 'Evelyn is the one I told you about, who made the mistake of growing too close to Max some years back.'

'Yeah, I guessed as much.'

'It was before she married Kit,' she added.

'And does Kit know?'

'No. And it must stay that way.'

She was about to make a move towards the door to go inside, when he said, 'Do you think that's fair?'

Surprised at his question, she said, 'It's not for me to judge what couples keep from one another. But I do know this, Evelyn has always tended to protect Kit and she would want to spare him any unnecessary pain.'

'Because she feels guilty?'

'I wouldn't like to say. But everybody has secrets which, for whatever reason, they keep from their loved ones.'

'I wouldn't keep any from you,' he said, his expression serious. 'I've already told you more about myself than I've told anyone else. I hope you realise what that means.'

Romily kissed his cold cheek. 'I do. I really do. But come on, let's go inside before we freeze to death out here.'

She led the way to the waiting room where she had sat many a time when here to visit Hope. The area had been festively decked out with brightly coloured decorations; there was even a small Christmas tree in one corner. Kit and Evelyn were already there and in the process of removing the many layers they'd worn to get here.

'Any news on Hope?' asked Romily.

Kit shook his head. 'No. Edmund and Annelise are with her now.'

'I doubt they'll let us all see her,' said Evelyn, unwinding the scarf from around her neck and sitting down.

'You're probably right,' said Kit, 'but she'll know that we came, that's the main thing.'

'Do you suppose there's any chance we might be able to get a hot drink here?' asked Red. 'I know we have the thermos flasks in the Land Rover, but it might be better to keep them for the journey home, just in case.'

'If anybody can charm a nurse into letting us use their kitchen,' said Romily with a smile, 'it would be you.'

'Hey Kit, you probably know your way round here pretty well, how about you come with me and help carry the cups back?'

'Did I just witness your American friend performing an act of international diplomacy?' asked Evelyn, when the two men had left them alone and Romily was sitting next to her.

'I believe you might be right. He mentioned that there had been a certain amount of tension between you and Kit on the way here.'

Evelyn sighed. 'I'm sorry that it was that blatant.'

'Max, I presume?'

'Yes. What on earth is he doing with Isabella? Apart from the obvious.' Her voice was taut with angry disbelief.

'I thought the same yesterday when he showed up,' said Romily. 'But as much as it pains me to say, he seems genuinely to care about Isabella. And from what she tells me, he looked after her extremely well when she was ill in bed with bronchitis. Haven't you noticed how attentive to her he is? She only has to cough and he's like a mother hen checking that she's all right.'

Evelyn didn't look convinced. 'But marriage. It's unthinkable. And they've known each other for so short a time. Mark my words, it won't last. He'll soon grow bored and start chasing after some other girl.'

'Trust me, I have the same concern,' Romily said, 'but if I had heeded the so-called warnings people gave me about Jack, I would have missed out on the love of my life.'

With a roll of her eyes, Evelyn said, 'You can't really think that Max could be the love of Isabella's life, do you?'

'I have no idea. But I don't think we have any choice but to give him the benefit of the doubt and let him prove himself.'

'I can't believe he's fooled you.'

'Evelyn, it's not a question of him fooling me, it's Isabella whom he has to convince.'

'But he's only been at Island House for twenty-four hours, you can't possibly be that sure of him. What would Elijah and her mother think?'

'Reluctantly they would have to do what we have to do, and that is allow Isabella to go her own way.'

'No matter the consequences and how painful they might be?'

Romily nodded. 'It's what you'll have to do with Pip and Em one day.'

Evelyn shuddered. 'Don't! I can't bear to think of that right now. Not on top of all this.'

'I'm sorry. But there's something you should know, and which won't please you. Max has told Isabella about you and him.'

Evelyn reeled back in shock. 'He did what?'

'*Shh!* He did it because he didn't want there to be any secrets between them.' At once Romily heard her words as an echo of Red's. She thought of her own secret which had lain dormant for so long. What would it take for her to share that with Red?

'Rubbish!' retorted Evelyn. 'Max's ego would have got the better of him and made him boast that I had been yet another conquest of his.'

It was hard for Romily to see her old friend who was normally the epitome of calm level-headedness so intractable. 'I don't think that's the case,' she said. 'He had too much to lose by sharing what he did with Isabella. She might have been appalled by his confession and ended things with him there and then.'

'And what if Isabella starts telling people? What if Kit gets wind of it?'

'He won't.'

At the sound of somebody clearing their throat, they both turned to see Red standing in the doorway with a tray of hot drinks. Kit was a few feet behind him.

Chapter Eighty-Two

In all the years she had known Edmund, Hope had never seen him cry. But then for that matter, nor had she ever cried in front of him. They were two of a kind in that respect; it was one of the reasons she had married him, knowing that they shared the same stoic instinct.

Yet here he was unashamedly weeping and telling her how much he loved her, that these past weeks had been the worst of his life. 'I'm so very sorry I shouted at you that afternoon,' he had said over and over, while Hope wept in his arms and apologised for being so vile to him.

Now, both of them calmer and with Hope feeling drained and her head throbbing with the effort of keeping her eyes open, Edmund explained that she was not the only one to be sent a poison pen letter, Evelyn had too, as had Florence.

'I know,' she told him, 'I've heard you all discussing it. Except sometimes I wasn't sure whether what I heard was real or something I was dreaming.'

'If only I had known that it was receiving one of those letters that was the cause of your unhappiness,' he said. 'Why didn't you tell me?'

Her throat so constricted with emotion, Hope could hardly get the words out. 'My pride,' she murmured. 'My wretched stubborn pride. Oh, Edmund, I'm sorry I doubted you.'

'It's I who should apologise. I should have done more to find out what was troubling you. I let you down and I'll never forgive myself for that.'

'It's not your fault,' she said, 'it's Arthur's.'

He looked at her with a frown. 'Your brother?'

She hesitated. With her head still a chaotic tangle of thoughts, she struggled to understand if what she'd said was based on fact, or something her brain had conjured up while she had been unconscious. But with the tornado of strange thoughts spinning around inside her head, she felt that Arthur was definitely at the epicentre of the maelstrom.

'He wrote the anonymous letters,' she said. 'I'm sure of it. Or I think I'm sure. Everything's all so blurry and mixed up. But I can't stop thinking that he's the reason I'm here.'

'Speaking now both as your husband and a doctor, you mustn't tax yourself,' Edmund said. 'Your mind and body are going to need time to recover.'

'You know I hate it when you mollycoddle me,' she said with a small smile.

'I'm afraid in this instance you have no choice in the matter.'

She sighed and turned to look out of the window. It was snowing heavily. Then as if mesmerised by the falling snow-flakes, it was as though two wires suddenly connected deep within her brain and gave her a jolt of clarity. 'It was Arthur who drove into me!' she exclaimed.

She turned back to Edmund and saw the alarm on his face. 'You saw him driving that day?' he said. 'It was definitely his Rolls?'

She wanted to say yes, but all she could remember of the accident was the darkness and a pair of dazzlingly bright head-lamps. 'I didn't actually see him,' she said, 'it was dark, but I know it was him. I just do.'

Alarm had now changed to doubt in Edmund's expression. 'He wouldn't leave you in the road though, would he? He's a rogue through and through, but to knock his own sister down and drive off, well it beggars belief.'

'My brother is capable of anything,' she said. 'And anyway, Julia told me what he'd done.' She caught her breath, realising what she'd just said. 'Julia! She knows the truth. She came here and told me that he did it, and that he refused to stop.'

When Edmund didn't say anything, just stared at her, as though assessing her mental state, she said, 'I know what you're thinking, that I have a screw loose, but I swear Julia was here. I didn't dream it. It was real!' Her voice sounded loud and shrill, almost hysterical. But she needed Edmund to believe her. 'Go and ask her if you think I've lost my mind.'

'I don't think anything of the sort,' he said soothingly.

With a rush of impatience, she waved her arm in the plaster cast at him. 'Please don't use your doctor's bedside manner voice on me. I've had quite enough of that from everyone else while lying here all these weeks.'

His expression softened. 'That's the Hope I know and love.'

'But you don't believe me, do you?'

'I don't know what to think for the simple reason I can't believe Arthur could be that callous. And why would Julia come here and betray her husband? Why not tell me? Or the police?'

Hope felt the strength of Edmund's gaze intensify as he studied her face. She in turn took in the face of the man she had been so sure she had lost. Lines that had not been there before her accident were etched around his bloodshot eyes and either side of his mouth. He looked exhausted.

'It's a medical fact,' he said evenly, 'and quite common, for the brain to play tricks on a person when unconscious. In this instance you might want to believe it's Arthur who did this to you because he's always been such a disagreeable brother.'

Her certainty wavered. Could Edmund be right? After all, it did seem extraordinary that timid Julia would have the courage to say anything remotely negative about her husband, never mind accuse him of running Hope over.

'What about the letters?' she tried. 'Don't you think that might be something Arthur would do? Just to cause trouble. It's what he did when we were children. He enjoyed taunting us and inflicting cruelty on anyone, or anything, that was defenceless.'

'I promise you, Hope, that if it is him, he'll pay for it. I'll make sure of that.'

To her dismay, his reassurance brought on another bout of uncontrollable weeping and he took her in his arms. She had been warned that her emotional state would be up and down in the days and weeks ahead.

'When can I go home?' she asked, when her sobbing subsided.

'Unfortunately, it's not for me to decide.'

'But you could persuade the doctors here that I'm well enough to leave, couldn't you?'

He kissed her, first one soft kiss on her left cheek, then her right. 'Only if I'm convinced you're well enough to be at home. And there'll be no work for you for the foreseeable future. You need a proper rest. Doctor's orders!'

'But I'll go mad if I have to lie here much longer, or if I don't have anything to do.'

'No debate, Hope. Your typewriter is out of bounds until I say so.'

'What about the letters I heard you and Annelise talking about, the ones the children from round the world have sent me? That wouldn't be too arduous replying to those, would it?'

'Hope, you have no idea how many there are. There must be at least ten large sacks of mail stored at the post office, as well as the ones already at the house.'

Even as Hope balked at being told what to do, the exhaustion she felt made her doubt she would cope with responding to one child's letter, never mind a sack of them.

'I've just realised something,' she said.

'What's that?'

'That I didn't dream about the bags of fan mail, they're real. Which means maybe I didn't dream that Julia was here, she really was.'

'If it puts your mind at rest, I'll check with the nurses to see if they know whether she visited or not. Would you like to see Annelise now?' He stopped abruptly. 'What is it?' he asked.

'It's Annelise,' Hope said slowly, 'something she told me . . . something . . . ' Her words ground to a halt as she tried to catch hold of a thought that was as insubstantial as a dust mote.

'What about Annelise?' he asked.

The thought danced away from her, and Hope shook her head. 'I don't know.'

'Don't force it, darling. Everything will slip into place in its own time.'

'You speak as though I'm suffering from amnesia.'

'Not at all. It's just a matter of giving yourself time to sift through the mixed-up contents of your head.'

'That sounds very patronising, you know.'

'Yes,' he said with a smile. 'It's a comment I'm sure I'll live to regret.'

I'm sure I'll live to regret . . .

The dust mote danced back towards her and Hope tried again to snatch hold of it. *Annelise.* It was Annelise who had used those words, or words very similar to them, about living to regret something she had done. What was it?

Oh, it was so annoying! Why wouldn't her brain work properly? Normally she had a mind like a filing cabinet and could instantly locate any fact or date she needed, but now she felt as if the cabinet had been ransacked and all the information she had stored away so carefully was thrown on the floor.

She watched Edmund leave the room and ignoring his advice not to force things, she cudgelled her brain to think straight. And then it came to her. But surely she was wrong. That had to be something she dreamt. Annelise wouldn't ever be so careless as to get herself into a mess like that, would she?

But the moment the door opened, and Hope saw Annelise she feared the worst. There were dark shadows beneath the girl's eyes, her skin was ashen, and she had lost weight. She also looked sick with worry. Instinct told Hope that the change in Annelise wasn't purely due to fretting about her. She surmised also that Edmund, despite being a doctor, had not put two and two together. Or had he been keeping this from her?

Hope summoned what little energy she had and smiled weakly at Annelise. 'Come and sit down,' she said. 'You look almost as bad as I feel.'

Annelise smiled too. But it wasn't her usual smile; it was too brittle and brimming with sadness. 'It's so good to have you back with us, Mums,' she said when she was seated by the side of the bed.

'Then why do you look so terrified?'

'Do I?'

'Yes you do. Would it be because I didn't dream that you told me you were pregnant, that you are?'

Annelise nodded and chewed on her lower lip. 'I'm sorry,' she said. 'I know how very disappointed in me you must be. But you need to know, whatever disappointment you feel, it's nothing compared to what I feel for myself. And I'm sorry I told you about the mess I've made of my life when you were unconscious.'

'I'm curious, why did you do that?'

'Part of me hoped it would shock you out of the coma. But it was also the coward's way of confessing my folly to you.'

'When I couldn't react?'

'Yes.' Annelise's lips quivered, and her eyes filled with tears. 'I'm so sorry. I've let you down. You and Edmund. And after everything you've done for me.'

Hope could feel her emotions unravelling again and fought hard not to give in to another loss of control. 'Please don't cry or you'll set me off too,' she said. 'Does Edmund know?'

'It didn't feel right to burden him while he was so worried about you. But Romily knows; she guessed.'

'In my experience it's never been possible to hide anything from Romily.'

'And I told Stanley.'

Hope looked up sharply. 'Is he the father?'

'No. It's a married man in Oxford.'

'Oh, Annelise, how could you?'

'I stupidly believed him when he told me his marriage was all but over. Which I know is the oldest trick in the book.'

'He must have been very convincing to fool you. You're by no means stupid.'

'He was. And I'm afraid I'm as stupid as the next naïve girl. You can be angry with me if you want to be. It's what I deserve.'

Hope's heart contracted at the sight of Annelise's anguish and she saw all too clearly that she had to do all she could to help. There was no point in being angry or disappointed. What Annelise needed was her help, not her condemnation.

'Edmund might accuse me of not being capable of thinking straight right now,' Hope said, 'but I have a suggestion. I think you should request a year-long sabbatical from St Gertrude's and just as soon as I'm deemed well enough to go abroad to convalesce, the three of us should go away together. Given my situation, the Dean is hardly likely to refuse your request, and not if I make a sizeable donation to the college.'

Her eyes wide, Annelise stared at her. 'But . . .'

'But what?'

'But then what do we do? Or rather, what do *I* do?'

'Goodness, you can't expect me to have all the answers after being in a coma for so long! But first things first; you must tell Edmund.'

'I can't bear the thought of disappointing him. Can I tell him in a few days, when he's recovered some of his old self? He's been so worried about you. As have we all.'

Thinking how she had wanted to give up on life, for it simply to be over, Hope succumbed to a shameful wave of guilt. It had been selfish of her to wish for her death. She had convinced herself that Edmund, and everybody else, would be better off without her. Now, knowing the torment that Annelise had been suffering and how scared she had to be of the future, Hope felt an overwhelming sense of love and responsibility to help the girl. She may have let Annelise down in the past by not always being as supportive as she could have been, but she would not fail her now.

'You're not to worry, Annelise,' she said, 'Edmund won't be disappointed in you. He loves you very much. Just as I do.'

With another wave of guilt, and her eyes beginning to close with exhaustion, Hope acknowledged that these were words she hadn't said often enough to Annelise. That would have to change.

Chapter Eighty-Three

Melstead Hall, Melstead St Mary
December 1962
Julia

Ralph had told Julia to wait for him in her parlour but the longer she waited, the more Julia's nerve went.

Could she really leave Arthur and the life she had here at Melstead Hall? And for what? To scrimp and save just as she had before Arthur came along? Maybe she could bear that for herself, but not for Charles. Wouldn't it be better to stay and try harder to please Arthur? Wouldn't that be a sacrifice worth making?

He had cared for her in the beginning, she was convinced of it. But at some point, that must have changed. She must have failed him in some way. *Failed to do her duty . . .*

That must be why he had sought his pleasure elsewhere, and with Miss Casey of all people. Had it been Miss Casey who had encouraged him to lie about the accident with Hope and then to threaten Julia by saying he would tell the police it was her behind the wheel of the car? With what she now knew, Julia wouldn't put anything past that woman.

What if she found a way to get rid of Miss Casey and then apologised to Arthur for all the upset she had caused him; would life then go back to how it once was? When it was bearable. When all she had to do was her duty.

No, no, *NO!* What was she thinking? She had done nothing

wrong. Arthur was a brute! A brute from whom she had to escape. She had to do it for Charles's sake, just as Ralph had told her.

But was escape really possible? Could she do it right this time?

When she was a child she had tried running away from home. She had filled a shopping bag with an apple from the garden, a clean nightdress, her toothbrush and hairbrush and a change of ribbon for her hair. Lastly, she had added her most treasured possession, a small doll called Polly. Her mother had given it to her a few months before she died.

The bag hooked over her shoulder, Julia had quietly opened the front door while her father was in his shed in the garden. She ran to the park and hid behind the pavilion. From her hiding place she watched the park keeper locking the gate. After tucking the key into his jacket pocket, he fastened on his cycle clips, climbed onto his bicycle and disappeared off down the road.

She made herself comfortable in the pavilion and hugging her doll close, she nibbled on the apple from her bag. It wasn't long before it was dark and cold and she regretted that she hadn't thought to pack a blanket or even another cardigan, but her decision to run away had been on the spur of the moment. She missed her mother so very much and her father always seemed cross with her.

To this day she couldn't remember how her father had found her in the park and got her out, but it was that night, at home, after he'd put her in the bath and dressed her ready for bed, that it started.

'I know you miss your mother,' he said. 'Just as I do. But you see, running away won't help. It makes thing worse. And it was a very naughty and selfish thing for you to do. You were only thinking of yourself, weren't you? What about me? Don't you care about my happiness?'

'I don't know why I did it,' she said, ashamed of herself. 'I just wanted to stop feeling the way I do.'

He'd stroked her hair. 'I understand. But what *you* have to understand is that you're old enough now to do what your mother did to make me happy.'

'What's that?' she asked.

'It's your duty to replace your mother,' he explained, his large rough hand now stroking her shoulder. She could smell the tobacco from his pipe on his fingers, combined with the earthy smell from what he'd been doing in the potting shed. 'Your mother wouldn't want me to be lonely,' he went on, 'so now that you're a big girl, it's your duty to make me happy. It's what your mother would have wanted. Do you think you can do that?'

'How?' she asked.

'I'll show you. It might hurt to begin with, but it won't always be that way.'

'Mummy, why are you crying?'

Her son's question, as he burst into the room out of breath, took her by surprise. Wiping away her tears, she forced her lips to smile. 'I was remembering something from a long time ago,' she said.

Closing the door behind him, he came towards her. 'Was it a horrid Christmas like the one we're having today?'

'No,' she said sadly. She held out her arms and he came into her embrace. Just as he always did. Her precious child. 'I'm sorry you're not having a good time,' she murmured into his baby-soft hair.

'It's not your fault,' he said, leaning back to look up at her. 'It's father. Why does he have to be so mean and nasty?'

'He's not always mean. I just think he's unhappy. People who are unhappy behave strangely.'

'Do you know what he's doing right now, this very minute?'

'He's not having another row with Ralph, is he?'

'No. He's drunk and smashing up the presents under the Christmas tree, including the one I put there for you. I call that pretty mean, don't you? He said I had to watch him do it, but I refused and ran off.'

'Oh darling, I'm sorry.'

'Don't keep apologising for something that isn't your fault. It's him. It's always him. I hate him. I hate him so much I never want to see him again. *Not ever!*'

'But he's your father.'

'I don't care. He's a fat pig of a man who I hate!'

Behind him the door opened again and fearing it was Arthur, Julia jumped up from where she was sitting, ready to shield Charles from his father's drunken fury. But it was Ralph.

'What have you been doing all this time?' she asked. 'I've been waiting here for ages.'

'Sorry about that, it took me longer than I thought to organise things properly. Now, are you both ready?'

Her nerve going again and frightened of the consequences of what Ralph wanted her to do, Julia looked at him anxiously. 'Are you sure running away is the answer? Won't he just come after us?'

Standing in front of her, Ralph looked at her sternly. 'Julia, listen to me. The man has been hitting the whisky decanter and right now he's downstairs going berserk with a hammer.'

'See, Mummy, I told you he was drunk and smashing the Christmas presents.'

'But—'

'No buts,' said Ralph. 'The mood he's in, there's no knowing what he might do next. And do you think for one minute he'll get more than a few yards on foot?'

'What about the car? He'll use that, won't he?'

467

Ralph smiled. 'No he won't. I have the keys.'

'Oh, Ralph, I'm not sure we're doing the right thing. If only you hadn't made him so angry, he wouldn't be in the state he is. Why don't we just apologise to him and—'

He interrupted her once more. 'That man was born angry. Now fetch your coat and come with me. Charlie-Boy, do you have your bag ready as I asked?'

'Yes. It's in my room.'

'Go and get it now and meet us on the landing. We're then going to use the servants' staircase and go down to the boot room.'

'What about Miss Casey?' asked Charles.

'I've locked her in her room.'

Julia stared at him open-mouthed. 'You've done what?'

'That's what took me so long, I had to wait for her to stop trying to calm my father down and go up to her room. Now come on, let's get out of here.'

Chapter Eighty-Four

Melstead St Mary
December 1962
Romily

At Edmund's insistence, nobody else was allowed to see Hope. She needed to rest, he had explained. He and Annelise were going to stay the night with her, even if it meant sleeping in chairs either side of the bed.

After clearing the snow from the windscreen of the Land Rover, and sharing round the food and drink they had brought with them, Romily embarked on the slow drive home. Kit and Evelyn had volunteered to go in the back again, leaving Red to have the more comfortable seat next to Romily. She was glad of his company. 'I doubt you anticipated spending Christmas Day quite like this,' she said to him.

'No, but then as I'm fast discovering, life with you is never boring, it's one surprise after another.'

'That's not a bad summation. Although I have to say, you're the biggest surprise to come my way in a long while.'

'A good one?'

'You're fishing again, Mr St Clair.'

'God loves a trier, Mrs Devereux-Temple. And so do you, if I'm not mistaken.'

She smiled, but kept her gaze straight ahead on the road, which was hardly visible beneath drifting banks of snow whipped up by the wind. The half-light of the afternoon was fast seeping from the leaden sky, and they were now reliant on the Land Rover's headlamps to guide them.

'What was that I heard you and Edmund talking about before we left the hospital? It sounded like something to do with Hope's brother being responsible for running her over.'

She told him in more detail what Edmund had shared with her. 'To anybody who doesn't know Arthur,' she said, 'it doesn't seem possible, but Kit and Hope could tell you many a tale of his sadistic and bullying nature when they were growing up.'

'Nice guy. I look forward to meeting him.'

'Careful what you wish for. I suspect he treats his poor wife, Julia, abominably.'

'Physically?'

'I sincerely hope not. I think he prefers mental cruelty as a means to control her. He makes all the decisions for her, such as what she should wear and with whom she can socialise. She effectively lives in a gilded cage at Melstead Hall.'

'It might sound like a crazy question, but does she love him?'

'Perhaps. She comes from a very different background, so I would imagine it's the type of love that's based on gratitude.'

'You mean she's from what you Brits consider an inferior class, so that gives him carte blanche to treat her like a dog, and she should be thankful?'

'I for one have never considered Julia my social inferior.'

'Have you never tried to intervene?'

'I've tried numerous times to talk to her, but she's so firmly under Arthur's thumb, she wouldn't ever be disloyal to him. Which is why it makes no sense that she would visit Hope and tell her that Arthur had run her over.'

'Unless the worm has turned, and she's had enough?'

'There is that,' said Romily thoughtfully.

She drove on in silence, and then when a strong gust of wind buffeted the Land Rover, she saw something moving in the falling snow ahead of them. At first she couldn't make out what it was, then as she slowed her speed to a crawling pace, Red, said, 'Hey, is that somebody in the road?'

'More than one person,' she said, as the light from the head-lamps revealed three figures, one of which was a lot smaller than the other two.

'They're waving to us,' Red said. 'Must mean they're in trouble. That's a kid with them, isn't it?'

It was only when Romily drew the Land Rover to a stop, the tyres biting into the snow and ice with a series of shuddering jerks, that Romily recognised who it was. 'You stay here,' she said to Red, pressing her shoulder to the door and shoving it open.

'The hell I will!' he replied, doing the same on his side.

The cold, stinging wind slapped her in the face when Romily stepped down from the Land Rover. 'If you're trying to get to Melstead Hall,' she told the group, 'you're going in the wrong direction.' She pointed back the way she had just driven. 'Hop in and I'll give you a lift.'

'No!' shouted Charles. He was clinging to his mother and even as the wind roared and sent the snow swirling around them, Romily caught the defiance in his young voice. 'We're running away,' he said, and not without a degree of pride.

'You've chosen a hell of a day for it, kiddo,' quipped Red.

'What's going on?' It was Kit and Evelyn, peering out from the back of the Land Rover.

'We've found some waifs and strays,' Romily shouted to them.

Ralph spoke next. 'Romily, I know this is an imposition, but we were hoping you might take us in for the night.'

'There's no reason why you should say yes,' said Julia. 'No reason at all.' She made a pitiful sight, shivering with cold and close to tears.

'Please don't say no,' implored Charles, 'we don't have any-where else to go. And it is Christmas.'

'I don't know who this boy is,' Red said with a smile, 'but he pleads a damned good case.'

Romily had no intention of leaving anyone stranded in the snow. 'Of course you can come to Island House,' she said. 'Now for heaven's sake, get into the Land Rover before we all die of hypothermia. Ralph, you sit in the front with Red and me, and Charles, you help your mother into the back and sit with your Uncle Kit and Auntie Evelyn.'

'You promise you won't take us back to father?' he asked with a heart-breakingly earnest expression on his young face.

'I promise,' she said firmly. 'And I never break a promise.'

Once everyone was seated and they were on their way again, and Romily had introduced Red, she asked Ralph to explain what was going on.

'It's Dad,' he said, wiping the melting snow from his flushed face. 'He's been treating Julia atrociously. I couldn't let him carry on the way he was. Not when he might then start on Charles. Romily, I know you and the rest of the family have never thought much of me, that I was too much of a chip off the old block, but . . . well, let's just say I've changed. For once in my life I wanted to do the right thing.'

'Does Arthur know what you've done?'

'He was drunk and raving like a lunatic when we slipped out. At some point he's going to realise Julia and Charles have gone.'

'Why escape on foot?' asked Red. 'A car would have got you away faster and that much further.'

'We set off in my Roadster with the intention of driving to Island House, but we ended up having to abandon it after we skidded off the road. But never mind that, there's something really important you need to know. About Hope.'

'I've a feeling I know what you're going to say,' responded Romily. 'You see, we've just come from the hospital. Hope is now fully conscious and says that Julia visited and told her that it was Arthur who ran her over.'

'It's true,' Ralph said. 'Julia's told me exactly what happened.'

'So that's how the worm turned,' Red said quietly when Ralph had shared with them what he knew.

'And that's not all,' Ralph said. 'We found evidence in Miss Casey's room that she's been sending Julia poison pen letters.'

'Miss Casey!' exclaimed Romily. 'You mean she's the one who's been behind these vile letters?'

'You knew that Julia had received them?' asked Ralph.

'No,' she said, trying to keep her eyes fixed on the road while shifting down a gear to negotiate a bend. 'But both of your aunts have had letters, as has Florence. And heaven only knows who else.'

Of all the people she had thought might be responsible, not once had Romily considered Miss Casey. The woman had been as good as invisible to her. Was that the problem? Had she taken offence at people not treating her better? But wasn't that of her own devising?

'It wouldn't surprise me if my father is involved,' said Ralph. 'I caught him and Miss Casey *in flagrante delicto* last night.'

'Dear God, poor Julia. Does she know what she wants to do next?'

'No. The only plan we had, and at my instigation, was to get away as soon as possible.'

Romily risked taking her eyes off the road to smile at him. 'I remember you being impulsive as a boy; you haven't changed then?'

'In that respect, no. What will you do if Arthur contacts you to ask if Julia and Charles are with you?'

'That rather depends on how long they stay. I can't keep him from seeing his son indefinitely.'

'You won't have to. With the right help and encouragement, Julia will be able to find somewhere of her own to live. I've extracted some money from Dad which he assumes I've asked for myself, but it's actually for Julia and Charles.'

'What if she decides to return to her husband?' asked Red. 'It's not uncommon for a woman who has been ill-treated by a husband to want to return to him.'

'That's what I'm worried about,' replied Ralph. 'But she'd be mad to do it. Do you know, my father even brought in a so-called nerve specialist from London who drugged her to keep her from leaving the house. That's how dangerously warped he is.'

Red let out a long exhalation of breath. 'What kind of a monster is this man? And how has he been allowed to get away with acting this way?'

Neither Romily nor Ralph had an answer.

Forty-five minutes later, and when Romily carefully turned in at the driveway, never had Island House been a more welcome sight. What an extraordinary Christmas Day it had been, she thought.

And what on earth would tomorrow bring?

Chapter Eighty-Five

Fairview, Melstead St Mary
January 1963
Annelise

In the days and weeks that followed Hope's recovery on Christmas Day, life had taken on a surreal quality. Fresh snow blew in almost daily, carried on an icy Siberian wind, and the temperature plummeted well below freezing.

Every morning when Annelise drew back the bedroom curtains at Fairview, she was greeted by an endlessly white landscape with hedges buried deep beneath snowdrifts and tree branches drooping with the weight of so much snow. Today, as she stood at the sink in the kitchen washing up the breakfast things and gazing out at the garden, she was entranced by the snow glistening in the bright sunlight. The sky was the purest of blues and the snow, so dazzlingly white, made her squint to look at it.

The weather had caused chaos up and down the country, particularly when it came to travelling anywhere. Thanks to the local farmers in the area, the main roads were passable, but it was a relentless and Herculean task to keep them clear. In some places, where the snow had been repeatedly pushed back and piled on either side of the road, it was akin to driving through a narrow gorge cut into cliffs of ice. Comparisons were continually being made to the winter of 1946 and 1947.

When Hope had been allowed home on New Year's Eve, the

475

journey to Fairview had been only marginally less precarious than the one they had made on Christmas Day with Romily at the wheel of the borrowed Land Rover. Three weeks on from that most memorable of days, Hope was still fragile from both her injuries and the effect of being in a coma. She suffered terrible headaches and her emotions went from high to low in a heartbeat. She tired easily and that made her crochety and impatient to resume her life as it was before. Privately Annelise and Edmund were of the same opinion, that Hope would need to accept that the pace at which she had pushed herself for so many years put too much pressure on her.

The washing-up now dried and put away, Annelise turned her attention to the coffee percolator. It was nearly eleven o'clock and Hope liked a cup of coffee and a piece of shortbread at this time of the morning. She had always liked routine and even more so now when she was banned from doing any work and had so little to do.

Under normal circumstances, Heather, their housemaid, would have washed up and made the coffee, but the poor girl had slipped on the ice walking home one day and twisted her ankle badly. There had been numerous such casualties in the village and Edmund had been inundated at the surgery. Their cook, Mrs Foster, had gone down with flu, so Annelise was holding the fort as best she could. She didn't object.

Being busy kept her mind off the baby. Term didn't commence in Oxford until next week and while normally she would have gone back well ahead of the start of it, she was in no hurry to return. If in fact she did.

Edmund's reaction to the news that she was pregnant had been far from the horror and disappointment she had dreaded. He had immediately declared himself a fool for not spotting the signs. 'Some doctor I am!' he'd said. He really couldn't have been sweeter. Which was not how he felt about the man who had been party to putting her into this situation.

With everything that had happened since Annelise had left Oxford to return home, Harry had barely registered in her thoughts. He had surprised her by telephoning Island House on New Year's Day to speak to her. It was the only contact number he had for her. Romily had taken the call and said that she would pass on any message he had for Annelise. Romily had known that Annelise had no desire whatsoever to speak to him and had informed him of the fact.

Annelise didn't care if it was unfair of her to keep Harry from knowing he was the father of the child she was expecting; she had to do what was best for her, not him. Had he really loved her, things might be different, but as it was, she had hardened her heart to him. Unlike her feelings for the baby. Every day that passed she grew more attached to the tiny life she was carrying. On the one hand it seemed irrational that she could feel anything for something she couldn't see or touch, but sometimes as she lay in bed at night, she found herself resting her hands on her abdomen and assuring the baby that he or she would be loved and cherished.

The coffee now ready, she took a tray through to the sitting room where Hope spent most of her time. Stanley had designed this part of the house, with its large picture windows and French doors, to catch the sun from morning to mid-afternoon. Such was the brilliant whiteness of the snow outside in the sunlight, the room felt artificially lit up.

With a pair of binoculars pressed to her eyes, and in her usual armchair with a blanket over her legs, Hope was observing the birds pecking at the crumbs of bread Annelise had earlier scattered on the snow-covered terrace.

'The blackbirds and robins have been fighting again,' she said, when Annelise placed the tray on the table next to her, carefully moving Hope's sketch pad out of the way. With her left wrist still in plaster, and her typewriter withheld from her, Hope spent most of her days reading the newspaper, listening to the radio and sketching. She had used up two pads already with delightful drawings of the view from her chair.

'For such innocent-looking birds, they're exceptionally aggressive,' Annelise said, pouring their coffee.

'That's what comes of having a fiercely territorial nature.'

'I wonder if that's what Uncle Arthur would claim excuses his vile behaviour, that he was merely being territorial.'

Hope lowered the binoculars and put them on the floor at her feet. She took the coffee cup Annelise held out to her. 'Nothing can excuse that dreadful man's behaviour. And I know it's not a charitable thing to say, but I don't possess a scrap of sympathy for him and what he's now going through.'

Annelise sat in the chair next to Hope. 'Nobody would criticise you for saying that, Mums. Not when we all think the same.'

The words *divine retribution* and *reaping what one sows* had been said many times since they had heard of the massive stroke Arthur had suffered on Boxing Day. Annelise and Edmund had been at the hospital with Hope, having stayed the night by her side, when Arthur had been brought in by ambulance accompanied by Miss Casey. It had taken the ambulance an hour to reach Melstead Hall, followed by another hour to the hospital. Of course, at this stage they didn't know about Ralph helping Julia and Charles to leave, and the reasons why. That came later. But what they did know was that Arthur was responsible for nearly killing Hope.

Were it not for him now being unable to move and barely able to speak, and not likely to live for much longer, Edmund would have had no qualms about informing the police so Arthur could be brought to justice for what he'd done. But justice, Hope maintained, had been served without any intervention on their part. She also didn't want it being publicly known that her own brother could behave so cold-bloodedly.

Julia had since moved back to the Hall with Charles and Ralph. Miss Casey had been given her marching orders and reported to the police for sending anonymous letters. Isabella's fiancé, Max, had subsequently surprised them all by unearthing a mine of information about Miss Casey's past.

It turned out she wasn't who she purported to be. Her real name was Bernice Reynolds and six years ago she had spent time in prison for conning the life savings out of an old lady for whom she worked.

A compulsive and scheming liar, this was not the first time she had been caught sending anonymous letters. The recipients, so Max had discovered, were usually married women. She targeted them for no other reason than she got a kick out of causing trouble between couples, of shattering their happiness. A psychologist might well say she was inherently jealous of any woman who had more than she did. Romily's theory that the letters were nothing but random shots fired in the dark was found to be spot on. It was awful to think of the harm and heartache the ghastly woman had so wilfully caused.

'Have you thought any more about our going away together?' asked Hope, breaking into Annelise's thoughts.

'I've thought about it frequently,' said Annelise. 'I'm worried about Edmund leaving the surgery in the hands of a locum for so long, but mostly I'm concerned that it would be too much for you, Mums.'

Hope tugged at the woollen blanket that had slipped off her lap. 'Whatever effort it takes, it will be worth it to escape the misery of this weather. I was thinking we could perhaps start our trip in Cairo, spend a few leisurely weeks there before cruising along the Nile. Edmund has always wanted to do that.

And just think how blessedly warm it would be. From Egypt we could then take a cruise around the Aegean.'

Annelise smiled. 'Edmund's been on at you for years to take a proper holiday, and now here you are planning a Grand Tour.'

Hope smiled too. 'Don't you dare tell him I said this, but he may have been right that I have focused on work too much. Lying in that wretched hospital bed, once I was fully *compos mentis*, and sitting here every day, I've had a lot of time to reflect on what's important in life. And it's family. Everything else is just frippery. Who will care in fifty years how many books I've churned out, or what riches I've accumulated?'

'But you can't dismiss the incredible pleasure you've given to the many children around the world who adore the books you've written for them. You could say they're your family too.'

'You sound just like my publishers,' Hope said with a dismissive tut. 'But I think the time has come for me to reconsider my priorities. So how about the three of us going to Egypt and then working our way round the Mediterranean and then maybe hiring a villa by the sea on the French Riviera? Or what about Switzerland? You could have the baby there quite anonymously.'

As good as it was to hear Hope talking about working less and enjoying life more, Annelise couldn't stop herself from saying, 'Then what? When I've had the baby, what happens next?'

'By then you will have decided what you want to do, and whatever decision you reach, Edmund and I will support you. Is there any more coffee?' She held out her cup.

The matter-of-fact way Hope spoke was so far removed from what Annelise had ever believed possible, it was difficult to take in. Was it the medication she was prescribed that made Hope so calm, or was this new Hope the result of having faced death head on and won?

'Has Edmund said anything to you about his idea?' asked Annelise.

'Yes,' replied Hope, taking the coffee cup she had just refilled. 'He put it to me earlier before he left for the surgery.'

'And?'

'I'm amazed it took him this long to come up with it.'

'You're not surprised by his suggestion?'

'I would have been more surprised if Edmund hadn't suggested what he has. You know how fond of children he is.'

'But what about you? How do feel about having a baby here?' Annelise chose her next words with care. 'You're not really overly fond of children, are you? You like them as a concept, but not as a reality.'

'How very succinctly you put it. But it's knowing that I failed you when you were a young child that makes me want to do better for you now. To help you all I can. Who knows, maybe I'll make a better grandmother than a mother?'

With a surge of emotion bubbling up inside her, Annelise had to put down her cup of coffee. 'Oh, Mums, please don't think you failed me, you didn't. Not once have I ever thought that. I just accepted the way you were. God knows it's what my child will have to do with me, because I'm never going to be perfect.'

Hope leaned over and patted her arm. 'Nobody is. But you won't be alone in the challenges you'll face; you'll have plenty of help.'

'Edmund seems to have everything worked out,' said Annelise, 'is that how you see it?'

'You and I both know Edmund has a much more positive way of looking at things than I do. But in theory I can see his suggestion working very well. He and I, with the help of a nanny of your choosing, will look after the child here while you continue your work at St Gertrude's and visit as often as possible.' She gave a wry smile. 'You can't imagine how absurdly excited Edmund is at the prospect of being a grandfather. It's most unseemly.'

Annelise had to laugh. She could easily imagine Edmund being a wonderful grandfather; he had always been such a good father to her, and a great uncle to Pip and Em. What she couldn't imagine so clearly was balancing her Oxford life with that of being a mother. Even a part-time mother. 'You make it seem so perfectly respectable and normal what Edmund has proposed, but what if they find out at St Gertrude's that I have a child?'

'Who will tell them? And if anyone does, you simply say a widowed friend of yours who was terminally ill asked you to be her child's guardian. And don't forget we have a history of doing that in our family, first me with you, and then Romily with Isabella.'

'But is it right to live with a lie of that magnitude?'

'Oh, Annelise, we live with lies all the time. But if I know you, you'll know when the time is right to be honest.' Hope suddenly shivered and once more tugged at the blanket.

'I'll put some more logs on the fire, shall I? By the way, Stanley's offered to come and chop some trees down if we run low on logs. He said it was the least he could do after Edmund let him stay here while he waited for a plumber to mend the burst pipes at his cottage.'

Hope sipped her coffee thoughtfully, then took a bite of shortbread. 'Stanley hasn't seemed his usual self recently. Would you agree?'

The fire nicely built up, Annelise sat down again. 'I would. Romily told me that he's thinking of leaving the village.'

'Really? Where is he planning to go, back to London? I didn't think he much cared for it.'

'All Romily said was that it might surprise everybody.'

Hope frowned. 'And he hasn't told you what he's planning? I thought he told you everything.'

Not anymore, thought Annelise sadly. She stared out of the window at the sculptured beauty of the garden in the slanting sunlight. With everything buried beneath a deep covering of snow, she thought how Stanley kept so much of himself hidden out of sight. But then, who didn't?

Chapter Eighty-Six

Chelstead Preparatory School for Girls, Chelstead
January 1963
Evelyn

The atmosphere at school was feverish with the dizzy-headed girls struggling to concentrate on their lessons. Evelyn could hardly blame them. All they wanted to do was be outside on the playing fields hurling snow at each other.

There had been no question in Evelyn's mind that she wouldn't open the school for the start of term; as far as she was concerned she had an obligation to teach her pupils and that was that. Thank goodness the members of her staff were similarly minded and either braved the treacherous roads in their cars as Evelyn did, or trudged through the snow with the kind of gritty determination they had probably shown during the war. Joyce Gatley, the games mistress, had taken to cross-country skis to make the journey every day, and a large number of the girls used sledges to take advantage of any downhill slopes. Morning assembly had been shortened to no more than a few minutes during which Evelyn tried to calm the girls and instil a sense of order to the start of the day.

First break was now over and a crowd of girls, flush-faced and as giddy as a herd of goats, was in the long corridor divesting themselves of their outer wear and shrieking their heads off.

'A little more decorum, ladies,' Evelyn said as she passed through the mêlée. An instant hush fell on the high-spirited girls, but was soon followed by stifled giggles when she pushed open the door to her office.

Seated at her desk, and after dealing with a number of telephone calls, she reached for her handbag. Opening it, she pulled out a letter which had arrived in the post yesterday while she was at work, and while Kit was over at Fairview seeing Hope. With the flying school closed until further notice, he spent most afternoons keeping his sister company. There had been something vaguely familiar about the handwriting on the envelope, and taking it through to the kitchen, she had been about to open it when she realised why the writing was familiar. At the same time, she'd heard Kit's key in the lock of the front door. Hurriedly she had stuffed the unopened letter into her handbag to read when there was no danger of Kit asking who it was from.

That moment was now.

> *Dear Evelyn,*
>
> *I know your first reaction, when you realise this letter is from me, will be to chuck it away without reading it. But please don't. I urge you to take a deep breath and read what I have to tell you.*
>
> *But before I do, I want to stress how disappointed I was at Christmas that we didn't have the opportunity to talk in private; had we been able to, I might have succeeded in allaying the worst of your fears. Hopefully I can do so now.*
>
> *I want you to know that I understand completely why you and Romily would sooner Isabella had brought Jack the Ripper home for Christmas! Perhaps that is an exaggeration on my part, but it makes the point I am trying to impress upon you, which is, I don't underestimate your distrust of me. But, and this I swear is the absolute truth,*

my feelings for Isabella are wholly genuine. No woman has ever turned my world upside down in the way she has. I'm well aware that you will have tutted or rolled your eyes as you read that, but I assure you, it's true.

I love Isabella and count myself the most fortunate of men that she loves me in return, which is why I have been totally honest with her. I didn't want Isabella to be con-fronted at a later date with anything that might hurt her. That was why I told her about the two of us at Bletchley. I have also taken the step of sharing with Isabella something I ordinarily withhold. I'm sure it won't surprise you that when I left Bletchley, and with the threat of the Cold War knocking on the door, I was recruited by MI5. It's very tame what I do, mostly vetting procedures for the Security Services. I've often thought that you would have been a perfect fit for the organisation.

And now I come to the crucial part of this letter which I hope will put your mind at rest, if indeed you ever had any doubts. But I raise the matter because of what you told me the night of your party. In early December, just after the smog began to clear, I visited my doctor for a specific test to be carried out. You may think it was an odd thing for me to do, but it was a measure of the way I felt about Isa-bella – I badly wanted (and always will want) the best for her, which in all seriousness isn't hitching herself to a man twenty-six years her senior! But thank God the heart is a fickle entity and for reasons beyond my comprehension, Isabella regards me as a worthwhile risk.

To my very great regret, the upshot of the test I request-ed from my doctor dealt me a personal blow – I am, it turns out, incapable of fathering a child. On Christmas Eve, on our way to Suffolk on the train, I shared this dis-appointment with Isabella, feeling it only right that she be

486

in full possession of the facts before our relationship went any further. As painful as it would be to let her go, I knew it would be the right thing to do if she wanted to be with a man who could provide her with children one day.

Of course, I am not so stupid as to rule out the prospect that sometime in the future she may desperately want a family of her own. If so, that is a hurdle I will have to deal with. But for now, Isabella and I plan to marry just as soon as we can.

So you see, Evelyn, if you ever had cause to worry that Kit wasn't the father of your delightful twins, then worry no more. As I said before, I am telling you this because you seemed so rattled by what you had been accused of in that anonymous letter – which we now know was the work of a scheming con woman. Although I must confess that I did have my own suspicions when I heard that you married Kit so hastily following our night together all those many years ago, and that you were pregnant a short time later. Whatever suspicions I had, I kept them to myself. I respected you too much to do otherwise.

I sincerely hope that this letter may go some way to help you believe my commitment to Isabella, and that in loving her, I have changed from the arrogant, self-absorbed young man you once knew.

With fondest and very best wishes,
Max

Evelyn stared and stared at the letter. Never had she been so wrongfooted. Every word contained a jolt of surprise, though perhaps not Max's line of work.

She slowly refolded the four pages of pale blue Basildon Bond notepaper and slipped them back inside the envelope. All the while her heart began to race and deep within her there was a trembling sensation. The trembling grew until suddenly it exploded, and with such force, it caused Evelyn to feel as light-headed and as giddy as the entire school of girls put together. Taking a steadying breath, she went over to the window and stared out at the snow. She had been ninety-nine per cent sure that Kit was Pip and Em's father, but that one per cent of doubt occasionally had the power to weigh on her conscience. But now she was free of the doubt. She was so happy with relief she could twirl around on the spot and hug the first person to walk through her office door!

The appearance, seconds later, of Bill Noakes, the school's notoriously grumpy caretaker, had her choking back a smile that would have made the Cheshire Cat look positively maudlin.

'Boiler's on the blink,' he said, regarding her with a dour expression and probably thinking his announcement would wipe the silly grin off her face. 'I've done everything I can to get it working again, but it ain't playing ball. I tried bashing it with a hammer, like I usually do, but nothing.'

Thinking the boiler might have finally objected to being hit, Evelyn offered to go and take a look herself.

'It'll take more than *looking* at it to get it going,' he said sullenly.

'Even so,' she said brightly, 'I shall still take a dekko.' If she could fix their rotten old oven at Meadow Lodge, she could jolly well try her luck with the school boiler!

Alone in the boiler room and feeling as though she could take anything on in her current mood, which was making her fizz like a bottle of champagne, she rolled up her sleeves. 'Now then old friend,' she murmured to the ancient boiler, 'I know this is a lot to ask of you, and you're probably worn out with the extra load expected of you during this cold weather, but if you could see your way to working again, I'd be so very happy. If only to prove you-know-who wrong!'

An hour had passed when, and with her hands covered in grease and grime and her hair falling loose from the clips holding it in place – not to mention a stream of curses having been muttered under her breath – the boiler stirred into life with a series of clunks and gurgling noises. Evelyn gave it a grateful pat. 'I knew you could do it, old girl. I knew you wouldn't let me down.'

Grabbing a grubby old towel from the back of a chair, she wiped her hands and gave thanks that by some miracle of birth she was born with a practical nature.

She also gave thanks to Max that he had gone to the trouble to write to her. She supposed she should feel sorry for him that he'd had the news he had from his doctor, and how that might affect his relationship with Isabella one day. But selfishly all she could think right now was that his inability to father a child chased away every last trace of the cloud that had been hanging over her since Miss Casey had sent that first poison pen letter.

Later, as she was crawling home in the car at a snail's pace, the light from the headlamps picking out yet more softly falling snow in the dark, she felt the past, which had been so much in her mind these last few months, had finally been put to rest. It was the future now that occupied her thoughts. Not just hers, but that of Max and Isabella. As unlikely a match as they were, they had as much chance as anybody of making it work. She hoped they did.

Letting herself in at Meadow Lodge, and with a spring in her step and a happy lightness of heart, she called out to Kit. 'Darling, I'm home!'

'In the kitchen,' he called back.

She found him on his hands and knees peering mournfully into the open oven. 'I was going to cook dinner for you, as a surprise, but the wretched thing is refusing to work. I really think it's time we replaced it.'

489

She laughed.

'What's so funny?'

'Life,' she said cheerfully, shrugging off her coat, then tossing her hat and gloves onto a chair. 'Life is just full of surprises. Now why don't you pour us a couple of glasses of Dubonnet and gin while I deal with the oven?'

On his feet, he kissed her. 'What would I do without you?'

She kissed him back. 'Since you're stuck with me forever, that's not something you're ever going to have to deal with, my darling.'

Her sleeves rolled up for the second time that day, she set about coaxing their dilapidated oven into life.

Chapter Eighty-Seven

Melstead Hall, Melstead St Mary
January 1963
Florence

'I never thought to see the day when we'd be standing here,' said Billy.

'Me neither,' agreed Florence, gazing round the crowded drawing room of Melstead Hall. Everywhere she looked there was a familiar face from the village. Many had come out of sheer nosiness, eager to have a snoop round the Hall and see if it was as dismal a mausoleum as legend had it.

Florence was guilty of the same curiosity and while the house itself was large and forbidding, and lacking in any homely charm, with a drinks party in full swing, it didn't seem too awful.

Frank Ifield singing 'I Remember You' on a radiogram helped to create a relaxed atmosphere. All the same though, it struck an odd note, a party to celebrate Julia Devereux's birthday while her husband was in hospital possibly breathing his last. Not that anybody seemed to mind very much. If this was her way of enjoying, or maybe even celebrating, her new-found freedom, Florence wished her well.

'I could do with a bite to eat,' said Billy, 'any sign of one of those waitresses we saw earlier with a tray of canapes?'

'I'm sure one will be round in a minute or two,' said Florence.

'Do you know what I really fancy?' he said.

'Surprise me.'

'A big fry-up when we're home. What do you say to eggs, bacon, sausages and a slice or two of fried bread? We could eat it by the fire, all nice and cosy like we used to.'

'Sounds perfect,' she said. 'But won't your mother be coming round?'

'Not tonight, I told her we'd be back late.'

Florence looked at her husband. 'If I didn't know better, William Minton, I'd say you have an ulterior motive.'

He winked. 'And you'd be dead right.'

She leaned in to him and kissed his cheek. 'How many times have I told you before, I'm always right?'

'I've lost count. But I just thought it would be good to have some proper time alone, now that George is back at his studies in London and we have the house to ourselves again.'

'I can see that you've put some thought into this.'

'I have,' he said, stepping aside to let another couple of guests pass by. 'But you know,' he went on, 'you're not always right. You were wrong not to tell me about those poison pen letters. You'd have saved yourself a lot of worry if you had.'

'I know that now,' she said, 'but at the time, I just couldn't bring myself to tell you.'

'I still can't believe you doubted me, that you thought I could be messing about with some woman behind your back.'

'That's the trouble with poison pen letters,' said Florence, 'they poison the mind.'

'Hello Mr and Mrs Minton, would you like something to eat?'

Florence turned from her husband to see Charles Devereux looking up at her with a tray of canapes in his hands. Florence smiled at the boy. How sweet he looked in his grey pullover, white shirt and tie and neatly combed hair. 'If you promise to call me Florence,' she said, 'I might just try one of those tasty looking sausage rolls. Do you think you can do that?'

He nodded and after she had helped herself, he offered the tray to Billy. 'Our new cook, Mrs Grundy, says that seeing as God gave us two hands, it's always better to take two of anything.'

Billy laughed. 'One for each hand; I like Mrs Grundy's thinking!'

'How are you liking your new school in the village?' asked Florence.

The boy's face lit up with the sunniest of smiles. 'It's great and a lot more fun than my stuffy old school. Best of all I can walk there and back and stay here with Mummy the whole time.'

'And have you made some nice friends?'

'Yes, Mrs Min . . . I mean . . . Florence. Some of us are going sledging tomorrow and then we're going to build the biggest snowman ever.'

'You'll have no shortage of snow, and that's a fact,' said Billy through a mouthful of flaky pastry. 'And you can tell Mrs Grundy that Billy Minton says her sausage rolls are delicious.'

'That's a rare word of praise from my husband's lips,' said Florence, 'so be sure to tell her, won't you?'

'I will. If you'll excuse me, I'd better serve some of the other guests.'

They were watching him go over to where Evelyn and Kit were chatting with Ralph and Annelise when the boy's mother appeared. Her hair nicely coiffed and wearing a navy blue slim-fitting, above-the-knee dress of fine wool with a matching cardigan draped over her shoulders, she looked elegant and poised. Remembering the dowdy shapeless dress she had worn to the party at Meadow Lodge back in October, and how awkward she had been that night, Florence was amazed at the change in her.

'I'm so pleased you both came,' she said graciously, looking and sounding like the perfect hostess.

'It was very kind of you to invite us,' said Florence. 'Happy Birthday to you.'

'Thank you. I hope people won't think it very odd having a party like this when Arthur is ... well ... given the situation, but Ralph wouldn't hear of not celebrating my birthday in style. I only agreed on the basis that everyone from the village was invited so I could thank them for their kindness these last few weeks.'

'Which was very thoughtful of you,' said Florence, thinking that Julia wasn't so much changed as completely transformed. 'We've just been chatting to your son,' she then said. 'What a charming and polite boy he is. You must be so proud of him.'

Julia smiled, her eyes searching for Charles in the crowd of guests. 'He insisted he helped,' she said, 'even though we have plenty of waitresses the agency sent us.'

'Is that where you found Mrs Grundy, your new cook? Charles mentioned her to us.'

'Yes, she's marvellous, and with any luck the agency will find a new housekeeper for me as well.' Julia gave a short unexpected laugh. 'A woman who doesn't have designs on being mistress of Melstead Hall, or one who enjoys concocting horrid letters.'

Surprised that Julia could joke in such a manner, Florence said, 'A number of us in the village owe you a debt of gratitude for discovering what Miss Casey was up to.'

'I didn't do anything particularly clever, I merely stumbled across the evidence quite by accident.'

'However you did it, we're all very glad you did, Mrs Devereux,' joined in Billy.

'Do please call me Julia. I hate everyone being so formal with me.'

494

'That was more or less what I said to Charles,' said Florence. 'I hope you don't mind.'

'Not at all. I'm just so happy that he now has the opportunity to get to know people here properly. This has always been his home, but until now it hasn't really felt that way for him. Which probably sounds peculiar, but that's the truth of the matter. Arthur didn't like for us to . . . ' she hesitated and fiddled with the string of pearls around her neck. 'He didn't like to share us with anyone else.'

'How is Mr Devereux?' asked Florence, noting that Julia had referred to him in the past tense.

'Not good, I'm afraid. Ralph and I have been told to prepare for the worst, that the end is sooner rather than later. His heart is just so very weak.'

What heart? Florence was tempted to ask. Instead she asked how much longer Ralph would be staying.

'He'll be here for a few more weeks, which will be a great help to me . . . particularly,' she lowered her voice, 'if there's a funeral to arrange.'

'Yes,' said Florence. 'I can see that would be a help to you.'

'Charles and I shall miss him when he does go back to London, we've grown very fond of Ralph. But he's found himself a job with a firm of stockbrokers. Now if you'll excuse me, I ought to chat with my other guests. Do have plenty to eat and drink, won't you?'

Florence watched Julia go over to chat with Max and Isabella, who had arrived yesterday at Island House for the weekend. Unfortunately, due to the awful weather, the play Isabella had been performing in had closed after a dramatic drop in audience numbers. Isabella didn't seem at all bothered, she was too busy being in love, Florence supposed.

'She's become quite the mistress of Melstead Hall, hasn't she?' remarked Billy.

Switching her thoughts back to Julia, Florence agreed. 'After what she had to put up with from that monster of a husband, I say good luck to her.'

Romily had told Florence in confidence all that she knew that had been going on here, but it was already common knowledge that Julia had been treated appallingly by Arthur Devereux. There was gossip too that he had run his own sister over and that he'd been carrying on with Miss Casey.

Seeing Stanley standing in the bay window on his own, his hands pushed deep into his trouser pockets as he stared out at the garden, Florence thought how glum he looked. Leaving Billy to chat with Reggie Potters from Holmewood Farm, she went over to Stanley.

'Penny for your thoughts,' she said.

'You know me,' he said despondently, 'I'm not a great one for parties, and this one feels plain weird, don't you think?'

'I think it's Julia's way of telling the village that Arthur is as good as dead and she's now carving out a new life for herself.'

'I know the feeling,' he said.

Concerned how morose he sounded, Florence said, 'Stanley, you would say if there was anything wrong, wouldn't you?'

'Why do you think there might be?'

'It's just a feeling I can't shake off. You don't seem yourself.'

He contemplated her for a moment, then when Elvis singing 'Can't Help Falling in Love' started up on the radiogram, he rolled his eyes and sighed. 'What the heck?' he said, 'it'll soon be widely known before too long anyway, so you might just as well hear it from me. I'm leaving the village.'

'Why? You came back because you felt you couldn't live anywhere else. You said this was your true home.'

'It's Annelise,' he said quietly, his gaze moving from Florence to where Annelise was making Hope comfortable in an armchair by the fire. 'I have to put as much distance between the two of us as I can,' he murmured. 'It's too painful living under the same sky as her.'

Florence had always known that Stanley had a soft spot for Annelise, but she hadn't realised just how strongly he felt. 'Does she know how you feel?'

'I made the mistake of telling her that I loved her, and it's ruined everything. I never should have said anything. I always knew I could only ever be a friend to her, but somehow I dreamt . . . well . . . you know what dreams are like, some come true, and some are simply nightmares in disguise.'

'Oh Stanley, I'm sorry. But surely it doesn't mean you have to leave? Annelise is going away with Hope and Edmund and then when they're home, she'll return to Oxford, and you won't have to see her so much.'

'Assuming she does go back to Oxford,' he muttered. He then clenched his jaw as if he was biting on something.

'Why wouldn't she go back?' asked Florence.

'Forget I said anything,' he said tersely. 'I told you I'm no good at parties, they make me say stupid things.'

She stared at him, puzzled. Then suddenly she remembered being out with Annelise and the girl falling over in the snow. Helping her to her feet, Florence had asked if she was all right. Annelise had said she was fine, but at the same time she had placed a gloved hand over her stomach. Not until now had Florence thought twice about that small, but what she now understood was a very instinctive gesture. Was this the real reason Annelise was going away with Hope and Edmund?

'Stanley,' she asked, her voice no more than a murmur, 'is Annelise pregnant?'

He hesitated. 'If she is, you didn't hear it from me.'

'And the father?'

'A married man in Oxford who had no intention of leaving his wife. And that's all I'm saying on the subject. Don't press me for anything more. But perhaps you now understand why I have to leave.'

'Where will you go, London?'

He shook his head. 'No. I'm emigrating to Australia.'

'*Australia!*' she repeated.

Florence didn't know what was more shocking, that Annelise was pregnant, or Stanley planning to emigrate. Many a time when he'd been a boy, Florence had taken Stanley in her arms and hugged him. She wished she could do the same now, especially if it would help make him change his mind. The thought of never seeing him again was just too awful to contemplate. As was knowing the pain he was suffering in loving Annelise and knowing he could never be with her.

'When do you think you'll go?' she asked.

'Just as soon as the necessary paperwork is completed.'

'But what about Tucker? What will you do with him?'

'I'm going to ask Kit and Evelyn to have him. Em seems to think they should have a dog.'

'Well, if they say no, Billy and I will have him. If you'll trust us.'

He almost smiled. 'Of course I do.'

'Does anyone else know what you're planning to do?' she asked. What she meant was, was there anybody else trying to put a stop to his plan?

'Romily knows,' he replied. 'I told her before she flew to Canada for her speaking engagement tour.'

'What did she think of what you're doing?'

'She said I had to follow my heart and do what felt right for me. Even if it was a terrifying leap into the unknown.'

That sounded exactly the kind of thing Romily would say. It was, after all, what she was doing right now. Except she wasn't in Canada on a speaking engagement tour, that was what Romily had told people so they wouldn't put two and two together. Only Florence knew where she really was and had been sworn to secrecy.

Secrets, she thought, there was no end to them.

Chapter Eighty-Eight

La Vista, Palm Springs
January 1963
Romily

Throughout the long flight to Los Angeles, Romily had rehearsed what she planned to say to Red when he opened the door to her. But not a word of it sounded right to her ears; it was too scripted. She needed to relax and to stop worrying that she was making a big mistake.

It was because she had decided to be more like her younger self – her young spontaneous and impulsive self – that she was now in a taxi and on her way to surprise Red. She had deliberately not bought herself a return ticket. What did she have to rush back for anyway? Island House would always be there for her.

Closing her eyes, she gave in to the memory of lying in bed with Red at Island House and their making love. They brought out the passion in each other, he claimed, and it was true. She felt she could give more of herself to him than she ever imagined possible. What she had come to feel for Red was equal to, if not greater than, the very deep love she had experienced with Jack. She had waited a long time for that to happen.

The thought of once again sharing a bed with Red immediately heightened her anticipation of seeing him, giving her butterflies in her stomach. She felt clammy, too, from a combination of excitement and nervous energy, and from wearing the wrong clothes.

When she left London yesterday, the temperature was barely above freezing, and she had been glad of her mink coat and woollen skirt and jacket. But here, mid-afternoon, it was seventy-two degrees Fahrenheit. She wished she hadn't been so impatient to get out of the airport and grab a taxi; she should have changed into something lighter. Fanning her face with her hand, her eyes on the passing sun-baked desert landscape, she wound down the side window to let the rush of air cool the flush of her cheeks. In the front, the taxi driver fiddled with the car radio, switching from one station to another until, through the crackling static, he found something to his liking. When he settled on Nat King Cole singing 'You Made me Love You' and began humming along, Romily smiled to herself. *Oh Red*, she thought, *you certainly did make me love you.*

He had reluctantly left Island House in the new year. A prior engagement with a film studio in Hollywood forced him to return, although he had been tempted to tell the studio that he was snowed in and there were no flights leaving Heathrow airport. Neither of which was true, and as Romily pointed out to him, he had to leave some time. 'Do I?' he'd asked. 'Are you sure I couldn't just stick around for ever? I wouldn't be any trouble.'

'You've been more than enough trouble already,' she'd teased him.

'The right kind of trouble?'

'Fishing again, Mr St Clair? What have I told you about that?'

She had gone with him to the airport to wave him off. Staying with him for as long as was possible in the departure area, sitting together at a table drinking coffee and suddenly finding it difficult to talk, she began to hope that a blizzard would prevent his flight from taking off. But not a flake of snow had fallen, and she had stood at the window watching his Pan Am DC-7C lumber along the cleared tarmac before soaring into the pewter-grey sky. Unable to face the train journey back to Suffolk that same day, she had stayed the night in London, already missing the man who had given her the best Christmas she could remember.

As eventful as Christmas had been, what with the extraordinary weather, Hope emerging from her coma, Ralph helping Julia to leave Arthur, and then Arthur suffering a stroke, Red had taken it all in his stride. He had fitted in perfectly, throwing himself into whatever needed doing without being asked – chopping logs for the fire and clearing snow, not just at Island House, but in the village with a small taskforce so that the elderly residents could get out to the shops. He had acted as an excellent barman whenever guests called and he had even charmed Mrs Collings, a feat Romily had believed could never be done.

Once he was back in Palm Springs, he and Romily slipped into a routine of telephoning each other almost daily. 'I'm the wrong side of fifty yet I feel like a teenager again,' he'd said during one call.

'Me too,' she'd laughed. 'It's absurd, isn't it?'

'Totally crazy. But I could talk to you all day, and then all night.'

'You might not think that when your telephone bill lands on your doormat.'

'I don't give a damn about that; I just want to know when I'm going to see you next.'

'Soon,' she had told him. 'Just as soon as life here has settled down again.'

'That family of yours can manage without you, you know.'

'I know that, it's just that I need to be sure that they're all right. So much has happened in the last few weeks, and their happiness is important to me.'

'How about your own happiness? Who's looking out for that? Apart from me, that is?' he added.

His question made her think that he had a point. She *had* spent a very long time not thinking about her own happiness, of always considering the needs of others before her own. Had it become too much of a habit, an unconscious need on her part always to be at the centre of things? If so, it was time to break the habit.

It was that thought that had encouraged her to book a flight to Los Angeles, and without telling anyone, not even Red. Florence was the exception. Dear Florence, what a good friend and co-conspirator she was.

Before she left Island House, Romily had done what she should have done years ago: she had burned Matteo's letters. It had not saddened her as she thought it might, watching the flickering flames devour the past; instead it had felt cathartic, a sense of letting go. Finally.

Back in 1944, and in the days after she had written to Matteo telling him it was over between them, that she would not be responsible for destroying his marriage, her emotions had ricocheted wildly, bouncing between heartbroken despair, self-pity and wild fury. In truth, her anger was mostly directed at herself for not being more careful. For allowing her reckless behaviour to get her into the mess she was.

Then one night, when she was alone in the cottage in Hamble, exhausted and feeling sorry for herself, she drowned her sorrows in a bottle of wine. By the time she had drained it to the last drop and made it upstairs to bed, she was consumed with drunken self-pity. Her last conscious thought before passing out was that she wished she could make the baby disappear from her life just as she had banished Matteo.

The next morning she woke with her stomach cramping painfully. Staggering to the bathroom, the pain causing her to cry out and double over, she realised that she was miscarrying: her wish had been granted.

She wept with guilt for hours afterwards. But she never told a soul. Not then, not since. She could never bring herself to admit the dreadful thing she had wanted to happen, that she had literally wished the baby's life away. The rational part of her could reason there was a world of difference between wishing something and it actually happening. But shame and remorse would not allow such an easy get-out clause. She was convinced that drinking so much alcohol had caused her to lose the baby; that a part of her had done it deliberately. That child would be eighteen now.

Remembering that shameful night, and the depths to which she had sunk, was as painful now to recall as it was then. She had tried to bury the memory inside that wooden box of letters she had hidden in the attic. It would have been better to destroy the letters, but she had kept them to punish herself, to ensure she never forgot. As if she ever could.

She never heard from Matteo again. For all his protestations of loving her and wanting to divorce his wife, he never did. He returned to Italy when the war was over and became an artist of some repute, many of his paintings portraying life through the changing seasons as a prisoner of war in England. She learned of his success when she came across one of his paintings that was due to be auctioned in London. The auctioneer's catalogue had written a piece about him, including his death two years previously. The article highlighted his time spent as a POW at Tilbrook Hall in Norfolk and that he was survived by his devoted wife, Maria, and their two adopted children.

In honour of the child she lost, Romily bought the painting

and ever since it had hung in her drawing room. It was another punishing reminder of her culpability.

The taxi driver came to a stop in front of the address she had given him. She settled the bill and with her handbag and fur coat hooked over her arm, she followed him up the path while he carried her heavy suitcase and typewriter case. Watching him drive away, and taking a deep breath to quell the resurgence of butterflies in her stomach, she rang the doorbell.

When the door was opened by an attractive flame-haired woman in tennis whites, the shortness of her skirt showing off a pair of shapely legs, Romily's heart sank.

But then why was she surprised? Of course he would be seeing other women while she was out of sight!

'Hello,' the flame-haired beauty said cheerfully. 'Presumably you were hoping to see Red?'

She was certainly seeing red right now, Romily thought, trying to think of something polite to say. Out of everything she had rehearsed during her journey here, this was not the scenario she had imagined. 'Yes,' was all she could muster.

Her hand on the door, the woman stepped back to let her enter, but then she noticed Romily's luggage. 'Oh, are you staying?' she asked.

'I doubt that very much in the circumstances,' answered Romily.

The woman closed the door and for the longest and most uncomfortable moment, stared at her. 'Are you English by any chance?' she asked, her head tilted to one side.

There was no faulting her detective skills. Or Red's taste in women; this one was a stunner. But at least she wasn't young enough to be his daughter. 'I'm as English as they come,' Romily said.

Her reply was met with an unexpected smile. 'I'll go and find

Red for you,' she said, 'the last I saw of him he was bashing away at that typewriter of his. Come on through and make yourself at home. Here, let me take one of those cases for you.'

'It's all right,' she said curtly, 'I'm perfectly capable of carrying them.'

Her comment elicited another smile. It was as if this beautiful woman was in on some kind of joke. Maybe she was used to foolish women turning up on Red's doorstep like this.

Well, Romily would have her say to him, and then insist he ordered a taxi to take her back to the airport where she would catch the first available flight home. So much for living more impulsively. Never again!

Ignoring the invitingly comfortable-looking sofas, she prowled round the large airy room she had been shown in to. She remembered it from her last visit. The white-painted walls were adorned with oversized abstract paintings, the colours rich and vibrant. The sight of a pile of her own novels on the glass coffee table made her want to hurl them through the sliding glass doors that led out to the garden.

She heard Red before she saw him; clearly her untimely visit had triggered a loud exclamation of shock from him. She heard laughter too from the flame-haired beauty, followed by a comment she couldn't make out.

The next thing Red was hurtling through the doorway. 'Romily! Oh my God, it is you! I don't believe it!' The shock on his face was priceless. But it was for the wrong reason; it was because she had caught him out.

'You better believe it,' she said coolly. 'Large as life.'

He rushed over to her and before she could stop him, he'd gathered her up in his arms to kiss her.

She pushed him away. 'I think you have some explaining to do,' she said, indicating the flame-haired beauty now standing behind him.

'I told you she had the wrong end of the stick,' the woman said with another of her infuriating smiles. 'For which, given your reputation, you have only yourself to blame.'

Even more infuriating, Red laughed. 'Romily, meet my sister, Patsy.'

Romily did a double take. 'Your *sister?*'

'Yep, she's a regular pain in the proberbial butt, always has been. I told you about her.'

'Yes,' Romily said vaguely, 'I . . . I do remember you mentioning a sister, but you didn't say how beautiful she was.'

'Nor would he,' said Patsy, stepping forward to shake hands. 'He only flags up my bad points. But I apologise for not saying who I was earlier, that was mischievous of me, especially as I'd guessed who you were. Now if you'll both excuse me, I have an appointment at the Racquet Club to keep.' She winked at Red. 'And don't worry, I'll be leaving town first thing in the morning to go back to Chuck, leaving you two love-birds to enjoy yourselves.'

'No chance you could leave before then, is there?' asked Red. 'I could help you pack if you like.'

She wagged a finger at him. 'Not a hope, I want the opportunity to get to know the woman who has finally captured your heart. I have a feeling Romily and I are going to be the best of friends.'

Red groaned. 'Just what I need, the two of you ganging up against me.'

When Patsy was gone, and Red had his arms around Romily, and they had kissed to make up for the time they had been apart, she said, 'Have I really captured your heart?'

'What the hell kind of a question is that? Damned straight you have!'

She kissed him again. 'You have no idea how delighted I am

507

to hear that. Or how relieved I am that Patsy is your sister.'

He frowned. 'I hope you didn't really think I was seeing another woman while—'

She silenced him with another kiss. 'It doesn't matter. I'm here now.'

'But you have to trust me, Romily. You really do.'

'I know,' she said with a sigh. 'It's just that it's a long time since I have trusted someone.'

'We'll get there,' he said with a smile. 'I promise. Now, is that your typewriter case I see?'

'I thought I might write while I'm here. Maybe write a new Sister Grace novel with a Palm Springs setting. Or maybe work with you on that film script for Gabe and Melvyn.'

'Are you planning on a lengthy stay?'

'I thought I could stick around until you're sick of me.'

'That'll be never, then. Unless—'

'Unless what?'

He loosened his grip and held her at arm's distance. 'I could swap you for Mrs Collings?'

She prodded his chest with a finger. 'Careful what you wish for, Mr St Clair.'

'Oh, I love nothing better than to live dangerously, Mrs Devereux-Temple.'

'Me too,' she said softly, thinking of Matteo's letters burning to ash in the fireplace back at Island House and finally releasing her from the past. 'Me too.'

Acknowledgements

I had always planned to write a sequel to *Coming Home to Island House*, I just needed a good idea . . . It came to me when my eldest son and his wife took me to Palm Springs, for which I am enormously grateful. While Edward drove me round the Movie Colony, a sought-after area once home to movie stars from the Golden Age of Hollywood, I had a flash of inspiration – I imagined it was the early 1960s and Romily Devereux-Temple was in Palm Springs to discuss a film script.

Of course, that initial spark of an idea was the easy bit, what followed was a year of putting words on the page, aided and abetted by agents Jonathan Lloyd and Lucy Morris, so a very big thank you to them.

Thanks must go to Genevieve Pegg for her editorial input, and to Sally Partington for her excellent copyediting skills. Also, thanks to Olivia Barber at Orion for the final push at the end. And not forgetting Team Orion who sent me the enormous bottle of fizz on my equally enormous birthday – cheers!

While I have used real events and places in creating my story I have, as I always do, taken a few liberties here and there to suit my purposes. I hope the reader will forgive me this.

A cherished home, a circle of friends and a summer that will change everything…

Linston End has been the summer holiday home for three families for many years. A rambling thatched house nestled on the water's edge on the Norfolk Broads, it's a haven of long, lazy picnics on the river, gin and tonics in the garden; a place to spend time together.

But this year, the friends are rocked by unexpected news, and it seems that Linston End will never be the same again. For some, this summer feels like the end. For others, it might just be the beginning. . .

Return to the start of Romily's story with this enchanting tale of one family coming together and finding their way.

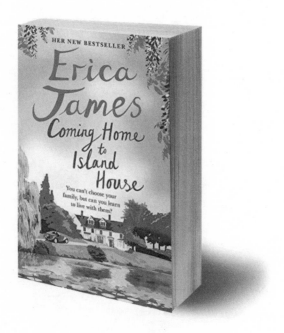

It's the summer of 1939, and after touring an unsettled Europe to promote her latest book, Romily Temple returns home to Island House and the love of her life, the charismatic Jack Devereux. But when Jack falls ill, his estranged family are called home and given seven days to find a way to bury their resentments and come together.

With war now declared, each member of the family is reluctantly forced to accept their new stepmother and confront their own shortcomings. But can the habits of a lifetime be changed in one week? And can Romily, a woman who thrives on adventure, cope with the life that has been so unexpectedly thrust upon her?

'A beautifully crafted and hugely uplifting tale of friendship, history and love. A real gem'
Isabelle Broom, *Heat*

Lizzie has an unfortunate knack for attracting bad luck, but this time she's hit the jackpot. After falling in love with her boss, she loses her job and is forced to move back in with her parents. She soon finds work at a care home for the elderly, and it's there that Lizzie meets Mrs Dallimore.

Mrs Dallimore tells Lizzie stories of her life – about when she left her home in America for England and her life truly began. These stories build a bond between the pair, one that will change everything Lizzie thought she knew about life, love and herself.

From wartime Bletchley to a modern day Suffolk village, this is a gorgeous tale of friendship and love.

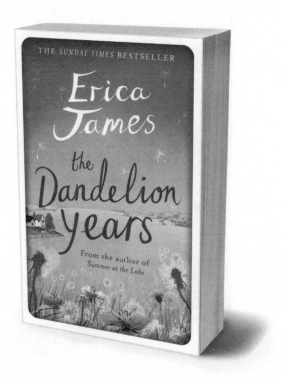

Ashcombe was the most beautiful house Saskia had ever seen as a little girl. A rambling cottage on the edge of a Suffolk village, it provided a perfect sanctuary to hide from the tragedy which shattered her childhood.

Now an adult, Saskia still lives at Ashcombe while she works as a book restorer. When she discovers a hidden notebook – and realises someone has gone to a great deal of trouble to hide a story of their own – Saskia finds herself drawn into a heart-rending tale of wartime love.

Set against the stunning backdrop of Lake Como, lost love, fate and second chances are rife in this compelling and poignant story.

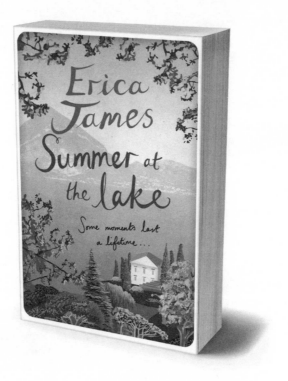

Lake Como – beautiful, enchanting, romantic . . .

For Floriana, it is the place where the love of her life is getting married to another woman. And she's been invited to the wedding.

And for Esme, it is where, over sixty years ago, she fell in love for the first time. So often she's wondered what happened to the man who stole her heart and changed the course of her life.

Now it's time for both of them to understand that the past is not only another country, it can also cast haunting shadows over everyone's lives . . .

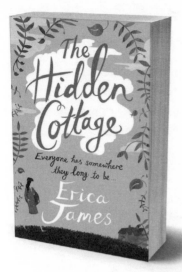

Mia Channing appears to have an enviable life. But appearances can be deceptive ...

Some shocks are in store for Mia when the family gathers for her son's birthday – her daughter, Daisy, decides this is the time to drop a bombshell. It's an evening that marks a turning point in all their lives, when old resentments and regrets surface and the carefully ordered world Mia has created begins to unravel.

A secret that changed everything ...

Katie Lavender is shocked to discover that the man she thought was her father in fact wasn't. She tracks her real father down to his home on the night he's hosting a party. As she hovers outside, Katie is mistaken for a waitress – an opportunity just too good to miss. Soon, she is within the family fold and they have no idea who she really is.

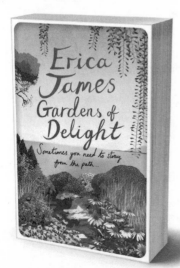

Sometimes you need to stray from the path ...

Three strangers attend The Gardens of Delight tour, visiting some of the most beautiful gardens in the Lake Como area of Italy. They come for a quiet trip but, of course, that's the last thing any of them are in for.

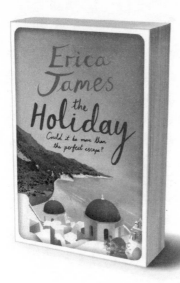

Could it be more than the perfect escape?

A long summer holiday on the beautiful island of Corfu is just what Izzy Jordan needs, but is she prepared for the romance and drama that she finds there?

Be careful what you wish for . . .

Ella Moore is recovering from seven wasted years of loving a man whom she thought she would spend the rest of her life with.

Ethan Edwards is a repeat offender when it comes to turning to women other than his wife for sexual consolation. When Ella appears unexpectedly in his life, he finds himself turning to her for very different reasons.

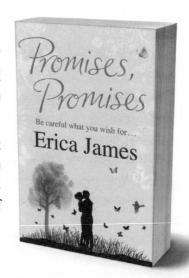

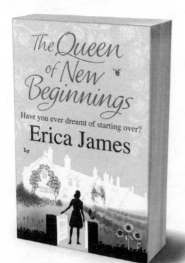

Have you ever dreamt of starting over?

Alice agrees to help out a friend by shopping and cleaning for the unknown man staying at Cuckoo House. Soon, she becomes suspicious that her strange and obnoxiously rude client has something to hide . . .

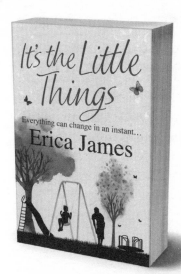

A story about how life can change in a heartbeat.

Dan and Sally Oliver and their friend Chloe Hennessey are lucky to be alive. They are all survivors of one of the world's biggest natural disasters – the Boxing Day tsunami. This is a compelling, moving and gripping story which looks at the tricky task of not taking anything for granted.

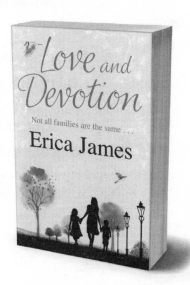

'A very moving novel about life, families and love' *Sunday Express*

Harriet Swift thinks she has the perfect life – then her only sister is killed in a car crash. She is forced to give up her well-ordered house to help look after her orphaned niece and nephew. And before long Harriet discovers things about her family she never believed possible.

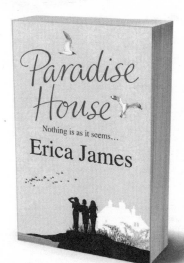

You can't choose your family . . .

Paradise House is a B&B which sits on the beautiful seaside resort of Angel Sands. A family run business, it's now down to Genevieve to maintain its smooth running – not an easy task, given that her father is suddenly a magnet for the opposite sex and her sisters have their heads in the clouds.

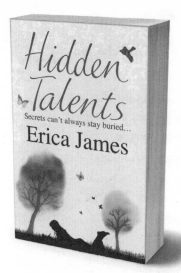

Secrets can't always stay buried . . .

A motley crew are thrown together when they join a creative writers' group. They all share two things in common – a need to escape and an intense need for their lives to be as private as possible. As they grow more confident in their skills, friendships develop, and gradually they come to realise that a little openness isn't always a bad thing.

Don't let life pass you by . . .

When Clara gives up her safe, conventional life and takes off with her young son on a three-month trip, she is soon forced to confront problems she thought she would never have to face.

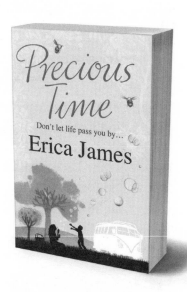

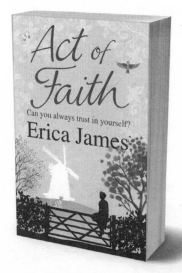

Can you always trust in yourself?

It's almost Christmas. Ali is persuaded to spend it with her friend Sarah – but that means also spending it with Trevor, Sarah's awful husband. When Trevor's cranky behaviour escalates, Ali takes it upon herself to play God with her friend's incomprehensible marriage. But her meddling has consequences even she could not have foreseen.

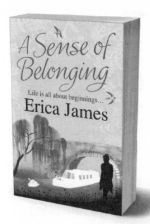

Life is all about beginnings . . .

Cholmford Hall Mews, a converted eighteenth-century barn, is far more than an exclusive home to its new inhabitants. In their different ways, all the newcomers are searching for something – love, peace, a sense of belonging. But will they find rather more than they bargained for?

Is it ever too late for a change of heart?

Ellen has been living on her own since her husband abandoned her to live with another woman. Having married once for love, she is now determined that the second time around it will be for money. Close at hand is Duncan, her not unattractive, and enticingly single, divorce lawyer . . .

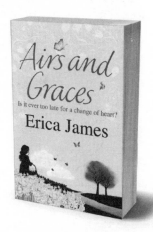

What do you do when your world falls apart?

Hilary had always thought she'd lived a charmed life until she discovers that her husband is having an affair. With her world turned upside-down, she doesn't know what to do – turn a blind eye, confront him? Or perhaps she should throw herself at attractive newcomer to the village, Nick Bradshaw.

After tragedy, how do you find love again?

Charlotte Lawrence, widowed at thirty-four, decides to return to all things pre-Peter, and that means moving back to the village of her childhood. It also means meeting Alex, a drop-dead-gorgeous neighbour – will this be the change she so desperately needs to heal?

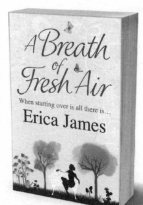

Help us make the next generation of readers

We – both author and publisher – hope you enjoyed this book. We believe that you can become a reader at any time in your life, but we'd love your help to give the next generation a head start.

Did you know that 9 per cent of children don't have a book of their own in their home, rising to 13 per cent in disadvantaged families*? We'd like to try to change that by asking you to consider the role you could play in helping to build readers of the future.

We'd love you to think of sharing, borrowing, reading, buying or talking about a book with a child in your life and spreading the love of reading. We want to make sure the next generation continue to have access to books, wherever they come from.

And if you would like to consider donating to charities that help fund literacy projects, find out more at **www.literacytrust.org.uk** and **www.booktrust.org.uk**.

THANK YOU

*As reported by the National Literacy Trust